DEEPEST RAGE
VORACIOUS VAMPIRES OF LAS VEGAS

EVE BALE

This is a work of fiction. Names, characters, places, and incidents either are the product of the author's imagination or are used fictitiously. Any resemblance to actual persons, living or dead, events, or locales is entirely coincidental.

Deepest Rage
Voracious Vampires of Las Vegas, Book 1
Copyright © 2021 by Eve Bale

Editors: Amy Briggs
Sonya Bateman

Cover designed by MiblArt

ALL RIGHTS RESERVED.
No part of this book may be reproduced or used in any manner without written permission of the copyright owner except for the use of quotations in a book review.

www.evebale.com

CONTENTS

About Deepest Rage   v

Chapter 1	1
Chapter 2	16
Chapter 3	28
Chapter 4	47
Chapter 5	52
Chapter 6	64
Chapter 7	75
Chapter 8	98
Chapter 9	113
Chapter 10	125
Chapter 11	132
Chapter 12	146
Chapter 13	152
Chapter 14	165
Chapter 15	173
Chapter 16	188
Chapter 17	203
Chapter 18	218
Chapter 19	228
Chapter 20	240
Chapter 21	257
Chapter 22	271
Chapter 23	283
Chapter 24	294
Chapter 25	307
Chapter 26	320
Chapter 27	333
Chapter 28	341
Chapter 29	345

Chapter 30	355
Chapter 31	357
Chapter 32	366
Chapter 33	378
Excerpt of Deacon: The Bladed (Spin-off series)	388
Excerpt of Cold-Blooded Alpha	393
Also By Eve Bale	399
Thank You	401

ABOUT DEEPEST RAGE

She wasn't the first woman to hurt him, but she'll be the last...

Centuries-old vampire Ethan Chambers is hellbent on exacting revenge on the woman who orchestrated his attack and torture four years ago. Tracking her at an elite vampire party in Vegas stirs his deep-seated hatred and desire for the only woman he's ever truly loved. But his thirst for vengeance only intensifies when another man has already staked his claim.

Former art teacher and callow vampire, Genevieve Althoff longs for the days when she felt safe and secure in the arms of her first love, Ethan, the vampire who turned her. Years after his death, Gen's finally able to find strength and courage in herself—until her protector and friend winds up dead. Now, someone clearly wants Gen dead—and will stop at nothing until she's destroyed.

Torn between his desire and detestation, Ethan struggles with his feelings for Gen. He can't possibly turn away when her life is in peril. But, she's resistant to his charms and tricks. Gen wants nothing to do with the finer side of the vampire world; she wants quiet, calm, and cozy. Ethan wants passion, pleasure, and pain. Together, they battle for control.

Can Ethan swallow his deepest rage to protect the only woman he's ever loved?

This is a dark paranormal romance. Due to adult themes, language, and steamy scenes this book is recommended for 18+

CHAPTER ONE

*E*than hunted her.

Nothing passed him by. Her every action, from the steady beating of her heart to the soft rise and fall of her chest, and the way her slim fingers curved around the stem of her champagne flute. He missed none of it.

Did she feel him watching? Did she have any idea he stalked her?

The man at her side said something which made her laugh, and leaned in close to brush a lock of chestnut hair from her face in a move that spoke of intimacy.

Possession.

Narrowing his eyes, he circled them, drifting closer as he willed her to see him.

Her head came up, turned, and her eyes searched the crowd. A pointless task.

With all the vampires thronging the ballroom of Eros on the Vegas Strip, and the dancing couples always in motion to the gentle plucking of a harp, it would be close to impossible for her to spot him.

But for a single moment, a single breath, he let her see.

The glass of blood-spiked champagne slipped out of her hand, exploding in a burst of red, pink, and crystalline shards when it hit the marble tile floor. One of his kin, who could never be accused of being tolerant, reacted at once.

There was a flash of fangs, glistening bright white against red-painted lips, and then a woman in a Grecian-style gold dress—the unfortunate victim of the shattered glass—launched herself at Genevieve.

But the lean man in the black silk shirt, with his long dark hair pulled back in a sleek man-bun was already nudging Genevieve aside, blocking the woman's attack with his own body.

Vincent Turner. Her leather pants and silk-shirt-wearing lover.

Her knight in shining fucking armor.

Using the thick crowd as a shield, Ethan downed his whiskey, noting how effortlessly Vincent—or Vince, he'd heard Genevieve call him—charmed the spite out of the woman in gold. Eventually she drifted away, apparently mollified by whatever Vincent had said.

His lip curled at how Genevieve gazed up at her savior, naked relief reflected in her expressive steel-gray eyes framed with their long, thick black lashes.

Four years ago, he had been certain he could trust her. That she loved him enough to give up her humanity and belong to him forever. Now he could see how much she had deceived him.

His? She'd never been his.

He'd been a mere stepping stone to something better. A path to high society parties in London, expensive jewelry, weekends in Paris, and a vampire lover who liked to pretend he was Prince Charming. Never mind that Ethan would have given her anything, everything.

No. She'd been after someone gentler, prettier, more charming.

Someone not him.

Well, it looked like she'd found it in Vincent fucking Turner.

Doubts had surfaced as his private plane crossed the Atlantic, delivering him back to the city which vampires had claimed nearly ten years prior: a city he'd left with the still-human Gen beside him six years later, excited to start their new life together in Prague. But now those doubts were vanquished in an instant.

It didn't matter that she was still the most beautiful woman he'd ever laid eyes on in her silky peach gown. She'd betrayed him—had left him to be tortured, and abandoned him at the moment of his darkest need. Her beauty wouldn't save her. Not after what she'd done.

Revenge was the name of the game, and he didn't care what it cost him.

After dropping his empty glass on a passing waiter's tray, he moved closer.

"You okay?" Vincent's British accent was soft with concern as he bent closer to Genevieve, with one arm curving around her slender waist.

A line formed between her brows. "I thought—"

"No need to worry about her," Vincent said. "I talked

her down, she won't come after you. But we can get out of here if you want?"

She nodded. "Yes Vince, let's go home."

And then Genevieve's hand was in Vincent's as he led her toward the exit.

A mocking voice whispered in his ear. *He'll be taking her to bed, you know he will. You saw the way he was touching her.*

His fangs exploded in his mouth at the thought of Genevieve lying naked beneath Vincent, of his feeding on the softness of her throat as he thrust inside her.

The sound of rushing blood filled his ears, and he stepped forward, his hand reaching for her, brushing against her wrist, her hand. He could have Genevieve back in his house, back in his bed before the night was out.

The phone in his pocket started ringing.

Genevieve's head started to turn, and he stepped back into the crowd, spinning around so his back was to her as he yanked his phone out of his pocket and answered it with a snarl. "What the fuck do you want, Rachel?"

His enhanced senses caught the exact moment Rachel's heart spiked at his sharp tone, but he didn't care. Rachel, his Vampire Agency Support Staff, or VASS, had known where he was going when he'd left home earlier. She knew better than to interrupt him. Especially tonight.

"The Claims Department has been in touch," she said, her voice cool.

He'd scared her, but Rachel never stayed scared for long.

"So, leave a message," he bit out, already lowering his

phone as he turned around to see what had happened to Genevieve and her wannabe rockstar lover.

Vincent continued leading her toward the exit, past the stage where a musician plucked at a harp.

"They've had a last-minute cancellation," Rachel said.

"When?" He weaved through the crowd, following close behind.

"In an hour," Rachel said.

Ethan paused to consider what the traffic would be like around the Strip. It was only eleven, late enough for the tourists to fill the sidewalks, and for the roads to be bumper to bumper full of cabs taking them to clubs and casinos on and off the Strip.

He wouldn't have time to do what he wanted and make it to the meeting on time.

"And if I don't take it?" he asked, as though he didn't know what the answer would be.

"The next available appointment isn't until next month."

"Tell them I'll be there," he said and hung up.

Stopping a few feet from the exit, he stuck to the shadows as he watched Vincent open the car door and help Genevieve in.

His stare locked on them. The hand on her hip was nothing less than a brand of possession.

Ethan's cell phone died as the glass, plastic, and metal cracked and crunched between his fingers.

Dropping the mangled mess on a passing waiter's tray, he ignored the curious stares around him and stepped out.

"You were quiet on the way home," Vince said as they stepped inside their mansion situated in one of the most exclusive vampire enclaves above the city.

Not the most exclusive, however. That was reserved for the most powerful, the wealthiest—as Vince had told Gen, Councilor August Mortlake, the only publicly known member of the Vampire Council. The body who ruled over all vampires in America.

"I think I saw Ethan," Gen murmured, leaning around Vince to pull the front door closed.

Shrugging out of his suit jacket, he paused while toeing off his leather boots beside the door.

"Doubt it was, luv," he said, tossing his jacket into the coat closet.

After slipping out of her high heels, Gen scooped them up and sighed in relief as she wiggled her feet in bliss.

Grinning, he took her shoes from her, grabbed her hand, and led them up the grand staircase. "Not even we can come back from the dead," he said.

It was always a relief to get home after a night out, and to step out of the painful heels and elegant dresses that Eros demanded. She always resented how Vince got away with black low-slung jeans or leather pants, and his black silk shirt half-buttoned. If she tried to dress like that, she wouldn't make it past the Bladed guarding the entrance.

But that was okay. We won't be in Vegas for much longer.

"But Vince, you didn't see him. You didn't see those flashing green eyes—so angry," Gen said as he led her into her bedroom. "He was staring at me like he hated me."

His room was next door, but whenever they returned from a night out, Vince always came to her room first to help her unbutton the back of her dress if she needed help, or wanted to talk.

After, he'd throw himself down on her bed while she went to finish undressing in her closet and pulled on a pair of sweats. Then they'd either lounge around in bed watching something on Netflix until it was late, or they'd talk for a bit until he went back out, and she would read in bed or sketch something in the sketch pad she'd brought from London, in which she was quickly running out of pages.

She hadn't thought to bring another, since she hadn't expected them to be in Vegas for as long as they had.

"Not that I think for even a second it was him, but why would he hate you?"

Because he couldn't have missed us dancing together, or your hand on my waist. Because Ethan had never liked it when another man touched her.

"I don't know," she lied.

"And most important, did you feel the bond?" Vince asked, crossing over to her balcony doors. Throwing them open, he stepped outside.

It had been Vince who'd explained to her all those years ago, when Ethan had left her and never come back, about the Master-Childe bond. About how it linked them together, and they would always know if the other lived or died.

She'd felt Ethan die. Had felt the connection between them extinguish in a second, and that was when she'd known she would die too. Because the only person she knew in Prague was Ethan, and he was dead.

But Vince had somehow, miraculously been there, and he'd saved her.

She hadn't wanted to live at all. Not without Ethan. But Vince had refused to let her give up. He'd given her a reason to live again when she thought she'd had none, not anymore.

"No," she admitted. "But maybe we weren't close enough for it to kick in. Maybe it's his ghost haunting me," she whispered, watching as Vince jerked his head away from the garden below, as if her words had startled him.

"Time and space don't matter. If it was Ethan, you'd have felt the Master-Childe bond. And like I said, what would he have to hate you for? You said he'd never hurt you, he was always gentle with you." He sounded distracted as he crossed over to her.

"He was... but maybe..."

"Shh, turn around," he interrupted, spinning her around until she faced the open balcony, and then he unbuttoned the back of her dress.

Gen stared out at the stars in the night sky, enjoying the cool breeze and the sweet fragrance of the roses drifting in from the gardens below.

"I'm sure it was him," she murmured.

"All you saw was a flash of green," Vince said, moving onto the next button, his breath cool on the back of her neck. "He's not the only fella with green eyes, luv."

She sighed. "It was Ethan, I'm almost sure of it."

If only he'd spoken. She would have known for certain

that it was him. All he would have had to do was call her name, just once. Genevieve. Because he never called her Gen, as everyone else did. She had always been Genevieve to him.

And the brief glimpse she'd caught of what the man had been wearing had convinced her it was Ethan. He'd always dressed in the same white long-sleeve shirt rolled up to the elbow, open at the throat, and black tailored pants.

Always he'd dressed the same way, from the moment she'd first caught sight of him at the bar in Hellfire, to the last time she'd seen him leave their Prague apartment.

"So, you saw his face, then?" Vince slipped the last button free, but he didn't release her as she expected. Instead, he stepped closer, sliding his hand over her hip.

She half-turned in surprise, but his hold stopped her.

"Vince, what are you—"

"Shh." He moved even closer. "Tell me why you think it was him."

It made her uncomfortable—his being so close, his hold on her mirroring the way Ethan had once held her. And it wasn't like him. Not when she'd always made it clear they were friends, that they could only ever be friends. Not after what she'd had with Ethan. She could never—would never love anyone the way she had him.

"Vince—"

Again, he interrupted her. "Relax. It's me, Gen. You trust me, don't you?"

Of course she did. This was Vince, the man who'd saved her life in Prague after Ethan had died. He'd been a stranger to her then, but he'd proven time and time again that she could trust him with her life. Not once had he ever betrayed that trust, not ever.

"Yes. You know I do," she admitted softly, trying to brush aside her unease in this new hold, this intimate embrace. Vince would never hurt her. In all the years they'd lived together in London, he had only ever cared about her happiness.

"Tell me, then. What makes you think it was Ethan?"

"For a second I thought I..." She paused and shook her head in confusion. "But it felt like him. I can't explain it."

Brushing her hair to one side, he bent his face to her throat. Then his hand rose from her hip, and fingers brushing against the strap of her dress, he eased it down her arm.

"It wasn't him," he murmured against her throat. "It's just your mind playing tricks on you. Don't you remember how you were the last time we were here?"

Gen opened her mouth to deny it, but she hesitated. It'd been a couple of years since they'd been in Vegas, and to say she'd been a mess was putting it mildly.

After Vince had saved her in Prague, he'd taken her to his home in a quiet, leafy suburb of London, in Richmond. It was close to a year before she could go a day without crying. Then he'd had the idea for them to come to Vegas for New Year's Eve as a way to unwind, and for her to see Tess, her friend and old roommate.

He'd thought it would help her recover. She'd nearly had another breakdown. And when they'd passed the gates which led to his home—a place she had lived for a short time—she'd been inconsolable.

In her mind, she'd seen Ethan everywhere, and it sent

her bouncing from sheer terror that he blamed her for his death, to a deep depression she'd struggled to emerge from. Things had gotten so bad that they'd returned to London after just a few days.

It was only once she'd settled back into her usual routine of painting and long walks in their neighborhood, before her mind had settled enough for her to come to grips with the fact she'd been seeing things. She had to remember Ethan was dead, and her guilt was making her see things that weren't there.

She'd been able to cope a little better with each visit they made, since it was the only thing Vince ever asked of her—to come to Vegas for New Year's Eve and have fun among their own kind. And it was an opportunity to see Tess.

"Maybe it's this place," she said, not sure if she was speaking to Vince or herself. "Maybe it's time we went home."

Vince's hand tugged the strap of her dress down past her elbow, and his lips trailed fervent kisses over her throat as one hand came up to span her stomach.

"Vince, what are you doing?" she murmured, trying to pull up the strap of her dress.

He didn't respond, and Gen tried to step away as his mouth on her neck grew more insistent. When she felt Vince's erection nudging against her lower back, she tried to pull away, but his hands tightened around her.

"Vince!" She gasped as the sharp edge of his fang traced a fiery line along her throat, even as the hand on her stomach came up to cup one of her breasts.

When the rich scent of blood tickled her nose, she tore

herself out of his grasp and reached a shaking hand to her neck, her fingers coming away bloody.

With one hand holding the front of her dress up, she swung around and blinked in surprise at the empty, glazed expression in Vince's eyes.

Something was wrong with him. His eyes were fixed on her, but there was a look in them that warned her he wasn't really seeing her.

It took a lot of alcohol to get a vampire drunk, more than she'd seen him drink that night. Vince rarely returned to their London home in a state which suggested he was. But when he did, mostly she was already sleeping.

Once, maybe twice, she'd hear him stumbling up the stairs in the early hours of the morning as she stood with paintbrush in hand in front of her newest creation.

It wasn't often she lost herself in the powerful need to create. But when the moment descended, she could and did paint for hours, and Vince would have to come and close the drapes in her bedroom before the early morning sun could touch her.

He hadn't been acting drunk at Eros, and he hadn't a moment ago. Was this some kind of a delayed reaction only catching up to him now? Or was this an urgent need for him to feed? Was that why he was continuing to stare, as if transfixed by the blood sliding down her neck?

"What's wrong with you?" she asked, taking a step back as Vince stepped closer, his dark eyes hooded as he moved toward her.

"Where you goin'? " he murmured as she backed away.

Her eyes searched his face as she tried to work out what was wrong with him. "Are you hungry? Drunk? Is that what this is?" she asked, feeling air playing with her loose hair like fingers as she stepped out onto the balcony

Vince didn't answer, only kept moving toward her.

His hands came up to his shirt, and in one violent motion, he tore it open. Buttons flew everywhere, and he shrugged out of his shirt, dropping it on the balcony floor.

"Vince, why aren't you answering me? What's going on?"

One hand came up to press against Vince's bare chest even as the other sought to keep her dress from sliding down.

Her back hit the balcony railing, forcing her to stop, and Vince's arms came down on either side of her, caging her in. His fingers ghosted up her bare arms, and he toyed with the straps of her dress.

For the first time, genuine fear rose until she was sure she could smell it, taste it in the air between them.

Something is wrong with him, and no one can help me.

Abandoning modesty in the face of something far worse, Gen gave up on trying to hold her dress up and used both hands to push him back.

"Stop it," she said when his hands slid the straps down her arms and the top of her dress fell, leaving her exposed.

Vince wrapped his arms around her and bent to kiss her neck, his tongue lapping at the blood. Reaching up, Gen gripped at his face, trying to push him back.

How could someone she trusted be behaving like a stranger?

"You're scaring me."

He murmured something inaudible against her skin

and pressed against her harder, grinding his hardness against her lower belly.

Panic surged through her, and Gen shoved hard, instinctively using her enhanced vampire strength to send him stumbling back.

"Stop it!" she shouted.

The back of his head hit the edge of the balcony door, and he raised his hand to rub at his head. Then he blinked at her as if he was emerging from a dream, eyes wide with confusion.

"Gen, what..." His voice trailed off as his eyes dropped to her bare breasts, and widened at the blood on her neck, her protective stance, and the panic in her eyes. Spinning around, his hands rose to his face.

"Shit, are you...?" He turned again, but then froze.

Gen yanked up her dress and stayed where she was.

"I'd like you to leave," she said, trying to keep her voice steady.

"Gen—"

"Get out!"

His back tensed, but he bent to retrieve his shirt from the balcony floor and strode back inside, disappearing from view.

She stood with her back against the balcony railing, staring at her bedroom door. But then, a sudden awareness of something in the gardens below—of someone watching her—had her spinning around to stare at the dark gardens below. But of course, there was no one there.

Great, just great. Now I'm seeing things—feeling things that aren't there.

Making her way inside and closing the balcony door behind her, she tried not to notice how much her hands were shaking as she rushed over to her bedroom door and turned the key in the lock.

For the first time in all the years she'd been with Vince, she'd locked a door to keep him out, trying not to think about the fact no locked door could keep any vampire out.

She perched on the edge of the bed and stared at the door.

What would she do if Vince came back?

CHAPTER TWO

*E*than had made it to the Council offices with only seconds to spare. But that'd been over thirty minutes ago.

Despite sitting in an empty room, more in keeping with a mausoleum than a waiting room, Ethan wasn't cold. Even if vampires could feel cold, he wouldn't have at this moment. His fury was enough to keep him plenty warm.

Opposite him was a large white slab of marble that someone had decided would make an adequate desk. At this monstrous desk was a woman with black hair in a severe bun, with sharp angular features wearing a tight black, sleeveless dress. She sat staring at him with large, dark eyes set in a pale, anemic face.

Although she had a razor-thin silver laptop open in front of her, she'd done little else but examine Ethan with eyes as cold as the room.

And since he'd destroyed his cell phone, he had

nothing to distract him from visions of Vincent taking Genevieve to bed.

He glanced at his watch again. Five more minutes had passed, and with it, the rest of his patience evaporated.

His decision to legitimize his hold over Genevieve with a stamped legal document from the Council had come to him shortly after his return to Vegas. It would mean that should she ever attempt to flee from him, he would have something tangible to wave in front of her face.

He wouldn't be surprised if Genevieve had forgotten all about the contract she'd signed after she'd agreed to being turned all those years ago. It was a document meant to ensure any humans accepting the change would fully understand that now, human laws no longer mattered. Only obedience to the Vampire Council—and to the vampire who turned them.

At the time, she'd barely glanced over it. Not that he'd pressed her to, since was mostly comprised of a long line of punishments designed to instill fear. He'd believed she would never need to know how determined the Council were to ensure order, especially now that they were, in Vegas at least, living openly among humans.

Being back in Vegas, remembering the power and the threat of the Council and the sword-wielding Bladed who served them by guarding the city, he had realized how the Council's obsession with ironclad contracts could serve another purpose.

His.

But if the unimportant bureaucrats who manned the

offices of the Council Headquarters on the Strip thought they could keep him waiting, he could do without it.

If he left now, he could reach the mansion that Genevieve and Vincent called home and make a start on the plans he'd been stewing over since his friend Aidan had emailed him the photographs that had put him on his private plane from Prague.

Rising, he jerked in surprised at the slight figure standing in the open doorway of the waiting room, watching him.

"Mr. Chambers?" the man said, his voice mild.

Ethan didn't respond at first. Instead, he examined the man closely. He'd neither heard nor felt anyone approach, but there he was.

The short man withstood the inspection with calm indifference, as if he was prepared to wait forever.

There was nothing at all remarkable about the man in the black suit with dark receding hair and wearing thin silver wire-rimmed glasses. He was so ordinary, he all but faded into the background.

"Yes?" Ethan said, hoping he would think Ethan had been reacting to his arrival, rather than leaving without a word.

"If you'll follow me," the vampire said, his expression unchanging.

The vampire's office was stark and utilitarian, as bland and lacking in personality as the man himself.

Stepping inside, Ethan watched the man round the black marble desk in the center of the room and sit, lifting his hand to invite Ethan to sit at the black leather armchair opposite him.

Only the thin lines bracketing mole-like brown eyes gave any indication of the vampire's age as he sat watching Ethan with a gaze which gave nothing away. Instead, his eyes served as dark mirrors reflecting Ethan's image back at him.

For a vampire to have been turned so late in life was unusual. Not only because the older the human, the less chance of survival from turning—but because vampires were vain, and very few vampires he'd ever known regarded wrinkles and age spots with anything other than disgust and pity.

Of course, there were exceptions, as there was with everything. But those were rare and only came about when a human could offer the vampire culture something valuable.

Perhaps the vampire had been a lawyer who'd never lost a case, or a Wall Street financial wizard? The Council would always have room for people like that within the gears of its offices.

"I am Mr. Knight," the vampire said, drawing Ethan's gaze from the small silver pin which marked him as a Council official. It was a miniature of a tiny, feathered quill, which was the only point of interest in the vampire's stark black suit and matching black tie.

"I believe you're seeking approval for a claim," Mr. Knight said, removing a thin file from a hidden drawer, and flicking through the pages. "A process which began over four years ago. Is that correct?"

"Yes."

"For there to be such a delay in issuing a right of claim

is most...unusual, Mr. Chambers," he said, a small frown creasing his brow as he closed the file.

"There were extenuating circumstances," Ethan said after a brief pause.

The brown-eyed vampire's expression did not change. "I imagine there might have been."

Ethan waited for the "but" he felt coming.

"But," the vampire continued, proving him right. "Because of the delay, there could be some...complications further down the line."

What was the problem with this vampire taking forever to say what he wanted to say?

Not only that, it sounded like Mr. Knight was on his way to turning down his claim ... and for whatever reason, he was drawing the process out instead of refusing the claim outright. But that was all right. He would make do without the claim if he had to. After all, he'd been prepared to leave even before the meeting started.

"I see," he said, working hard to hide his increasing frustration.

"Do you?" the vampire asked. "Do you really?"

"You're implying there can be a challenge to my claim," Ethan said.

He'd done a lot of digging around since he'd returned to Vegas, and it hadn't been hard to learn that she was living a life far removed from the vampire politics of Vegas in London.

From what he understood, there wasn't even a Claims Department in Europe. So, the only way she'd know she had the ability to challenge the claim he was pressing to enforce over her would be if he told her, which was something he had no intention of doing.

"Mm, perhaps it's best I garnish you with the legal paperwork so you can become more acquainted with the consequences. I fear—"

"That won't be necessary," Ethan interrupted, his temper rising at the vampire's pedantry. He rose. "If you're going to reject the claim, then get it over with," he snapped.

Mr. Knight stared at him, his face a mask of bland indifference. Yet in the silent regard, Ethan felt a tension rise in the room. He couldn't see it on the vampire's face, but there was a distinct feel to the energy of the room that spoke of a rage simmering just beneath the surface.

"The vampire in question... a Genevieve Althoff, is living with a Vincent Turner at their primary address in Richmond, London. Is that correct?"

For a moment Ethan stood undecided, not knowing if he should leave or stay. Not used to indecision, he returned to his seat. He'd hear the man out for another couple of minutes, and then he would leave if he felt the vampire was wasting his time.

"Yes," he said, not surprised that the Claims Department and this Claims Advisor, in particular, had done his homework. He didn't seem the type who failed to cross his t's or dot his i's.

"It is my duty as senior claims advisor within the Council Department to ensure you are aware of all the consequences of your late filing."

"But not Genevieve?" Ethan asked, wanting to be sure things hadn't changed in his long absence.

Those unreadable eyes seemed to sharpen. "The care and education fall to a Master to provide for and nurture his Childe. As I'm sure you're aware."

"Of course." Ethan nodded as he reclined in his chair, more relaxed now that things were heading in a more positive direction than they had been before.

"Genevieve Althoff has been living under the care of Vincent Turner for three years and seven months," the vampire said, leaning forward with his eyes fixed on Ethan. "Your claim could be construed as tenuous at best."

Ethan's jaw firmed. "She is my Childe."

"Miss Althoff's agreement to being guided by you is not in dispute, Mr. Chambers. After all, we have her signature agreeing to the change right here." Mr. Knight gestured to the file on the desk, though his eyes did not leave Ethan's. "Which adds a certain vigor to your claim."

"She belongs to me," he bit out.

"But you have been absent from her life for three years and seven months. Is that true?"

"Yes," Ethan said. "That's right."

For a long moment the vampire stared at him without speaking, his thin white hands folded over the file on the desk as he examined Ethan.

Ethan couldn't help but feel a trickle of unease throughout the clinical examination, but he withstood it in silence.

He didn't know how he could have forgotten that his return to Vegas meant being back under the ever-watchful eyes of the Council, and the Advisors who served as the public faces of the Council.

As ever, the members of the Vampire Council

remained hidden within the upper echelons of the vampire enclaves, high above the city.

Still, they would have eyes and ears everywhere, even in Europe. He doubted they would have no knowledge of how he'd been lured and ambushed nearly to his death in Prague.

After all, this Advisor knew exactly when Genevieve had started living with Vincent. But would they understand the nature of his return? Would they care about his plan to revenge himself on Genevieve and Vincent?

Without breaking his stare, Mr. Knight reached one hand into a drawer beside him. His hand emerged with a black stamp. Flipping the file open, he brought the stamp down with surprising force on the front sheet.

"Granted," Mr. Knight said, closing the file

Ethan blinked in surprise. Then he felt anticipation coursing through him. He rose. It was early enough that he might have enough time to go to the mansion Genevieve and Vincent called home, and drag her from it.

"A courier will deliver a notarized copy to you within forty-eight hours," Mr. Knight said, sliding the file into another hidden drawer.

Ethan turned away. His mind was already picturing how Genevieve would react at finding him standing at her front door.

Vincent would have to die, of course. But depending on how much Genevieve fought him, that would determine how much he'd make Vincent suffer before he put him out of his misery.

"Mr. Chambers?"

"Yes?"

"Until the claim has been notarized and delivered to you, Genevieve Althoff is not to be touched."

He stopped. "What!"

"As we Advisors serve as the hands of the Council, it is for them to finalize this and other claims. Until they do, Genevieve Althoff retains the status of unclaimed vampire."

Ethan felt a wave of burning anger rising deep inside, and for a second he considered seizing the interfering pencil-pusher and ripping his head off, even though he knew it would cost him his life. No one killed a Council Advisor and lived for long after.

"Are you telling me," Ethan bit out. "That until I receive the form—"

"You are not to touch Genevieve Althoff. I'm sure I've made myself clear?"

"And if I do?" Ethan's voice was silky.

But Mr. Knight had already turned to retrieve another file from a different drawer. Just before he opened it, he paused and glanced up at Ethan as if he'd forgotten he was there.

"I shouldn't have to remind you of the consequences of disobeying the Council, should I, Mr. Chambers? Not when they have already excused a past infraction once before."

Ethan silently swore.

Vampires never forgot, and the Council least of all. They wouldn't have forgotten his role in seeking revenge for a willful act of violence delivered on his friend Aidan's bar and employees ten years ago.

Yes, the Councilor had stayed their hands back then,

but they'd had the eyes of the world watching them at the time.

Now, there were no reporters swarming Vegas' streets armed with cameras to report on the historic first months following the vampire's purchase of Vegas from a near-bankrupt US government.

If the Council wanted to act, Ethan could be lying dead in a dark alley, his head separated from his shoulders by the Council's armed guards—and there would be nothing he or his friend Aidan could do to stop them.

Saying nothing, he stalked out of the office, his footsteps ringing sharply on the marble floor.

He should have known better than to think he could walk in and get what he wanted without the Council doing all it could to remind him he was nothing more than a cog in their machine. But now that he'd made his intentions clear, he was forced to accede to the bland-faced Council workers' demands.

He'd wanted to make sure Genevieve didn't have even a hint of a chance to wriggle out of his trap. Now, because of his choice, he had to play by the Council's rules.

When he stepped outside the marble and glass office building in the center of the Vegas Strip, a sleek black Mercedes S-class started up, its engine purring as it pulled up beside him. Not bothering to wait for the driver to open the door for him, he jerked open the door and slipped inside.

"Get me the fuck away from this place," he snarled.

His driver said nothing as he started for Ethan's home in the Hills.

They couldn't have gone more than a couple of blocks when red traffic lights forced them to stop. That was when he spotted her. A young woman in her early to mid-twenties with long blonde hair and wide blue eyes, wearing a short red dress which revealed more skin than it hid.

Ethan's fangs throbbed in anticipation, and he felt them lengthen as he focused on the long line of her white neck. No woman would walk around Vegas with their throats exposed like that—least of all in the middle of the Strip—unless they were in search of dark pleasures. Everyone knew it was asking for trouble. But that was okay. Right now, trouble was exactly what he was after.

"Pull over," he barked without taking his eyes off the blonde woman who stood in line, waiting to enter some club.

The car slowed, and Ethan pushed the door open.

Already he was getting attention as people turned to see what was going on.

In a black Mercedes with black tinted windows, there was more chance of him being a vampire than not, and the tourists milling about knew it. Some raised their phones to snap pictures or record him.

Ignoring the tourists, Ethan raised his hand in invitation to the woman who watched him like the rest of them. He didn't even need to enthrall the woman before she was turning away from the club and crossing toward him, her eyes bright with excitement, grasping at the hand Ethan offered her.

Then he closed the door, shutting out the world, his focus now on the speeding drumbeat of the woman's heart. Placing a warm hand on his thigh, she flashed small white teeth in a shy smile.

His gaze dropped to her hand, and for a moment he observed it with cold detachment before he turned the hand over to examine the thin blue veins on her wrist. He had no interest in her body—he knew she'd never satisfy him—and his hunger wasn't for sex. It hadn't been for a long time.

But his rage... his rage still burned like a living thing, needing to be fed. So he'd take what she offered, and if it ended with her body lying in one of Vegas' many dark alleys, then so be it.

She wouldn't be the first tourist who'd gone in search of dark delights and didn't live to regret it. Everyone knew what could happen in Vegas, and if they didn't... it wasn't his job to teach them the error of their ways.

CHAPTER THREE

"The last thing I want is to go to another party," Gen said as she wandered along the clothes rails in Louis Vuitton while Vince trailed behind her.

"It's just a party," he said, picking out a short sequined gold dress and holding it up to her.

She ignored it. "I'd rather not have a repeat of last night."

Vince glanced at a hovering sales assistant.

"She's human, Vince," Gen said, turning to leave. "It's not like she can hear me from over there."

When he took her arm, she tensed and pulled away.

"I've already said I'm sorry, luv. I don't know what came over me. One minute I'm unbuttoning your dress, and the next you're staring at me like I'm some kind of animal."

He sounded sorry—more than sorry, in fact. Full of anguish from what he'd done the night before.

"So, what happened? Were you drunk or hungry, or what?"

Blowing out a gusty breath, Vince raked a hand through his hair. "I don't know. But you must know—" He reached out a hand to her again, but when she took a step back, his face fell.

"You know how I feel, Gen," he continued, dropping his hand. "You know how much I care about you."

Despite her guilt at seeing his face twisted in a mix of agony of despair, she shook her head. What he was saying wasn't new to her. He'd admitted his feelings years before, and in return she'd had to break his heart by telling him she didn't feel the same way.

"You scared me," she murmured, letting him see the truth of it in her eyes. "I was too scared to do anything but stare at the door for hours, terrified you'd come back."

Vince looked devastated. "I would never hurt you. Gen, you have to believe me. That wasn't me."

"Is everything okay?" the sales assistant who'd been hovering nearby said, edging closer.

"Yes," Gen said, "we were just leaving."

She turned and headed for the exit, Vince following behind. She hadn't wanted to come to the mall in the first place, but Vince had been so insistent about making things up to her after the way he'd behaved, it'd been easier to just give in.

But things were awkward now between them, and it felt so wrong. She'd always trusted him, since he'd saved her life and was her closest friend. How was she supposed to just forget what had happened ... and what if it happened again?

"Genny?" Vince murmured.

But she didn't respond. If she did, she'd only say something that would hurt him. So, they wandered through Crystal's shopping mall, moving with the vampires and humans clutching shopping bags as they drifted in and out of the designer stores.

She'd thought getting out of the house for a couple of hours would distract her from what'd happened between her and Vince. But once again, going anywhere in Vegas only made her feel worse.

Turning away from another human couple whispering to each other as they stared at her, she gritted her teeth and tried to look unconcerned. Even in jeans and a T-shirt, they always seemed to recognize what she was, and it left her feeling like an animal in a zoo.

"I want to go home, Vince," she said as he tugged her into Versace.

"And we will go home," Vince told her.

"You don't have anything a little stronger, do you, sweetheart?" he asked a sales assistant at the entrance holding a silver tray of champagne glasses.

The slender woman with wide brown eyes and pouty red lips flushed, and Gen sighed as she wandered further into the store, declining the offer of a drink.

It was being fawned at like they were celebrities, or being stared at with fascinated horror, wherever they went.

Vince downed his champagne in one go and returned the glass to the tray.

"You've been saying that for weeks," she reminded him.

"It's Vegas, luv. We're here to have a good time."

"We *were* here to have a good time—for New Year's

Eve. But now it's the middle of February and we're still here."

Vince plucked a red silk dress from the clothes rail and held it up to her.

"Why don't you try this one on?"

"No. And I stopped having a good time here a long time ago," she said as she walked away. Catching the sales assistant still watching them, she turned back.

"So, let me make it up to you."

Usually, it worked. His British accent was her weak spot, and he knew it. But this time her patience had run out.

"I'm going back, Vince. I've had enough. You know how I feel about this place," she said, turning away again.

There was a brief flash of panic in his eyes before he shoved the dress back on the rack and followed her. She didn't go far, turning to lean against the wall while he stopped in front of her, his back to the store.

He rested a hand on the wall over her head and bent down to peer down into her eyes, keeping his distance when she flinched.

"We'll go back to London soon. I promise. But please, let me take you out and we'll dance and laugh and have fun. It'll be like New Year's, and I know you had fun then."

She didn't even try to deny it. Not when Aidan had thrown such an amazing party that even she hadn't wanted it to end.

Not wanting to immediately admit Vince was right, she turned away to take in the boutique with its rows of expensive designer dresses, thin sales assistants in tight knee-length black dresses, and a woman with long black hair who'd entered the store and stood scanning the rails.

Vampire, she thought. The woman was a vampire.

As if feeling Gen's eyes on her, the woman looked up and smiled. Flushing at being caught staring at the stunning woman with startling blue eyes, Gen tore her gaze away. God, she was just as bad as the tourists.

She sighed. "Okay, fine. One last party." At the wide grin spreading across his face, she glared at him. "But this is it. I need to feel normal again, and I can't do that here."

She missed her quiet daily life, and she missed her painting. If Vince wanted to stay in Vegas longer, that was fine by her, but she was tired of being on show—of feeling like a freak. The only thing Vegas had to offer her was a reminder of everything she'd lost.

"I'll make arrangements. Now," he said, towing her across the store. "I think I've spotted the perfect dress."

"Is everything ready?" Ethan asked, his attention on the photograph in his hand and not on the woman standing in front of his desk.

"Yes."

"And the letter?" he asked.

"It hasn't arrived," Rachel said. "Not yet."

He knew he was expecting too much for the claim to have arrived so soon, since he imagined it would take time for the adviser to forward the documents to the Council. So, after he'd blunted the worst of his rage on the blonde woman he'd picked up on the Strip, he'd returned to his home in the Vegas Hills.

After spending hours doing serious damage to his crystal decanter of whiskey, he'd closed the ultra-blackout blinds and heavy drapes before retiring to bed as the sky lightened from true darkness to an indigo-purple dawn.

But it may yet arrive tonight, he thought. Vegas was the home of vampires now, and business carried on throughout the night. It remained what it had always been —a city that never slept.

"That is all," he said, his eyes still on the photograph in his hand. "You can go."

But there was a brief hesitation that made him glance up. One of the greatest strengths of his VASS was her decisiveness and her efficiency. She didn't hesitate.

When he looked up, he saw that her attention was on the photograph. She didn't need to see it to know what it was. After all, had he not spent more hours than he could count sipping whiskey as he stared at it in the days following his return to Vegas?

"Sire," she said, her voice soft.

Rachel had come to him by way of the Vampire Agency Support Staff training academy, a secret body of humans who had served vampires for hundreds of years.

Their role over the years had morphed from vampire slaves to something more in keeping with the new world they lived in.

As long life had forced vampires to embrace an ever-changing world, the VASS also had to evolve in a society more reliant on technology. Mindless servitude was no longer enough. Intelligence and forward thinking soon became what the VASS were known for among the vampire population.

And Rachel, he hadn't been surprised to learn, came from a well-respected family whose parents also served as VASS, as had their parents before them.

Capable, loyal, and unwaveringly dedicated—those were the hallmarks of the DeLuca line, and Rachel's character hadn't diverged from them.

While Ethan had spent the last several years in Prague, Rachel had in the intervening years continued to function as his hands and his eyes in Vegas. She had kept his home clean, his paperwork ordered, and any number of tasks completed efficiently in his absence.

Though her petite frame and elfin features suggested fragility, the tone of her voice was anything but. When she spoke, it always surprised him how someone he'd taken on straight out of training could be so self-assured.

But the hesitancy, the softness in her voice... this wasn't his Rachel speaking, and it made him suspicious. "What is it?"

"If... if you don't mind me saying so, maybe you might be happier if you..." Rachel's words trailed off.

Returning the photograph to the top drawer of his desk, he leaned back in his chair, the sound of creaking leather breaking the sudden silence between them.

His eyes never left her face. "Drop it? Move on? Is that what you were about to say?" he asked, his voice a mere thread of sound.

Rachel could read his moods faster than almost anyone, even his vampire acquaintances. Looking at her face, he saw the moment she realized she'd made a mistake. However, the only sign of her discomfort was in the slight tightening of her fingers around the black tablet she held in one hand.

"Come on, Rachel, now's not the time to clam up. Please, enlighten me! Should I be spending my time finding some other woman to fuck?" his tone mild.

"I only meant—"

He rose without warning, and although he saw her eyes widen, she didn't move.

"Perhaps you didn't want me to find just anyone, is that it?" he asked, prowling toward her.

"Sire," she murmured.

"Someone like you perhaps? Is that what you were thinking?" he asked, his voice cold now, telling her without words what he thought about her—about anything ever happening between them.

She reacted as if he'd slapped her. Then she straightened, and her face settled into a blank mask. But he could still hear the beating of her heart and knew the mask she wore was only that—a mask.

She took a step to one side. Not a retreat, but a deliberate turning away from him. "I was thinking to save you from more heartache, but I can see now I shouldn't have bothered. Don't worry, I won't make the same mistake again."

Turning smartly, she left his office, closing the door behind her with perfect calm. Showing that Ethan hadn't penetrated her resolve enough for her to lose control. That he wasn't worth it.

Deep in thought, Ethan massaged the nape of his neck

as he stared at the closed door before he returned to his desk.

He knew how Rachel felt about him—how she'd always felt. It wasn't easy to hide a body's biological responses to a vampire who could see, smell, and hear the physiological signs of desire.

It'd been clear to him when they'd been introduced at the VASS Offices several years ago, but she'd been young then, and he wasn't interested in innocent human girls.

But over the years, as he'd bounced around between Europe, New York, and Vegas, he'd watched her mature in body and mind.

He'd known when she'd had her first sexual experience—which had surprised him, since he'd thought she'd be the type to wait for love. But it hadn't lasted long, and she'd made no mention of seeing anyone else since.

For a moment he'd toyed with the idea of letting something—brief though it might be—happen between them.

But then he'd met Genevieve at Hellfire, and after that... well, the idea of taking any other woman to bed, human or vampire, had sailed right out of his head.

He glanced at the clock. Nine. Genevieve and Vincent would be on their way to Eros, or there already. They didn't go there every night; he'd watched them enough to know that. But it was Valentine's Day evening, and he had no doubt Vincent would want to take Genevieve out, if only to show her off.

Mr. Knight had made it clear what would happen if he went near her, but as Ethan's gaze fixed with unnerving intensity on the closed desk drawer, the consequences mattered less and less.

He'd been living a quiet life in Prague, seeing no one, keeping to himself, and wandering the dark cobbled streets of a city he'd once loved.

Every night was a battle to keep the burning rage at bay, knowing if he gave in to it for even a moment there would be no stopping him. Aware if he let it loose, he'd set the world on fire.

So, he'd fed on the bagged blood a local Czech VASS filled his refrigerator with, and he drank too much. He wandered the streets, and he slept. That'd been the pattern of his days and nights for years.

And then two weeks ago, he finally opened the email Aidan had sent, railing at him for again missing his New Year's Eve party. There'd been photographs attached, and it was like a strike of lightning shooting through his body when his eyes focused on the couple on the very edge of the shot.

A woman with a mass of rich chestnut hair gazed up at her partner, the long line of her bare neck exposed in a clingy black strapless gown. An intricate mask with a large vibrant peacock feather framed her eyes.

Pressed against her was a lean man wearing a matching mask with one arm wrapped around her waist, the other holding her chin as his lips pressed against hers.

He'd known at first glance it was Genevieve.

How could I not know her?

He tried to convince himself he didn't care, that it didn't matter that she'd left him. But when he saw the next picture... the way she was laughing up at Vincent, like no one and nothing else existed...

Even now he had a vague memory of picking up his phone and telling Rachel to prepare for his return. Sheer, unadulterated rage had powered his movements, and then before he knew it, he was on his private plane and back to Vegas, plans whirling around in his head.

His eyes returned to the clock on the wall. It was nine-fifteen. He was in Vegas, and he knew where Genevieve and Vincent would be tonight. Grabbing the new cell phone that he'd had Rachel replace from his desk, he stalked out of his office.

It was late by the time Genevieve and Vince climbed into their car. The driver didn't need to be told where they were going, and so he started the winding turns down the Vegas Hills, down toward the bright lights of the Strip in the distance.

As they reached the black iron gates at the foot of the exclusive vampire residences high above the city, the Bladed—the armed guards who served the Vampire Council—waved their driver through.

As always, dressed in black shirts and pants, their eyes covered with mirrored wrap-around glasses, they stood with one hand on the distinctive black leather-handled short swords that identified them as what they were.

Gen shivered at seeing the cold-faced vampire guards, completely devoid of expression. She doubted anyone human would ever dare to try their luck against them.

There were more than a few rumors of how misbehaving human tourists weren't always fortunate enough to be given a second chance before they were ruthlessly deprived of an arm, or a leg. Sometimes even a head.

As usual, young women in lace and leather outfits drifted around the enclave gates, waiting for a vampire to leave. On seeing a car approach, they rushed the gates and aimed their phones at the car.

Not that it would have done much good, Gen thought, watching them try to peer through the car's tinted windows as they drove past the small huddle.

"Remember the girl who ripped off her top and threw herself on the windshield?" Vince asked, and Gen couldn't help but giggle at the memory.

While she and Vince hadn't spoken a lot since they'd returned from shopping, just knowing that her time in Vegas was ending had improved her mood. Soon Vegas would be a distant memory when they returned to London.

"As if I could ever forget. What she hoped it would achieve, I have no idea," she said.

"I do," Vince said, winking at her.

It was easy being with Vince. So much so, a part of her still struggled to believe he'd scared her so badly, and at times she wondered if she'd overreacted.

She wanted to forgive him and move on, especially when she caught the despair in his eyes when he looked at her. He cared about her—more than cared—and it wasn't hard to see that keeping her distance from him was hurting him.

When he'd first taken her to London to heal from

losing Ethan, she'd had the impression that she wasn't alone in trying to get over a painful event. But whatever it was that had hurt him, he never mentioned it.

Once he'd let slip a name, a woman called Lily, when she'd asked him about his life before he'd been turned. There'd been such haunting sadness in his eyes, she wondered if it was a woman he'd loved before, and being turned had meant he could no longer be with her.

Had Lily been a former love who'd hurt him, or perhaps even died? She didn't know, since Vince always found some way of changing the subject whenever she pushed.

Now she caught the same lingering sadness in his eyes when she turned to him. He was doing a good job of hiding it, but it was there. If she was being honest with herself, it had been there since she'd let him kiss her on New Year's Eve.

She shouldn't have agreed to it, not now that she could see it would have only reminded him that theirs was a friendly type of love, and not a romantic one.

The smile fading from her face, she reached out to take his hand. "Vince…"

"Genny, we've talked about this. You don't have to—"

"But I feel like I do. I can't help but feel like I'm keeping you from finding happiness with someone else. Instead, you're tied to me, protecting me, letting me live in your home, and I'm—"

Vince squeezed her hand and moved closer. The ever-present humor in his dark eyes disappeared, and for one rare moment, his eyes were serious.

"Our house. And you're not keeping me from being with anyone. I want to be with you."

"Then why do I feel like I am?"

"Because you're a good person," he said, his lips curling into a cynical grin. "A much better person than I am, if I'm being honest, luv."

"But don't you want something more?" she asked, pushing in a way she'd never done before. Perhaps being back in Vegas was making her crazy again.

Vince leaned back in his seat, though he still kept hold of her hand as he turned to gaze out the window. Their car sped through the Vegas streets, passing hotels and casinos before getting mired in the traffic on the Strip.

He was silent for a moment before he spoke. "Sometimes I do. But I know I can't compete with Ethan. I know how much he meant to you."

She shifted her gaze from his profile to the people they passed on the sidewalks, to the vampires and the humans melding together on the streets as they laughed, danced, and drank.

"Do you think that's what I'm doing? Asking you to compete with him?"

Vince turned to her with a sad smile ghosting across his face. "No, but I'd understand it if you were. First loves have a powerful hold on you."

Ah, so that was what Lily had been, then. A first love—much as Ethan had been to her.

Sighing, she sat back in her seat and turned to stare through the windshield at the lights ahead, at the people spilling out across the road at a traffic light.

"He was," she breathed. "But he's gone, and every time

I'm here, it's like I'm haunted by his ghost. I need to move on, but something inside me doesn't seem to be able to."

"Come here," Vince said, tugging at her hand. Unbuckling her seatbelt, she slid over to his side.

Curling his arm around her shoulder, she rested her head against his chest and gazed out of the window. This was what she needed, she thought—breathing in the clean scent of Vince, just simple uncomplicated comfort.

When their car pulled up outside Eros, Gen felt her heart lurch as a spike of fear shot through her. She hadn't thought to ask Vince where they were going tonight, but she should have known it would be Eros, the last place she'd seen the man with the striking resemblance to Ethan. There one second, and gone the next.

She felt Vince's eyes on her and tried to steady her racing heart.

"What is it, luv?"

She laughed, but even to her, it sounded fake. "Nothing, I'm being silly."

Easing her away from him, he peered down at her in silence.

Not for the first time, she wondered at her reasons for not letting anything happen between them.

He was handsome in a way that the girl she'd been when she'd lived her quiet, unremarkable life in a small town in Ohio with her religious parents never would have been able to refuse.

She was reminded of the times she'd sneak CDs she'd borrowed from her friend Tess, since nothing but Christian music or certain types of country were allowed in their home.

There was no way they'd have ever allowed her to listen to rock music. Not with all the swearing, or the CD covers emblazoned with tattooed and heavily pierced musicians all dressed in black. So, she'd listened to them in secret, under her covers with a pair of Tess's headphones in the dead of night while, they slept.

With his shoulder-length black hair held back with a tie, and the glint of silver studs in his ears, she struggled to understand how she'd never been interested in anything more than friendship with Vince.

"Spill," he said.

"Vince, we have to get out. We're causing a backup," she said, peering over his shoulder as at least two black Mercedes waited behind them.

Behind towering black fencing on either side, tourists waited with phones ready to capture arrivals at one of the few venues lining the Strip that no human could enter.

For a moment Gen was convinced Vince was about to tell her to screw the waiting vampires, that he only cared about what was wrong with her. But then he sighed and pushed open his door.

"We'll talk later," he said instead. She couldn't help but compare him to Ethan at that moment.

Ethan wouldn't have cared if traffic backed up for an hour. He wouldn't have let me step out of the car until he got to the bottom of what was wrong with me.

Taking his hand, she stepped out and tried to ignore the flash of cameras from the tourists. Teenage girls especially seemed fascinated by Vince, so she knew he was getting more attention than she was. But then again, at their age, she couldn't deny the appeal of beautiful vampires with pale skin and tight leather pants.

Stopping for a moment, she gazed up at Eros's exterior with its black painted windows and burnished metal bars.

"You look scared," Vince said.

She turned to him and realized he'd been watching her as she stared up at the building. "Do I?"

"Mm."

She smiled. "It's nothing, I'm okay," she said and breathed a sigh of relief when he didn't push. Grateful that he always took her at her word.

"Have I told you how beautiful you are tonight?" Vince said as he guided her toward the entrance with a hand on her hip.

Glancing down at the long black beaded dress which fit like a glove, she shrugged. "If you say so."

She'd grown too accustomed to the baggy men's shirts she'd taken to wearing around their London home, and she'd made no secret of her desire to get back to normalcy. Designer dresses and expensive jewelry had never held any kind of appeal to her. Give her easy and relaxed comfort any day.

"Sorry, sweetheart, but paint-splattered men's shirts just ain't done here," Vince said, winking at the giggling teenage girls recording them on their phones.

Gen spluttered with laughter when, without warning, Vince turned to her and dipped her, bent, and kissed her.

She couldn't help but overhear the sighs of pleasure at what must have seemed like a romantic moment between two vampire lovers. They were eating it up, just as Vince knew they would.

Closing her eyes, she played along, cupping Vince's jaw with both hands as she tried to stifle her laughter. From the squeeze of warning on her right hip, Vince was all too aware of it.

Then he was lifting her and leading her inside as Gen caught sight of one woman fanning herself with her phone. The moment the doors closed behind them, both she and Vince burst out laughing.

Despite her earlier unease, she was having a great time. Vince was determined to deliver on his promise of a good time, and it was working.

They'd danced non-stop since they'd arrived, and when they weren't dancing, he was making her laugh by telling her the rudest jokes he could think of. He didn't seem to care about the disapproval aimed his way, and after a while, neither did she.

"No more," she begged off. "My feet hurt and my sides ache from your terrible jokes. I need a break."

"You sure? I promised you a good time."

"I'm having a great time," she smiled.

"Then I'll get us some drinks." His eyes searched for a waiter. "Wait here, I'll be right back."

"I'll come with you," Gen said, glancing at the cold faces around her warily. He'd be leaving her in the middle of the dance floor alone, and she wasn't sure she'd gotten over what'd happened the last time.

"No need. I'll only be a minute, then it's back to dancing." He winked at her and turned to leave.

Halting him with a hand on his shoulder, she brushed a kiss on his cheek. "Thanks, Vince."

"No need to thank me. The night's not over yet," he said before disappearing into the crowd.

Still smiling, Gen moved out of the way of the dancing couples. Eros was busy as it always was, and with jazz on offer instead of the usual classical music, the atmosphere was a lot less cold.

But as much as she was enjoying tonight with Vince, it was time for her, for both of them, to return to London. She'd talk to him about it again when they returned home, she decided.

A hand landed on her shoulder and grinning, she turned.

"Did you not find—" She stopped. Stared.

A hand, cold and unforgiving, clasped her waist and jerked her toward him. Her hands went up to press against an equally hard chest for balance, as her entire world tipped and swayed around her.

"Ethan!" she gasped.

There was no response from the grim-faced man with the firm jaw and stubborn chin who stared down at her with tortured, verdant green eyes. His thick, raven-black hair was just a little too long, brushed the nape of his neck.

With his arms trapping her against him as her hands came up to clutch him in a vain attempt to steady herself, he danced them through the thick crowd of people.

His hands were cold and hard, and his face... somehow managed to be even harder.

CHAPTER FOUR

*E*than said nothing as he whirled Genevieve across the dance floor and outside to the gardens, where thick vines and dappled willow trees shielded those below from the moon's rays.

The sound of car horns, people laughing, and music drifting in from neighboring clubs and bars surrounded them. Each new sound fought for dominance, and each won, if only for a moment.

They were alone, but they might not be for long, so Ethan continued until they reached a small fountain surrounded by mature trees, deep within the lush oasis in the center of the Vegas strip. Only then did he step away.

"Ethan?" Genevieve whispered, disbelieving. She continued toward him, her hand drifting up to his face as the start of a smile drew his attention to her dusky pink lips. "You're alive!"

In the second before she touched him, his hand shot out, and he caught her wrist. Then he stilled as he smelled it. Smelled her. Sweet orange and coconut drifted from her skin, and he shook with the need to either thrust her away or crush her against him.

His hand clenched around her thin wrist as he fought for control, and she winced in pain. "You have one night," he said, dropping her hand as he stepped away from her.

He could read the confusion in her eyes. "How can you be alive?" she whispered.

When she stepped closer and reached for him, he bared his teeth, and she froze.

"You have no right to demand any answers from me," he snarled.

For a moment a tense silence fell between them as he stared down into her steel-gray eyes, daring her to continue.

She gazed up at him, her eyes wary. "Okay," she whispered. "No questions. But—"

The sweet scent of her wrapped around him until all he could smell was her. "You have one night to say goodbye to your lover."

She parted her lips as if to speak. But when she saw his face harden, she stopped.

"You will not kiss him." He stepped closer as the memory of Vincent and Genevieve's passionate kiss outside Eros turned his words into a rage-filled growl.

"You will not touch him." He edged even closer, his fangs lengthening, the way they had at the sight of Vince's hand on her hip as he'd guided her inside.

Genevieve inched back a step as he crowded her.

"You will not fuck him," he snarled, scenting the sharp fragrance of her fear in the air.

Backing up until she hit a tree and couldn't retreat any further, she opened her mouth, but froze when he reached out and wrapped his hand around her throat. Ethan felt her hard swallow beneath his hand.

"You will not leave Vegas. If you attempt it, I will know. I will come after you. I will kill him, and I promise you it will neither be quick, nor painless. And after that..." He gently squeezed her neck.

"And me? What will you do to me?" she whispered.

He leaned toward her. So close he felt her body trembling against his.

"Whatever I want." He dropped his hand and stepped away as she slid down the tree, as if her legs had lost all ability to support her.

Ethan watched from the shadows as Vincent stepped out into the garden, his eyes searching until he focused on Genevieve's slumped form at the base of the tree where he'd left her.

A small part of him was relieved at Vincent's interruption. He couldn't be sure if he'd been about to choke the life from her, or plunge his fangs into her neck and drink from her.

At the thought of tasting her spicy-sweet blood, he felt his cock harden in response. He'd underestimated the effect she would still have on him, but that was okay. He had time to prepare himself. He wouldn't let his own body's response catch him unawares again. The last thing he wanted, the last thing he would ever want, was her back in his bed. She couldn't be trusted. Not after her betrayal. Not after she'd abandoned him to be tortured in Prague.

From deep in the shadows, his eyes drank in Genevieve's terror as she shook and Vincent demanded to know what was wrong. But all she did was shake her head and repeat that she wanted to go home.

"Was there someone here with you?" Vincent asked her, his gaze searching until Ethan felt it settle on his hiding spot.

"Did someone scare you?" Vincent rose from his crouch beside her.

In the shadows, Ethan grinned in anticipation. Would Vincent dare to face off with him? Because he was ready and waiting.

Genevieve's desperate grasp halted Vincent as he rose.

Ethan's growl was soundless as his eyes focused on that small, soft hand wrapped around Vincent's arm. And though he'd made no sound, Genevieve blanched as if she heard it, and she yanked her hand away.

"I want to go home," she said, stumbling in her haste to get up.

When Vincent turned away from him to steady Genevieve, she slipped out of his grasp and took off at a near run. Vincent was left with little choice but to follow her or be left behind.

Ethan watched them leave before scrubbing a hand over his face. He could still smell the fragrance of her on his skin, and for a moment he closed his eyes and inhaled a scent he hadn't smelled in nearly four years, a scent he hadn't ever expected to smell again.

"One night," he murmured to himself as the door slammed shut behind Genevieve and Vincent, leaving him alone in the dark shadows.

"Just one more night."

CHAPTER FIVE

"Go see Tess? What do you mean, go see Tess?" Gen demanded after they rose the following night.

It'd taken several hours before she finally stopped shaking, and then the tears had started. The sight of her blood-red tears still managed to be as disturbing as the first time she'd seen them, and deep down she doubted she'd ever get used to it.

But at least she didn't have to worry about forcing herself to relax so she could sleep, or about nightmares chasing her from her bed. Not anymore. When she slept now, everything stopped—thoughts, dreams, nightmares... and her heart.

"It'll be a while before we come back to Vegas," Vince said, his eyes glued to his phone. He glanced up at her, clearly distracted. "You should take the opportunity to say goodbye to her face to face, while still you can."

Gen stared at Vince in shock. "What are you talking about? Did you not hear anything I told you about

Ethan…about what he said? We can't leave Vegas. Not now."

"Everything'll work out. Just relax, luv," he said, his attention back on the phone in his hand.

"Vince, you didn't hear him. He meant every word he said. He'll kill you."

"And you're sure it was Ethan?"

"Are you being serious?" she shrieked. "Of course it was him. You don't think I wouldn't recognize—"

Then he was there, wrapping his arms around her. "Look, I'm sorry. I didn't mean it. I've got something else on my mind right now."

The fear that Ethan might be watching, that he'd burst into the house and see Vince hugging her, made it impossible for her to relax.

"Go visit Tess while I get you packed up. Soon this will all be a distant memory."

"But he—" she mumbled into his chest.

Vince's arms tightened around her. "Hush. Go see Tess, and when you get back, we can leave. We can go back home to London. Just like you wanted. You do trust me, don't you?"

She couldn't deny that all she'd wanted was to go back home with Vince and to return to her painting. But now, with Ethan back from the dead, was she supposed to pretend she hadn't seen him? And what if he came after them? He wasn't stupid. It wouldn't take him long to figure out where they'd gone, and then what would he do?

Then there was the not-so-small matter of her feelings for him. Didn't she still love him? Wasn't that the reason she hadn't been able to move on from him?

Sighing, Genevieve scrubbed a hand over her face at the memory of Ethan staring down at her with eyes filled with hatred. How had things gotten so crazy all of a sudden?

Taking her silence for acquiescence, Vince nodded as if everything was decided, and nudged her toward the front door before he returned to his phone.

Not knowing what else to say to convince him to listen, she left. She'd never been any good at confrontation, and this was just another in a long line of arguments she had chosen to walk away from.

The problem with having such strict parents and being an only child was it was always two against one. Over the years, it'd been easier to just do as she was told, since her parents always had an answer for everything. Right up until she'd been paired with Tess during biology in her freshman year of junior high school.

It'd been Tess who'd given her the first taste of freedom, and it was Tess who had run to Vegas as soon as she'd graduated high school to take whatever job she could that would put her up close and personal with vampires.

Tess had always been convinced they existed, and when they revealed their presence to the world and claimed Vegas… that was it. Her goal was set. She would move to Vegas, and there she would convince them to turn her. There was nothing more that Tess wanted.

After Gen had graduated high school and gone through teacher training at a local community college, she'd applied and been accepted at a small school as an art teacher and followed Tess, devastating her parents.

They hadn't spoken to her for months. And then shortly after they'd started taking her calls again, she'd met and fallen in love with Ethan. Once she'd agreed to follow her heart and be turned so they could be together forever, that had been the final nail in the coffin. He was a devil in disguise, according to her god-fearing parents, and that had been that.

She hadn't spoken to them since.

Tess would know what to do, she thought, walking past the suitcases lining the hallway. She'd calm her fears and reassure her that Ethan couldn't mean what he said.

Opening the front door, she spared one last glance at Vince before she stepped out, admitting to herself that regardless of what happened, her gut warned her she wouldn't be seeing Tess for a long while.

Ethan reached for the door handle, poised to step out of his car when Genevieve pushed the front door open, allowing him a glance inside before she emerged.

She was dressed in a pair of blue jeans and a V-neck cream angora sweater, which served to make her olive-skinned complexion appear paler than usual. With her thick glossy curls caught up in a loose bun, and her skin bare of makeup, she was as beautiful as ever.

Parked on the sidewalk outside the neighboring home, he was left with little choice but to pretend he'd dropped something as she climbed into a red Mini Cooper and drove past him. No longer in danger of being spotted by her, he started his engine, but then he stopped.

She hadn't given the impression of someone poised to flee the country. She didn't even have a bag with her, and she'd need her passport at the very least, if she was returning to London. Still, for a moment he sat undecided. Should he follow her and see where she went, or should he stay and keep an eye on the one person his gut warned him needed watching?

When Genevieve's car headlights disappeared from view, he turned the engine off and sat back in his seat, tapping his fingers on the wheel as he waited to see what Vincent would do.

Once she'd revealed who had so terrified her in the garden, Ethan had no doubt escape would be the first thing that crossed Vincent's mind. He doubted Genevieve would try to leave on her own—he'd scared her too much for that. But Vincent... Vincent was an unknown.

Then again, he'd seen Vincent's face as he'd danced with Genevieve the night before. He knew what that softness in his eyes meant. The question was whether Genevieve was more important to him than his self-preservation.

There was no way he'd be letting Vincent disappear without at least one confrontation. After what Vincent and Genevieve had done to him... it wasn't happening. Vincent would have to be completely lacking in intelligence to not be able to read between the lines. He must know a reckoning was coming.

Glancing at the envelope on the seat beside him, he considered going in and confronting Vincent. But unexpected movement from the house stopped him with his hand again on the door handle. Seeing Vincent's white face in an upstairs window with a phone pressed to his ear had him pausing in thought.

"What are you up to?" he murmured to himself when seconds later he heard a car approaching.

Glancing at his rear-view mirror, he saw at once that it wasn't Genevieve returning from her errand. Instead, a limousine with black tinted windows pulled up outside the mansion, and a figure swaddled in a heavy black cloak with a large hood stepped out.

A thin white hand snaked out from the deep recesses of the car and pulled the car door closed. Then the hooded figure, so completely wrapped in thick black fabric that Ethan had no way to tell if it was a man or a woman, started for the front door.

Something about the slow and measured steps up the stone stairs suggested it could be a woman. There was even something vaguely familiar about the stride, but shaking his head, he brushed aside the thought. It couldn't be the person he was thinking. She was dead—had been dead a long time.

But Ethan had no way to know for sure, and from the way the front door was wrenched open before the figure could knock, evidentially the mysterious guest was expected. The limousine drove away, and Ethan returned his gaze to the pale blue three-story mansion.

Vincent's face was devoid of the easy humor which seemed to be his hallmark whenever Ethan had seen him. Instead, his brow was furrowed, and after he shot a nervous glance behind his cloaked guest, he stepped aside to let them in before hurriedly pulling the door closed.

Just who had Vincent invited over? And why had he waited until Genevieve had left the house to do it?

Tess laughed until she cried. Then shaking her head, she sat rocking back and forth on a playground swing beside Gen and stared into the distance.

"Vince is an idiot," she snorted, her bright cherry hair managing to be as vivid in the darkness of the night as it was during the day.

"Hey!" Gen said, offended on Vince's behalf.

"If he thinks Ethan's going to let him—and you—slip away like that, then he is. And you're an idiot too, for agreeing to it."

"I haven't agreed to anything,"

"Then what're you doing here?" Tess said sharply as she pushed off the ground to start up her swing. Gen watched her for a moment, and then kicked off too.

"It wasn't a terrible idea, my coming to see you. We hardly see each other anymore as it is."

She was starting to get the impression that she wasn't welcome whenever she visited Tess. And that was another thing—it was never Tess coming to see her. But at least this time she'd agreed to join her on the swings outside the apartment they'd used to share. At least that was something.

"Things change all the time. Except me, that is," Tess said, a note of bitterness in her voice.

Gen didn't like to agree, but Tess was right. Since she'd moved to Vegas, Tess was still wearing the same black leather, lace tights, and black eye shadow. She was still working at the vampire club downtown and had ever-increasing bite marks on her neck. The only thing that'd changed about her was she older, with more lines and fewer smiles on her face.

"You could change if you wanted to. Maybe think about leaving Vegas?" she suggested, knowing almost before Tess spoke what her answer would be. Before she'd even stopped speaking, Tess was already shaking her head.

"I can't leave. Not when I still have a chance of being turned. A waitress not far from Hellfire was turned a few weeks back. She's moved into a hotel on the Strip with him. She's forty, if you can believe it. If they can change a pudgy forty-year-old with wrinkles, no matter what anyone says, one of them will change me."

"But what if they don't?" Gen asked. This was a delicate subject, and the last thing she wanted was to upset Tess, but sooner rather than later her friend had to accept the thing she'd always wanted might not happen before her life was over.

"They will. I just have to be patient."

She made sure her voice was soft. "It's been nearly ten years, Tess."

"I know how long it's been, Gen," Tess snapped.

Gen sighed. "I didn't mean to upset you. I just think you're pretty amazing as you are, you don't need—"

"What do you know about what I need and don't need?" Tess asked, her voice hard as she pushed harder at her swing.

Gen let her swing come to a gentle stop and watched Tess swing higher and higher.

"You couldn't care less what happened to me from the moment you got yourself turned, and you're only here to rub my nose in it."

"That isn't true. I didn't come here—"

"No. No, you didn't. It just happened to you without you even asking for it. And me—who wants it more than you ever did—gets left behind, as vampire after vampire falls over themselves for you."

Gen watched as Tess launched herself out of the swing, landing on her feet with a stumble. But she didn't turn around.

"You don't deserve it," Tess said, her voice thick. "And you don't deserve Ethan, either. I'd do anything for—well, it doesn't matter, does it? You have it all, and still, it's not enough for you."

"I didn't know he was alive, Tess," Gen said, standing from the swing. Tears filled her eyes, but she didn't care about having blood-red tears now. Not when Tess was about to walk away from her. "I didn't know."

Tess's back was straight. Unbowed as she walked away.

"Well, let's hope that's enough to save you from Ethan. We all know how vampires deal with betrayal, don't we?"

Gen watched her friend go. She remembered the nights they snuggled on the couch, shrieking with laughter at a TV show, or sometimes nothing at all. They'd been friends for years, and she knew Tess enough to know not to even try. All she could do was give her time. Maybe in a day or two, her anger might have burned itself out. But there was no forcing Tess to listen when she didn't want to.

"Goodbye, Tess," she murmured, blinking back the tears from her eyes.

Ethan's gaze was curious as he examined the stone facade of the mansion Genevieve and Vincent called home. He'd done—or rather he'd had Rachel do—some digging, and she'd discovered that the mansion was one they'd stayed in before. The home was in fact owned by Vincent.

From his house-hunting efforts several years ago, he knew homes in this neighborhood cost upward of a couple million or more. Then there were the designer clothes, the exorbitant membership to Eros, and the private plane.

So where did all the money come from?

It could only be Vincent's Master. A Master who lavished a fortune on both Vincent and Genevieve, but who chose to remain hidden. Through all his digging, he'd never managed to get any closer to who it was.

His cell phone vibrated, and Ethan glanced at the text message from Rachel.

It read, *No private plane booked. Another way?*

Responding with a question mark, he tossed the phone back into the seat beside him. With all flights from the States to Europe coming dangerously close to arriving during daylight hours, the safest way to travel would be by private plane.

Since he trusted Rachel was thorough enough not to

have made a mistake, he guessed Vincent must have planned something else. Though what, he had no idea.

When car headlights appeared behind him, a glance confirmed it was Genevieve returning from her errand.

He sank a little in his seat as she pulled up in the driveway. But instead of getting out, she sat unmoving for a long moment.

Unable to see her face, Ethan frowned in thought as he considered her slumped form. Evidentially, whatever errand she'd ran hadn't been a good one, and he watched as she stepped out of her car and rubbed at her eyes with the back of her hand.

Seeing it, despite her unforgivable betrayal, a part of him—a very small part—wanted nothing more than to go to her and wrap his arms around her.

When she entered the house and closed the door behind her, Ethan felt something stir inside him … some feeling of disquiet. He'd seen something when Genevieve left the house earlier, and again when she'd returned. What was it that had his instincts screaming that something wasn't right?

Closing his eyes, he thought back to what he'd seen— the stranger arriving, Vince letting them in, the stranger's car leaving. He'd seen… suitcases in the hallway. So, he'd been right about Vince making a run for it. But how was he planning on leaving, if not on a private plane? He couldn't see Vincent taking Genevieve back to London any other way.

Then it clicked. What he'd seen. When Genevieve had opened the door to let herself in, the suitcases were no longer there. And then he remembered the cloaked stranger had never left.

His heart lurched in warning, and then he was moving without conscious thought. Phone, keys, and the all-important stamped claim left behind with the car door wide open as he sprinted after Genevieve.

CHAPTER SIX

"Vince?" Gen called, closing the front door behind her. "Vince, I'm back. Where are you?"

She'd expected to find him in the lounge on his phone, but instead, the elegant glass and muted pastel decorated room, which put her in mind of expensive boutique hotels, was empty—and the suitcases he'd left beside the front door were gone.

Glancing up the staircase, she let out a sigh of relief when she saw them propped against the wall outside her bedroom.

"Have you changed your mind about leaving, then?" she said, starting up the stairs. "I told you it wasn't a good idea. Maybe if we all just sat down, you, me, and Ethan, I'm sure we could work something out."

With Vince leaving the suitcases outside her room, she'd expected to find him inside. But the room was empty. He wasn't usually so quiet, and the few occasions she'd been the one to go out and he stay in, he'd at least called out a quick hi if he was busy with something. But it wasn't like him to be this quiet.

Growing increasingly concerned, she turned to try his room. Maybe he was in the shower and couldn't hear her?

But then she stopped.

Because the room wasn't empty at all. The chunky heel of Vince's combat style boots—boots he never took off—peeked out at her from the far side of her bed. Blood rushed to her head, and she fought against the frantic desperation to run and never stop running.

Taking a hesitant step forward, she took another, and then another before she came to a sudden stop, like a train suddenly running out of track. Because just like the room, the boots weren't empty either. There were feet in them. Vince's feet. Horror—it was sheer, unadulterated horror holding her immobile when she saw the rest of him.

His head was missing. Someone had cut off his head.

Lacking awareness of how she'd got there, she came to herself on the floor with one hand pressed tight against her mouth and the other hugging her knees to her chest. The strange, keening cry she heard echoing all around her wasn't the anguished sound of an animal in pain. It was the sound of her heart breaking.

Because Vince was gone. There'd be no healing from this. No vampire could survive decapitation. It'd been Ethan who'd been the one to tell her that, on one summer night as they'd sat on the swings outside her and Tess's apartment.

She remembered his brief pause after she'd finally given in to her curiosity about vampires.

"If you stake a vampire, or use holy water, will it kill him?"

The question was quiet, but the words rushed out of her mouth before she could change her mind again, and let another opportunity to learn more—to know more—slip away.

His gaze was focused, and she felt the weight of his stare as he took his time deciding whether she was someone he could trust or not. Then he looked away, and for a second she felt a stabbing pain in her heart because he didn't trust her and it... hurt. It surprised her how much it hurt.

But then he spoke. His voice was casual, as if he were talking about the weather, all the while his eyes fixed on something in the distance.

"The business of staking a vampire is complicated," he said. "Holy water will annoy a vampire, in the same way a human would be annoyed at someone soaking their thousand-dollar strictly dry-clean only designer shirt. But the stake... there's not many who can summon the will to stab someone through the heart while looking them right in the eye. It takes a special kind of person to do that." He turned to eye her then, as if to see how she was taking it.

Mouth hanging open, she could only stare at him in shock.

"And another thing is force," he continued in the same casual tone. "Not many people are strong enough to do it. I guess that's where the old stories of people using mallets to stake sleeping vampires in their coffins came from."

Licking suddenly dry lips, she pushed off the ground and resumed swinging. Only now had she noticed she'd come to a complete stand-still. The movement helped—if only a little—to distract herself from the horrifying thought of someone plunging a stake into Ethan, while he lay helpless and unprotected in his sleep.

"So, you're saying the myths are right, then? That if a

person was strong enough, if they used a mallet, they could kill a vampire?"

"If the vampire were very young. A young vampire is easier to kill—even a car crash could do it. It takes time for immortality to... take. Decades, in fact."

Listening to him talk was both fascinating, yet equally terrifying. She was hearing things no one else knew, and a small, hidden part of her hungered for more. To hear that newly turned humans could still be as vulnerable as the rest of humanity, was something she could imagine the Vampire Council would want to keep hidden.

"But not an older vampire?"

"No," he said.

"And are you an... older vampire?"

He turned to her with the corners of his eyes creased in mirth, an easy smile on his lips.

For a moment she wondered what he'd do if she leaned over and kissed him. Would he kiss her back, or would he tell her she'd gotten the wrong message, and he wasn't interested in art teachers who didn't go out, rarely drank, and were tucked up in bed by nine?

As if sensing where her thoughts had drifted, his eyes darkened and excitement shot through her that he might be the one to kiss her. But then he shook his head with a faint smile still on his face and turned away. "Old enough," he said.

She wanted to know how old he was, but something in the way he answered her made her realize he would not tell her. Was it considered rude to ask a vampire his or her age?

"So, what would I have to do, then?" she asked.

"Persistent little thing, aren't you?" he said with a smile in his voice.

"Yes," she said without turning to face him. He had a dangerous smile, a far too distracting one, especially when it revealed the dimple on his right cheek.

"Beheading," he said.

Spinning her head around, she sucked in a breath as her swing shot out from beneath her, nearly sending her crashing to the ground.

Before she could blink, he'd caught her. Was holding her close enough for her to smell the whiskey on his breath, the woody-citrus scent of his cologne, and see the vivid green of his eyes which reminded her of new grass in spring.

"What?" she whispered.

He leaned closer, cupping her jaw with one large hand as his eyes dipped to her lips. "To kill me, you would need to behead me."

Her eyes widened in shock. "Why would you tell me that?"

"Maybe I've started to trust you," he said, leaning closer. "Am I making a mistake?"

The sound of water dripping in the bathroom brought her back to herself. It was impossible to know if she'd been sitting on the floor for two minutes or two hours. Time didn't seem quite so important to her right now. Nothing did.

In the back of her mind, she was aware the sound had always been there. But it was like she was hearing it for the first time, and it pulled her out of herself, out of her memories. It was such a strange thing for her to focus on when Vince was lying dead in front of her.

Brushing at the wetness on her cheeks with the back of her hand, she rose. As if in a trance, she started toward the bathroom, drawn by the noise like a moth to a flame.

The bathroom door was closed, and something about it almost drew her from her dreamlike state. After she showered, she always shut the bathroom door to keep the steam out of the bedroom. At least she was sure she had. And with Vince having his own bathroom, he never used hers.

But she could see the door was open a few inches. Had she been distracted by thoughts of Ethan and not closed the door all the way? Or was this something else?

Still, the lingering sense that something wasn't quite right wasn't enough to stop her. Was Vince's head inside? Had someone killed him and left his head for her to find in the bathroom? She shook her head as she pressed forward. She couldn't think about that now. Perhaps not ever.

The metal door handle felt cold in her hand, and she gripped it tighter. She'd turn off the dripping faucet. After that, she had no idea what she would do, where she would go. *But it could all come later. Much later.*

She started to push the door open.

A hand flashed past her face, close enough that she felt the stir of air against her skin. Then it clamped down hard on her mouth, forcing back the scream barreling its way up her throat. A second hand joined hers on the door handle, and the bathroom door was slammed shut with enough force for the air to ruffle her hair.

Then, urged back against a tall, muscled body, she thrashed and struggled as she was forced step by step out of the bedroom.

"Stop struggling. It's me."

It took her far longer than it should have for the words

to form a coherent shape in her mind. And then she understood. Ethan. It was Ethan. What was he doing...? Had he been the one who...?

Then she was struggling again. Harder now. Remembering what he'd said. She hadn't kissed Vince, but Vince had packed their bags. Had Ethan known that Vince planned on leaving, and killed him as he said he would?

Fighting a desperate battle now, she nearly sent them tipping down the stairs with her violent struggles.

"For fuck—" Ethan growled.

He stopped, and between one breath and the next, Gen went from standing to being flung over Ethan's shoulder as he moved with vampire speed.

One moment he was forcing her down the stairs, and the next he was shoving her into the passenger side of a black Mercedes with tinted windows, and slamming her door shut.

Before she could even think about trying to run, he'd poured his large body into the driver's seat and was glaring at her as he started the engine.

"Don't even think about it," he snarled.

Shrinking away from the rage in his eyes, she pressed herself against the door, as far away as she could get from him.

He slammed his foot on the accelerator, and they peeled away from the mansion in a squeal of burning rubber. She jerked forward in her seat from the sudden movement.

"Put your seatbelt on," Ethan snapped.

She couldn't help but wonder why all of a sudden, he sounded so very far away, like she was on one island and he was on another, and he had to shout to make himself heard.

She wrapped her arms around herself. All she could think about was Vince's head. Why couldn't she stop thinking about Vince's missing head?

Ethan glanced at Genevieve in the seat beside him. If he was in any doubt about her state of mind, the glazed sheen in her eyes and her lack of response made it clear how badly she was coping with Vincent's death.

"Genevieve?"

He wasn't surprised when the only response he got was another tear sliding down already bloodstained cheeks.

Sighing, he reached over and after snagging her seatbelt, snapped it into place.

At least she'd reacted when he'd sworn at her, but now it was like she couldn't hear him at all. Or like he didn't even exist to her anymore.

There was something about the sight of her tears sliding silently down her cheeks that made him feel strangely uncomfortable.

Shaking his head, he concentrated on getting them back to his home in the vampire enclave set a little higher in the hills, and guarded by more of the Bladed guards.

He didn't know what'd been behind the bathroom door, but he knew it couldn't have been anything good. Not with Vincent lying dead on the bedroom floor and his head missing. Whatever it was had made his hackles rise, and his first and only instinct was to grab Genevieve and run.

Why someone would not only kill Vincent, but also leave his body splayed out for her to find, he didn't know. Perhaps he'd pissed off the wrong Master, and this was payback—but whatever mistake he'd made, he'd certainly paid a hefty price for it. Still, whoever it was had done Ethan a favor, and he wasn't about to complain about it.

Rachel was waiting for him in the entryway, her gaze on Genevieve as she stood silently beside him. "Do you need me to—"

"No. You can leave. I want you back at the house early tomorrow, I have a task for you," Ethan said.

Though he could feel her curiosity as he led a placid Genevieve up the white marble staircase, she didn't ask any questions.

"Of course," Rachel said. "Good night, Sire."

Lifting a hand in farewell, he didn't turn round as he continued to lead the docile Genevieve up the stairs and into his bedroom, closing the door behind them. A thought struck him unexpectedly. It'd once been their bedroom, not just his. For a short time, they had lived together, and those months had been the happiest of his life. He glanced at her, expecting to find some reaction, some emotion—but her gaze was devoid of all expression.

Leaving her standing beside the king-size bed, he returned moments later with a damp washcloth and a white T-shirt.

"Close your eyes," he said.

Genevieve's gaze remained fixed at a point above his right ear.

He caught her chin and angled her head so they were eye to eye. "Close your eyes," he repeated, injecting force into his words.

After a brief pause, her eyes fluttered shut.

In silence, Ethan wiped the blood from her face with gentle fingers before tossing the cloth at the foot of the bed. Then he caught the bottom of her blood-stained cream sweater and eased it over her head.

For a moment his gaze lingered on the soft swell of her breasts peeking over her simple white cotton bra. But forcing his eyes away from temptation, instead he tugged the T-shirt over her head.

Better he didn't even think about taking off Genevieve's bra—not when his fangs were already extended, and his cock was already straining against his pants. It'd be asking for trouble, and he knew it.

It was like dressing a life-size doll, he thought. Genevieve standing still, staring into the distance as he slid her jeans off her by lifting first one foot, and then the other. Then he was pulling the white linen covers back and easing her into the bed before tucking the covers around her.

He stared down at her as she gazed up at him—or rather, through him. When Ethan saw her eyes filling with tears, he leaned down so he could speak directly into her ear.

"Sleep," he ordered, for a moment forgetting Genevieve couldn't be enthralled, which surprised him considering it had been the thing that had caught his attention in the first place.

He'd seen her in his friend Aidan's bar, a human girl firmly, yet politely telling a vampire who'd approached her that she wasn't interested in being anyone's dinner. Not tonight. Not ever.

But maybe he wasn't the only one who forgot, because she obeyed him as if he'd been the one to push her into oblivion.

Her heartbeat slowed, beating once, twice more, and then stilled. When he lifted his head, her eyes were closed and fresh blood tracks ran down the side of her face and onto the white pillows.

He reached out to touch the softness of her cheek but caught himself before his fingers could graze her skin. Pulling his hand back, he formed it into a tight fist and turned away. There was one reason, and one reason only he'd brought her back to his home and into his bed, and he'd do better to remember that.

There was no room for doubt or weakness or anything else which threatened to turn him away from his goal.

Striding from the room, he shut the door behind him. He needed a drink … a big one.

CHAPTER SEVEN

In the second before Gen opened her eyes, she tensed. This wasn't her bed, and she never wore a bra to bed.

Then it all came back to her—finding Vince's body, Ethan throwing her over his shoulder, and then ordering her to sleep. Which meant the only place she could be was in Ethan's bed.

Without conscious thought, she was out of bed and moving, rushing toward the bedroom door before she stopped. She glanced down at the white T-shirt that hit her mid-thigh. She couldn't go out like this.

She needed pants first, and later—much later—she could think about why Ethan had undressed her, and why she couldn't remember him doing it.

Spinning around, she crossed over to the closet on the other side of the room and yanked the door open. Her eyes widened in surprise at the racks jam-packed with enough clothing to fill a high-end boutique.

Most, if not all the clothes, still had their tags attached. Finally managing to shake off her disbelief, she grabbed the first pair of jeans she saw and didn't stop to pull off the tag before she shoved her legs into them. They fit her perfectly, which made her pause for another second.

Shoes were going to be a problem. The only shoes here were heels, and most of them at least three inches. Heels would only slow her down, she thought as she closed the closet door. They didn't exactly fit the bill for sneaking out of a vampire's mansion.

Breathing a sigh of relief when she managed to open the door without making a sound, she tiptoed down the stairs, the marble floor cold beneath her bare feet.

There was no sign of Ethan as she continued down the grand staircase, her eyes fixed on the large white front door across the entryway.

She had no idea what time it was, but she sensed enough time had passed for it to be the next day, that the sun had long since gone down and it was safe for her to venture out. Everything else was a mystery she could work on solving later, once she'd gotten out of Ethan's house before he did to her what he'd done to Vince.

She'd taken one step outside when she stopped. Memories struck without warning, filling in the gaps between what she remembered and what she'd forgotten. Of Ethan wiping the tears from her face, of his undressing her and putting her to bed.

Those weren't the actions of a killer.

Ethan had reacted like there was something to be feared behind the bathroom door, something she hadn't sensed. And the way he'd snatched her up and tossed her over his shoulder, the speed he'd carried her away, suggested whatever it was had been bad. If anything, he'd been acting like he was protecting her.

Closing the front door, she headed for Ethan's office. It'd been a long time since she'd been back in the house she'd briefly called home, and she knew if Ethan was going to be anywhere, he'd be in his office.

Ethan knew the moment Genevieve woke. He would always know the sound of her heart beating.

Sitting back in his chair, he shifted his focus away from the email he'd been composing to his accountant. It'd been impossible not to hear her wrenching open the closet door, creeping down the stairs, and rushing toward the front door. He'd started to rise, but then she'd stopped, and so had he.

It'd come as no surprise she'd try to run away from him, but he had no intention of letting her get far.

As he waited to see what she would do, he knew one thing was certain—she wasn't getting away. Not when he hadn't even begun. But then he heard her close the front door and start toward his office. Settling back in his seat, he waited.

The feel of her eyes on him told him when she'd reached the doorway, but he didn't immediately raise his from the laptop screen. When he did, he found her standing in the open doorway watching him, her expression filled with a softness he hadn't been expecting.

"I see you changed your mind about leaving, then," he

said, closing the laptop lid and leaning back in his black leather office chair. It was both harder and easier to keep his expression blank with her in his home after all this time.

She was the woman he would have dreamed about if vampires could dream. The woman he'd loved, hated and craved all these years.

His again.

As she took a small step inside his office, his gaze lowered. She'd been about to run out of the door in nothing more than bare feet, a T-shirt she'd slept in, and a pair of jeans? Not even taking the time to put on a pair of fucking shoes? His face hardened at the sight.

Returning his focus to her face, he saw in the seconds that had ticked by, her gaze had shifted to wariness.

"I... I didn't remember," she said, fiddling with her hands as she stood just inside his office. "About what you did for me. I, er, for a moment I thought you had done it. That you..." Her words trailed off.

"Killed your boyfriend?" His tone was silky.

She swallowed. "He wasn't my..."

Pausing when she picked up on a small shift in his expression, she cleared her throat. "Anyway, I realize you probably saved my life, and I wanted to say thanks. And for what you did after, you know, for taking care of me."

He stared at her. Silence reigned as Genevieve raised a hand to tuck a strand of hair behind her ear. His continued silence was making her nervous—he could see it in her eyes, in the way she couldn't quite meet his—but he didn't care.

He picked up his cut crystal whiskey glass and took a long draw from the fiery amber liquid without taking his eyes from hers. "So, you were running away because you believed I was responsible?"

"Well, I..." She paused. "In the garden, you said you'd kill him if we tried to leave."

"Yes. Yes, I did."

At his lack of denial, unease crept across her face.

"Ah, I see you haven't completely absolved me of all responsibility, then. So even now you still believe I played a part in your lover's death?" he asked.

Her silence made him smile. But it was a cold and humorless smile. "Well, it wouldn't make a difference whether I had or not. You would have been returned to me by one of the Bladed long before the night was over."

He lifted the lid of his laptop, and hit send on his email before moving onto the next message awaiting his response.

It was a message from his accountant about some real estate in London he'd been considering as a long-term investment property.

"I don't understand," Genevieve said, sounding confused. "What do you mean, I would've been brought back to you?"

Ethan kept his eyes on the screen as he typed up a quick response.

"I'd have thought I was clear enough, but since you've had a shock, I suppose I can afford to be generous." He stopped typing to glance up at her.

"I've been formally recognized by the Vampire Council

as your Master. Which means you leaving without my express approval would result in... harsh consequences. After all, we can't have young vampires running around without a firm guiding hand, can we?" he asked sharply.

He was well aware that things could have gone badly without his quick maneuvering. Vincent's murder had surprised him, and it could have upset his careful plans, but this complication had also opened some doors. Doors he planned to make full use of.

"But I don't have..." She stopped when Ethan glanced up at her. "I've been living with Vince in London. I thought you were dead. I don't understand how the Council can decide to—"

Saying nothing, he retrieved a piece of paper from his desk. It was the claim form he'd retrieved from his car after he'd left Genevieve sleeping. Though it was more than a little creased from where she'd sat on it, it was still perfectly legible. Sliding it across the desk, he tapped at the top of the form with one finger until she came close enough to read it.

"As you can see, this confirms you are my Childe. Mine to educate. To teach. To nurture. That is my duty as a Master. Something the Council takes very seriously, especially when more and more young vampires have to be put down because of their lack of control."

Her eyes skimmed over the claim, growing wider and her face paler as she read, and then she came to an abrupt stop.

Ethan hid his smile. "Ah, I see it's all coming back to you now," he said, slipping the claim form back into a drawer.

"I remember signing this," she whispered. "But I live in London now. I can't stay here." Genevieve sounded panicked at the thought.

"You have no reason to return to London," he said. "What with your boyfriend dead. Then there's the matter with his Master…"

Here he paused briefly, waiting to see if he might find out who Vince's Master was—something neither he nor Rachel had been able to learn.

"I never met his Master," she said distractedly.

What did she mean, she'd never met his Master?

Rachel had discovered that although the property in Vegas and a couple of homes in London had been in Vince's name, he had to have been bankrolled by someone else. Because twenty years ago Vincent had been human, and he'd had another name.

He'd been Jake Walker, a talented street musician who performed on his guitar in Covent Garden. A man who had dreams of making it big but had disappeared one day, leaving behind a guitar he'd rarely been seen without.

It was clear what had happened to him. Along the way, perhaps by chance or by design, he'd caught the attention of a vampire … the one who'd turned him.

"Wait! What's going to happen to Vince? I mean, he's dead, murdered. And his killer is out there, maybe planning on killing someone else. And his body..." Genevieve sounded close to tears. He forced himself to ignore her response.

"Will be found by his VASS... I'm assuming you employed one?"

"Well, yes. But—"

"Then I imagine his body will be disposed of," he said.

"What do you mean...disposed of?"

He shrugged. It didn't concern him in the least what was done with Vince's body.

"Either his Master will claim it, or they won't. It hardly matters which," Ethan said, keeping his voice light, ignoring the horror on Genevieve's face. "And this Master of his…"

Still distracted, she shrugged. "I don't know, he never talked about his Master. There was a woman, but I think she was an old girlfriend…"

Ethan lost interest.

It was, of course, a possibility that Vince's Master was a woman. After all, Vince had been handsome in a pretty kind of way, and female vampires often did like to surround themselves with pretty young men. But he doubted it.

Vince had been based in London, and Ethan had more than a few friends and acquaintances in and around Europe. There were no female vampires who could successfully hide themselves as well as this one had from him and Rachel.

No. Vince's Master was a man. Likely one with his own reasons for wanting to keep his identity a secret from Genevieve and the vampire population for some strange reason. Or perhaps he was just crazy. It was known to happen with older vampires.

"You mean there won't even be an investigation? Or a funeral? I can't just do nothing. He deserves a funeral, at the least. Everyone does. I don't know his Master, but I could do it... organize one. I could take his body back to London, and—"

Ethan seized his laptop with one hand and launched it at the wall on the other side of the room in one fluid motion. It exploded on contact. Fragments of glass, metal, and plastic showered them from all angles like confetti.

Then he turned his gaze from the remains of his computer to Genevieve, who stared at him with wide eyes, her heart racing so fast it was all he could hear in the silence of his office.

He stood and stalked around his desk. The closer he got to her, the wider her eyes grew. She raised one hand toward him as if to halt his progress, but he ignored it as he continued to back her against the wall.

"You are pushing me," he bit out. "To the very edge of my limits. If I were you, I would be more concerned with survival, and less about that dead boyfriend of yours. Have I made myself clear?"

"Yes, I—"

"Good. Now get out."

"But I—"

"I swear to heaven and hell. If you make me repeat myself, Genevieve, you will regret it," Ethan snarled.

When he saw fear flood her eyes, he took a step back.

She didn't hesitate. She flew out of the room.

At the top of the stairs, Gen stopped. She didn't know what she'd done to make Ethan so angry with her, but it didn't matter. This wasn't about her—not anymore. This was about Vince, about making sure he was treated with respect.

To stand back and do nothing while the Council disposed of Vince's body like he didn't matter, wasn't an option. Because he did matter. He mattered to her.

He'd saved her life in Prague. For her to do anything less than her absolute best would be a mockery of everything he'd done for her. So, turning around, she started back down the stairs, stiffening her spine as she went. This was a confrontation she wasn't backing down from, no matter what. Because there were some things you just didn't walk away from, and this was one of them.

She found Ethan standing at his window, gazing down at the twinkling lights of the Vegas Strip in the distance, a full glass of whiskey in his hand and his back to the shattered remains of his laptop.

Telling herself the only reason she had for not venturing any further inside the room was to avoid stepping on sharp fragments, she cleared her throat.

His eyes focused on her with unnerving intensity as he sipped at his drink. She remembered the taste of his whiskey kisses, rich and smoky and caramel-sweet, but that wasn't all she hungered for. There was something in watching his throat work as he drank which made her hunger in a way she'd never felt before.

She knew it had everything to do with being a vampire, about satisfying a different kind of hunger, even as he gazed at her over the rim of his glass with hooded dark eyes, his day-old stubble making her fingers itch to touch.

Turning away from temptation, she found herself staring at the space on the wall above his desk. He'd gotten rid of her painting, the gift he'd told her was the best present anyone had ever given him.

Once, a long time ago, she'd dreamed of turning a silly little hobby into a career. A hope that she could turn her passion to draw, to paint, into something more. But then her dreams had crashed into the unmovable wall that was her parents' will, and their insistence that being an artist would put her on a path to unemployment checks and crappy apartments.

So, she'd swallowed her wild dreams and settled for a career as an art teacher. At least then she could still nurture passion for art in kids, even if she couldn't nurture it in herself.

It had been Ethan who'd picked up a sketch pad she'd left lying around her apartment with Tess and, after flicking through, discovered the rough sketches she'd done of him.

One night she'd found herself unable to stop seeing Ethan nursing a squat glass of whiskey at the bar of Hellfire, and so she'd run out to buy a pad and pencils, and spent hours sketching him from memory.

He'd stared at it for the longest time, and then torn it out, carefully folding it and tucking the paper in his pocket.

Not knowing what to say, she'd been too embarrassed to offer up any comment in case he thought she was weird for drawing him when she'd only known him for a couple of days. But instead, he'd turned to her and said,

"I want another one. A painting this time. One I can hang over my desk."

And that was when she'd known he'd liked it.

Tears pricked her eyes, but she forced herself not to cry. She couldn't afford to give into them, not now. Not when the only reason she was here was because of Vince.

Forcing her mind away from his destruction of something she'd worked on for weeks, something she'd known he'd loved, she squared her shoulders and met Ethan's eyes.

"Look, Ethan, I'm sorry for whatever I've done to upset you. I really am, but I can't do nothing about Vince," she said firmly.

She'd seen the way his jaw tensed, as if he was grinding his teeth whenever she said Vince's name. Evidently, he thought something had happened between them, and until she could make him see how wrong he was, she'd try to avoid upsetting him.

A spark of humor lit his eyes. "Is that so?" he asked, his voice soft.

For a moment she wavered. There was something there, some dark shadow flickering in his eyes that made her want to retreat. It warned her she was approaching some invisible line, and that there was a very real possibility he might actually hurt her.

Shaking her head and trying to convince herself this was Ethan, and Ethan had never hurt her before, she cleared her throat and continued.

"It's important. His life was important, and so is finding out who did it. He didn't deserve to have his head..." She braced herself as dizziness swept over her at the sudden, jolting memory of Vince's headless body

"I see. And that's your priority, then? To investigate the death of your lover?"

It was on the tip of her tongue to tell Ethan that Vince hadn't been her lover. But when he narrowed his eyes, she promptly closed her mouth. The last thing she needed to do was antagonize him, she thought. Especially when she needed his help with Vince.

As long as Vince had his funeral, and she did everything she could to find out who'd killed him, it could wait.

"Yes," she said, and then hesitated. "But I don't know anything about investigating a murder. Perhaps the Council might—"

"The Council couldn't care less about a vampire killing, unless it's someone of a higher status than your friend was," Ethan interrupted, his voice cold.

"Higher status?" she asked. "And what does that mean?"

"Important," he said. "Powerful, extremely wealthy, and well-connected."

She scowled. "So, because my friend is none of those things, they won't do anything?" she asked, shocked once again by how little vampires cared about each other. It was one thing seeing it in action at Eros, but it was another thing hearing it from Ethan's lips.

"Why should they? If a Master wants to go after the person responsible for the murder of his Childe, so be it. If not…" Ethan shrugged.

Staring at him in silence, she rubbed at her temples.

"I get what you're saying, but how is his Master even supposed to know Vince is dead?"

Ethan's gaze sharpened. "His Master will know."

"Right, the Master-Childe bond," she murmured, Vince's words returning to her. And then she blinked at Ethan. How could they be in the same room as each other, and yet she could feel no awareness of him on a deeper level?

It had been there, the first night he'd awoken her after he'd turned her in Prague. She'd felt the thread tying them together that made her aware of his presence in a way she'd never been aware of anyone else before.

When he'd said he needed to go out and deal with some business and he hadn't come back, the thread linking them together had stretched and become as insubstantial as gossamer thread, until finally it had snapped. That was when she'd known he was gone. Dead. And that he wouldn't be coming back.

But he hadn't died. He couldn't have, if he was standing right in front of her. Yet the bond between them was still missing. How could that be?

"And if Vince's Master doesn't want to find out who's responsible?"

Ethan shrugged, looking bored.

She stared at him. "So, nothing is done?"

"Have you considered that this may be to your benefit, his mysterious Master staying away?"

"I don't understand. How could—"

"It would be no stretch of the imagination to believe you played a part in his Childe's murder."

"And why would—"

Ethan raised his glass to his mouth as he studied her, a

thoughtful expression on his face. "We'll get to that. But first, about this funeral you're so keen to have…"

It struck her not only was she broke, she'd also never planned a funeral before in her life. But it couldn't be that hard, could it?

"I don't mind. It'll be small, so it wouldn't cost a lot. And I'd get a job after to pay you back. What do you think?"

Vince had always paid for everything, and he'd refused to entertain the idea of her getting a job for even a second. He'd told her it was his role to provide for her, not that she'd put up too much of a fight. Ethan had been the same way, and it hadn't taken long for her to accept this was just the way vampires were.

But now with Vince dead, she had no money and no belongings of her own. She had clothes back at their house, and photos and her paintings in London, but she didn't see Ethan agreeing to let her go and retrieve her stuff. So, at the moment she was wholly and completely reliant on him, at least until she could find a way of getting back on her feet—however long that might take.

As someone who'd worked all through college and gone straight into work after, she never imagined she'd be approaching her thirties with so little to show for all her hard work.

"Of course," Ethan said nodding.

The tension fell away from her shoulders. Perhaps he wasn't as angry as he'd been earlier. Maybe it was something else that'd set him off.

Ethan finished off his whiskey. "And in return, I'm sure I can look forward to your complete and utter obedience."

She blinked at him. "I'm sorry, what?"

"Your obedience," Ethan repeated casually, as if he couldn't see how horrified she was by the word. As if she hadn't told him what her parents had been like, how strict they were, how desperate she'd been to build a new life for herself free from their constant interference.

If it had been up to them, she'd have been married and pregnant the second she graduated college—or better yet, not gone to college at all.

Marrying someone from their church that she didn't love wouldn't have made her happy. But that wouldn't have mattered to them. Her mother had as good as told her when she'd said the pastor's son was interested in getting to know her better, and that she hoped it would lead to a more permanent relationship.

The kind that ended with her giving them grandkids. At least five of them.

Still, she shook her head in disbelief. He couldn't possibly mean what she thought he did, could he?

"I don't think I understand."

"Then I guess I need to make myself clearer, don't I?" he drawled. Leaving his empty glass on the windowsill beside him, he folded his arms across his chest as he leaned back against the wall.

"Among other things, you will attend the events I believe will educate you and give you the exposure you need to be a vibrant member of the vampire community. Any questions?"

Did she have any questions? Her mind bubbled, fairly overflowing with them, but with Ethan eyeing her as a hawk would a mouse, she struggled to shape the thoughts into a coherent sentence. So, she decided to start with something small. Something simple.

"Will I have to call you Master?" she asked, already mentally cringing at the thought. There had been a brief mention of it in the contract Ethan had shown her, amongst the long line of punishments she had to look forward to if she ever thought about stepping out of line or causing trouble for the Council.

She could say with utter certainty that the old Ethan wouldn't have asked her to, but this new one... she had no idea what he would demand of her.

His expression was inscrutable as he examined her. "You consider this as more important than a funeral for your friend?"

"No," she said, shifting in place under his unblinking gaze. "No, it's not."

"Let me be clear, Genevieve. As a Childe—my Childe—you haven't earned the right to act independently in vampire affairs. In this case, you taking responsibility for organizing the funeral would be superseding the rights of your friend's Master."

"Your Childe? But wait a second—"

"Only the Master can make arrangements for his Childe's final resting place. And I have my doubts he'll provide it, given that following the death of his Childe, you—his... friend—are now with me. I would think his Master might feel a touch... betrayed at the short time frame it took for you to change addresses," Ethan said with a neutral expression on his face.

"But I didn't... that isn't what happened. Surely you can explain—"

"And how might I do that, if I don't know who he is?" he asked, his voice mild. "Even if I did, do you think he would believe that it was lucky happenstance for me to be there? I hardly think he's going to take my word for it. Do you?"

She stared at him. It felt like somehow along the way, she'd lost complete control of the conversation, and Ethan was firmly in the driving seat. She'd always known, just as everyone else did, that vampires were devils in business—but she'd never been on the receiving end of it before.

Ethan was right, though. She didn't know who Vince's Master was, but things didn't look good. His Master would assume she and Ethan had something to do with Vince's death, and their history would only make them appear guilty, as if they were trying to get rid of Vince so they could reunite.

Gen knew she wasn't a particularly strong vampire, not when there were vampires who were hundreds, perhaps thousands of years old. Not long ago, she'd been a normal twenty-two-year-old middle-school teacher.

It didn't help matters that since moving to London with Vince, she'd all but ignored the aspects of her vampire self. Other than drinking a couple of pints of bagged blood several times a week, she'd done little else but paint and enjoy midnight walks in their local parks.

The idea that a powerful Master vampire would come after her, looking for revenge for something she hadn't done, made her lightheaded. She had no knowledge or skills to even begin to able to defend herself.

"I, uh. I think you might be right," she murmured, feeling faint.

Ethan, however, seemed unconcerned. "But I'm sure I can use my authority to persuade the Council to grant a simple funeral."

"What about his killer? Is the Council going to do anything about that?"

"As I said, Genevieve, they don't care. Only a Childe's Master will care."

"Why do I have to give you something for you to agree to the funeral? Why can't you agree because it's the right thing to do?" she asked.

He smiled, but it was an empty thing, devoid of any real feeling. "Is it?"

She didn't have a choice, not really, and he knew it. What else would she do? She didn't know anyone else, and there was every chance going it alone would only lead to her ending up in a bigger mess than she was already in.

"All right then. I agree. But I want your help to find out who killed Vince."

"Granted," Ethan said.

"And I want to go back to London when this is all done, and the claim torn up. I'm not staying here forever," she said, even though she knew it was a long shot.

The thought of never going back to quiet normality was making her desperate. Vampires lived for a long time. *She* would live a long time, and the thought of years, of decades in Vegas would drive her crazy. It was only a matter of time.

Ethan's harsh laugh startled her, making her jump.

"You think this is a permanent arrangement? This claim is nothing more than paperwork, mere details, and temporary at that. Did you think I wanted to keep you?"

Ethan drawled, his gaze running up and down her as if he was trying to work out what it was he'd ever seen in her.

She struggled to hide her reaction to his cold inspection. "But from what you said about the Council formalizing it, I assumed it must be perm—"

"If it were up to me..." Ethan crossed the room toward her, broken glass from the laptop screen crunching beneath his shoes. "I'd be happy to never set eyes on you for the rest of my life. But unfortunately, I'm a victim in all of this as much as you are."

Gen blinked in surprise. From the harsh lines of his jaw to the dark slash of his eyebrows over penetrating vivid eyes, there was nothing about him that screamed victim. He was an alpha male, pure and simple.

She couldn't imagine anyone making Ethan Chambers do anything he didn't want to or didn't choose to do himself, and she didn't bother hiding her disbelief.

"So, this isn't your idea?" she asked, not knowing if she felt relief or bitter disappointment.

"All vampires must accede to the wishes of the Council, as they were quick to remind me when I returned to Vegas. But as I said, this arrangement is little more than a temporary duty, one I don't see lasting longer than a month."

"You mean I can go back to London?"

"And how do you plan on doing that, seeing as the only things you possess at this moment are the clothes on your back?"

She sighed. "So, what then?"

"I will see to my duties as Master, and once the

Council has been satisfied, then I will go my way. And you can go yours."

"And if we haven't discovered who killed V—my friend by then?"

Ethan shrugged as he started for the door.

"Then it would be in your best interests not to piss me off. Otherwise, I do nothing, and at the end of the month I leave and you're on your own. After all, it's not like I care about who killed your friend or why. Just know that right now, I'm the only person in the world who can help you."

"And I can leave Vegas?"

"You can take the resettlement money and go whatever you like," Ethan said.

"Wait a minute, what resettlement money?"

"Oh, didn't I mention it earlier? As your Master, I'm contractually obligated to leave you with a set-up fund after I break the claim. Something in the region of a hundred grand."

Genevieve stared at him. "You didn't say anything about that."

"Oh, did I forget to mention it? Anyway, it's a relatively pain-free process. Just a matter of filing some paperwork."

All lingering reluctance disappeared. Vince would have his funeral; she'd have Ethan's Vegas connections to investigate who'd killed him. Then in a month, she could be back in London, with more than enough money to take her time figuring out what she wanted to do with the rest of her life, instead of having to rush into something.

She'd be stupid to turn it down, and if she had to call Ethan "Master" a few times, then it would still be a good deal. As long as Vince got his funeral, everything else was a bonus.

"Okay, so what do we do now?"

"Now I'm going to show you what it means to be a vampire," Ethan said, leading the way out of his office.

"I know what it means to be a vampire," she said a touch defensively.

"You know what your friend taught you. And I doubt it's very much. He was no more than a Childe himself."

She opened her mouth.

"Now," Ethan said. "When was the last time you fed?"

She struggled to remember. "Um, the night at the party at Eros. I had a glass of—"

"That's exactly what I'm talking about. True vampires do not sip at their blood from a wine glass," he said.

She was starting to get a bad feeling about this. "Uh, where are we going?"

Ethan stepped through the lounge. Hesitating a moment, she followed him in.

On the couch, Rachel sat reading something on her tablet, her legs crossed at the ankle. Sitting opposite her was a guy in his late teens or early twenties, with shaggy blond hair and the heavy muscles of a college football player. But it was his eyes that caught and held her attention. His brown eyes were hollow and empty, and he sat so utterly still that Genevieve knew there was nothing natural about it.

Enthralled. He had been enthralled.

"Who is this?" she asked, tearing her eyes away from him.

Rachel glanced up from her tablet, but the college

student didn't react at all to her voice—just continued to stare straight ahead with vacant absorption.

"Dinner," Ethan said, his voice mild as he took a seat beside Rachel.

The bottom fell out of her stomach, and she retreated a step. "What!"

"Oh, there's no need to worry about sharing," Ethan said. "I intend to hunt later; this one is all yours."

CHAPTER EIGHT

*E*than examined Genevieve curiously as her eyes remained locked on the enthralled college student sitting opposite him.

His instincts had been proven right then. He'd caught her strangely nervous reaction when a waiter at Eros had offered her his throat. There were feeding rooms at the exclusive venue on the Strip for just that reason. But in all her visits to Eros, she had never ventured inside the private rooms, although Vince had.

So he'd gambled that there was more going on than simple nerves. What he was witnessing now was genuine anxiety. A strange reaction indeed to a simple matter of feeding—but useful for him, he thought.

Now he had another way to torment her. Excellent.

"Is something the matter?" he asked, all innocence.

She startled violently, her eyes darting toward him, as if she'd forgotten he was even there.

"Is something..." She licked her lips. "No, nothing is... I just wasn't expecting to find…"

"An enthralled human?" he asked as he settled back on the couch, crossing one leg over the other.

"Well, yes," she murmured.

"It's clear you haven't been drinking near enough, so think of it as me doing you a favor. This way you get a nice easy meal, instead of dealing with prey fighting to escape," he said with an offhand shrug.

She blanched noticeably, and although he could feel Rachel's curious gaze on him, he ignored it. He'd always been careful to keep the truth of how most vampires regarded humans hidden from Genevieve. He'd thought he could trust her then, but now he knew otherwise. She deserved no such careful treatment.

"Prey?" Genevieve's voice was a thread of sound.

"Yes. Are vampires not predators?"

"I guess?" Her response more of a question than an answer.

"And are you not a vampire?"

Her life must have been very sheltered for her to be this hesitant, this horrified, by the idea of feeding on an enthralled human. She was acting as if she'd never fed from the vein at all, something he knew from personal experience wasn't the case.

"I am," she said hesitantly, the scent of her fear starting to overpower the sweet orange fragrance of her skin.

Uncrossing his legs, he leaned toward her. Her eyes kept drifting away from him, as if she couldn't quite stop herself from turning to the man who sat so docilely opposite him.

Her heartbeat increased the longer she hovered by the doorway. While she hadn't tried to run from the room yet, listening to the frantic pace of her heart, he knew it was only a matter of time. Fight or flight. It would happen soon. Since she'd never been much of a fighter, he could guess which response it would be.

"You need to learn to control your heartbeat," he said after a long moment.

"I... what?"

"Your heart rate is out of control. You're on your way to a collapse. Surely you know that?"

Her hand rose to hover over her chest. "You can hear it?"

Frowning, he leaned back in his seat, sensing he wasn't alone in his surprise. He could feel Rachel's shock, even if he couldn't see it. Genevieve was lacking information that most, if not all vampires should know. Information even Rachel, his human VASS, knew.

Her having lived in London for all her vampire life didn't excuse the fact that there were some pretty fundamental things she should know, but didn't.

Why Vincent and his Master hadn't revealed these things to her didn't make sense to him. Not when he struggled to count on one hand his kin who would turn down the opportunity of having another vampire be subservient to them. What vampire wouldn't appreciate a healthy dose of power and control?

"Once you've fed, I'm sure you'll find it easier to control yourself," Ethan said when Genevieve made no other comment.

Now that he'd made her aware of her racing heart, it slowed a little—but still it continued to beat far faster than it should.

"You want me to... to feed?" she asked.

"Yes, as all vampires must."

"And he won't..." Her words trailed off as her eyes returned to the solidly built college student.

"You are quite safe." He smiled. "You could go at Chad with a carving knife, and he wouldn't lift a finger to even defend himself. Though I wouldn't attempt that if I were you. Getting blood out of leather is murder."

Genevieve swayed.

"I, er... I have to..." She turned to leave.

"Did you already forget our little arrangement?" Ethan drawled.

Gen couldn't see a way out of it, not with the way Ethan was looking at her. She could try to lie, but Ethan had always been able to see right through her.

Sighing, she reluctantly turned to face her unwanted meal. Rachel was watching her, and although she'd remained silent, she could practically feel the judgment oozing from Ethan's impassive VASS.

But it wasn't like she could even be angry at Rachel. After all, she was facing a vampire who didn't drink from the vein. It sounded like a joke. She felt like one, too.

Ethan's gaze moved from her to the empty seat beside the enthralled college student. Sighing loudly, she crossed the room and sat, perching on the very edge of the couch, ignoring him as his lips quirked in a rare display of humor.

Other than the two black couches which faced each

other, there was little to focus on besides Ethan, Rachel, or the enthralled student. If there'd been even a rug somewhere, there was little doubt in her mind she wouldn't have hesitated to use it as a hiding place.

She'd never been a big fan of Ethan's fondness for minimalist interiors. To her, it was cold and devoid of personality. Never had she wished for something, some painting or object, to focus on more than she did at this moment. But no, there was nothing—nothing at all. So, her attention remained fixed on Ethan's ear, because she couldn't quite bring herself to meet his eyes.

"No," she said. "I haven't forgotten about our arrangement."

"Then I don't see what your problem is. You drink bagged blood, don't you?"

"Some people eat chicken, but they can't touch raw meat. They have to wear gloves or get someone else to prepare it," she said. Then she winced. She sounded like an idiot, and the look on Ethan's face made it clear he didn't disagree.

He continued to stare at her in silence.

Pressing her lips together, she tried not to think about the laptop he'd destroyed in his office. She especially tried not to think about how much closer she was to him now than she'd been in his office.

"I'm not forcing you to do this, Genevieve. You can leave any time you want," Ethan said with perfect calm.

That's right. She could. She could walk right out and lose everything she wanted. There'd be no funeral for Vince, and no justice for him either. And that was just the start of it.

First, she'd have to find somewhere to stay during the day—and with the only person she knew in Vegas currently not talking to her, she was already at a disadvantage. And her parents... well, there was no way they'd take her in, even if she could find a way back to Ohio before the sun came up.

Then there was the matter of having nothing. No money, no clothes, and no passport. She'd be a sitting duck waiting for Vince's Master to show up and rip her head off. So yeah, she could leave. But both of them knew she wouldn't. Not if she wanted to keep on breathing.

"I'll stay," she said eventually. "It's just that I'm used to—"

"That stops right here. I can see I have my work cut out for me," he said, his eyes sweeping over her like he was figuring out where to start with her.

Her lips tightened. He was eyeing her like she was a broken thing. As if she was a thing in desperate need of fixing. What had happened to him that he was treating her like this? What had she done that was so bad?

"I don't feed... in the traditional sense," she mumbled a touch defensively, feeling the unmistakable need to explain herself, especially when her eyes met with Rachel's carefully blank expression.

"In the traditional sense?" Ethan's voice was dry, and his face was a blank mask of cold indifference.

"I mean I don't drink... from a person."

"It's blood." Ethan's voice was colder now than it'd been a moment ago, and hearing it made her heartbeat thump harder and faster.

"But I don't drink from... you know... the source." She

winced as she said it, wishing she could take it back but knowing it was too late.

Yep, definitely an idiot.

Where had her intelligence gone? She'd gone to college and been a teacher, for God's sake. What had happened to her?

Briefly, Ethan closed his eyes and pressed his fingers to his temple, head bowed as if he was trying to ease away the beginnings of a headache. But vampires didn't get headaches, even though she desperately wished they did. It might have even offered her a way out of this impossible situation.

When he pulled his hand from his face, his expression was much as it'd been before, except something deep in his eyes hinted that his patience was running out.

"You drank from me," he said.

Standing, she took a few casual steps away, trying to make it seem as if she needed to stretch her legs. As if she wasn't trying to escape the intensity of Ethan's stare or the woody scent of his cologne. Or that she wasn't in desperate need of some distance from him.

God, his words are awakening feelings I haven't felt in so long. Too long.

She hadn't expected him to still be wearing the same cologne he always had, or been prepared for the effect it would still have on her mind, or on her heart.

She loved him, pure and simple. Had loved the way he looked at her like she was the most beautiful woman in the world, the way he'd listened to her with all of his attention. And there'd been this shadowed part of him he sometimes let her see that she ached to fill with love.

He'd been hurt before. She had seen it in him even before his friend Aidan had pulled her aside one night and told her to be careful with his friend, but she'd never been able to get Ethan to open up about who had hurt him. Aidan had told her that he'd been alone for a long time, so it had to have been bad.

"Well, yes." She stopped in front of the sliding glass doors which led to the rose gardens—a place where she'd once loved nothing more than to surround herself in their sweet perfume for hours at a time. "But that was different," she said, turning when she felt movement at her back.

"And how," Ethan was stalking toward her, "was it different?"

"I don't know, it just was," she said as she fought to stand her ground.

When he veered to her right at the last moment, and stopped at a glass side table that held a crystal decanter and several glasses, she quietly released a deep sigh of relief.

"So, you never drank from Vincent?" he asked as he poured himself a glass of whiskey.

"Yes. Once."

Vince had told her she'd been hours from death, but there were more blanks in her memory than actual images. The only thing she remembered with any real clarity was that Ethan was gone, dead, lost to her forever. There was only so much pain she could take, and thinking about what she'd lost that night was something she avoided doing at all costs.

But the memory of the hunger was still there. She

doubted she'd ever forgotten the hunger that'd nearly overwhelmed her. It was unlike anything she'd ever experienced before. All she'd been was a creature that craved … and hungered. In a way, she'd been glad of it. At least it'd gone some way to distract her from the agony of the emptiness in her heart and soul.

"And how was it?" Ethan's eyes were intense as he watched her. "Drinking from Vince?"

She shrugged. "I don't remember," she said.

Ethan stared at her in stark disbelief. "You don't remember?"

"It was a long time ago. And it was only once," she said, knowing she was sounding defensive but unable to help herself when the expression on Ethan's face was all but accusing her of lying.

His doubtful expression didn't change, so she tried to explain.

"I hadn't fed in... a long time. Vince said it wouldn't have been safe for me to drink from a person, and he didn't have any bagged blood at the time," she said, noting the open interest in Rachel's eyes.

The VASS was paying such close attention to what she was saying, it was making her uncomfortable. What had happened between her and Ethan, between her and Vince, was private—and she didn't want to talk about it with anyone but Ethan.

"And you never drank from him again?"

"I didn't see the point. Blood is blood, whether it's from a person or a bag. It's just a matter of sating a thirst." She shrugged.

Then she realized how closely he was watching her. And that he'd stopped drinking.

"Is it?"

Glancing at Rachel, and then back at Ethan, she couldn't help but feel like she was doing something wrong, saying something wrong. "Yeah."

Ethan didn't sound convinced. "And with me? Was it just sating a thirst?"

Her mouth went dry. Felt her gut clench tight as her body flushed from hot to cold, and then back again, as if she was feverish. Without conscious thought, her gaze shifting to Ethan's throat and the pulsing vein there. Rachel's presence was completely forgotten.

Licking dry lips, she forced her eyes away from his throat and found that Ethan's gaze was fixed with intense and hungry focus on her mouth. The grip he had on his glass warned her he was in danger of crushing the crystal if he didn't ease up.

"No," she murmured, after a long pause. "No, it wasn't, but it's you. It's bound to feel different with you."

He tore his eyes from her mouth, and right then she'd have given absolutely anything to know what he was thinking.

Draining the contents of his glass in one fluid motion, he placed the glass on the table with deliberate calm. Then he was turning and walking away from her, his face an impenetrable mask.

"Wait, where are you going?" she asked as he strode toward the door.

"Out. Meeting."

"I thought you..." And then she stopped.

Why was she still talking? He was giving her a way out, literally offering her a way out of this situation on a plate—and she was trying to stop him? What the hell was wrong with her?

But Ethan didn't respond. He just kept on walking.

There was no doubt in Ethan's mind as he slipped behind the wheel of his matte black Mercedes S-class that he was running away. Bit by bit, every time he was forced to engage with Genevieve, his will was being worn down.

Although his mind warned him against the dangers of giving in to want, his body couldn't help but be triggered by memories of her. Of inhaling the sweet fragrance of her skin, caressing the warm silk of her hair, and having her lying naked and eager beneath him.

Grinding his teeth, he tightened his hands on the steering wheel and tore out of the enclave gates, aiming his car downhill and in the direction of the Strip.

If he didn't get a handle on himself, he could see himself spending more time fucking Genevieve, instead of doing what he'd come back to Vegas to do in the first place.

What made it worse was knowing if he touched her the way he wanted to, she wouldn't have stopped him. He'd read it in her eyes. She'd wanted him as much as he wanted her.

The scent of her desire had been spicy-sweet and intoxicating. She'd been thinking about feeding from him, and seeing the naked want in her eyes had been so unexpected, he'd nearly lost control of himself.

If Rachel hadn't been there, there was no doubt in his mind he would have ripped the jeans from her and taken her against the wall while she fed from him. But to his relief and disappointment, Rachel had been there—so, thank fuck—had been the college student, to act as a buffer between them.

His cock was still hard and throbbing with need, and he fought to control his arousal. Taking a moment to adjust himself in his pants, he tried to concentrate instead on the freedom he always felt when he drove with no real direction in mind.

Without quite knowing how, he found himself driving through the quiet back streets of downtown Vegas. For a second he toyed with the idea of stopping in at Aidan's bar, but almost immediately rejected it. The way he was feeling right now, just on the edge of losing control… being anywhere public had the potential to end badly for anyone who even looked at him wrong.

Never mind the fact that his friend would want answers. He'd take one look at Ethan's face and know something was up. Since he'd returned to Vegas several days ago, he'd stopped in at the bar only briefly on a night he knew it would be busy, and he'd been vague about what had brought him back.

Aidan would have known Genevieve had returned to Vegas, since she'd gone to his New Year's Eve party, and Ethan was sure he'd link his return with Genevieve—but the less his friend knew, the better. The last thing he needed was Aidan taking her side, or trying to convince him not to go through with his plans.

Although he and Aidan had emailed in the years since he'd been living in Prague, the messages had been brief.

He was fine. No, he would not be returning to Vegas, and no, he didn't want to talk about Genevieve. And that was that.

Pulling up beside a red swing set in a playground surrounded by overgrown weeds and dying grass, for a long moment he could do nothing but stare.

The memory of Genevieve sitting in the swing beside him washed over him, her head thrown back as her peals of laughter rang loudly in the quiet night. He couldn't remember what it was he'd said to set off her laughter.

Or maybe he didn't want to.

Glancing at the apartment building across the road from the playground, he saw the lights were on in Tess's apartment. A look at his watch told him it was ten. He'd have thought she'd be at work already, but with bars often open until six in the morning, she could just as easily be working a late shift.

Finally, he got out and crossed over to the swings, ignoring a passing human couple who paused to stare at him. Trying to imagine how he would react to seeing a smartly dressed vampire in a crisp white shirt, tailored pants, and leather shoes swinging in an overgrown playground at night, he had to admit it deserved at least a second look.

As usual, it didn't take long for his thoughts to return to Genevieve. It was like she'd been completely sheltered from vampire life in London, a place that had a bustling nightlife to rival Vegas. She'd remained as human as she was when Ethan had first met her.

He narrowed his eyes as he thought back to what she'd said about feeding. There was something deeply wrong about how she viewed it, but he couldn't put his finger on what that was.

All he knew was that feeding could be sexually arousing, comforting, or self-indulgent, but it was never just sating a thirst. And why had she gone so long without feeding in the first place? Why did he have a feeling there was a lot more she was leaving unsaid?

He told himself he didn't care. What did it matter to him what had happened after she'd left him? But it surprised him that Vincent had let her get to that point; he must have known how dangerous it was for a vampire to go so long without feeding.

Already Ethan could see the effect it was having on Genevieve. The natural golden undertones in her olive skin had been stripped away, and she was pale. He'd seen the way she was curling her toes from the floor when she'd sat, as if her feet were cold. All tell-tale signs that her body was crying out for blood.

He felt himself growing hard again at the thought of her mouth moving hungrily on him, at the sounds of her feeding, and he groaned in frustration. He remembered all too well how it'd felt with her feeding from him as he'd pounded into her soft, warm body, and it'd been unlike anything he'd ever felt before. He'd never come so hard in his life.

Squeezing his eyes shut, he struggled to get his breathing back under control. He'd drive around for a little while longer, and then he'd go back. And this time Genevieve would feed. But first, if he wanted to regain control of his own raging emotions, he needed to deal with his hunger.

He noticed the human couple murmuring to each other as they continued to watch him from the side of the road. From his seat on the swing, he could smell the faint trace of sweet juice and alcohol on their breath.

They must live nearby; likely they were returning from having a couple of drinks in the city. But they weren't drunk—buzzed, if Ethan had to guess the level of their intoxication. All it took was a slight nudge, and they were drifting toward him with eager smiles.

He stood from the swing and waited for them to come to him. "Excuse me." He smiled. "There's something I'd like your help with. My car is just over here."

CHAPTER NINE

*T*ension filled the room. Since Ethan had walked out several minutes ago, Rachel had not said one word. Instead, her sole focus seemed to be on pretending Gen didn't exist. Finally, the silence grew so taut, she turned from her view of the landscaped gardens outside the sliding doors and faced Rachel.

She wasn't getting the sense that Ethan would be rushing back anytime soon from wherever he'd disappeared to. He'd said it was to go to a meeting, but that hadn't been what she'd been thinking as he stalked away from her.

If anything, it'd felt like he was running away from her, which made her stare after him in confusion long after he'd disappeared from view.

She knew Ethan, and Ethan didn't run from anything.

But regardless of where he'd gone, she couldn't ignore the fact that she'd been granted a golden opportunity. If anyone could help her get to the bottom of what she'd done to piss Ethan off, it was his VASS. If, that was, she could get her talking.

"Rachel?"

Rachel glanced up from the tablet in her hand, her expression frigid. "Yes?"

With that one word, Gen regretted having said anything at all. There was something in Rachel's eyes that warned her a confrontation—which she'd never been a fan of—was on the horizon.

"I just wanted to say thank you for everything you're doing for me. It can't be easy, having double the amount of work all of sudden," she said with a tentative smile, hoping a compliment or two might work in her favor.

Her words were met with silence.

"And, well… I wanted to say I appreciate everything you do for Ethan as well. I always thought you do a great job of looking after all of his needs."

"I do, do I?" Rachel rose from the couch, her eyes narrowing.

If she'd thought Rachel's expression had been cold before, now the pale blue eyes sparkling from her elfin features were positively glacial.

"Yeah?"

When Rachel started for the door without a word, Genevieve decided to do what she should have done at the start and go for honesty.

"Rachel, have I… done something to upset you in any way? I can't help but feel like I've done something wrong."

"Maybe you're just seeing things." Rachel's hands were white as they gripped the tablet.

"I could be," she said slowly. "But I don't think I am."

"So, you're accusing me of lying. Is that it?" Rachel spat out.

The sudden rage on Rachel's face made her pause. "No, I was—"

"Then if you'll excuse me, I have a great deal of work waiting for me. I'll leave you to your... whatever it is you're doing," Rachel said, her eyes spearing her with such cold hatred, Gen couldn't but help flinch.

Yep. I've definitely done something to piss her off.

But what had she done? Try as she might, she couldn't think of anything she could've done to make the usually reserved Rachel hate her. Sure, things had been a little strained at times between them—but there hadn't been anything like this outright hostility.

Sighing, Gen tried not to let the encounter sour her. Then she caught sight of the slim black cordless phone on a side table. She stared at it as she debated the merits of calling Tess. What was the worst that could happen? Tess not answering?

It wasn't like she was Ethan's prisoner or anything, and he hadn't said anything about her not being able to use the phone. Not that it'd come up in conversation yet, but still, it was a phone call. To Tess. He could hardly kick up a fuss about it, could he?

Hesitating, she thought back to his mercurial moods, and then she made a decision. For the first time since being in Vegas, she felt truly alone. Vince was dead, Ethan was treating her like public enemy number one, and Rachel was following in the footsteps of her boss. She needed to talk to someone or she'd go crazy.

In no time at all, she was across the room with the

phone in her hand as she dialed Tess's number, doing her best to ignore Chad's blank stare as he sat on the couch across from her.

Even though she was sure he wasn't watching her, wasn't about to harm her, she was alone, and if Ethan's thrall suddenly failed... well, she didn't have the first idea of how to enthrall someone herself, or even how to defend herself.

She'd never been put in a position where she'd had to test her preternatural strength against anyone. Until Vince's strange behavior, that is—and even then, her reaction had been instinctive, just like she'd lived so much of her vampire life.

Feeding from Ethan had been a natural reaction from their making love the first night she'd woken as a vampire. And feeding from Vince... well, she'd been more dead than alive then.

There was so much she didn't know. Maybe Ethan was right that Vince had been too young to teach her the things she should know—things he would have told her if he hadn't disappeared from their Prague apartment.

But regardless of what Ethan ended up teaching her, killing or using her strength to hurt anyone was something she'd never be able to do. Even if it meant he refused to help her track down Vince's killer.

To deliberately strike out at someone, a human someone that she could kill without meaning to, terrified her—perhaps more than the idea of being hurt herself.

Because that is who I am now. A vampire afraid of an enthralled human. No wonder the Council was demanding that Ethan educate me.

Alert to any sudden movement from Chad, she held the phone to her ear as it rang, and rang, and rang. Then she hung up and tried again.

If ever she needed a friend, it was now. No one back home would understand. She couldn't even call her parents, who wanted nothing more to do with her after she'd let Ethan turn her. They were too god-fearing to want anything to do with their vampire daughter.

The ringing stopped so suddenly, it took her a moment to notice.

"Tess?" Excitement thrummed through her. Had Tess forgiven her already? "Tess, it's Gen, are you there?"

But there was no response.

"Tess, it's—" The phone cut off mid-sentence.

Despair started to set in as she stared at the phone in her hand. It looked like she was on her own.

Ethan found her staring into the middle distance, deep in thought, the phone dangling from her hand as she pressed her forehead against the glass sliding doors.

His gaze lingered for a moment on the phone in her hand. Just who had she been calling? Tess, maybe? Or was it someone else?

On the couch opposite her, Chad had yet to move, and wouldn't. Not until Ethan released his hold on him.

He'd fed well on the couple at the playground, but now as he examined the long line of Genevieve's throat, he was suddenly ravenous.

"Genevieve," he said.

The phone thumped to the floor, and her head whipped toward him so fast he heard a bone in her neck crack.

Then she spun back around to face the sliding doors, lifting a hand to rub at her eyes. Not that there was any point in her doing it. Ethan had already caught the streaks of blood on her cheeks she hadn't managed to wipe away, and her eyes were red. She'd been crying.

"Oh, Ethan, you scared me," she said, her voice husky as her eyes shifted to Chad before she bent to retrieve the phone from the floor.

"Where's Rachel?" he asked.

She shrugged, a slight lift of one shoulder as she looked away. "I don't know."

Truth and lies merged.

There was something she wasn't telling him. Something in the way she looked away from him made him think she didn't want him reading the expression in her eyes. She was lying about Rachel, and she'd been crying. What had happened in his absence?

When his cell phone rang, he pulled it from his pocket and glanced at the caller ID. Rachel. "Where are you?"

"Picking up your dry cleaning," Rachel said.

Ethan raised an eyebrow. If there was one thing Rachel always delayed until the last possible minute, it was going to the dry cleaners, because the heat always destroyed her poker-straight hair.

She didn't have to tell him. He always saw it in the faint air of embarrassment as she patted at the frizzy ends of her usually straight hair when she didn't think he was looking. And with at least a couple more days until his dry cleaning needed to be collected, he knew something must have happened between her and Genevieve for her to have decided to go pick it up now, rather than later.

"Okay, I'll see you tomorrow." He started to hang up, never taking his eyes off Genevieve.

"But it's early. I thought we could go through your filing cabinet?"

While he'd been in Prague, Rachel had kept the house cleaned and in order, but she hadn't touched the paperwork in his filing cabinet. A lot of it he needed to go through himself, and he knew without looking that it would be a big job. Bigger than he was ready to tackle anytime soon.

"We'll do it another time. Anyway, it's probably for the best you aren't around tonight," he said, never taking his eyes from Genevieve.

Because he was watching her so closely, he caught her head swivel. She realized he was watching her, and then she jerked back around to face the garden.

Tucking his phone back into his pocket, he crossed over to Chad. He'd found the college student near one of the shopping malls while Genevieve had still been sleeping, and it'd taken little effort on his part to persuade him to climb into his car.

"Genevieve."

She jumped and turned to face him again. Her eyes turned wary when she saw him squatting beside Chad. He held his hand out to her. "Come here."

Cautiously, she approached him until she was standing beside him.

"Give me your hand." Bracing himself, he was

conscious of her doing the same as he folded his larger hand around her smaller soft one.

The breath she'd been holding since she'd started toward him gusted out, and he waited for her breathing to settle before he spoke.

"There is little I need to show you." He tugged her closer.

"We are predators, and predators instinctively know when and how to attack. So, on a subconscious level, you know where to bite." It was a battle to keep his voice cool and indifferent as he spoke, when the memory of the erotic pleasure-pain of her first bite surged through him.

All of a sudden, the cool touch of her hand was an unbearable temptation. With the couch beside them, it would be the easiest thing in the world to tug her onto it and follow her down.

She cleared her throat. "Could you, er, remind me," she said, flushing. "About where to bite. I'm not sure I remember, with it being so long ago."

He could feel his face harden. Could feel his desire cool. It was a long time ago, and he'd do better to remember that. Both of them were very different people now.

"This is the best place to strike," he said, moving her hand over to Chad's neck, and placing her fingers at the joint of his neck and shoulder. "You can get a steady flow of blood going with minimal effort, but you need to avoid the jugular vein."

"Why? It's the biggest vein, right?" Genevieve asked.

"Yes. But for now, you need to learn control, and feeding from the jugular when you're hungry isn't always the best idea. Unless you want to kill, of course." His voice was mechanical, that of a teacher and nothing more. A part of him wondered what he was doing.

He should be making her suffer, not be doing what he said he would when his words had only been a ploy designed to prevent her from running. Because he knew Genevieve. She was no fighter. In times of great stress, she always ran.

Genevieve gulped. "Right. No jugular."

"You'll need to sit close beside him. I'll make sure to stop you when you've had enough."

A nervous laugh escaped. "Won't I stop when I've had enough?"

Ethan said nothing. How did she know so little? Could she not even understand the power of bloodlust when drinking from the vein?

"Although it's normal for a vampire to drink to excess, to gorge, it isn't always motivated by greed. Perhaps he craves something more. Pain. Death. You must know and understand when and how to stop."

Genevieve perched on the edge of the couch beside Chad. Close, but not close enough. He gave Chad a silent command to bend his head toward her, but he wasn't prepared for her reaction. Without warning, she sprang to her feet, away from him.

Ethan gripped her hand tighter and held her fast.

"Easy," he murmured.

The beat of her heart, the sound of blood pumping around her body was loud, and he watched her, waiting for it to ease.

"Sorry, I just…" She cleared her throat, her face flushed

with embarrassment as she settled back down on the couch. "So, what do I do now?"

Ethan could read reluctance in every line of her body. Her heartbeat was still unsteady, and the hand in his was tense. But despite her obvious signs of fear, she was doing everything she could to look calm and collected.

"Put your mouth where I showed you. Your fangs will extend the closer you come to feeding," he murmured, feeling his own extend as he watched her.

She didn't respond. Her lips settled against Chad's neck and her eyes drifted closed—and strangely, her heartbeat started to slow, to ease into a steady rhythm. Matching the calm pulsing of Chad's.

"Now," he breathed. "Bite."

Genevieve bit down, and the sound of Chad's gasping breath was overly loud in the quiet room.

He was never entirely certain if it was in pain, or it was pleasure. The two were linked so closely with each other, even Ethan couldn't say which he was reacting to when he'd been bitten by Genevieve, and by others before.

He watched her feed with hooded eyes before his gaze drifted down to her mouth, and to her throat. Her throat undulated as she drank. Knowing what she was feeling, his own hunger stirred at watching her sate hers, though he'd not long since had his fill of the couple in the playground.

He didn't notice it at first because of his intense focus on making sure she drank enough. That, and trying to tamp down his raging erection.

When he did notice her feeding wasn't going the way he'd expected, he encircled Chad's wrist with one hand. It was just as he'd thought. The college student should have been awash in fierce emotion—but there was no desire, no pain, no desperate clinging need for the feeding to never stop.

For all intents and purposes, it was as if Genevieve wasn't feeding at all.

Once Ethan moved his hand to her bare arm, he understood the reason why. All he could sense from her was a clinical sort of detachment, as if she were merely going through the motions.

It was no wonder the college student was feeling nothing at all. She wasn't getting the least bit of enjoyment from the experience, and so Chad's emotions were echoing hers.

He glanced at his watch and prepared to forcefully separate Genevieve from Chad. But then she was lifting her head, lapping at her bite and standing, even as she wiped at her mouth with the back of her hand.

Blinking in surprise, he followed her to his feet. "Genevieve?"

Her skin was radiant, glowing with health as she turned to him. "Yeah."

"What was that?" Ethan asked.

How had she found the self-control, the will, to stop herself from feeding when he'd felt her hunger beating down at her? He should've had to pry her from Chad. It didn't make sense.

"What was what?" she repeated.

"Why didn't Chad feel pleasure, or pain, or anything? Why didn't you?"

"I told you." Genevieve moved away from him, from Chad. "I only felt it with you."

CHAPTER TEN

It was late. Hours had passed, and Ethan still hadn't returned from taking Chad back to the Strip as he'd said he would.

Gen should be sleeping already—but knowing it would be twilight soon, knowing he was still out there, her mind refused to even think about closing her eyes.

She'd done something wrong, again, and she didn't know what it was. The truth of it had been in Ethan's eyes as he examined her before he told her to go upstairs. It had everything to do with her feeding.

She couldn't help the way she felt. Whose fault it was, she couldn't say.

Vince hadn't ever pushed her to feed from the vein, so she'd never considered it might be unusual, and it was easy not to when their London VASS always made sure the fridge was stocked with bagged blood.

She found her eyes filling with tears again despite her determination not to cry anymore, since Ethan had already caught her at it when he'd quietly returned from wherever he'd gone.

But it was hard not to when she thought about Vince. His body would have been discovered by their VASS Paul by now; probably it had been the night before. Thinking of where his body would be taken, and what the Council would do with it, made her swallow hard.

And the bathroom—there'd been something about the bathroom that had made Ethan rush her from the house. She hoped Paul was okay, and that nothing bad had happened to him.

Try as she might, whenever she thought about Vince, at the forefront of her mind now was the way he'd scared her on her balcony, and the sight of his body on her bedroom floor. Which wasn't how she wanted to remember him. She wanted to focus on his kindness and how caring he'd been, like how he'd treated her in the days he'd first taken her with him to London.

It'd been the fourth or fifth night they'd been in London. She'd been such a mess then that she had little memory of those first days. There were vague memories of him encouraging her to drink, but she'd rebuffed all of his attempts to get her to drink the glass of blood he'd brought her.

The idea of drinking blood, of even raising the glass to her mouth, had filled her with tension. She'd dreaded it with every fiber of her body, but Vince had been insistent. Once she had the first sip, he'd told her, her body would crave it and any disgust would disappear.

"And was it like that the first time you drank?" she'd asked him, in one of the rare nights she wasn't a sobbing mess as she

sat on the couch in the bright and sunny lounge, which overlooked the wild park she'd later come to fall in love with.

His smile was sad as he tugged her feet into his lap. "No, Genny. No, it wasn't."

So she took the glass because she'd been the one to put the sadness there. He'd made it his mission to care for her since he'd brought her to London. Each night he tried to get her to drink, and prodded her into showering, and dressing, and even going for a short walk. The last thing she wanted was to be the cause of his upset when he'd done so much for her.

"No one's ever called me Genny before," she admitted, swirling the thick liquid in the glass, the clenching in her stomach turning into a soft rumble. "Ethan—"

And then she had to stop because the tears were forming again, and the dark wall of grief that had consumed her was on its way to crushing her again.

"It will ease," Vince had said softly as she'd fought to hold the tears at bay. "This pain you're feeling is still too sharp. It won't ever completely go away, but one day you'll learn it won't kill you."

"Why are you helping me?"

"Because you needed helping. Now drink. You can even plug your nose and close your eyes if you want."

Darting a glance at him, she raised the glass and prepared to plug her nose. "Will it help?"

"I don't know, but it's something to try," he'd said in his slightly dry British accent.

Surprised into laughter, she'd plugged her nose, squeezed her eyes shut and tossed the contents of the glass back. And he'd been right. As the first drops hit her tongue, she'd suddenly been ravenous, and the glass had been empty far sooner than she'd have believed possible.

She blinked rapidly as the memory of the comforting presence of Vince that night, and of his hands resting lightly on her feet in his lap, faded away. Her thoughts now, without conscious effort, turned to Ethan. She couldn't stop thinking about him, always. He never remained out of her thoughts for long.

Ethan should have been back already, but he still wasn't. Even after she'd done as he'd told her and come up to bed. She'd had a quick shower and brushed her teeth before turning off the lights and crawling under the sheets. And that was how she'd stayed. For hours. Tossing and turning as she tried not to think about Ethan and the way he was making her feel.

Being around him, close enough to touch, but the fury in his eyes warning her away, was driving her crazy. Sometimes she was sure he wanted her as much as she wanted him. And other times, he looked at her like he hated her. Should she have known Ethan was alive and gone to find him?

She flipped onto her back, more restless than ever. It felt like a lifetime ago when he'd curved his arm around her after they'd made love, and murmured in her ear that she need never feed off anyone but him. But now he expected, was practically demanding she feed off some guy he'd dragged in off the street to be her prey.

Her lips twisted at the word. Prey. When had humans suddenly become prey? Had he thought of her that way when she'd been human, or was that something recent, something tied to whatever it was she'd done?

When the door was suddenly shoved open, she sat up, twisting to face it. Ethan stood frozen, his form outlined by the hallway light. His green eyes shone as he stared at her. Neither one of them moved or spoke. And then he stepped inside and shut the door behind him, plunging the room once more into darkness.

She watched him move toward her, his steps unhurried. Blinking rapidly, she struggled for several seconds to trigger her night sight. Then it flared to life, and all of a sudden, everything came into sharp focus.

With a mouth gone dry, her hands tightened around the sheets as Ethan yanked his shirt from his pants, and after unbuttoning the first few buttons, pulled it over his head and tossed it on the floor.

Her eyes traced the corded muscles of his chest and the defined strength of his forearms. She remembered the strength in those hands, remembered how they'd felt running over her body. God, it'd been so long since he'd touched her. Too long.

His hands moved to his fly, and then he stopped. She swallowed. Hard. Staring at his hands, she willed him to continue, but as the seconds ticked by she realized he wasn't going to do what she wanted. Lifting her head, she met his stare head-on. His expression was unreadable.

He dropped his hands from his pants, and as he stalked toward her, she lost the ability to breathe. Then he was there, bending over her. His smell was pure Ethan, the woody, smoky citrus cologne he always wore, his favorite whiskey, and the distinctive scent of his skin that was him, and him alone.

The lightest brush of his fingertips danced across her

jaw, and her eyes fluttered closed as she tipped her head to the side. She felt the barest graze of his knuckle at the junction of her throat at the exact spot she'd bitten Chad, and sucked in a breath at the sharp spike of need, of want. Her stomach cramped, and heat flooded through her. Was he going to bite her?

He bent closer. Close enough his breath was hot against her neck. As his erection pressed against her thigh, she held still, waiting to see what he would do. She heard him mutter something under his breath—but whatever it was, she missed it.

"Mm?" she said.

He bent closer. So close, she could feel the heat coming off him, could feel the barest brush of his body against hers, and then she felt the rough stroke of his tongue against her neck. Her body tensed in anticipation, her nails digging into the sheets, even as her body arched so her breasts pressed flush against his chest.

He froze.

Confused, she opened her eyes and found herself stretched out beneath him. When had she lain down? It didn't matter when—all that mattered was discovering the reason why Ethan had stopped. Releasing her death grip on the sheets, she started to reach for him.

"Ethan?"

He stared at her neck, even as he backed away from her. Then he stood, the muscles in his back tense as he bent to retrieve his shirt from the floor.

"Where—" She scrambled to sit up as he strode toward the door.

The door snicked with finality behind him, and Gen

stared at it in shock before flopping onto her back. Staring up at the ceiling, she tried to calm her racing heart.

Her panties were damp, and her breasts were sore and aching. He'd wanted her, she'd seen it, felt it. And yet he'd gotten up and just... walked away. Why put her—why put both of them—in that state, and then walk away?

CHAPTER ELEVEN

*E*than examined the gift box Rachel had left on his office desk at his next rising. It was small, about the right size to hold a man's watch or a woman's bracelet, beautifully wrapped in silver foil and secured with a blood-red bow.

But it wasn't the gift wrap that held his attention. It was the overpowering sweet perfume that didn't quite manage to hide the sour, pickle-like smell of whatever lay inside. Formaldehyde. He would know the smell anywhere.

His father and brothers had been fond of hunting, and they'd used the chemical to preserve the heads of the animals they'd killed. But that had been a long time ago, and he tried not to think of that time, or of his family anymore.

Ignoring the bundle of letters that Rachel had left for him, Ethan pushed aside his empty glass of warmed blood, slipped the ribbon off the box, and opened the lid. The smell of decay was unmistakable when the body of a small brown mouse, lying in a bed of tissue paper, was exposed to the air.

The odd angle of the mouse's head left no doubt as to how it'd met its fate. But other than the macabre gift, there was no note, no message at all.

Since he couldn't recall having pissed anyone off enough recently enough to having them sending him such a strange gift, he assumed it had something to do with Vincent and Genevieve.

It would be a vampire, though, he thought as he took a sip from his glass. Given the reason he'd returned to the Vegas in the first place, he would know better than most how much vampires liked to play their games.

Was this the killer's way of telling Ethan that he knew Genevieve was under his roof?

Investigating Vincent's murder hadn't interested him in the least. It was nothing more than another way to tie Genevieve to him, once he'd seen how important it was to her. But this gift made him curious.

Between the gift and Genevieve's strange feeding habits, he had questions he couldn't answer. So, he picked up his phone and made a call.

"Aidan. Yeah, it's me. What's happening at the club tonight?"

Genevieve held up the skimpy black silk dress he'd pulled from the closet and tossed at her moments before.

"I'm supposed to wear this?" She eyed the dress with nothing short of growing horror.

He could understand her discomfort. The dress was backless, dipped low at the front, and was very, very short.

"Yes," he said, turning to inspect the row of high-heeled shoes he'd had Rachel fill the closet with.

Behind him, he could hear her shifting around in the cool linen sheets. He closed his eyes in a vain attempt to shut out the image of all that soft golden skin, and the dark silk of her hair as she sat cross-legged in nothing more than a t-shirt. *His* t-shirt.

"To investigate Vince's murder?" Her tone was one of disbelief.

Opening his eyes, he bent to scoop up a pair of black five-inch stilettos, and turned to toss them on the bed beside her.

"To ask some questions," he said, crossing his arms across his chest.

"And I can't do that in jeans? Or sneakers?"

She sounded wary. Nervous, even.

Perfect.

"It's a dress and heels. Surely you wore such clothing when you went out with your..." he paused. "Friend?"

"I did, but Ethan, it wasn't anything like—"

"Master," Ethan interrupted.

She blinked. "What?"

"I've decided I prefer you calling me Master," he said in a cool voice.

If what'd nearly happened between them had taught him anything, it was that he needed to keep his distance. And he needed to make sure she kept hers. But at least he'd managed to stop himself before things went too far.

Though it'd meant a long, cold shower before crashing in one of the spare bedrooms, the alternative was much worse. The last thing he needed was feelings, warm feelings, coming into play. On either side.

"But I've never worn heels this tall before. What if I trip and fall?" She sounded desperate now, and Ethan didn't pause as he started for the door.

He needed to find Rachel and have her make sure any future gifts—if any were forthcoming—were tucked away in his office. If Genevieve opened one and linked it with the murder of her boyfriend, there'd be no stopping her from running then, regardless of the consequences.

"Then if I were you, I'd take short steps. And if you fall..." He stepped out of the bedroom. "Well, you're a vampire. I'm sure you'll survive."

She muttered something under her breath. His lips twitched at the swear word he'd never heard her say before. Wiping all trace of humor from his face, he turned around.

"What was that?"

"Nothing," she muttered her eyes on the dress in her lap.

He didn't move.

"Master," she bit out, her voice overly loud.

"Get dressed. We leave in thirty minutes," he said and started for the stairs.

The car ride to the club was silent, and Gen didn't know what to say to break the terse atmosphere, especially when she was feeling so uncomfortable.

Not wanting to complain and risk having Ethan leave her behind—or even worse, change his mind altogether about investigating Vince's murder—she said nothing as she tried to deal with the fact that she was going out in what was essentially nothing more than lingerie.

She wondered if it was Ethan or Rachel who'd decided on the clothes, and the makeup she'd found in the closet and bathroom. Either way, everything fit her perfectly, and the makeup was flattering, although there was more of it than she was used to wearing.

So, she'd kept things simple with an Urban Decay smoky eyeshadow pallet she'd found, and followed it up with a slick of blood-red Chanel lipstick, before brushing her freshly washed hair and leaving it down to finish drying naturally. Ethan hadn't exactly been generous with the time he'd allotted her to get ready.

But his reaction when she'd come down the stairs had been more than a little disappointing. Dressed in his usual white shirt with rolled-up sleeves and black pants, all he'd done was glance up at her from his phone, nod, and lead the way out to their waiting car.

Now they sat quietly beside each other as their driver, nearly hidden behind a tinted glass screen, drove them to Hellfire.

The parallels between this moment and when she and Vince had laughed on their way to Eros suddenly struck her, and her eyes burned at the thought that she'd never see him again. He'd never try to make her laugh, or comfort her the way someone who truly recognized and understood her pain would.

She couldn't help but wonder if Vince had felt betrayed at her arguing against them leaving Vegas, when all along she'd been the one pushing for it. Had he suspected it was only a matter of time before she left him to go back to Ethan?

Fighting to control the tears threatening to fall, her shoulders shook as she kept her gaze firmly pointed outside the window.

By the time their car pulled up outside Hellfire, she felt like she'd finally gotten a grip on her emotions.

Not waiting for Ethan to open her door the way he always had, she stepped out and took in the line of people queuing outside.

At the door of the red and black-fronted building were two large guards with blank expressions on their faces, swords strapped around their hips and dark sunglasses wrapped around their eyes. Standing behind a red velvet rope, a female vampire in a tight leather dress with a clipboard waved in a couple of people at a time.

Gen was conscious of Ethan circling the car as she started toward the bar. But his hand on her bare upper shoulder stopped her. Startled, she glanced up at him. He was staring down into her face, and his expression was unreadable. Something about the way he examined her held her immobile.

It felt like for the first time since he'd reentered her

life, he was seeing her—really seeing her. And the rage, the emotion she saw more often than not lighting his eyes was absent. Lifting his free hand to her face, he brushed his thumb under her right eye with a gentle touch.

"What? Is my makeup smudged?" she asked, voice soft, not daring to move with his hand still on her face.

When Ethan continued to study her, she drew in a breath and held it as his fingers moved over her jaw and tucked a strand of hair behind her ear.

And then he lifted his head as if remembering they stood in the middle of a busy sidewalk in downtown Vegas, with the car door open and people milling all around them. Dropping his hand from her face, he grabbed one of her hands,

"Come on," he murmured as he led the way to the club entrance.

Inside, it took a moment for her to get over the wall of heat and noise which hit her full in the face. She followed behind Ethan as he guided them through people standing about talking and drinking, nodding along to dance music.

She craned her head as they passed the bar and the dance floor, searching the black and red interior, but couldn't spot Tess anywhere. With Tess's distinctive cherry red hair, there was no way she could have missed her. Disappointed, she reminded herself they'd only just arrived, and there was still plenty of time for her to spot Tess later.

Ethan stopped at the booths reserved only for vampires. She'd slid in and was tugging at the hem of her dress before she noticed he hadn't joined her.

"Stay here. I'll get you a drink," he said, and before she could stop him, he was gone.

Ethan sipped at his beer as he waited for Aidan at the bar. Glancing behind him, he could see Genevieve had barely touched the glass of champagne he'd had a server deliver to her. Instead, her shoulders were slumped as her gaze roved around the bar.

Despite an unexpected reluctance to leave her alone, he'd shaken off the feeling and walked away from her. It didn't matter that the idea of her crying made him feel things he didn't want to feel, or that something inside him rebelled at leaving her alone, looking small and lonely.

He had questions for Aidan. Questions it was better she wasn't close by to hear the answers.

"Long time no see," Aidan said, clapping him on his shoulder as a wide grin stretched across his face.

It wasn't like his friend to be so outwardly cheerful, he thought, eyeing Aidan in his usual black on black suit and shirt, his dyed platinum hair shining all the brighter in the bar's dark interior.

"That it has," Ethan agreed as Aidan motioned to the bartender.

"And what's this I hear about you claiming a Childe?" Aidan asked, his voice barely audible in the loudness of the bar. Even when he was angry, Ethan hadn't ever heard him sound anything other than calm and in perfect control.

"Not just any Childe." Ethan swigged from his beer as Aidan knocked back the shot of vodka the bartender had slid toward him.

Aidan raised his eyebrow. "Really?"

"Genevieve," Ethan said.

Aidan studied him with a mild expression. "Mm. I thought I'd heard something to that effect. So, where is she?"

Ethan tipped his head toward Genevieve's booth. She sat straight, likely in an attempt to prevent the front of her dress from gaping open, even as her eyes continued to search the bar as he'd seen her doing since they'd arrived.

"I thought she was with another guy?"

"He's dead," Ethan said bluntly.

Aidan paused in the act of reaching for a second shot the bartender slid over. "Is he, now?"

Ethan raised his hands in innocence. "I had nothing to do with it. When I went to claim her, he was already dead, and she'd found him that way. He'd been decapitated, and I had the distinct feeling someone was trying to lure her into the bathroom for some nefarious purpose."

He kept his tone casual, unaffected. Like the thought of something happening to Genevieve didn't matter, trying to hide the spike of panic that'd surged through him the moment he'd realized someone was waiting for her in the house. But when Aidan's gaze sharpened, he saw that he hadn't succeeded.

Aidan had always seen far too much. If anything, it appeared that since his bar had been attacked by anti-vampire elements when his kind had initially settled in Vegas, he was more watchful than ever.

It no doubt had a lot to do with how the Vampire Council had handled, or rather not handled events, and Aidan's bar and employees had ended up paying the price for their failure to act.

"Is that so?" Aidan examined Genevieve. "How's she doing now?"

"Scared. But determined to find out who did it. Now, with someone sending me a dead mouse, I'm more than a little intrigued to find out what is going on, and why."

"A dead mouse?"

"Yep," he said, "preserved and covered in perfume so Rachel wouldn't smell it when she accepted the mail."

"Well, that's real classy. And you've got no idea who it is?"

"None. Which is why I'm here. I was hoping you could tell me if you know of anyone who'd want the ex-boyfriend dead."

Aidan looked Ethan straight in the eye. "I do. One person, actually, and he's sitting right in front of me."

Ethan rolled his eyes. "Since I know I didn't do it, and I know you don't think so either, we can move onto whoever the real culprit is."

"What makes you think they were after him? They could've been after her, since I'm guessing you didn't get the gift until after you brought her home?" Aidan said, his gaze still on Genevieve.

"Maybe they are. Too early to say either way. What is it?"

"Is she looking for anyone in particular?"

Ethan remembered that Tess worked at the bar, though that'd been years ago when he'd first met Genevieve. "Probably Tess."

"Tess?"

"Her old roommate. Small. Cherry red hair."

The confusion on Aidan's face smoothed away. "Oh, she doesn't work here anymore. She stopped turning up for her shifts."

"Really? I'd have thought she was the kind to always find a reason to stay."

"You and me both. But you never can tell sometimes. Oh, looks like Gen's made a new friend," Aidan said, the hint of a smile on his face.

Ethan started to correct Aidan as he turned to find a man in a cheap navy suit leaning over Genevieve. Over the noise in the bar, it was impossible to hear what the man was saying to her, but going by the frozen smile on her face, whatever he was saying, she didn't like it.

Strangling the urge to grab the man by the back of the neck and force him away from her, he turned around… and found Aidan eyeing him curiously.

"What?"

"Nothing. But go ahead, you look like you have a question."

Aidan's powers of observation still managed to surprise him, even after all the years they'd known each other. Then again, if the shit-storm they'd been through a few years back had taught him anything, it was that Aidan's ability to read people was often more right than wrong.

"I wanted to ask you about feeding."

Aidan smirked. "Really? I'd have thought you'd know enough about it by now. But, if you need advice at your age, then maybe—"

"Shut up," Ethan grinned. "Have you heard of any of our kin who don't feel anything when they feed from the vein?"

"No emotion?" Aidan asked, raising his hand to the bartender for another round of drinks.

"Yeah. No pleasure or pain, just… sating a thirst?"

Aidan waited until the bartender put their drinks down and walked away before he leaned toward Ethan with a frown on his face.

"Yes. Funnily enough, I have. Do I need to be concerned?"

"No." He took a swig of his beer. "I'm asking for a friend."

Aidan raised his eyebrow but didn't comment on his flimsy excuse. "Well, tell your *friend* that more often than not, it's the result of a traumatic turning. Is it with all feeding?"

"Not all. Not with one," Ethan said.

Interest sparked in Aidan's eyes. "Only one? Well, that's... novel. So, was the turning traumatic in any way?" he asked, sipping his vodka.

He thought back to his turning of Genevieve, and he shook his head. "No."

"Not even immediately after?"

He hesitated.

Aidan sighed and leaned closer. "Look, I'm not pushing to know the details, but I'm guessing this has to do with Gen?"

Ethan didn't respond.

"I'm getting the impression you still blame Gen for you being ambushed. You know I have my doubts about that, but you claimed her, which means there must still be something between you. But some guy is over there pawing at her, and you're over here acting like it doesn't mean shit to you, when I can see that it does." Aidan's voice was mild.

Just in time, Ethan managed to stop himself from turning around at Aidan's words about Genevieve, but it was close. Real close. Instead, he picked up his beer with a casual shrug.

"You're reading too much into things."

"Am I?" Aidan's lips twitched before he gave a low whistle at something happening over Ethan's shoulder. "Then maybe you're not interested in seeing what Gen and that oily businessman are doing to each other in that booth?"

The muscles in his neck strained with effort as he spun around, immediately realizing his mistake when he saw Genevieve sitting alone, sipping at her champagne as she gazed back at him. He swung back around to glare at Aidan.

"I don't pry. You know me well enough for that. But this feeding issue your... friend is having is nothing to mess around with. You need to create a link that triggers an emotional response to feeding. The stronger the emotion, the better the connection. It's not a quick fix, either, and the sooner you start the fix, the more opportunity there is for it to stick," Aidan said, standing.

He considered the sober look in his friend's eye. "You sound worried. How big of a deal can this be?" he asked.

"Think about it, Ethan. Feeding should never be a matter of going through the motions, especially for a new vampire," he said with a knowing look. "Not when it's what we need to do to survive. Continue to view it like it doesn't matter, and it becomes easier to put it off, and eventually to start resenting it."

Ethan took a moment to absorb what Aidan was telling him. "What happened to the vampires you knew about?"

"They went longer and longer without feeding, and then eventually... well, eventually they went too long. I'm sure I don't need to tell you what happened then," Aidan said and walked away.

"I'll call you if I hear anything about your other problem," he added, lifting his hand in farewell.

CHAPTER TWELVE

Gen didn't know what Aidan had said to put such a hard look on Ethan's face, but whatever it was, it'd left him staring at her across the length of the bar for a solid ten minutes.

Then it was as if something had snapped him out of it, and he was telling her they were done. Looking into his face, one glance had been more than enough to warn her to not even bother with questions. He didn't look to be in an answering kind of mood.

Now, as she glanced out the window of their car, she saw they weren't going back to Ethan's house. Instead, they were heading toward a part of the city where she'd never ventured before. A place where tall black iron gates stretched high into the sky, and the ever-silent Bladed barred the way in to a world of power and excessive wealth.

As they made their ascent up the highest reaches of the most secure vampire enclave in Vegas, and most likely the world, Gen could only catch brief glimpses of towering mansions and yet more iron gates in the distance.

The only thing that moved on the road was the Bladed. In their black-on-black uniforms, the only reason she saw them at all was because she had the benefit of night sight.

When Vince had told her about this place, she'd never imagined that she'd actually see what lay behind the black iron gates. But here she was, brought here by Ethan, because of something Aidan had said to him over a beer in his bar. Why else would they come? Was Vince's killer hiding among the most powerful of those who lived beyond the iron gates?

Tugging at the dress determined to crawl up her thighs, she turned to Ethan when her questions threatened to choke her. But when she saw the hard line of his jaw, the tightness of his lips, and remembered a similar look on his face just before he destroyed his laptop, she closed her mouth and looked away.

She was just in time to see yet another iron gate in front of them. There were more Bladed guarding this gate than she'd seen before, and in the dark tree-lined roads, she sensed more hidden even from her vampire sight. A couple of the Bladed stood holding radios as they motioned a line of sleek black Mercedes up to the gate, one by one, toward what seemed to be the last gate they'd enter. The gates leading to the highest point of this vampire enclave.

Soon they were at the head of the line, and Ethan lowered the window as a Bladed approached. The guard said nothing, and neither did Ethan. Gen watched as Ethan slipped the same black card out of his wallet and handed it over to the waiting guard, as he'd been doing at each of the five checkpoints so far.

It was examined more closely this time than all the others before the guard handed it back. Neither of the men spoke a single word. And then the Bladed stepped back, and she and Ethan were on the move once again.

The sight of the cream plantation-style mansion with Greek columns, wooden shutters, and a wraparound balcony on the second floor took her breath away. In a word, it was gorgeous—easily the most beautiful house she'd ever seen.

She'd been expecting an ultra-modern mansion, not something straight out of *Gone with the Wind*. She stared up at it, transfixed. In the midst of leaning over to get a closer look, Ethan spoke for the first time since he'd sat her down at a booth in Hellfire and left her there.

"You're wondering why we're here," he said.

Startled, she turned from the window to find Ethan studying her with such intense focus, she itched to ask what he was thinking. But instead, she cleared her throat, nervous but not knowing why. "I am."

"Aidan has a lot of connections. If anything of interest happens, he usually knows about it before anyone else does. He said no one he knows had a reason to kill your friend."

"No one? Really?"

"Except me, that is." In the darkness his green eyes glittered, daring her to say something. Perhaps to accuse him again.

"Oh," she said.

"So, that leaves two options. It could either be Vince's

Master, or another vampire with a grudge against Vince's mysterious Master." He glanced at the mansion they were fast approaching.

"And you're sure it was another vampire who did it, not a human?"

"If you've ever tried to kill another vampire, you'd know it's something most humans are not capable of doing."

She fought to keep her face as expressionless as Ethan's. "And have you," she paused. "Ever tried to kill another vampire?"

For a moment he was silent as he continued to gaze at the mansion.

"Tonight, we're going to be surrounded by some of the oldest and most powerful vampires in the world. Very few of them will appreciate being accused, directly or indirectly, of killing another vampire's Childe. Some will choose to view it as a game. You won't know which until one separates your head from your body."

She gulped as fear spiked through her. "So that's why we're here, then, to ask questions? That's what Aidan was telling you?"

"You won't be asking the questions, I will. You're here for a different purpose."

"To watch for any signs of guilt?" she asked.

Ethan scoffed. "Vampires this old don't look guilty. They don't look anything except bored."

"What makes you think it's one vampire? Why not two, in like a partnership or something?"

"There's a reason vampires prefer to live in houses so

distant from each other. We're not social creatures like the wolves are."

Interest stirred. Vince had hinted at the existence of werewolves in London, but she'd never seen one. However much she wanted to know more, in the grand scheme of things it wasn't important. Not when it came to finding out who'd killed Vince.

"I still don't understand why an old vampire would want to kill him."

"Because that's what they do," Ethan said. "If they can't get to the object of their hate, they will strike at the next vulnerable target. More often than not, it's the Childe who pays the price."

She eyed Ethan, wondering if he had a lot of enemies, but she wasn't quite brave enough to ask him. "I see."

"It would be wise if you don't follow anyone into any side rooms. You're likely to find entertainments of which some even the oldest among us would find… uncomfortable."

"Okay. No side rooms," she said, getting the real sense she might not walk out alive if she wasn't careful.

"And we'll be expected to dine."

"Dine?" she asked, confused. "At a dinner? But we don't—"

"No," Ethan said, cutting her off as their car came to a stop in front of the entrance.

Her eyes widened when a servant dressed in the black and white uniform of a British butler approached their car. She guessed it made a strange kind of sense the disgustingly rich vampire who lived in a Southern plantation-style home would have actual servants, instead of using VASS.

"Not that kind of dinner. Oh, and try not to act too surprised about the blood." Ethan opened the door and stepped out.

Tearing her eyes from the butler, she spun to face him. "The blood?" she asked. "What blood?"

CHAPTER THIRTEEN

Fear and determination fought for dominance in the depths of Genevieve's eyes as Ethan guided her up the front steps with a hand on her lower back, past the imposing stone columns and through the front entrance, where two silent Bladed stood guard on either side of the door.

Inside, her heels clicked across the marble floor, her eyes fixed straight ahead. Conscious of a blush staining her cheeks, he studied her out of the corner of his eye, confused as to what had caused it. But one swift glance at the women in floor-length white dresses lining the foyer was enough to reveal the source of her embarrassment. In her short black dress, it was impossible not to notice the difference.

As they cut a path through the mingling crowds in the hallway, through open French double doors and into the dining room, male appreciation followed her. He couldn't blame them. Her long, slender legs were a honeyed gold that seemed to go on forever in her heels and were worthy of the attention.

Glancing at Genevieve to see if she'd noticed the lack of silverware on the table, he found her gaze fixed on the couple performing onstage. They were the only humans in the entire room, and Genevieve wasn't alone in being entranced by the music they were creating.

The middle-aged man with salt and pepper gray hair played the violin like he'd been born to it, and his slim doe-eyed partner sang with such sweet beauty, it was no wonder they had so completely captured Genevieve's attention.

While Ethan didn't know a lot about classical music, the song the woman sang was a familiar one. If there was one thing everyone knew about their host, it was his weakness for sweet soprano voices accompanying Prokofiev's haunting melodies.

As Ethan's gaze moved around the room, it soon became clear that it wasn't only the human couple's music causing a stir. Even here she was managing to attract attention. While some eyed her with vague curiosity, the look of one spotting a new face and wondering who she was, there were a few lingering stares which suggested a darker interest.

He wouldn't have been surprised if a large part of her appeal lay in her difference from the other woman in the room. While they were immaculately dressed, their makeup and hair perfectly in place, they had the appearance of statues. Of beauty not quite real, something to admire from a distance.

In contrast, Genevieve now gazed about her with

undisguised interest. Her eyes sparkled with excitement as she absorbed her elegant surroundings.

She turned to him with a smile. "Wow," she said. "I don't think I've ever been to a home this beautiful before. It's incredible."

"This is old money. Very old," he said, pulling a chair out for her to sit.

"Old, Ethan? Did I hear you calling us old?" A blond man appeared beside him as if he'd been waiting for the perfect opportunity to slip into the conversation. Knowing their host, Ethan wouldn't have been surprised if he had.

"You'll offend us, saying things like that to your beautiful friend. Introduce us." Lucian's words were nothing less than an order as he continued to stare at Genevieve.

He gave a small bow of apology. "I meant no offense. Genevieve, this is Lucian. He's the owner of this home and our host. Lucian, this is—"

"I believe I know who this is," Lucian interrupted.

Her smile was genuine and sweet, and Ethan could see Lucian both noticed and appreciated it. "Hello, Lucian, pleased to meet you."

Lucian laughed. "Oh, please. Not so formal. May I...?" He paused to take her hand, and flipping it over, he pressed his lips on the inside of her wrist in a lingering kiss.

Blushing, she glanced nervously at Ethan.

"Stunning," Lucian said, without releasing her hand. "Absolutely stunning."

Ethan stared at the slender hand Lucian was clasping

so tightly, feeling a surge of emotion at his proprietary grip.

Gritting his teeth, he weighed up the odds of walking out alive if he dared to do what his instincts were telling him to do. He hesitated. Which was all the time Lucian needed to start leading Genevieve away.

"Now, as I can see it is your first time here, I couldn't possibly allow you to miss out on the best view of the entertainments to come. You must join me at my table," Lucian said.

"Lucian." Ethan reached out to snag Genevieve's free hand. Caught between one vampire and another, she came to a sudden stop, forcing Lucian to stop as well.

"I appreciate your kind offer, but this is Genevieve's first time here. I'm sure she'd rather watch than be a player, at least this time around." Ethan made sure Lucian couldn't fail to miss the steel beneath his words. She was his, and he wasn't letting him take her anywhere.

Lucian stared at him, dark shadows appearing in the bright blue of his eyes, and for a moment the young-looking blond man with the angelic face was both ancient and evil. Genevieve's hand tightened in his, and he knew she'd also seen the darkness stirring within him.

Finally, Lucian sighed.

"It seems Ethan is not willing to share you this evening. Perhaps you might come back and sit beside me next time? I'm sure once you see what you've missed out on, you'll be most upset that Ethan deprived you of so much excitement," Lucian said, sounding young than the shadows in his eyes suggested he was.

Genevieve glanced at Ethan in question, but when he subtly shook his head no, she turned to smile at Lucian.

"Thanks for the invitation. You have a beautiful home, and I can't stop looking at your chandelier. I've never seen anything quite like it before, it's beautiful."

Ethan saw the effect her praise had on Lucian. His chest swelled with pride and his smile widened.

"Oh, yes, it's one of a kind. Most people don't even notice it anymore. But I wouldn't be afraid of it falling. We haven't had an accident like that happen in... nigh on three hundred years now. And then, it only affected one table. It was a fortunate escape for my other guests, particularly since we were so busy that night."

"Three hundred years? These parties have been going on for as long as that? Wow! I feel like I've become part of history or something." She laughed.

"It's a good thing I'm not as vain as I used to be with all this talk of age," Lucian said with mock disapproval, his sparkling blue eyes betraying him.

"Is it very rude of me to ask how old you are, then?"

"If you come again, I may whisper it in your ear. It wouldn't do to let anyone else in on the secret, now, would it?" Lucian winked at Ethan.

Ethan forced a smile on his face. "No, I suppose it wouldn't."

But before Lucian and Genevieve could continue their conversation, there was the faint sound of a bell ringing. The musicians paused their performance and turned as one to Lucian.

Genuine reluctance was evident as Lucian smiled

down at Genevieve. "I'm afraid I must tend to tonight's entertainments, but it's been a pleasure."

After squeezing her hand briefly, Lucian turned and threaded his way through the tables, heading in the direction of the musicians.

Sinking into the seat Ethan had started to pull out for her earlier, she'd barely gotten comfortable before she was turning to him, her eyes curious.

"There was a lot Lucian said that made me wonder," she murmured. "But I didn't think it was a good idea to ask him lots of questions."

Ethan nodded, trying not to think too long or too hard at his relief when Lucian had been called away. "And you were right not to. Lucian is... old. Very old. And the old are always drawn to the young and curious. He liked you, which can be a dangerous thing."

"Really? But he wanted us to join him at his table."

"As I said, it's not always safe to catch the attention of Lucian. His friends rarely survive it."

"Did he mean what he said about the chandelier? At first I thought he was joking, but now I'm not so sure."

"He wasn't joking. A chandelier snapped and crashed into vampires sitting at a table underneath," he said, taking advantage of his opportunity to appreciate the fluid lines of Genevieve's throat as she glanced up at the chandelier.

"Really? I don't see how it could have snapped. It looks reinforced to me."

Ethan flagged down a passing server and took two glasses from his tray.

"The reinforcements came later. The original fixtures weren't so sturdy back then."

"And it snapped? Did anyone survive?"

"None. What the chandelier didn't do, the flames from the candles finished off."

Genevieve sipped at her glass of blood-spiked champagne while she scanned the room. Ethan noticing she drank it in the same way she had the champagne at the bar—with faint interest, but little in the way of real enjoyment.

All around him, the open appreciation of the champagne spiked with a heady mix of adrenalin and excitement was obvious. But not for Genevieve. She alone seemed blind to the potent emotions contained in her glass.

So that was another thing Aidan had been right about. It would be interesting, he thought as he discreetly watched her, to see how she responded to tonight's entertainment. "How's your drink?"

She smiled at him. "It's nice, thanks," she said, her gaze lingering on the musicians who'd resumed their performance.

"Nice?" he echoed, a twist to his lips.

"Ethan." A voice spoke from directly behind him.

But Ethan didn't immediately turn around. Instead, he picked up his glass and drained it. Beside him, he could feel Genevieve's eyes on him, and he knew the rage he felt rising from the pit of his stomach was already spilling out of him, all before he'd even taken one look at the man standing behind him. It didn't bode well at all.

Returning the empty glass to the table with a gentleness he didn't feel, he rose.

"I heard you were here this evening, but I didn't think you came to these sorts of events anymore."

Ethan made no response to the man with the faint Italian accent before he met Genevieve's curious eyes. "I'll be back in a moment. Stay here."

Although her gaze shifted from him to the man standing beside him, he made no move to introduce them. Instead, he walked far enough away from Genevieve that she wouldn't be able to hear what he said, and then he turned to the man who'd quietly followed him.

In all the years that'd passed since Ethan had seen the vampire who'd turned him, nothing about him had changed—at least in terms of his appearance. He was still the dark-haired and dark-eyed man who looked to be in his thirties, with a touch of sadness about his eyes and a slight downturned mouth.

"Dante. What are you doing here?" Ethan asked, fighting to keep his voice casual as he worked hard to hide the violent emotions simmering just below the surface of his mask of indifference.

Dante smiled. "I heard you'd claimed a Childe."

"She was mine to begin with. I merely formalized it. Not that it has anything to do with you. But since it was a recent event, I imagine you were here even before that," Ethan said, feeling Genevieve's eyes on him, wishing now he'd left her at home. Wishing he'd stayed at home.

"Ethan, I am not your enemy," Dante said, his black eyes as unreadable as ever. His accent was heavier now than it'd been before. He must have returned to his native Italy for it to be this thick.

"I've only ever wanted the best for you."

"That, Dante, is not quite how I remember things. Perhaps in your old age, your memory is slipping," Ethan said, his voice sharp.

He felt a sudden spike of interest from those listening. No doubt they were excited beyond measure at having managed to secure ringside seats to the unexpected public reunion between an estranged Master and his former Childe.

But he wasn't about to give them what they wanted. He'd leave it up to Lucian to find a way of entertaining those who struggled to find any real enjoyment in anything but the most shocking of acts anymore.

"If that is what you have chosen to believe," Dante said, keeping his gaze trained on Ethan, his eyes as equally aware, if not more so of how many ears would be turned their way. "Then, you may do so."

"The first course is due to start soon," Ethan said, glancing up at the couple on stage who appeared to be winding down their performance. Looking to the side of the stage, Ethan saw a brief flash of Lucian's blue eyes as he watched the performers from just offstage.

"I'd appreciate it if you would say what you came here to say, so I can return to Genevieve." He turned in time to catch her wave at the offer of another drink.

"There's something I need to tell you, but not here. Come with me outside," Dante said, nodding toward the double doors leading to the terrace.

But Ethan was already shaking his head. After the

rumors he'd heard about what went on out there, of the humans Lucian made certain weren't enthralled before they were hunted down in some kind of sick game, he had no intention of stepping out there. Not for any reason, least of all to talk to a man he had no interest in talking with at all.

The hunts had been the reason he'd stopped attending Lucian's blood-feasts in the first place—that, and his having met Genevieve. For the first time in a long time, he'd felt something akin to shame, and he hadn't wanted her to know he'd ever attend the depraved entertainments that Lucian took such pleasure in putting on.

"I'm not interested in anything you have to say. Now, if you'll let me get back to my evening..."

Dante eyed him with a faint look of disapproval. "Are you sure, Childe? She does not seem to be the sort to enjoy the games Lucian likes, and neither are you. At least you never used to."

Ethan found himself hating him for his perceptiveness. "I am not your Childe," he snapped.

One of Dante's heavy, jet-black eyebrows rose. "I see you have forgotten a great many things I have taught you."

As Ethan opened his mouth to respond, Dante raised his hands in a sign of peace.

"Ethan, I am not here to duel with you about the past. I need to talk to you about something else. It is important."

"It's always important," Ethan said, snatching up a glass from a passing server's tray, and drained it in one swallow. "But, as I said, I need to get back to Genevieve."

"Your Childe?"

"Yes. She's my Childe."

"And you're sure of this?" Dante ignored the server offering him a tray.

For as long as Ethan had known him, Dante had never drank blood in any other way than directly from a vein, and he abstained completely from alcohol of any description.

"Yes. I am."

"And how does she feel about that? Does the name trouble her, as it did you?" Dante asked with a small smile.

His patience starting to run thin, Ethan let his frustrations show. "I don't see why it matters what I call her."

"Mmm. I heard whispers she was living with another vampire in...London, I believe it was?"

He forced himself not to respond. Why was he getting the sense Dante was trying to provoke him?

"But now Vincent, I believe was his name, is dead. Some believe you had something to do with it." His smile turned secretive.

"Then they don't know me very well. If they know me at all, that is." Ethan said pointedly.

"Perhaps it would have been better for you to leave Genevieve with Vincent. Better yet, perhaps you should have let them return to London."

"Better?" Ethan asked. "Better for who, exactly?"

"For you. And perhaps for her, too," Dante said enigmatically.

Ethan itched to shake whatever it was Dante was hinting at out of him. "And what is that supposed to mean?"

Dante blinked at him in perfect innocence. "Just that,"

he said. "Perhaps it would have been better for you not to have claimed Genevieve at all. For both your sakes."

Ethan stepped forward. "What are you trying to say? Did you have something to do with it? And when did you arrive in Vegas? Aidan didn't say you were here."

"Despite what you believe, Aidan doesn't know everything that goes on in Vegas."

But before Ethan could respond, Dante shifted his focus to the stage. "The first course is starting," he murmured, and on the heels of his words, the violinist and the soprano's performance came to an end.

At the conclusion of the performance, the vampires broke off their conversations and turned to the stage. The soprano stepped forward and curtsied to the crowd, her disappointment plain to see when she was met with silence.

Then it was the violinist's turn to step forward, bending formally at the waist in an old-world style bow. Silence greeted him as it had greeted her. But the violinist wasn't finished yet. He raised the violin bow in his left hand and the violin in his right.

There was a stillness now that hadn't been there before. A hunger in the silence. Ethan glanced at Genevieve, who sat with her elbows resting on the table, as captivated by the violinist as everyone around her.

Ethan turned back to the stage just in time to see the violinist retreat behind the soprano, as if inviting the silent audience to focus its attention on her.

But, behind her, the violinist lifted his bow, and before the soprano could react, he sliced it sharply across her throat. Blood—thick, red, and hot—showered down. The singer fell to the floor without a word, a pool of blood spreading around her still form.

Applause burst out.

Then the violinist raised the bow. Blood dripped slowly onto the stage. His white suit was still untouched, having avoided the worst of the blood. There was another hush as the vampires stared in silent expectation.

Ethan turned to Genevieve when he saw the violinist raise the bow to his own neck with a gentle smile. She stared at the stage; her face was pale and flecked with blood. Her hand crept up to her mouth as she watched. Her eyes widened with horror, and she flinched as the splatter of blood hitting her face announced the climax of the violinist's performance.

"Welcome to my home, ladies and gentlemen. I am Lucian, and tonight I will be your host. The first course, a little something to get the blood pumping, has been served. Enjoy."

The lights went out to thunderous applause.

"As I said," Dante murmured from close beside him. "She doesn't look the sort to enjoy entertainments as dark as this."

CHAPTER FOURTEEN

"Here." Ethan placed a fresh glass of blood-spiked champagne in front of Gen. He was back from his conversation with the darkly handsome Italian vampire he hadn't wanted to introduce her to, but his return was no real comfort to her. Not when they weren't leaving yet. Not when she could still feel the blood drying on her face.

"I'm not thirsty." Her voice was low, stunned. She reached to scrub at her face without conscious thought, and Ethan's hand snaked out and caught at her wrist.

It hadn't been the first time he'd stopped her. Before, his eyes had flashed in warning, but this time he leaned in close.

"Don't," he murmured in her ear, her eyes caught by the vampires near the stage holding their glasses under the blood dripping from the stage. "Lucian is watching."

She turned, and her gaze clashed with Lucian's, his eyes glittering with feral pleasure as he tipped his glass toward her. Forcing a smile, she raised the glass Ethan offered her. Her hand was shaking, and she found herself unable to stop it.

Sagging in relief when Lucian turned to speak to one of the servers, she replaced her untouched glass on the table and faced Ethan with something close to desperation. "Who was that vampire you were talking to?"

For a while, at least, distraction might be enough to get her to stop thinking about the blood on her face, the bodies on the stage, and the dread that worse was still yet to come. Hadn't Lucian said this was only the first course?

"The vampire who made me." His voice was stripped of emotion, and it took her a moment for his words to sink in.

"Your Master?"

"No," he said, shaking his head as if words weren't enough.

She started to speak, but his attention had shifted to the French double doors.

"The second course," he murmured.

Sucking in a breath, she fought the urge to run. How could she have forgotten Ethan's words in the car? He'd warned her about the blood, but she'd been so caught up with the beauty of the house, his words had slipped from her mind.

It took everything in her to make herself face the double doors; aware that she was the only one not looking. She'd already been the center of attention with her dress. The last thing she wanted was for it to happen again.

Servers filed out in a single line, and a beautiful woman in a short white dress with long dark hair, bare feet, and a hand tucked behind her back stepped in. The door closed firmly behind her. Sinking low into an extended curtsey, she paused with her hair shielding her face. She was greeted with painful silence.

Gen's hands tightened around her glass as the woman rose, her movements graceful and smooth, like that of a trained dancer. Her gut clenched and her heart started to race as the woman revealed what she'd been hiding behind her back.

It was a small, sharp silver knife, and its luster was plain to see under the bright lights of the chandelier above. A murmur of excitement spread, and when Gen glanced at Lucian, his smile was wide enough to reveal the hint of fang between his lips.

Genevieve didn't speak a word as their driver took them home. There were still a few hours left until dawn, but Ethan couldn't see himself venturing down to the city to feed. He wasn't feeling in the mood.

Beside him, she still clutched the damp cloth the driver had pressed into her hand when they'd returned to the car. Her face was an unchanging mask of horror.

Ethan was himself covered in blood, and the scent of it, the heady adrenaline and pain-laced mix that Lucian had "served" them still clung to him.

When the driver came to a stop, Genevieve was out of

the car in a second. But before she reached the door, Rachel was there, cool and professional, even after she got a good look at Genevieve's blood-splattered face. It was nothing she hadn't seen before.

Ethan resumed wiping at his face with a damp cloth as he watched Genevieve slip out of her heels and run lightly up the stairs.

"I'm guessing Lucian's didn't go well?" Rachel asked as she shut the front door.

"It was the same as usual."

"Well, it looks like it proved to be a disappointment."

"What makes you say that?"

"Her face, and the fact you're here and not downtown feeding. Not that I'm surprised about her. But you, I'd have thought you'd be—"

"Why are you still here?" he snapped.

It would be just like Rachel to pick up on what he hoped she wouldn't.

He'd thought he would enjoy the taste of Genevieve's fear when she realized the sort of place he'd taken her to, and the knowledge that she couldn't leave. But that hadn't happened.

Her terror hadn't filled him with the glee he'd expected. She'd gazed at him as if he were a monster, and the look as he helped her up from her seat had killed any desire he had to venture down to the Strip, or downtown.

He should've been relishing her horror. Instead, he just felt... flat.

"You had a message from the Council. They want to know how Genevieve wants to dispose of Vincent's body," Rachel said.

Ethan stared at her. "What?"

"As Genevieve was his partner, they've permitted her to dispose of the body as she sees fit." She dug a note out of one of her pockets, as upstairs the sound of a shower started up.

"But I didn't put a request in." He scanned the note as he started for his office. "Are you sure? That doesn't sound like the Council at all."

"You're right, it doesn't. It sounds like someone's trying to do her a favor," Rachel said, following behind him.

"Any word from his Master?"

Rachel shrugged. "Nothing. I guess whoever it is doesn't care."

"Not all Masters do," he murmured.

"And you're sure it's a man?" Rachel asked, following him into the office. "Because I've been talking to a couple of the VASS from London, and—"

"Rachel, as much as I admire your initiative, you're barking up the wrong tree," he said, heading straight for his decanter of whiskey.

"But according to them, there isn't anyone who would have a reason to do this," she said, sounding stubborn.

Taking a sip from his whiskey, he sighed. Rachel was intelligent, capable, and a VASS like no other, but he was starting to regret having given her so much free reign. And he'd made a mistake in telling her about the dead mouse that'd been delivered. He should have known she would have an opinion. She always did.

"It just doesn't seem like the thing an old male vampire would do. It's too…" she paused to search for the word that eluded her. "Subtle. Especially the perfume. It's exactly the sort of thing I could see a woman doing. Even a human one, if she felt scorned or something. Maybe—"

"Rachel." Ethan lowered his glass from his lips. It was best he nipped this in the bud before she launched into some farfetched theory of who could be behind his strange gift.

"You are too young to understand the way we vampires are."

Her jaw tightened. "That may be the case. But I understand women, and I'm telling you—"

"You're telling me, are you?" he asked softly, the first stirrings of anger awakening. "Is that what's happening here?"

Rachel recognized at once where this was heading—where his mood was going, and promptly snapped her mouth shut. After a brief pause, she cleared her throat.

"I apologize, Sire. It won't happen again."

He nodded, his mind turning to the matter of Vincent's body and how best he could use it to his advantage.

That the Council hadn't just cremated the body and delivered the urn to Vincent's Master was unusual, but perhaps the identity was as much of a mystery to them as it was to him. Which left him in a position he hadn't expected of being able to give Genevieve the simple funeral she'd wanted.

"Also, Aidan called and said an old family friend has arrived in town. He said you'd know who he meant."

Ethan smirked. So much for Dante's claim about Aidan. "Anything else? Any mail?"

"None."

"You can go home now. I'll see you tomorrow."

After Rachel left, he sat and thought over the strange conversation he'd had with Dante. What had he been talking about? And had it been him who had contacted the Council about Vincent?

Dante had a lot of friends in the city. It'd been rumored he'd even turned down a Council seat, but that'd been years ago. Ethan didn't know if he still kept in touch with his powerful connections, but even if he did, why would he want to help Genevieve?

Then there was the matter of Vincent's mysterious Master who didn't seem to care about his murder. He'd expected some form of retaliation, especially since he looked to have the most to gain by killing Vincent, but there'd been nothing. Nothing except the dead mouse. What kind of message was a preserved dead mouse?

Rachel's little theory about a woman being behind it was impossible. He had no scorned women in his past. There was only one woman who may have felt he'd scorned her, but that was another life ago, and she'd been dead a long time.

Upstairs, the shower shut off, and he heard Genevieve moving from the bathroom to the bedroom. He'd told her they were going to Lucian's to ask questions about Vince's murder, and he hadn't done that. He wondered if she'd even noticed.

Finally, shaking his head to clear away all the questions crowding his mind, he sent off a quick email to the Council offices letting them know he'd bring Genevieve down to discuss the arrangements for Vincent, and then headed upstairs.

He found Genevieve in bed, already sleeping, her damp dark curls spread over the white pillow and her lashes forming half-moons on her tearstained cheeks. Then he turned away and started undressing.

CHAPTER FIFTEEN

The second her heart resumed beating the next rising, even before she opened her eyes, Gen knew she wasn't alone. She could already feel the intensity of someone watching her and knew it could only be one person.

She opened her eyes.

While she lay flat on her back, lying on his side beside her, resting his head on one elbow, was Ethan. His green eyes were dark and fathomless as he stared down into her face.

She didn't know how long he'd been awake and watching her. But it was long enough for him to be fully dressed, and to have opened the drapes to flood the dark room with the light of the moon's rays outside.

Licking dry lips, she met his stare head-on. "Why did you take me to that place last night?"

As soon as she started speaking, Ethan's eyes dropped to her lips. He reached a hand toward her, but his fingers stopping just shy of touching her.

She swallowed and edged back. "It wasn't to investigate Vince's murder," she said when he didn't respond. His expression didn't change at her mentioning Vince's name, and she wouldn't have cared if it had. After what he'd put her through, she didn't care about anything.

His lips quirked in a humorless smile. "Wasn't it?"

"No. It felt like..." She forgot what she'd been about to say as heat pooled in her belly when he moved closer, his eyes on her mouth a physical caress. She shook her head to clear it. "It felt like you wanted to punish me... to hurt me."

"Is that what you think?" he asked.

She was running out of space behind her. The bed was only so big, and she hadn't started off in the middle of it. As if he knew she'd keep on going until she wound up on the floor, he placed a hand on her hip. It wasn't a hard grip, but it was enough to stop her.

The heat of his hand was like a hot brand, burning through the thin sheets and the T-shirt she'd worn to bed. She froze like she'd been electrocuted.

Then he was lying half on top of her, a muscled thigh pinning one of her legs down to the bed. It felt good. Better than good. It was like a homecoming, having his weight settling down over her, and she struggled against the need to soften under him. Still, that wasn't enough to shut off the relentless voice in her head telling her it didn't matter, that he'd scared her, and sex wouldn't change anything.

But Ethan shifted until he was bracing a hand beside her head, his face hovering close to hers, close enough for his breath to brush against her lips and make them tingle. And then the voice went strangely silent.

She lay beneath him, body quivering with nervous anticipation as he shoved at the sheets between them, fully exposing her t-shirt clad body to his gaze. When his eyes dipped to her breasts, she felt her nipples harden beneath his attention, and a buzz of excitement warmed her lower belly.

Shifting his weight so even more of his weight was pressing her into the bed, his free hand came down to trace the outline of her lips with a single finger. It was slow, deliberate, and without conscious thought. Her mouth parted, and she was drawing the tip of his finger into her mouth, sucking lightly.

The flare of heat in his eyes warned her seconds before he tugged his finger from her mouth and bent his lips to hers.

Her hands came up and shoved against his chest, halting him, which caused a flicker of surprise to flash across his face before it disappeared. Despite her body wanting more, she couldn't forget last night. She couldn't forget him exposing her to sights she'd never be able to forget.

"And why would I want to punish you?" His eyes were lazy as they roamed across her face.

"I don't know," she said, trying to ignore the need to trace his six-pack abs beneath her hands. Desperate to ignore the urge to slip her arms around his waist and tug him closer.

His hand traced the line of her jaw, continued down the

side of her neck and crept lower, glancing over one breast, her stomach, and then settling on her bare thigh. Her eyes widened, and he smiled. When his hand slid up her thigh, under the hem of her t-shirt, and his fingers traced the edge of her panties, she grabbed desperately for his hand.

"Ethan!" Her voice was sharp with panic. "What are you doing?"

"Master," he corrected her, voice mild.

She shook her head frantically.

"No?" Humor was evident in his voice. "I could make you beg for it. Make you scream, and writhe, and beg me to never stop, and it wouldn't even take me licking you between your legs to do it. All you have to do is call me your Master."

Nerves frazzled at the thought of Ethan's tongue moving over her. Her body sagged, softening against him as the fight went out of her. Tugging his hand free, he skimmed his fingers up her thigh to the junction between her legs.

One finger nudged aside her panties and brushed against her sex. She jerked, sucking in a sharp breath as she waited to see what else he would do. But he did nothing. Above her, he examined her coolly.

Trying to slow her racing heart, she opened her mouth, but the only sound to emerge was a wanton moan as he angled his finger upward, sliding through the slick folds of her sex. Her head fell back against the pillow and her back arched.

Ethan's lips curved in a smile. "If you want me to stop, just say it."

His finger brushed against a hard bundle of nerves,

and she gasped as she writhed beneath him. And then he was pulling his hand back as if about to stop. She grabbed at his shirt to stop him and frantically shook her head.

God, how had she forgotten what his touch did to her? This went beyond want. She needed this. Needed him.

"That's not enough," Ethan said, his gaze watchful as he slowly started to press one finger inside her.

Her eyes slammed closed even as her legs fell open, a breathy moan slipping out between her lips. But then he stopped, just like that, half inside her, and she groaned in frustration as she forced her eyes open.

"I need to hear you say it." His voice was husky and the muscles in his face tight, as if his touching her was having just as much of an effect on him as it was her. He started to draw his finger out of her, and her inner muscles clamped around him as if to hold him inside her.

Shifting beneath him, struggling to remind herself what Ethan had done, that his decision to take her to a blood feast had hurt her, she shook her head again.

"I won't—" She broke off with a shuddering gasp when Ethan thrust his finger deep inside her.

Bending his face to her neck, he caught her earlobe between his teeth and gently bit down. She moaned at the unexpected pleasure-pain of the bite.

"You were saying?" he murmured against her neck, letting her feel the sharp edge of his teeth, of his fangs.

Heart pounding loudly as her stomach muscles quivered at the feel of his finger lodged inside her, she tried to remember how to breathe—and that was when she felt it. Felt his cock, hard and hot and throbbing, brushing against her inner thigh, and she tightened her grip on his shirt as his lips moved over her throat. He'd barely touched her, and she was ready to come just from the touch of his finger.

"Ethan, please!" she all but begged.

He started to withdraw his finger, even as his lips moved away from her throat. "That isn't the magic—"

"I won't say it," she said in a rush, even as her body followed his retreat as if determined to keep him within her.

"Because of last night?"

She narrowed her eyes, letting him see the determination on her face. "I'm not going back there. Or anywhere else like that again."

But with his hand still between her legs, and his finger lodged deep within her, sounding firm was close to impossible.

He smiled, not at all convinced. "Is that right?"

"Yes," she whispered, starting to slide her hands beneath his shirt. God, she needed to touch him, needed it like she needed air.

"Have you already forgotten about your promise to be obedient? Your willingness to do anything for your friend? Or does your word mean nothing?" His voice was cold now. Cruel.

Her hands paused at his words. She squeezed them into fists. Forced them back down again to the bed.

"My word means everything to me. You know it does."

"Do I?" Ethan asked, lifting his head and slipping his hand from between her legs, leaving the muscles of her sex clenching, and her aching with need.

They stared at each other for seconds that felt like

hours. For a moment some emotion—pain, or anger, or something else—stirred in the depths of his eyes, but then he blinked, and it was gone again.

"Get up. You have a funeral to plan."

And then instantly, between one breath and the next, he was at the door, ready to walk away from her.

She sat up, surprised. Both by his sudden withdrawal and by what he'd said. He'd started something between them, and again he was leaving her—leaving them both unsatisfied. She knew he wanted her as much as she wanted him. But it felt like he'd just been toying with her, and again she had no idea why.

"Ethan, what happened to us?" she whispered, her heart in her throat.

He turned away from her. Opened the door to leave.

"You tell me, Genevieve," he said, stepping out the door. "You tell me."

What the fuck had he been thinking?

He was barely restraining himself as it was. The last thing he needed was to be making things even harder for himself by starting something with Genevieve that could only end one way.

But even as he silently swore and stalked down the stairs, he knew it was only a matter of time before he slipped up again. He hadn't intended on touching her, but seeing her sleeping in his bed, wearing nothing but his t-shirt, smelling of him... he hadn't been able to help himself.

Then her eyes had fluttered open, and he was helplessly reaching out to touch her before he'd even realized what he was doing. And when she'd sucked his finger into the heat of her mouth… his cock throbbed again at the memory of the gentle pressure of her lips. What he wouldn't have given at that moment to have her wrap her mouth around his cock.

Even now he struggled to ignore the tantalizing scent of Genevieve's desire. It was a battle he lost. Lifting his hand, he drew the sweet, musky scent of her sex deep into his lungs. He craved the taste of her in a way that nearly had him rushing back up the stairs. She'd still be in bed, waiting for him. Ready for him.

Gritting his teeth at his cock straining the front of his pants, he paused at the entrance of his office to try and wrestle himself back into some sense of calm. And that was when he smelled it.

Tensing, he raised his head as all thoughts of Genevieve were shoved aside. He opened his office door and stepped inside. He stopped and stared at the shoe-box sized gift waiting for him on his desk, the smell of death and decay unmistakable.

Like the last gift, this one was no different in its professionally wrapped silver foil and a red bow. The only difference this time was the size, and whoever had sent it hadn't bothered with quite as much perfume this time. It was as if the sender cared less about hiding the true contents from Rachel—but even still, human senses weren't enough to pick up the scent. Not yet.

After crossing the room, he tugged the ribbon free and slipped the lid off the box. He was met with the body of a dead rabbit lying in a bed of tissue paper. Like the mouse, its neck was broken, and the smell of formaldehyde lingered on its fur.

While he'd long become inured to the sight of death, the senseless killing of some helpless creature for someone's amusement triggered a need to lash out at whoever was playing such a sick game.

About to return the lid to the box, his eyes caught on a tiny silver card matching the foil wrapping, with a name etched in calligraphy. He stared at it. There was no message, only a name—Genevieve Althoff. Unease skittered through him at the sight.

Replacing the lid on the macabre gift, he couldn't help but feel this was leading to something worse. First a mouse, and then a rabbit. What else would follow? A dog? A horse? A person?

When Ethan heard Genevieve coming down the stairs, he shoved the box under his desk, at the same time making a mental note to tell Rachel to leave his packages in the garage from now on.

If this was going to get worse—and he had a feeling it would—the last thing he wanted was for whatever new delivery to end up on his desk, or for Genevieve to inadvertently get to it before he could.

She was still wearing his t-shirt and nothing else when she popped her head in, almost immediately wrinkling her nose. "What's that smell?" she asked, glancing around.

"Why aren't you dressed?"

"I wanted to find out where we're going," she said, gazing about as if trying to locate the source of the lingering foul sweet-and-sour scent.

"I told you." He moved to block her view of the desk and what lay beneath it, trying not to think too closely about why he was so eager to hide the gift from her. After all, hadn't revenge been the very reason he'd returned to Vegas? Wouldn't revealing this dark gift offer him the perfect opportunity to scare her?

Or had Aidan been right? Had he claimed Genevieve for a reason other than revenge? Reasons like feelings. Warm feelings.

"You said I was planning a funeral. Are we going to a vampire mortuary? Or does someone come here? Should I wear jeans, or should I—"

"Wear whatever you want," Ethan snapped.

She stared at him. "Okay. I'll do that," she murmured before stepping out of his office.

They sat in a waiting room almost identical to the one Ethan had sat in at the Claims Department. Same building, but different wing. There was the same white marble flooring and huge slab of a desk, where the receptionist sat tapping away at a laptop. She even looked like she could have been the sister of the receptionist in the Claims Department, if you didn't look too closely at her.

They'd been waiting for no more than five minutes when a somber man with pale blue eyes and precisely center-parted light brown hair cleared his throat to get their attention. But unlike Mr. Knight, Ethan had at least heard this vampire's approach and was already turning to greet him.

"Mr. Chambers, Miss Althoff, I am Mr. Ember. If you'll please follow me this way," he said.

Standing, Ethan followed behind Genevieve as the Council official led the way to his office. She'd decided on a simple sleeveless, knee-length black dress made of light cotton that skimmed her curves. As he followed in her wake, a coconut scent drifted from her mass of long dark hair and tickled his nose

"Now," the vampire said, closing the door behind them and gesturing toward two empty chairs. "I take it you're here to discuss what you want to be done with the remains of Mr. Turner?"

Ethan glanced at Genevieve after they'd taken their seats. This had nothing to do with him. "She is," he told the official before turning his attention to his cell phone.

"Yes. I'd like to plan a small funeral for him. But I'm not sure how I'd go ahead with that. I didn't even know there was a Council department that dealt with funerals."

Ethan started scanning emails on his phone.

"Well, Miss Althoff, funerals are only a small part of my responsibilities as Senior Advisor within the Final Arrangements department. I mostly handle new transitions and work with the lottery winners. As you can probably imagine, it can be an overwhelming experience for the newly turned."

Taking a quick peek into Genevieve's face, he caught her interest sparking at the vampire's words. Great, now he'd be forced to sit through her questions about the lottery—something she'd always pushed at him to tell her more about when they'd first met.

Her friend Tess had been desperate to win, but the

odds of winning the annual opportunity for one human between the ages of eighteen and thirty to be turned were astronomical. Genevieve had told him that it'd been the reason Tess had decided to move to Vegas in the first place.

Not that Tess would've been the only human to move to Vegas with the aim of convincing a vampire to turn her. They weren't hard to miss—the human men and women who oozed desperation as they clung to a vampire after a feeding, or threw themselves at any and all vampires unfortunate enough to cross their path.

When Vegas had initially become the property of vampires, Ethan had found himself caught in the crosshairs of more than his fair share of these desperate souls. Hence his reason for moving away from the more tourist-hit areas and spending more time downtown in Aidan's club. Tess, at least, had taken one look at his face and recognized almost from the start to not even bother.

None of the drama surrounding the first lottery winner had taken away from people's desire to begin a new immortal life. Though no one knew how the winner was chosen from the doubtless millions of entries, the fact that Genevieve was sitting in front of someone who could answer the questions people would have killed to know, meant there was little chance she'd let the opportunity pass her by.

"Really, the lottery? I have a friend—"

"Genevieve," he said, giving her a pointed look. "We have time to accomplish one task here. Pick one."

She looked devastated by his words, but let out a heavy sigh. "Okay. Fine."

The vampire observed them in silence.

"Please, call me Gen, Mr. Ember. That's fascinating. The thing is, I can't think of anyone to invite. I didn't know his Master, and we didn't live a very sociable life in London. Well, Vince was more social than I was, but I didn't meet his friends. I don't even know if he had anyone close enough who'd want to make the journey here."

"And there is no one here you'd like to invite?" the vampire asked.

"I could see if our VASS, Paul, might want to come." She paused. "But that still doesn't seem like enough people."

So why then, Ethan couldn't help but wonder, had she been so insistent that Vince have a funeral in the first place, if there wasn't even anyone to invite?

"But it's important," she burst out, as if she'd read his mind. "Doing something to mark his death is important. My parents…" Here she stopped, and although his eyes were on the phone in his hand, he'd stopped paying attention to the message on his screen.

He knew they'd cut her out of their lives after she'd told them about her decision to have him turn her. At the time she'd been distraught, and he'd comforted her, holding her for hours while she'd cried.

Eventually, when she'd stopped, she'd admitted how guilty she felt that her upset was an equal measure of sadness, and of relief that they wouldn't be able to bully her into choices she didn't want to make anymore. Now he wondered at her bringing them up, when she'd left Ohio to be free of them.

"My parents were religious," she said after a brief pause. "Me? I... I tried to be the same, but I wasn't. Not deep down where it mattered. But they taught me that saying goodbye is important, and I still believe that, if nothing else. Even if I'm the only one there," she said softly.

Ethan felt her eyes on him, as though waiting for him to say something—what, he couldn't imagine—but then his phone was vibrating in his hand, and he saw there was a message from Lisette with an answer to a question he'd asked earlier. He tapped out a quick response.

"It's not about the number of attendants, but how they felt about Vincent. Is it not more important to have people who cared about him, rather than having a roomful of those who did not?" Mr. Ember said.

"Yes, of course. I think Paul would want to be there. Do you need me to—"

"Oh, there's no need. My office will do all of that—contacting Paul, dealing with the cremation, preparing the floral arrangements, those kinds of things."

Ethan heard the sound of the vampire's pen scratching across paper.

"But where would we hold it?" she asked.

"Perhaps Mr. Chambers might agree to use a room in his home?"

This time, at feeling both the advisor and Genevieve's eyes on him, he raised his head and tucked his phone away. "You can contact my VASS, Rachel, to coordinate things with her," he said, rising. "If that's all, we have an appointment."

Ethan opened the door for Genevieve after she'd thanked the advisor.

"Where are we going? Is it about the funeral?" she asked.

"Something like that. We're going to Mustards."

"Mustards?" she asked as they left the Council offices.

The noise on the Strip of the tourists thronging the streets, laughing and shrieking for reasons Ethan couldn't understand, drivers almost ceaselessly beeping their horns, and a cacophony of music crashed into them the moment they stepped out onto the street.

He'd decided not to bother with a driver tonight, so after unlocking his car that he'd parked outside, they climbed in.

"A casino on the Strip," he said, putting the car in reverse as she snapped her seatbelt on. He raised his eyebrow but didn't comment on her continued need to use something she didn't need. Then he remembered how he had done it for her when she'd been too mired in shock to do it herself. Deliberately, he forced his thoughts away from his action.

"We're going gambling?" she asked, surprised.

"No," he said, pulling out into the Vegas traffic. "We're going to see a friend."

CHAPTER SIXTEEN

Before she'd met Ethan, visiting the casinos had never held much of an appeal for her. Not when all the money she earned was spent long before payday.

Teaching middle school in an inner city hadn't exactly been a high-paying job. So, she'd always been conscious that she had to be frugal and budget.

Gambling would just be throwing money away she couldn't afford to, especially when she needed every dollar and every dime to make ends meet.

Then when Ethan had warned her against going to the Strip on her own, it'd given her another, better reason to stay away. Vampires hunted on the Strip, and she had no interest in seeking out a vampire's dark kiss.

Now, as they passed the Bladed guarding the front entrance of one of the Strip's vampire-only casinos, she was both excited and disappointed in equal measure that the casino didn't look any different from what she'd seen on TV and in movies.

Ethan was silent as he led her through the red-carpeted entrance and past the vampires in suits and cocktail dresses at the slot machines. It was mostly silent except for the sound of the machines, and the ringing and clanging as levers were lifted, pushed, and pulled.

Coming to a stop, she blinked in surprise as she stared at the vampire in an expensive suit and watch in front of her. He clutched an oversized plastic cup filled nearly to the brim with coins he fed into a slot machine. The gold and silver of his watch shone brightly under the harsh overhead lights.

"Genevieve!" Ethan called sharply from several feet away.

Startled, she gave the vampire one last lingering look before hurrying to catch up with Ethan.

He was silent as they passed the tables where bored croupiers in mustard-yellow vests and matching bow ties waited beside their tables.

At nine, she'd expected there to be more gamblers, but most of the gaming tables were empty except for a couple at the roulette wheel. Maybe they hunted first, and saved the gambling for later?

Curiosity finally won out. "Ethan, why were those vampires playing the slot machines?"

She turned to watch the vampires feeding coins into the slot machines, one right after the other, on autopilot. With their eyes focused in unblinking intensity on the machines in front of them, it didn't look like they'd be moving anytime soon.

Ethan's hand on her arm surprised her, and she glanced at him with a question on her lips. But then she saw that he'd stopped her from walking into a poker table and was steering her into a roped-off bar area where the staff was still setting up for the night.

"It's Vegas. Everyone plays the slot machines."

A bartender looked up from slicing lemons and nodded toward a half-closed door. "Go ahead," he told Ethan. "She's expecting you."

"But not like that. I mean, surely you can't win all that much from those machines, right?" she asked.

Ethan shrugged. "It depends. Some you can win millions. The ones here… maybe a few thousand."

"That's what I thought. The vampires back there didn't look like they needed the money. I'm sure I saw one of them wearing a Rolex."

They climbed a set of stairs up to a glass-fronted office overlooking the casino main floor, and Ethan knocked on the metal door. "It wasn't a Rolex," Ethan said, turning to face her. "It was a Patek Phillippe. Very rare."

The name sounded familiar, but she struggled to remember where she'd heard it from before. "A what?"

"A Patek Phillippe. I think only four of that particular design were ever made. There was an auction a while back, and one sold for nine million. I think it made most of the papers."

She stared at Ethan, her mouth gaping open.

"You're telling me some guy was wearing a nine-million-dollar watch while he fed quarters into a slot machine, hoping to win a couple of thousand? Why would he do that? What's the point?"

Ethan started to speak, but it was a female voice filled with humor who answered. "Because it's fun, and even stupidly rich vampires deserve to have some fun on the slot machines in Vegas."

Lisette wasn't what Gen expected a casino owner to look like. She was a petite woman with a razor-cut chestnut bob, and severe bangs which revealed almond-shaped, doe-like eyes.

She didn't look like the stereotypical hard-faced, money-hungry casino owner with the protruding belly and power suits she'd seen on TV and in the movies. But since this was her first time in a casino, what did she know about casino owners?

As Lisette poured Ethan a whiskey, Gen took advantage of the opportunity to examine her. There was something about her style and her easy confidence that she liked. The slim, navy pant-suit and white peasant blouse she wore suited her perfectly, giving her the look of a French actress or model.

When she pulled a metal case from her suit pocket and lit a cigarette, Gen found that it fitted with her style rather than detracted from it.

Once she would have been surprised to see a vampire smoking, but not anymore. That'd been something else she'd learned over the years. Vampires couldn't be killed by fire. It was something some were deathly afraid of, but it couldn't kill a vampire outright—not the way she'd always read it could.

Ethan had smoked when she'd first met him at Aidan's bar, when she'd gone looking for help for Tess one night.

It had disturbed her seeing him with a cigarette in one hand and a lighter in the other. And as time went on, the more often she'd seen him with it, the harder it'd been to hide how much it had bothered her.

Finally he'd asked, and her fear that he'd set himself on fire had poured out of her so fast, it was a wonder he'd been able to understand a word of what she'd said.

He'd stared at her for so long, she'd thought that this was it. She'd finally scared off the one guy she wanted more than she'd ever wanted anyone else.

"You're afraid?" he'd asked.

"Yes," she'd responded.

"Of me... setting myself on fire? Why?"

"Because I don't want anything to happen to you," she said, her voice getting softer as the intensity of his eyes increased with each passing second.

"I see."

And then he hadn't said anything else. But after that, she'd never seen him with the lighter again, and he no longer smelled of tobacco. She'd known then that he'd stopped smoking for her, because of what she'd said.

When Lisette offered her a drink, she waved it off. She hadn't liked the taste of hard liquor and had only really enjoyed having a glass or two of white wine with Tess.

God, she hoped Tess would start speaking to her again. Without her, she was completely friendless, and it was all over something she couldn't help.

"I'm guessing you're here about Dante?" Lisette asked Ethan, sinking into a French-style white chaise lounge. Ethan sipped at his whiskey in his armchair beside

Lisette's delicate antique mahogany desk, while Gen drifted over to the window overlooking the casino.

She watched the bartenders wiping surfaces, restocking spirits, and cutting lemons as Ethan and Lisette continued their conversation behind her.

"What makes you think that?" Ethan asked.

"Because you're here, and you're only here when it has something to do with him. What has he done this time?" Lisette asked.

Something about the question caught her attention, and she shifted her focus, and her gaze, back to Ethan and Lisette. They looked comfortable with each other, relaxed in each other's presence, as if they'd known each other for a long time—and she couldn't help wondering who Lisette was to Ethan.

Why did Ethan think Lisette would know something about Vince's murder when she didn't look, or act, any older than he did?

"I'm not sure yet, but he was very quiet about getting here. You must know why he came back?"

"To see you, I imagine. Genevieve, darling. Are you sure I can't get you something to drink? My heart is positively breaking with you standing there without a drink in your hand. Perhaps you might like something from the bar?" Lisette asked, appearing almost silently beside Gen and leaving a trail of smoke to snake around them.

"No, I'm fine, but thank you,"

Lisette inhaled as she gazed out of the window for a long moment, and then she tilted her head toward Gen with a coy expression on her face. "How very polite... perhaps I might interest you in a taste of Enrique?"

She had no idea what Lisette was talking about. "Enrique?"

"My head bartender. He's really quite delicious, like a full-bodied red wine. Very rich, but delicious. But I'll have to insist you restrain yourself from gorging. Only he knows how to make my martinis just the way I like them," she said, wagging an immaculately burgundy-painted finger at her.

"Oh, no. I was—"

"Watching?" She inhaled and blew out another tendril of smoke. "I'd heard that about you. I don't know how you do it, watching without feeling the slightest inclination to—"

"Lisette!" Ethan barked.

Lisette let out a throaty chuckle, and Gen eyed Ethan curiously. What had Lisette been about to tell her, and why hadn't Ethan wanted her to? It sounded like Lisette had been mocking her, perhaps for not enjoying the blood feast.

They probably thought less of her because of it, and she found she didn't care. She knew they looked at her as a disappointment for not letting go of her humanity, but it didn't matter. If that was the kind of entertainment they liked, that was fine by her. She refused to feel less-than for not taking pleasure in another person's pain.

"No need for ruffled feathers," Lisette said, a faint French accent subtly coloring her words for the first time. "I was only playing."

Ethan's voice was sharp as he regarded Lisette coolly. "Whatever you want to call it, stop it. Now, tell me about Dante. What's he doing here?"

Lisette sighed dramatically and drifted away from Gen, back to the seat she'd abandoned. "And how am I supposed to know?"

"Because you two are close. Closer than you'd want to admit to anyone," Ethan said.

Gen examined Lisette's petite form and a face that suggested she couldn't be any older than her mid-twenties. Could Lisette be Dante's Childe? Was that what Ethan was hinting at when he said they were close?

When Lisette turned burnt-sugar eyes on her, as if she'd felt Gen's gaze, a smile twisted her lips. "Ethan, you need to educate your Childe. I see she is getting quite the wrong impression altogether," Lisette said.

"The wrong impression?" Gen asked. "About what?"

"About me," Lisette said, putting out her cigarette in a small glass dish on a side table beside her. "Ethan's Master—yes, I know you don't like the title, Ethan. Perhaps maker might be preferable? But whatever the name, he did make you."

Ignoring the dark glower on Ethan's face, Lisette reached for her silver case to light up another slim cigarette before turning to her.

"Dante and I are old friends, and Ethan believes that Dante has been causing mischief. Am I right?" She glanced at him.

"I believe he's up to something," Ethan admitted, sipping at his whiskey.

All of a sudden, she remembered what Ethan had said to her in the car outside Lucian's home. He'd said something about a Childe being the victim when a Master decided to seek out vengeance.

"But why would Dante want to hurt Vince?" she asked Ethan, confused.

"Vince?" Lisette said, pausing. "Oh, you mean Vincent? You believe Dante had something to do with that?"

Ethan drained the contents of his glass and set it aside before he spoke. "Who else could it be? And you must admit, his return to Vegas is more than a little coincidental."

"Ethan, despite what you might think, Dante is not looking to hurt you. Even after what you did," Lisette said.

What was Lisette talking about? What had Ethan done to his Master that would be worthy of revenge? About to ask him, she missed the opportunity when Ethan spoke over her.

"And what if he thought he was doing me a favor?"

Lisette eyed him in silence.

"Are you saying you think your Master—er, the vampire who made you—killed Vince because he thought that's what you wanted?" Gen asked, shifting her gaze between Lisette and Ethan for confirmation.

"It is possible," Lisette said with a Gallic one-shoulder shrug.

"But what about the leaking faucet?"

Now that she thought about it, Gen was sure someone had been trying to lure her into the bathroom. Ethan's reaction at the time certainly suggested it. Only she had no idea what that reason was, and if Ethan knew, he wasn't sharing.

"What faucet?" Lisette asked.

But Gen didn't answer, because something in Ethan's

face was telling her someone had wanted to harm her. "Did he think you would want me dead too?"

Ethan continued to say a whole lot of nothing.

Lisette tutted. "Well, after you—"

"Thank you for your hospitality, Lisette, but Genevieve and I really should be going." Ethan's face was wiped clean of all expression as he stood and started for the door.

"And Lisette, if you see him, tell him I want to speak to him." He paused with his hand on the door handle. "And tell him to stop sending the gifts. I know what he's doing, and it isn't going to work."

"Gifts?" Gen asked as Ethan opened the office door and ushered her out, all the while ignoring her question.

Following Ethan past the bar, she couldn't help but notice that a Spanish man with tawny-bronze skin and heavy dark brows had stopped polishing the bar and was staring up at Lisette's office. The look on his face was entranced, as if the rest of the world no longer existed for him.

And gazing back at him was Lisette, who stood in the open door of her office, her gaze full of dark hunger as it met the man Gen took to be Enrique.

There was something about the look in her eyes, something that made her reassess Lisette's age. In that brief moment, she felt she was seeing Lisette as she was. Not as an attractive, young-looking French casino owner, but as a predator with its eye fixed on prey.

"Ethan," she said. "I know it's rude to ask, but how old is Lisette?"

He shrugged. "No one knows," he said. "But there have

been rumors she's one of the oldest vampires in the city. And likely Dante's Master."

As Ethan waited for the red light to change, beside him he could almost feel the questions bubbling over in Genevieve's head as she sat in silence.

"Why did you wait four years to tell me you were alive, Ethan? And why am I getting the feeling I'm the last one to find out?"

Clenching his hands around the steering wheel at the underlying hurt in her voice, Ethan felt the long-simmering rage begin to stir. He felt her gaze on him now, though he didn't turn to face her—not yet.

"If I were you," he murmured, letting her hear the threat in his voice. "I would stop right there."

"Stop where? You tell me Vince was murdered by your Master, and Lisette is hinting that he wants me dead too. What did I do? Why are you so angry at me?"

In her voice, Ethan heard a wealth of frustration. As if she were the victim in all this. As if he were the one to blame. And even though they were at a red light in the middle of the Strip where people surged down sidewalks, screaming, laughing, and chatting, at that moment none of it mattered.

Turning to Genevieve, he caught her forearm and yanked her toward him, ignoring the snap of her seat belt as it tightened across her.

"You. Do not get to demand, ask, or request anything from me. I will give you the answers I think you deserve.

And right now, you can bet your ass you don't deserve shit from me. So, sit back, shut up, and hope I calm down enough not to toss you out on the street and take my chances with the Council." Ethan's voice was a low-pitched snarl, his face so close to hers, he couldn't miss the fear bleeding into her eyes.

Behind him, cars beeped their horns, but he ignored the sound as he waited to see if she dared to ask him another question, or if she'd try to run.

But into the tense quiet, his cell phone vibrated and he dropped her arm to answer it. "What?" he snapped without looking away from her.

There was a brief pause, and then Rachel spoke.

"Sorry to interrupt you, but you need to get back home as soon as you can. Something arrived. A gift, and… well, it's probably best you see it for yourself."

Ethan hung up as he turned away from the still-silent Genevieve. He saw the red light was now green, and he was holding up traffic. Swearing under his breath, he drove on.

When he pulled up in front of the house, Rachel was already waiting outside the front door. To his right, he could see the garage doors were half-open.

Genevieve didn't speak as she unbuckled her seat belt and slipped out of the car. Ethan watched as she walked into the house, her hands lightly rubbing at her upper arms. He hadn't thought he'd grabbed her hard enough to hurt her, but then he remembered the seat belt had been pulled across her upper arms and shoulders.

For a moment he was tempted to follow, to see if he'd hurt her, but then he shook his head. What did it matter if he hurt her, when the only reason she was with him in the first place was so she could get a taste of what she'd put him through?

"Trouble?" Rachel asked as he climbed out of his car.

He glanced at the garage doors. "You tell me."

She looked like she wanted to say something about Genevieve, but evidently, she'd learned from the last time she'd offered up an unwanted opinion.

"A package arrived while you were out..."

"And?" he probed.

"Well, it's a good thing you told me to leave the packages in the garage from now on. Because once I smelled it, to be honest, I didn't even want to touch it. But someone left it right outside the front door, and I wasn't about to leave it there," Rachel said, her nose wrinkling in disgust as she eyed the garage.

Ethan could already smell it, could already guess what he'd find. His only real surprise was that Genevieve hadn't. "I'll deal with it. You can go home."

"Are you sure? I mean, maybe I could..." Rachel started, then stopped when she saw the look on his face.

"What? Go begging to the Council for help because I'm being sent unsavory gifts?" he asked, tone mocking. But when he saw the genuine concern in Rachel's eyes, his expression softened.

"Look, I know who's responsible, and it'll stop soon.

Go home. I'll see you tomorrow night," Ethan said, starting for the garage.

He heard her turn back to the house, likely to grab her bag and coat, as he entered the garage and followed his nose to the smell of decaying flesh and death.

The package was even larger than the one he'd received earlier, and it proved he'd been right to worry about things escalating. Two gifts sent in one day, with one being left outside his home with no sign it'd even been sent via courier. Had it got to the point where Dante was making personal deliveries now? Was he that desperate to scare Genevieve off?

Grimacing at the foul stench emanating from the large foil-wrapped package addressed to Genevieve, he tugged open the red ribbon and removed the lid.

He regarded the bloody remains of the dead creature with silent pity. While he felt no affinity for wolves or shifters, not when they were too territorial for his liking, seeing what Dante had done to this one wasn't a comfortable experience.

He knew no wolf pack would ever choose to make Vegas their home. Not when too many of his kind hunted the city, and with the lack of forests for a wolf to run and hunt. So, this wolf must have been a lone one. Young, vulnerable, and easy prey for such an old vampire as Dante.

If Genevieve had seen what had been done to the wolf, he knew without a shadow a doubt she'd have taken it as the warning it appeared to be, and run regardless of whether she had anywhere to run to or not.

Sighing, he pulled out his phone and left a message

with the Council to collect the remains of the wolf and dispose of it. The last thing he needed was for the wolves to discover what'd been done to one of their kind, and have to deal with a long and bloody fight with the shifters.

Leaving the garage door slightly ajar so the Council clean-up crew could enter without his needing to be there, Ethan headed straight to his office and started making calls.

CHAPTER SEVENTEEN

Gen wiped the steam on the bathroom mirror, her eyes latching onto the fading red mark on her shoulder. When Ethan had yanked her over to his side of the car last night, she hadn't imagined it would be enough for the seat belt strap to leave such a vivid red-black bruise behind.

It hadn't hurt at the time, and it still didn't, but seeing it made her wonder if he'd wanted to hurt her. Or if he didn't know his own strength.

As the nights wore on, she couldn't help but feel he was inching closer and closer toward breaking point, and she didn't know if he would kill her or have sex with her. It was impossible to know which, especially when she'd woken to find the covers pulled over her and the imprint of his body to show he'd slept beside her.

Then there was the whole matter of the closets full of brand-new, high-end designer clothes, and the bathroom cabinets stocked full of her favorite Philosophy sweet-orange honey shower gel, and Shu Uemura coconut shampoo and conditioner.

None of it was making any sense to her, and Ethan going from hot to cold was leaving her in an almost constant state of anxiety. If she didn't have Vince's funeral to keep her focused, she'd have climbed out of the car back at the traffic light and hitched a ride out of Vegas, regardless of the consequences.

But then what would she do? Where would she go?

She wouldn't last five minutes before Ethan would no doubt have the Bladed come and drag her back if she were lucky—and if she wasn't, he would find her himself.

God, when this is all over I really have to figure out what I'm going to do with the rest of my life. If I even manage to survive it, that is.

Turning from the mirror to go and get dressed, she tried to run through some ground rules that might stop her from losing her mind. She'd keep her distance from Ethan and try not to ask him any questions.

Ethan clearly believed she'd abandoned him or betrayed him in Prague, even though she hadn't even known he was still alive. Talking about it was only enraging him, and despite her need to fix whatever was broken between them, maybe she wasn't supposed to. So, she wouldn't anymore.

They'd been given a second chance, but sometimes things just weren't meant to be. She'd loved him, and if she were being honest with herself, a part of her always would. But it didn't look like he'd ever forgive her, not with how he was treating her.

It would be best for her to focus her attention on

figuring out who had killed Vince, and then she could return to London and think about re-building her life.

Alone.

With a towel wrapped around her body, she opened the bathroom door, but stopped when she saw a burgundy velvet dress—so dark it was almost black—waiting for her on the bed. On the floor was a matching pair of six-inch high heels that made her fear for her ankles.

After crossing over to the bed, she picked up the dress and couldn't stop herself from grimacing when she saw it was little more than a sleeveless sheath. Which meant no bra, which meant there was no way Ethan—or anyone else—wouldn't see the fading marks on her shoulder. If anyone asked her about them, what would she say?

She tried to think what it said about her staying, even after he'd hurt her. And for a moment she wavered, undecided. Should she leave? Should she go to Ethan and tell him she wouldn't wear the dress? Then she remembered everything Vince had done for her, how caring he'd always been.

And this wouldn't be forever, she told herself.

Ethan's moods were mercurial as it was, the last thing she wanted was to say something, or do something to upset him, especially when he'd agreed to help her.

So, sighing, she tossed the dress back on the bed and started getting ready. It looked like they were going out again, and the best she could hope for was that this time they'd be staying away from blood feasts. She didn't think her nerves could take it.

"Something happened," Aidan said as he leaned against the bar beside him.

Ethan turned to face him, and for a few seconds, he considered lying.

"What makes you say that?" Ethan said, taking a long draw of his beer.

"I can always tell. You know that. Now stop pussy-footing and tell me what happened." Aidan raised his hand for the bartender to bring him a drink.

"I lost my temper."

"I see," Aidan said, turning to look at Genevieve, who sat alone at the same booth he'd left her in before.

Only this time she wasn't even pretending to want to be there. Her blood-spiked champagne sat untouched, and she gazed blankly at the dancers on the dance floor, her chin propped up on one elbow. Even though the club lights were dim and she was several feet away, Ethan couldn't miss the red mark on her shoulder.

He hadn't seen it when he'd pulled the covers over her. Not when she'd been lying with her face turned away from the door. But if he had, he doubted he would have picked out a dress that revealed it.

He remembered seeing a mark like that on a medical TV show years ago. A man had gotten in a car crash and his seat belt had saved his life, and the deep bruising it'd left behind had been a testament to the impact of the force of the crash. He hadn't thought he'd been that forceful, but clearly, he'd lost more control of himself than he'd realized.

When she'd come down the stairs in her dress, clutching her heels in one hand he'd opened his mouth, ready to apologize.

But the cold determination in her eyes had stopped him. She didn't want his apology. All she wanted was to find out who killed Vincent, and then she could disappear from his life. It'd been clear in her eyes. All she cared about was Vincent.

Swallowing his apology hadn't been easy, but he'd done it. It was easier to shove everything—all his pain, all his rage—behind a thick wall in his mind as he told her they were going to Hellfire.

With the ultra-blackout blinds covering all the windows in his home, there was little chance of any hint of sun peeking through. He'd risen as soon as the sun had set.

He hadn't wanted Genevieve to find him sleeping beside her, and although he knew he should take advantage of one of the five other spare bedrooms, he found he couldn't stay away.

When Aidan had called and said he needed to see them both, that he'd discovered something he needed to share, he hadn't been able to hide his relief. Knowing, or strongly suspecting Dante was one thing, but actually proving it—that was another thing. Although he had connections in the city, Dante and Aidan had much more.

"Want to talk about it?" Aidan asked.

As usual, there wasn't any judgment in his friend's voice. He'd have been surprised if there was. But this was Aidan. Still, he knew Aidan wouldn't have missed the mark on Genevieve's shoulder, and he was smart enough to put two and two together.

"Not really," Ethan said, a touch defensive.

He swallowed another gulp of beer, even as he wished it was something strong enough to bury the burning feeling in the pit of his stomach he was trying to ignore.

"And I'm guessing you still haven't told her what exactly happened to you in Prague?" Aidan asked.

Ethan regretted it now, having broken down and revealed to Aidan what had happened to him in Prague. He'd planned never to tell anyone, but in a call after he'd spent days, weeks recovering from his agony and from losing Genevieve, his emotions had gotten the better of him.

It had all poured out—his being lured to an abandoned part of Prague, his capture, and his eventual torture to death and beyond. Even on the phone, Ethan had caught Aidan's fury as he decided to come to Prague and track down whoever had done it. To make them pay for what had been done to him.

But Ethan? He just hadn't cared enough to do anything.

All he'd cared about—all he'd wanted—was to be alone with his pain.

Besides, he had known at least one culprit was Genevieve. Why else had she disappeared to London with a pretty British vampire the moment he left?

He never wanted to ever think about it ever again, and a part of him, a small part, resented Aidan for bringing it up now. Especially at a time when he was struggling with his feelings about losing control, the way he had last night on the Strip.

Revenge had brought him to Vegas, of that there was no doubt. But seeing a mark on her? A mark he had put there? It ate away at him in a way he had never expected.

He tightened his grip around the neck of his bottle. "I shouldn't have to."

"I'm not trying to piss you off, but keep squeezing that bottle like that, and you'll be making a mess all over my newly polished bar. Ease up, my friend," Aidan said.

Sighing, he pushed the half-empty bottle aside. He didn't want it anyway. Not with his control sorely lacking already. "She knows what happened in Prague."

"She's been with you, what... a couple of days now?"

"Three," Ethan corrected him instantly.

"Ah, so we're keeping count now, are we?"

He wasn't surprised to find Aidan grinning at him when he lifted his head, looking unrepentant.

"Shut up," he said, even as his lips curved into a reluctant smile. "What should I do?" he asked in the next breath.

"How about you pretend she had no idea what happened to you."

Ethan raised an eyebrow.

"I said pretend," Aidan repeated. "Think about it for a minute. Is she acting like someone who would willingly leave you for dead to run off with a secret lover?"

Ethan turned to examined Genevieve as she sat, her eyes on the crush of people on the dance floor. Her lips were turned down at the sides, and her shoulders were slumped. In short, she was looking utterly miserable.

"No," he murmured.

Beside him, Aidan was silent.

But then he remembered the agony of Prague. Of somehow making it back to the apartment and finding her gone. The certainty that she'd abandoned him. "But that doesn't mean she didn't. She's had four years of preparing to face me," he growled.

"Is that what you really think?" Aidan asked, giving no outward sign of what he thought.

Ethan took another long swallow of his beer. "I don't know. Maybe she did, maybe she didn't. But she should have been there. Instead, she takes off with some guy the moment my back is turned. Which happens to be right after I turn her. Tell me that doesn't look suspicious as fuck?"

"Okay. I admit it looks shifty. But in all the years since, you ever get any closer to figuring out who did it? Because it couldn't all have been Gen—if it was her at all—that is." Aidan asked, raising his hand for another round of drinks.

"For a moment I thought that it might have been Vincent," he said.

Aidan snorted. "Vincent?"

"I said for a moment, okay? But once I looked into him, I knew it couldn't be him. He's—he was too young. He didn't have it in him to do something like that."

"But now you think it's Dante?" Aidan asked, reminding Ethan of the long phone call they'd had before he'd followed Genevieve to bed.

"Who else could it be?"

"And you think he hates you that much?"

"After what I did to him, what do you think?" Ethan asked.

He needed to change the subject, and quickly.

Now was not the time for him to be thinking about how he'd publicly rejected the vampire who had turned him, and the way he'd done it. Some said it was the very reason Dante had left Vegas to return to his native Italy in the first place.

It was rare that a Childe turned against his or her Master the way he had with Dante, and the rumors had been rife for years. He was still surprised Dante hadn't just killed him, but Dante had always been a mystery to him despite the decades they'd known each other.

"Fair enough," Aidan said after a brief pause. "What I'd like to know is how Gen and Vince met if she'd never been to Prague before."

"Her name is Genevieve, and she could have lied. Whose side are you on, anyway?" Ethan asked.

"She was quite explicit in my calling her Gen. And I'm on the side of truth, of course. But I met her. She never struck me as the type of person who'd do something like that," Aidan said, studying her thoughtfully.

"People change. Or sometimes they only show you the side of them they want you to see. And once you've given them what they want, their reason to hide that side disappears."

"So why is she with you? Why did you claim her if you don't trust her?"

"I have my reasons."

Aidan studied him, and Ethan forced himself to meet his look with bland indifference. But when Aidan raised his eyebrow and shook his head, Ethan knew he might fool anyone else, but he wasn't fooling Aidan.

"I heard you took her to Lucian's?"

At Aidan's casual tone, Ethan was immediately suspicious.

"So? And you still haven't told me where Dante might be hiding."

Aidan shrugged. "And how am I supposed to know? The man has had years to build himself more dark corners to burrow in than anyone will ever find. Anyway, I heard even with all the entertainments, and Lucian's special champagne—what I wouldn't give to get my hands on his champagne supplier—"

"Wait a minute. You demanded I bring Genevieve along or you weren't telling me about Dante." Ethan glared at him.

"I lied," Aidan said calmly. "But, as I was saying, the rumors are circulating even faster than the ones about whether you killed Vincent to reclaim Gen."

He narrowed his eyes. "You're trying to distract me. If you didn't bring me down here for news about Dante, why did you?"

Aidan took a sip from his glass. "I've been thinking about what you told me, about your 'friend' with the feeding problems. You remember that, Ethan, don't you?"

Ethan turned to his drink, wishing now that he'd never opened his mouth.

Beside him, Aidan continued. "So, I was thinking maybe the friend might be Gen, and then I thought there might be something I could do to help."

Ethan turned to Aidan. This, he realized, was the real

reason for his demanding he come down to Hellfire and bring Genevieve with him. "Help?"

Aidan grinned. "Yes. Since I've met someone—"

"What? You never mentioned you were seeing anyone."

"It's early days, and she's not one for shouting it from the rooftops. You know how it is,"

"I do. Well, I'm happy for you." Ethan said.

But he was surprised, since Aidan had made no secret of his intention to stay out of anything even resembling a relationship. Even while Ethan had been in Prague, Aidan had remained the resolute slut, given what he'd said on the phone.

He wasn't the sort to 'see someone.' Sleep around, yeah, but seeing someone? Not since Aidan had lived in New Mexico had his friend had a serious relationship. And that one had ended badly enough to turn his friend from the relationship type to the casual commitment-phobe he was now.

"I'm glad you are, to be honest, I thought you might not be, what with her being an old friend of yours. But since you and Gen are back together, I'm guessing that boat has long sailed." Aidan clapped Ethan on the shoulder.

"Old friend?" Ethan asked. Aidan hadn't dated in a long time, and Ethan could number the female friends he had on one hand. "Lisette?"

Aidan snorted. "She'd chew me up and spit me out in a heartbeat. No, from your days in Europe."

There was only one woman he could think of, but there was no way Aidan could be talking about her. Not when her remains were buried at a tiny cemetery in Prague.

"But enough about her. Gen's looking this way. Just smile and nod at her." Aidan's hand squeezed his shoulder.

Confused, Ethan turned to see Genevieve sitting at her booth, except she was no longer alone. A man in a black t-shirt sat beside her, and she was looking more than a little uncertain as she met Ethan's eyes.

The hand on his shoulder tightened, and Ethan glanced at Aidan, who was smiling at Genevieve. "Smile and nod," he said, without moving his lips.

Ethan smiled and nodded. The look of uncertainty smoothed away from Genevieve's face, and she turned to the man beside her.

Why was he getting such a bad feeling about this all of a sudden?

"Aidan," Ethan murmured. "You want to explain what's going on? And what that bartender is doing with her? I didn't think you let anyone but our kin into those booths."

"Ordinarily you'd be right. No humans sit in those seats. But tonight, I made an exception. Andy works the bar, and I trust him implicitly. He's the only one I trust to have Gen feed from."

"You want her to feed on your bartender? In public?" Ethan stared at Andy the bartender chatting easily with Genevieve. He looked fit and strong, with tanned forearms and a wide mouth full of straight white teeth, and something he'd said was making her smile.

Gradually, all the tension in her face and shoulders seem to ease away from her the longer they spoke. Ethan found himself narrowing his eyes the longer he watched them chat to each other.

"Andy will shield her, so no one will be any wiser about what's going on. Don't worry. He knows what he's doing."

"She's never fed like that in public. She won't do it," Ethan said, not sure who he was trying to convince—him or Aidan.

"Andy is very convincing, and she knows it's what you want. So why would she refuse?" Aidan asked.

It was on his lips to continue arguing. But then he saw the faint smile on Aidan's lips, and how closely he was watching him. It was as if he were waiting for some kind of reaction. So, he snapped his mouth shut, reached for his beer, and started to drink, stopping halfway when he realized his bottle was empty.

"You want another?" Aidan asked, all innocence.

"Why not," Ethan said, fighting his every urge to turn around and see if Genevieve was feeding. Suddenly the need to know what was happening behind him became as urgent as breathing.

What if Andy was making her feel things she'd only ever felt with him? What if her feeding turned into full-blown sex in the booth in the middle of Hellfire? Would he be able to watch and do nothing?

But he kept his eyes on the bar in front of him as the bartender slid another beer his way. He took it but didn't drink.

"Thanks. So, tell me about this old friend of mine. How did you meet?" Ethan said, desperate to distract himself from what could be happening behind him.

"Ah, that I could never tell. But suffice to say it was an extraordinary experience. She wondered when you were coming back to Vegas, suggested I drop you an email. I didn't think that was all it would take to get you to come back."

But Ethan was hearing only bits and pieces of what he was saying. His every sense was attuned to Genevieve's booth. He couldn't be sure, but for a second he thought he'd heard a woman moan, and his heart ratcheted at the thought.

Had it been Genevieve moaning in a blood-induced climax? Was there the sharp tang of blood—Andy's blood—in the air?

"I have to say that I'm a little jealous. Andy is one lucky guy," Aidan said with his back against the bar, not even trying to hide his pleasure at what he was seeing.

And that was it. That was all it took.

Ethan slammed his beer bottle back on the bar and spun around. But all he saw was Genevieve drinking from Andy. It was all perfectly innocent, and Aidan was right—it was almost impossible for any human onlooker to guess what was happening. Andy shielded her from view so well that looking at them, it appeared as if they were embracing each other.

His gaze lingered on her face. But as if she could feel his gaze on her, her eyes flickered open and locked with his.

Then her pupils dilated and her silver-gray eyes darkened, turned liquid, and it was like he could feel her mouth on his throat. Lust kicked in. Hard. Andy must have felt it too, because all of a sudden, the bartender was tugging Genevieve closer, and her hands were curling up to grip the back of Andy's shirt.

Her eyes half-closed in pleasure. Ethan's cock hardened painfully, and at that moment, the only thing he cared about was being inside Genevieve.

"Ethan? Ethan?" He knew Aidan was calling him, but it sounded faint. Distant. Barely audible over the sound of his heart thudding against his chest.

Something inside him snapped, and he stood, his eyes never leaving Genevieve's.

CHAPTER EIGHTEEN

Gen struggled to keep up with Ethan's ground-eating strides in her towering heels as he marched them out of Hellfire and to their waiting driver.

When the bartender with an easy smile had appeared at her booth to tell her Ethan expected her to feed on him, she'd considered walking out. The thought of feeding in public—in front of everyone—turned her skin to ice.

But Ethan was watching, and he'd made it clear he expected utter obedience from her. Now he wanted her to do something he knew she'd never done before. Slowly, deliberately, he was twisting her into something she wasn't. Because this wasn't her. She didn't feed in public or go to blood feasts. She didn't do any of this. But she wanted Vince to have a funeral, and she wanted to find his killer. And this was the price she had to pay for what she wanted.

After this was over, she would never return to Vegas again. And she would think long and hard about how she could support herself, earn her own money, and be in a position where she wouldn't be reliant on anyone again.

Maybe she could do what she'd always dreamed of doing and start selling her paintings? Would anyone even want to buy art she created? I mean, who exactly was she? What made her work worth paying for?

There'd been no reason in her mind to think this feeding wouldn't go the same way as the first. And so, as she drank from Andy, she let her mind wander. But suddenly something *was* different. She felt different. There was an awareness, a heated intensity moving over her face, drawing her attention away from Andy and forcing her to open her eyes.

Ethan's vivid green eyes pierced her right to her core, with the intensity of physical touch. Unlike anything she'd ever felt before, it was like a brush of fingers across her skin. And then she was tasting passion and desire in Andy's veins, was craving it as her gut clenched and moisture flooded her panties. Andy was groaning and crushing her against him, his hands on her waist no longer gentle but eagerly moving over her, even as he tilted his head to grant her better access to his throat.

But deep down, it wasn't Andy's blood she craved. It wasn't his hands she felt touching her, holding her to him.

Then she was moving, pulling away from Andy, even as he tightened his grip around her. Standing, she could only watch, her eyes on Ethan stalking across the bar, his gaze locked on her.

In his eyes, she saw hunger unlike anything she'd ever seen before. His face was carved as if from stone, and even as she felt a flutter of fear in her belly, the need, the craving for him drowned it out.

He cut a path through the crowd, and people scrambled to get out of his way, though he didn't even seem to notice. His eyes remained fixed on her in a way that made it seem like the only thing that existed at that moment was her. That the only thing he wanted was her.

Ethan didn't speak. Just shackled her wrist in an unbreakable hold and headed straight for the exit. As she fought to keep up in her heels, she felt eyes on her back. Turning, she found Aidan watching with a faint smile of satisfaction on his face.

Then they were stepping out of the bar, and the last thing she glimpsed was Aidan raising his hand in farewell.

The moment the driver slammed their door shut, before he'd even had time to walk to the front and climb into the driver's seat, Ethan was tugging her into his lap. She went willingly, her mouth dry at the dark heat in his eyes. He wanted her, and he was going to take her.

Sat astride him, the hem of her dress rose. Ethan's hands slid up her bare thighs, the tips of his fingers lightly skimming her skin, making her suck in her breath at the heat of his touch.

Eyes never moving from hers, he eased the hem of her dress up her thighs and to her waist. Clutching at his shoulders, she stared down into his eyes, neither of them looking away as one of his hands held her dress up, and the other tightened around the waistband of her panties.

She gasped, shocked when the material tore, and then she was exposed as Ethan stripped away the remains of her panties. Startled, her eyes shot up and through the back window, could see they were now in motion, being driven down the Strip full of people, and she was naked from the waist down. Face hot with embarrassment, she reached for the hem of her dress, started to tug it down.

But Ethan caught her wrists with one large hand before lifting his other hand from her waist. The sound of his zipper in the silence had her eyes widening, even as anticipation surged through her.

For the first time, his gaze shifted from her eyes down to her lips, and she licked them in anticipation. He was going to kiss her, she thought. She was going to feel the press of his lips moving against hers.

Releasing her wrists, his hand slipped up her back and curved around the nape of her neck, while his free hand tightened around her waist. With increasing pressure, he pressed down on her nape, telling her without words what he wanted.

At the first brush of his cock butting against her sex, she froze. He felt too thick, and the head of his cock too wide. He'd fit inside her before, but that was years ago and she hadn't been with anyone since.

But she didn't move. Didn't say no, didn't do anything but watch him, her breath coming out in a near pant. They were in the back of a car in the middle of the Strip, and she was naked from the waist down as the tip of his cock pressed teasingly against the entrance of her sex.

It was making her hotter and more excited the longer she stayed like that. Biting her lips to try and contain the desperate need burning through her, she shifted slightly, settling more firmly against him.

His hands tightened around her waist, and his eyes

darkened until they were almost black. Liquid pooled at the heat in his eyes as he stared at her lips as if hypnotized by them. She got even wetter, and his nostrils flared as if he could smell her need. But he still didn't move.

She couldn't take any more. If she didn't do anything… if he didn't, she was going to lose her mind.

Sucking in a breath and closing her eyes, she sank down on him. His growl made her tremble, she felt the rumble of it deep inside her, and then he was thrusting upward into her. She cried out as her muscles rippled around him, struggling to adjust to his size.

She was so utterly filled with him, she could feel every vein, every throb from his cock lodged inside her. And still, he watched her with dark eyes that burned with an intensity that made her inner muscles clamp tightly around him.

He said nothing, and neither did she. But for a second, for one brief second, she saw a battle raging deep in his eyes. He was thinking about pulling out. Leaving her, like before. She could see it in his eyes.

Shaking her head, she wrapped her legs around his waist, and he slipped in another couple of inches until he was seated fully inside her. They both groaned.

His hand tightening at her nape, he bent his head to her throat. Her body tensed in anticipation at the heat of his breath on her neck. Then his tongue flicked out, touching her throbbing pulse. His tongue moved, glided over her neck, the brush of his fangs making her shiver. And then he bit down.

Screaming at the pleasure-pain of his bite, she gripped at the muscles of his shoulders as he drank.

God, it was even better than she remembered. How could she have forgotten the agony of need he made her feel?

Holding her against him with one hand fastened around her hip and the other around her nape, his mouth was insistent as he fed on her, his hips rocking against hers almost unconsciously. She felt the pressure of each suck between her legs, and the sound of his feeding made her writhe against him.

She was close. She was going to come, and she wanted—needed him—to come with her. She was desperate for him to want her the same way she wanted him.

"Ethan..." she moaned, her hands sliding down his arms, searching for bare skin, fighting with the buttons on his shirt.

Then his tongue was lapping at her, sealing the bite, and at Ethan's urging, she bent her head to his neck. It didn't enter her mind to hesitate, to wait. She needed the taste of him in her mouth. Now. Her fangs were already extended, primed for feeding. She bit down.

He roared and gripping her hips with both hands, lifted her body from his and slammed her down on him. She forgot to swallow, choked, and the blood—*his* blood slid down his neck as he drove himself into her, each thrust deeper and harder than the last.

Frantic now, she ripped at his shirt, tore it open as she bent to his neck to lap at the blood there, conscious of buttons flying this way and that, even as she ground down to meet his thrusting hips.

The air was heavy with the musky scent of sex and the sharp tang of blood, and the only sound she could hear over the pounding of her heart was of flesh slapping against bare skin.

Then Ethan was slipping out of his shirt, even as he was shifting forward, urging her down onto the floor. She arched her back as he settled his weight between her legs. He was driving into her now, so deep she couldn't tell where he ended and she began, but it didn't matter. None of it mattered.

All she could feel was Ethan, his cock swelling inside her. His face was a grimace of concentration, harsh with strain, and sweat dotted his forehead.

Tilting his hips, the angle of his penetration shifting ever so slightly and she gasped as it propelled her closer to the edge.

His hands caught hers and raised them above her head, pinned them to the ground as the pressure between her legs continued to grow. She moaned. The desperate sound seemed to trigger a more frantic response in him—as if he could sense how close she was and was racing to meet her.

Her back bowed, even as she thrashed her head from side to side.

"Look at me," he snarled.

Her eyes fluttered open. Eyes she hadn't realized she'd closed.

He thrust again, the tip of him touching her cervix, and she moaned, an echo of the last. His eyes darkened. He did it again. And again.

"Let go. Now." His voice was tight as one of his hands left her wrists, reaching between them to brush against the tight bundle of nerves above where they were joined.

She came apart screaming in his arms. He followed seconds later with a deep groan, and liquid heat filled her as his body strained against hers.

She didn't know how long they'd been lying on the floor before she realized the car wasn't moving. Above her, Ethan's weight was heavy, but not uncomfortable as he lay lodged inside her, still hard despite him finding his release. But not wanting to move yet, she opened her eyes and tilted her head so she could try to see out of the car window.

Outside, the unmistakable sight of Ethan's white stone home greeted her. Somehow, the driver had not only made the thirty-minute journey from the Strip, but had left the car without her being aware of any of it.

She should feel embarrassed by it, that there was no way he couldn't have heard what she and Ethan had been doing, but it'd felt too good for embarrassment to sink in yet.

"Ethan?" she murmured, running her hands up his bare back. Inside her, his cock twitched, and she gasped in response.

Slowly, he lifted his head from her neck and gazed down at her, his eyes still dark with passion. Even though he'd driven her above and beyond any pleasure she'd ever known, she wanted more. Gazing into his eyes, she could see he wanted it just as much as she did.

Her eyes drifted over his face as he started to rock gently against her, as if he couldn't quite help himself from moving. She sighed at the feel of him, even as her eyes caught on the trail of blood on his throat. Lifting her head, she followed the blood trail with her tongue.

Above her, Ethan growled low in his throat and deepened his thrusts. Her head fell back against the soft car floor, and he followed, one hand digging into her waist. Then he stopped and pulled back. She didn't even try to hide her soft sound of complaint as he eased himself out of her.

"On your hands and knees," he growled, already turning her.

Liquid pooled at his words, and the way he looked down at her as he said them. She rolled onto her side with Ethan's hand still gripping her waist and managed to get her shaking knees beneath her.

Holding her breath as he covered his body with hers, her every thought was on him, on waiting for him to move. One of his hands curved around her front, brushing over her bared breasts. Feeling the tip of him nudging the entrance of her sex, she tensed in expectation as he brushed her hair to one side and dropped his face into the crook of her neck.

He drove himself into her, and she let out a shuddering moan. All she could do was grit her teeth as he surged within her, too fast for her to even try to meet the violence of his thrusts with her own. Instead, she closed her eyes as heat spiraled outward from her belly. Sweat collected between her breasts as the tension in Ethan's grip on her hips warned her of the looming explosion.

He thrust once, twice, and then she came screaming, pushing back, even as she ground against his hardness, her orgasm tearing through her with a violence that stole the last of her strength. He groaned, holding her tightly against him as his cock jerked inside her. Then his body was pressing her inexorably down to the carpeted floor as her knees slowly collapsed beneath her.

She closed her eyes and sank into oblivion.

CHAPTER NINETEEN

Despite his intention to walk away once he'd stripped Genevieve and deposited her beneath the sheets in bed, Ethan did none of that. Instead, the creamy-gold skin of her bare back called to him like nothing else, and for once he didn't fight it. So, after kicking off his shoes, he lay on his side next to her and trailed his fingers up and down the smooth line of her back.

After wrapping Genevieve in his shirt, he'd carried her into the house, past Rachel with her tablet in the lounge, and his driver sitting opposite her. Neither said a word to him, and he didn't stop long enough to comment either.

His thoughts were on the woman in his arms. He wanted her again, and he had every intention of waking her the second he had her in his bed.

But when he gazed down at her face, took in the dark half-moons of her lashes on her cheeks, something in him had gentled and he'd left her to sleep.

He'd been rough with her, he thought, touching the

bruises on her hips in the shape of his fingers, rougher than he'd been with her before, but she hadn't looked like she wasn't enjoying it.

The muscles of her sex had clasped so tightly around him at his first thrust, it'd nearly been all over before he'd even started.

He felt himself harden at the thought of his cock wrapped in the heat of her clenching muscles again. Fuck, how could already want her again?

As if sensing his frustration, Genevieve stirred and opened her eyes. She rolled over until she lay on her side facing him. "Hey," she murmured, a soft smile on her face.

He didn't answer right away, just continued to stare into eyes filled with warmth. His hand brushed over her hip, and she raised a hand to trail her fingers over his bare chest.

"Hey," he whispered.

Her smile widened, and his eyes dropped to her dusky pink lips. To the slightly fuller top lip that he itched to suck. He bent toward her.

Then the memory of the last time he'd done just that came out of nowhere and hit him right between the eyes, and his smile froze.

"What is it?" she asked as he dropped his hand from her waist and perched on the edge of the bed.

"I'm not going anywhere," he said, his voice soft. "I'll be right here waiting for you."

Though he heard sheets rustling as Genevieve sat up, she didn't speak.

He didn't turn around. "That's what you told me. Do you remember?"

"I know I said that, and I waited for you. But—"

He rose. Turned to face her. She sat with her knees drawn up, and the sheets pulled up to cover her breasts. She looked innocent, vulnerable even as she gazed back at him, her eyebrows knitted in concern.

But he knew it was all a lie.

"Stop," he snarled, pacing. Unable to stay still. "Just stop. I don't want to hear your lies."

"But I'm not lying. I don't know what—"

"Fine," he snapped. "Aidan told me to pretend you didn't know what happened to me in Prague. So fine, how about we play pretend?"

She frowned, even as her hand tightened around the sheet. "Happened to you? What do you—"

He stalked toward her until he was bent over her, his face so close to her he could read each shifting emotion in her eyes the moment she thought it. Then he spoke.

"Well, you heard the call I got from my VASS about a problem with picking up the blood from the blood bank." He waited until she nodded before he continued.

"I found his body. But before I could do anything, I was ambushed. Tortured. Died and brought back to suffer more, because clearly, I hadn't suffered enough. They flayed the skin from my back. Cut me open with knives. Crushed my bones. And then gave me enough blood so I'd heal enough for them to pick up and carry on. And through it all, I knew I had left you alone. Newly turned. With no way for you to call anyone, since I knew you didn't have a cell phone, no blood in the fridge, and no knowledge of how to survive. Knowing that if I didn't find the strength to escape and get back to you, you would die an agonizing death." His voice was low, controlled, but she flinched with each word as if he were shouting.

Tears filled her eyes until finally, they overflowed. He watched as her face crumpled in slow motion. Then he bent to speak into the shell of her ear so she couldn't miss a single word. "I escaped."

"They relaxed their guard, and I escaped. And I came to you. I didn't care who saw me, I didn't care about hiding what I was, or that dawn was only minutes away. I cared only about finding you. Saving you."

Genevieve was weeping now. Openly weeping, her head bowed, one hand raised to her mouth as if to contain her cries.

"Imagine my surprise," he continued. "When I crawl into my apartment, voice hoarse from screaming, thinking you couldn't answer because you were dead. And instead, I find you gone."

He barked out a harsh laugh, and she jumped as if he'd scared her.

"I'm glad you were the one to find Vince's body. Clearly, the universe understands poetic justice. Did you know I imagined every corner I'd find your dead eyes staring back at me? But you were gone. And then I passed out. After I recovered, I went looking for you. And do you know what I found?" His voice was low, just above a whisper.

Although she was no longer crying aloud, her shoulders still shook, and as he watched, she raised her head. Blood-red tears slid silently down her face and dripped down to paint the sheets red.

"I asked you a question. Do you know what I found?" he growled.

"That I was gone. With Vince," she said, her voice husky with tears.

"Yes. Gone with Vince," Ethan said, starting for the door. "Whose funeral is tomorrow. Or did fucking me become more important than Vince?"

Stepping out, he closed the door with quiet finality. As he left her behind, heading for a spare bedroom to shower and dress, for the first time he had serious doubts about having brought her back into his house.

He'd flung the truth of what happened to him in her face, and despite knowing she was lying, despite knowing she couldn't be telling the truth, something about the way she'd looked at him was making him doubt himself.

He couldn't afford to let that happen. Not when he knew he was right.

It was Vince's funeral, and she was alone in the room Rachel had prepared for it, waiting for Paul to arrive. Gen didn't know where Rachel had disappeared to, nor had she seen Ethan either, since she'd risen hours after sunset when the sky was truly black. But she knew they were somewhere in the house. Likely avoiding her.

She should be thinking of Vince. Of how she was going to say goodbye to him, because she wanted to say something, even if it would only be her and Paul there. But instead, thoughts of Ethan consumed her. Someone had tortured him. Nearly killed him. And he blamed her for it.

Somehow, she had to make him see that if she'd had even the slightest sense he might still be alive, she'd have stayed, even knowing it would have cost her life. Because she still loved him. But now she had to make him believe she was as much of a victim as he'd been.

He wouldn't listen to her now if she tried to tell him about how long she'd waited for him to return. Things had been just as desperate as he'd said—she'd been alone, starving, with no way of reaching out to anyone. By the time she realized Ethan wasn't coming back, she was in too bad of a state to leave the apartment and try to borrow a neighbor's phone.

Not that she'd even known Rachel's number. Maybe she could have called Tess for help, but with her every thought centered on her hunger, she doubted she'd even have been able to focus on anything else. Probably she would have attacked and killed whoever opened the door to her.

She'd caught sight of the state of Vince's neck after he'd managed to pry her off him, and she'd been horrified. She'd ravaged him.

For the first time, she'd recognized she was no longer human. After Ethan had changed her, of course she'd known it. She'd felt the difference, been nauseous at the thought of food, and she hadn't been able to tear her gaze from the pulse beating at his throat. And there'd still been the taste of something metallic and rich in her mouth when she woke—his blood, though she couldn't remember having drank from him as he'd told her she'd need to, to be turned.

Ethan didn't believe she'd waited for him, but she had. And someone had lied to him and told him she hadn't. It didn't make sense to her who would want to hurt her—hurt him like this. It's like they wanted Ethan to hate her. But why? What would Dante have to gain by torturing Ethan and making him hate her?

Lifting her head at the sound of someone knocking at the door, she rose from her seat and prepared to meet Mr. Ember and Paul.

She hadn't thought Mr. Ember would stay for the funeral. She thought he'd send someone to deliver Vince's remains, and that would be the end of it. But he'd made it clear he was staying, and she couldn't help but feel relieved there'd be one more person to celebrate Vince's life.

Rachel had also surprised her when she'd stayed after showing Mr. Ember and Paul into the reception room she'd chosen for the ceremony. Gen couldn't be sure if she'd made the decision to attend on her own, or if Ethan had told her to.

No one could have accused Rachel of going overboard with the preparations, but that was okay. Gen had asked for simple and small, and that was what she got.

On a black fireplace was the only significant change to the room. A black urn polished to a high sheen stood alongside an elegant floral arrangement of white roses, but it was the urn that'd held her gaze since Mr. Ember had placed it there.

It was impossible to look away from it, even as they'd made small talk before he'd taken a seat alongside Rachel and Paul on the couch.

There was no sign of Ethan, not that she'd expected him to hold her hand through Vince's funeral. Not after what he'd said. But it hurt. Even though she hadn't expected him to be there, she couldn't help how much his not being there hurt.

Finally, it was time to begin. Smoothing the invisible creases from the front of a black silk dress she'd found in the closet, which was probably a little too clingy to be suitable for a funeral, she crossed over to the fireplace. She took a few deep breaths to steady herself and turned around.

Mr. Ember gazed up at her with his hands crossed primly over his knees, looking up at her with a trace of pity in his eyes. It'd been almost impossible to hide the signs that she'd spent most of last night, and her rising, crying. No amount of makeup had managed to hide her red-rimmed eyes.

Beside him sat Paul, her and Vince's Vegas VASS. Like Rachel, he wore the look of VASS everywhere—calm, and yet still managing to look as if he was prepared for anything. But she guessed they must be, given theirs was an organization that had existed as long has vampires had needed humans to serve them as they slept, Ethan had once told her. Only these weren't mindless slaves, but truly dedicated partners who had served vampires for generations.

Next to Paul, Rachel sat gazing up at Gen with blank indifference. At least now it made sense why Rachel hated her. The VASS were always loyal to their Masters, and Rachel was more so than some of the others because of the trust Ethan had given her. Rachel would probably hate her forever, regardless of whether she managed to convince Ethan otherwise.

She cleared her throat. "Thank you for coming."

"When I asked for Vince to have a funeral, I didn't even know if vampires had funerals. I'd never been to one before, and Vince..." She stopped. Swallowed hard. Forced herself to continue.

"Vince would have said I was being silly for insisting on one. Not when he didn't believe in heaven or hell, or devils or angels, or... anything to do with an afterlife. But I'd like to think he would have appreciated being remembered in some small way. I think everyone deserves to have that." Her vision blurred, and she blinked to clear it.

"Vince saved my life," she said, wiping at the tears spilling over her cheeks with the back of one hand. "He spent more time than he should have trying to make me laugh, trying to make me happy. He made sure I had everything I could ever want, and he never thought about his own needs, even when I told him he deserved so much better than me. But..." She paused to wipe at more tears.

"He wouldn't want me crying over him like this. He'd want me to be happy. I wanted you to know—I wanted someone to know that he was a good person who didn't deserve to die. And, well, that I'll miss him. That I already miss him."

She turned now to the fireplace, and to the urn it hurt

to look at. Placed a hand on it and smiled. "Goodbye, Vince. I miss you already."

After a brief pause, the soft sound of clapping surprised her. But then she felt the air stir beside her. For a moment she hoped it might be Ethan, but turning, she found it was Mr. Ember.

"That was well said, Genevieve," he said, handing her a cloth handkerchief.

She smiled, trying to hide her disappointment. "Thank you for agreeing to this, for coming. I appreciate it."

"It's important to recognize those we lose," he said with a gentle smile. "I believe Rachel has seen about some refreshments. I'll leave you to have a moment with Vince while I speak to Ethan about another matter."

Gen's heart constricted and her eyes darted to the doorway. But when she looked, there was no one there. "Ethan?" she murmured.

"Yes, he was there a moment ago. If you'll excuse me," he said and slipped out of the room.

She turned to watch him go, thinking about Ethan. Had he been there all along? Had he heard what she'd said about Vince? And why hadn't he wanted her to know he was there?

"Hello, Mistress."

She jumped and turned to the figure who'd quietly approached. It was Paul. She'd forgotten he was even there. "Oh, hi Paul, sorry I didn't' see you there. And I told you to call me Gen."

He shook his head. "Oh, I'm sorry to have startled you. But I couldn't possibly, Mistress," he murmured.

He'd never called her by her nickname, but she never stopped insisting.

"It's my fault. I'm in my own little world and forgot I wasn't alone. I'm sorry."

"There's no need to apologize," Paul said, his soft brown eyes serious.

"But there is, and not only for that. You must have been the one to find Vince. I'm so sorry, but I fell apart and Ethan had to—"

"You have nothing to apologize for. There wasn't anything you could have done, and well... we VASS are trained to handle almost anything. It must have been a shock to you."

He was kind, Gen thought as she studied him. His expression was one of genuine concern for her, and she squeezed his shoulder in appreciation.

"How are you, Paul? I can't imagine it was easy for your contract to end without warning like that. Have you found another position already?"

He blinked at her. "I'm not sure what you mean? You extended my contract until the end of the year."

"Extended your contract?" she asked, not attempting to hide her confusion. "How could I do that, when Vince was the account holder?"

Paul blinked at her. "No, Mistress, the account holder is not a—"

"Paul, I hope I'm not interrupting you about to reveal personal details of an account to someone who's denied they were the holder of that account?" Rachel interrupted, her voice cool.

Paul flushed a deep red and lowered his head.

Gen turned to Rachel, who stood at the door clutching a tray filled with glasses of blood and wine.

At that moment she didn't care that Rachel hated her for something she hadn't done. She didn't have any right to take her anger out on Paul, who hadn't done anything wrong.

"I'm sure Paul didn't mean—"

"To break VASS rules?" Rachel asked, gliding into the room with one eyebrow raised in question.

"I don't see that it is. I mean, Vince and I—"

"Regardless of what your relationship was," Rachel cut in again, holding the tray out to Gen with an expression that demanded she take a glass.

Gen helped herself to one filled with blood after giving Rachel a look of bemusement. Why did Ethan not have a problem with her drinking blood from a glass now, when it'd enraged him before?

"If neither you nor Vince was the account holder, then Paul is breaking some pretty specific rules that contravene sharing personal account holder details. As I'm sure he's well aware. Isn't that right, Paul?" Rachel approached him with the tray.

Gen watched as Rachel held the tray out to Paul. She didn't get a chance to see if Paul would face Rachel down or turn down the offer of a drink, because Mr. Ember chose that moment to slip back into the room.

"I see Rachel has returned with refreshments. Excellent. I'll take a glass of blood, if I may?"

CHAPTER TWENTY

"You said it wasn't another blood-feast."

Ethan glanced over at Genevieve and shrugged. "It isn't."

As he strode down Eros's hallway, conscious of her hurrying to keep up, he turned in time to catch her when she tripped in her six-inch-heels and nearly went flying across the marble floor.

She felt warm in his arms, her waist slender—and with her breasts smashed against his chest, it felt good. Too good.

Her mouth parted, and she blinked those liquid metal eyes up at him. But he dropped his hands from her waist and stepped back.

"Come on, let's go."

"So, what is it then, if it isn't a blood-feast?"

She was struggling again to keep up with his long strides and he slowed. "A bacchanalia."

"A what?"

"You'll see."

"Oh."

When she didn't ask him again about what one was, he glanced over at her. Her lips were pressed in a tight line, as if she couldn't trust herself to say any more in case the questions he could see she was desperate to ask him would come flooding out.

Did she think that was the way to quiet his rage? To stop asking him questions?

He doubted she'd ever been to a bacchanalia before, least of all one in the back rooms of Eros.

Going by what he'd heard from outside Vince's funeral, it sounded like Vince hadn't shown her anything that might make her uncomfortable about her new vampire life.

But Vince was gone now, and Genevieve was his to do with whatever he wanted. It was about time she took a step outside the light and into the darkness. And if that hurt? Well... no one got through life without some pain, right?

"It's a celebration of sorts," he said.

"A celebration of what?"

"Pleasure."

He felt her turn to look at him. "What ki—"

She tripped, her heels probably catching on the hem of her floor-length dress, and he caught her, this time leaving his arm around her waist. "Don't you think it's about time you learned to walk in those things?"

He felt her bristle before she tried to step away from him, but he tightened his arm around her.

"I'd like to see you try," she muttered beneath her breath, probably thinking he couldn't hear her. Despite himself, he found himself turning his head away so she wouldn't see his smile.

She looked beautiful in the dress and heels. Not that he was about to tell her, he thought as they reached the double doors leading to one of Eros's private rooms.

Pushing open one of the doors, he urged her forward, feeling her startle in surprise when she saw what awaited her on the other side.

Glancing down at her, he took the opportunity while she was distracted to study her. The black silk of her dress looked liquid and inviting, gliding down the swell of her breasts, clinging to her hips as it fell to the ground, leaving a tantalizing glimpse of bare leg, arm, and most of her back.

Gradually increasing the pressure of his hand on her hip, he stepped into the dimly lit room. All around them, vampires were in the throes of ecstasy as music with a low bass pulsed from hidden speakers.

In booths large enough to fit dozens were bodies, some naked, some half-writhing, the musky scent of sex hanging heavy in the air. Genevieve's steps slowed, and her eyes widened as she stared in open fascination. Ethan nudged her forward, and she looked away, her cheeks stained red.

But that wasn't the only sight that caught her eyes in the low-ceilinged space, painted completely black and fitted with soft black carpets that seemed to absorb all sound. On low tables, vampires cut red dusted powder into thin lines. Others fed with wild abandon as they reclined on low-backed velvet chaises.

His gaze moved over them as he searched for Dante's

distinctive lean frame and the harsh lines of his face. Instead, he only saw more vampires concerned with finding pleasure.

He stopped at the bar stretching along one side of the wall and turned to Genevieve, finding her staring with her mouth hanging open at a couple in the throes of sex. The woman sat on the very edge of the bar with her legs wrapped around her shaggy blond-haired partner, who stood thrusting between her legs.

For a moment he watched Genevieve's flushed face, heard her heart racing as she watched the couple fucking on the bar, and then he caught her arm. "Genevieve."

Her mouth snapped shut, and she spun to face him, guilt in her eyes. "What?"

"Wait here. I need to look for Dante."

Absolute panic spread across her face. "What? But what if..." Her eyes moved around the room, and she gulped. He couldn't just see the terror in her eyes—he could smell it.

This was what he wanted, wasn't it?

For a second he considered walking away and leaving her. But then he turned at the feel of eyes on them and caught sight of a man in a dark corner staring at Genevieve with narrow-eyed focus. It was a look full of dark promise. He knew what that look meant.

"If someone approaches you, just tell them you're not interested."

"But I don't get it. I thought you brought me here for this. To celebrate pleasure?"

She was right. This was exactly why he'd brought her.

That, and a text message he'd received from Lisette when he'd risen that night.

But the thought of coming back to find some guy fucking her on the bar while he drank from her made his fangs extend. Rage filled him. He positively shook with it.

He didn't want to leave her, but Lisette had said Dante would be here tonight, and he needed to put a stop to the gifts before they continued to escalate.

Dante might claim to not be fond of playing games, but he was a vampire, and an old one at that. There was no way Ethan was taking him at his word. If Ethan didn't find and stop him, his games would only continue.

Bending down, knowing his eyes were dark with rage, he pulled her flush against him. He knew the moment she felt his erection pressing against her lower belly, because her eyes widened and her stomach tensed against his hardness.

"Is that what you want? To fuck someone else?" His voice was low gravel.

She shook her head and moved closer, her body softening against the hard press of his. "No. The only one I've ever wanted has been you," she said, her voice pitched low for his ears only.

Ethan stared down at her. He felt the impact of those words right through him. And even though he knew she couldn't mean them, that they could only be a lie, he'd have given anything for those words to be true.

Without letting himself think too much about what he was doing, he slipped his hand around the nape of her neck and tugged her close before pressing his lips against hers in a hard, possessive kiss. Her hands wrapped around his waist, and then he was lifting his head as he released her, turned, and walked away.

After Ethan left, Gen glanced around her before pulling up one of the stools lining the bar.

"Mm, I'm going to take a stab in the dark and say it's your first time here."

Turning to the speaker, she saw it was the woman who'd been having sex on the bar. The guy was busy stuffing himself back into his pants, and she flushed when she caught sight of a little more than she'd intended.

The woman beside her barked out a laugh. "Yep, that confirms it," she said, swiveling her stool around to face Gen.

"Yeah, I've never been to a place like this before," Gen said, not sure if she'd ever be brave enough—or if she'd even want to have sex as openly as everyone around her was.

"Well, I'm Selene and this is Max. Say hi, Max," Selene said, catching the shaggy blonde vampire by his flapping shirttail and yanking him closer.

Max grinned at her, unabashed at literally being caught with his pants down. There was something inherently sweet and harmless about him that she couldn't help responding to.

She stuck out a hand. "Hi, I'm Gen," she said.

Max peered down at her hand without taking it before turning with a raised eyebrow toward Selene. "Babe?"

"What?" Gen asked, looking between Max and Selene, whose smile had dimmed.

Sighing, Selene flagged down the bartender. "Three tequilas with lime," she said, ignoring Gen as she shook her head no.

"You're going to need it by the time I'm through with you," Selene said, tucking a lock of her poker-straight black hair behind one ear.

They made a strange pair, she thought as she studied them. Max, the stereotypical surfer guy with shoulder-length blond hair and blue eyes, and Selene with long black hair, dark mysterious eyes, and pale skin.

"I don't understand. Why would I need tequila?"

"Because clearly, you're a very new vampire. Too new to be left alone in a place like this, knowing as little as you do." Selene knocked back her tequila and followed it with a bite of lime.

Grimacing, Gen waved aside the offer of the shot. "What do you mean?"

"You don't shake a vampire's hand," Selene said as Max did his shot of tequila.

"Why not?" Gen asked. "It's just a handshake."

Selene downed the last shot before signaling the bartender to pour another round. "Not if you want your neck to remain as bite-free as yours is. By the way, how is your skin so golden? Have you just fed?"

"No, I've always been like this."

"Well, I'd be careful with pretty skin like that. It's very tempting," Max said, eyeing her neck, all the while wriggling his eyebrows suggestively at her.

Gen clasped a hand to her neck, feeling self-conscious

and a little afraid. But when Selene reached out to smack Max sharply on his arm when she saw what he was doing, she found herself liking Selene all the more.

"Will you stop doing that? You're scaring her. Sorry, he's harmless, really he is. But he's not wrong."

"About shaking hands?" She was stunned.

How could no one have ever told her? Not Ethan, or Vince. Even Tess, who worked in a vampire bar, had never said anything about not shaking hands. Had Tess assumed she knew? Was it common knowledge?

Since she'd never gone to any parties without Vince, or Ethan, it had never come up. As Lucian had done at the blood-feast, sometimes vampires had planted a kiss on her inner wrist when she was with Vince, but she so rarely went out. Ethan had never taken her to any vampire events before. She'd been human then, and he'd always warned her to keep her distance from vampires, since they didn't always appreciate personal space. Had that been what he meant?

"It's seen as kind of an invitation for feeding. Coming to a place like this, it's one of those unspoken rules, you know? How old are you, if you don't mind me asking—and I don't mean age-age, I mean vampire age. How long have you been a vampire, honey?"

"About four years now," she said.

Selene's look of concern deepened.

"And your Master didn't explain this to you when he turned you?" Selene asked quietly, nudging a tequila shot over to her.

This time she took it but ignored the lime. As expected, it burned all the way down, and after she'd finished spluttering, she remembered why she hated tequila.

"No. He... he couldn't. Something happened," she said, being deliberately vague.

There was no way Ethan would be happy to hear her sharing their history with strangers, as nice as Selene and Max were. "It's complicated," she said after a pause.

Selene looked intrigued. "So, you were alone then?"

"No, I was with another vampire."

A brief flare of recognition flashed in Selene's eyes, but it disappeared so quickly, she couldn't be sure she'd seen it.

"And he didn't tell you either?"

"No. We never went to places like, uh, like this. I didn't even know they existed until Ethan brought me here."

"Ethan?" Selene asked, glancing briefly at Max, whose own expression went carefully blank.

Seeing the exchange, Gen realized she'd said something she shouldn't have.

"You know him? You've heard about what happened? Please don't tell him I said anything."

"We won't say anything. Promise. But he should've told you, at least before leaving you alone here." Selene gazed in the direction Ethan had gone. "Which makes me wonder what else he's not telling you."

Before Gen could respond, she felt the presence of someone close behind her.

"I don't know who 'he' is, but I'll happily tell you everything you need and want to know about anything and everything."

Selene glanced up, her lips tightening, and Max's open

expression closed. They'd seemed so open and friendly, but whoever this stranger was, he was no friend of theirs.

Turning, she took in the tall, not-unattractive vampire who moved to stand at the bar beside her, his arm angled in such a way that he seemed about to touch her.

"Sorry, I'm not interested," she said, leaning away from him.

He lifted his gaze reluctantly from where he had it pointed down her dress, and when she saw the smile on his face, she leaned even further away from him. There was something about it that made her feel dirty, and more than a little uncomfortable.

"I'm Jason. You must be Genevieve, I saw you at Lucian's, but you slipped away before I could introduce myself," he said, holding his hand out to her.

Looking at him, she knew there was no way Ethan would have let this vampire anywhere near her, regardless of how he felt about her. Her eyes dropped to his hand, and she was ready to hug Selene for not only having told her about what handshakes could mean, but also for both her and Max staying with her.

"As I already said, I'm not interested."

"Not even for a passing hour, if you will it..."

Gen leaned back from his hand as it inched toward her arm.

"I don't think you're listening to her," Max said, his voice uncharacteristically hard.

"And as you can see, she's practically tipping out of her chair in her eagerness for more," Selene added sarcastically.

Jason lazily eyed Max and Selene. "Really, Selene, this

has nothing to do with you. I'd have thought you'd learned by now to not interfere in things that don't concern you, given what happened with Daddy dearest."

Before Selene could respond, or Genevieve could think too much about what he was talking about, Jason bent closer, his eyes on her bare neck. Cursing herself for deciding to put her hair up, she swore never to do it again. It was leaving her feeling far too exposed for her liking.

Standing, she edged behind her chair. But it was only a stool and didn't serve as any real barrier to Jason. He moved closer, even as she backed away. She didn't have to look to know Selene had risen, as Max was shifting her behind him.

This was going to turn into a fight. It was in the air, in the way the vampires around them were turning to see what was going on.

It was on the tip of her tongue to call out to Ethan. The music wasn't loud enough that he wouldn't hear her, she tried to convince herself. It wasn't like the room was all that big. He would hear her, and he would come and stop Jason from whatever he planned.

"Genevieve, is everything okay?" Ethan's cool voice said from behind her.

All the tension slipped away at the sound of his voice, and she couldn't quite stop herself from letting out a sigh of relief.

Ethan was there, and going by the disappearance of Jason's leer, he knew as well as she did his game was up.

"Yes. Everything's fine. Jason was just leaving, weren't you?" she said, feeling confident now with Ethan stepping forward to stand beside her.

"Good," Ethan said, his eyes never moving from Jason as the vampire turned and stalked away. Then he turned to Selene and Max.

"Thanks for staying with Genevieve. But we need to leave now."

Waving at Selene and Max as Ethan steered her away with a hand on her lower back, she didn't miss the look of concern on Selene's face and wondered what it meant.

With their car stopped at a red light, she tried not to think about what would have happened to her if Selene and Max hadn't been there to defend her.

She'd been a perfect target—naïve, vulnerable, and weak. And if she'd been human when she'd met Jason? Would she have survived the encounter? Something in his eyes told her no.

Had she never let herself think about how much the humans in Vegas were at the mercy of the vampires? She glanced at Ethan, who'd been quiet since they'd got in the car. From the quality of his silence, tense rather than contemplative, it didn't look like he'd had any success in finding Dante.

"Ethan?"

He didn't take his eyes from the road. "Hmm."

She'd told herself she wouldn't ask Ethan any questions, not when all they seemed to do was make him angry, but she had to ask him this one.

She couldn't get the thought out of her head that something had happened to Tess. Tess, who was human in a city that she was learning more and more functioned as the hunting ground for vampires.

"I'm worried about Tess. I haven't heard from her, and she wasn't at the club either time we were there."

Ethan glanced at her, distracted. "You have a fight? Tess could always be temperamental. It's not like it'd be the first time you fell out."

He was right. After all, she and Tess falling out was the reason she'd moved in with Ethan in the first place, years before. "Yeah. We argued. But—"

"So, give her time. She'll get in touch when she's ready to talk."

"Yeah," she murmured. She wasn't convinced, but there was something in Ethan's voice that told her he wasn't really hearing her. "I'll do that."

Since Ethan's office door had remained closed after Mr. Ember had caught sight of him outside Vince's funeral, she hadn't seen him at all the rest of the night.

Then Paul and Mr. Ember had left after an awkward half-hour sipping their drinks, and Rachel had followed Ethan into the office. So, she'd spent the night staring out into the garden, worrying over Tess when another call to her went unanswered.

Because he wasn't snarling at her, she was tempted to ask again about Tess, even knowing there was a strong possibility it would only piss him off. She couldn't let go of the idea that something was wrong. She'd lost one friend already, and she didn't—couldn't lose another.

Maybe it was having nothing to do that was making her so anxious. Or it could be grief. Not only was she mourning the loss of Vince, but also a part of herself, since most nights in London she was used to sketching or painting—something she hadn't done for days now.

And she'd left her sketchpad in her and Vince's home. Not that she could see herself stepping foot in the place ever again to retrieve it. In her mind, that place would always be linked with Vince's strange behavior, and with finding him dead.

She needed a creative outlet or she'd lose her mind. But more importantly, she needed to know Tess was okay.

He'd disappeared into his office, closing the door behind him the moment they got back to his house, and Gen hovered in the hallway, undecided.

She wanted to ask him about what Paul had said at the funeral and see if he could find out who'd been responsible for the extension of his contract. It was probably nothing, but it was something out of the ordinary that might prove to be useful.

He was distracted, though, and she knew that if she pushed him, it'd only cause him to lash out at her again. Which meant she was on her own.

As she passed the lounge, her eyes latched onto the phone. Aidan, she thought. He'd been nice to her when they'd first met, and Tess had always said that unlike some of the other vampire bar owners, he seemed to genuinely care about his staff.

So, deciding it was better to try rather than to not know, she slipped into the lounge and picked up the phone. Hesitating for a second, she quickly dialed Tess's number from memory. No answer. Again.

Then it was a few seconds' work to dial the number Vince had given her for the Council directory and ask to be connected to Hellfire.

With the phone ringing in her ear, she kicked off her heels and started pacing. What if Aidan didn't answer—and if he did, what if he couldn't help her?

"Hellfire. Aidan speaking." His words were almost completely drowned out by dance music in the background.

"Aidan. Hi. It's Genevieve—Gen," she said, raising her voice as she clutched the phone tighter.

"Gen, hi. You okay?"

There was a sound of a door closing, and she could suddenly hear him much clearer. He must have left the bar and gone to his office, she thought.

"It's about Tess. Is she working tonight? I haven't heard from her in a couple of days, and I didn't see her at the bar."

Aidan said nothing for a moment, and her heart lurched. "What is it? What's happened?"

"Maybe you should speak to Ethan," Aidan suggested, his voice soft.

"Speak to him about what? What aren't you telling me?"

He sighed. "Tess stopped showing up for her shifts. Didn't Ethan tell you?"

"No. He, er, no he didn't. So, she doesn't work there anymore?"

"No."

"And she said nothing about another job?"

"I'm sorry, Gen, but no. She stopped showing up for her shifts, and all my staff are told when they start that two missed shifts mean an automatic firing. I can't afford to keep staff on who don't do the work."

"And you're not worried something's happened to her?"

"This isn't the first time something like this has happened Gen. Not with Tess, but with other staff in most of the bars in the city, to be honest. Either they have an unpleasant experience, they get fed up with the shifts, or they find something better. Whatever the reason, they all leave eventually," he said, sounding tired.

She stared at her shoes beside the couch. Tess had been happier at the club than anywhere else. She wouldn't leave Vegas, either—not after what she'd said at the park.

"Gen? Are you still there?"

"I'm here. I just don't know what to do."

"You could try talking to Ethan about it. Maybe he could—"

She laughed, but there was little humor in it. "You think I haven't tried? He thinks nothing's wrong."

"You should keep trying," he said. "He does care about you. Give him time."

"I will, Aidan, but I—"

Turning to resume pacing, she halted in surprise at the sight of Rachel standing in the doorway, staring at her.

She'd been about to tell Aidan that it wasn't easy, that she wasn't sure Ethan cared about her at all, not anymore. But there was no way she was about to say any of that with his VASS standing right in front of her.

"I have to go, but thanks."

"Call me if you hear anything. Or if you need any help, I'll see what I can do on my end."

She couldn't help the brief smile that flashed across her face as she turned away from Rachel. If nothing else, at least Aidan had listened to her about Tess, and maybe he'd call in a couple of days to let her know Tess was working in another bar after all.

"I will, thanks. Bye."

She bent to return the phone to the side table. "Hi, Rachel, did you—"

She stopped because the doorway was empty, and Rachel was gone.

CHAPTER TWENTY-ONE

"Can the driver take me to the desert tonight?"

Ethan looked up from his laptop to find Genevieve standing outside his office, staring down at her bare feet.

"Why do you want to go to the desert?" he asked.

When she raised her head and he saw the bleak despair in her eyes, he knew that letting her out of his sight was the last thing he would do.

"I asked you a question," he said, closing his laptop.

She looked away. It was clear from her wan face and red-rimmed eyes that since rising the night after their brief visit to the bacchanalia, she must have been doing little else but crying. Which explained why she hadn't come down to ask him about Vincent's investigation. Not that he would've even heard her, he thought as he silently studied her.

He'd been so busy calling and messaging anyone who might know where Dante might be. But like Aidan had said, Dante had managed to crawl into a dark hole somewhere, and no one could say which hole it was.

He couldn't even get a response from Lisette, who was now ignoring his messages—which wasn't pissing him off as much as it normally would. She'd been the one to tell him Dante would be at the bacchanalia in Eros, so he was blaming her for what'd nearly happened to Genevieve.

He'd seen the way Jason had been watching her, knew it was only a matter of good timing and Genevieve's new friends that'd prevented the vampire from making his move.

Everyone knew what he was like, prowling at the periphery of blood-feasts and other parties as he hunted for the newly turned and vulnerable among them. He wasn't exactly known for taking no for an answer, and he'd nearly gotten his hands on Genevieve. It'd been all he could think about as he drove them home the other night.

Then his hopes to be left alone while he worked at regaining his control had faded the second he'd stepped through the front door and known Rachel was waiting for him in his office.

She'd spent several minutes dropping unsubtle hints that he couldn't trust Genevieve. That she was still convinced it was a woman doing all of this, and if he would let her explain, she was sure she could link it back to when he'd been in Europe. Not just Europe, but Prague.

"Rachel, if this is some farfetched idea about Genevieve being behind this, I don't want to hear it," he'd finally snapped, needing to be alone.

"That isn't what I'm saying at all," she said quickly, resting her hand on his arm.

He stared down at the light weight of her hand, and then he raised his gaze to her face. "This has to stop, Rachel. Nothing is going to happen between us."

Yanking her hand away, she'd flushed at his rejection.

"I wasn't—this isn't—"

"You're a good VASS, Rachel. But that is all you ever will be. Though if you keep pushing, you might not even be that if you don't drop this. And now."

She'd left, blinking rapidly. Whether it was because of his rejecting her advances, or because of his threat to get rid of her, he couldn't say.

Rachel was becoming a problem, and he needed to carve out some time to talk to her before her jealousy morphed into outright animosity toward Genevieve, or she said something that would interfere with his plans.

Plans that had seemingly ground to a halt without his noticing.

And now here was Genevieve, coming to him in bare feet, one of his shirts falling to her knees and vulnerability in her eyes.

"I just want to go to the desert," she whispered.

"It's late." There was no give in his voice. "And you're too young to be out this close to dawn."

"I won't be gone long."

He leaned back in his seat. What was she trying to hide from him? "Tell me why, and I might consider it."

Her eyes shot up to his, and then darted away. Yep, he thought, definitely hiding something.

"Nothing," she murmured.

"Then no. If it's nothing, as you say, then my answer is no." Lifting the lid of his laptop, he made as if to return to his work.

There was a long pause.

She'd never been secretive like this before. But he was patient. He could outwait her. He opened an email from his accountant, had started scanning an update on a couple of his riskier investments when she cleared her throat. He looked up from his screen.

Her eyes were on the side of his head, maybe his ear, and the words burst out of her as if she expected him to interrupt her. "I want to spread Vince's ashes. He never got to see a sunrise, but I did, and... I think that's what he would've wanted."

When he continued to gaze steadily back at her, her eyes darted to his before she looked away again, as if she hadn't wanted to meet his eyes.

He glanced at the blinds, mentally calculating how long it was until dawn and what the traffic would be like. Then he closed his laptop and rose. "What are you waiting for? Go put some shoes on."

She blinked at him in surprise, but then turned and hurried up the stairs, as if afraid he'd change his mind.

"I didn't, er, I wasn't expecting you to take me."

He glanced at her in the seat beside him with Vincent's urn clutched tight in her lap. "I'm your Master, which makes you my responsibility."

"Sure," she said, a note of disappointment in her voice.

"Where am I going?" he asked as he drove out of the enclave gates one of the Bladed had opened for him.

"The ridge," she said. "If you turn left, then—"

"I remember where it is."

She'd told him about the ridge that overlooked the Strip on one side and showcased the vast expanse of the Nevada desert on the other, not long after they'd first met.

He doubted he'd ever forget how she'd first described the place to him. Of the way the sun had kissed the edge of the desert in the far distance, and of how standing looking down at it all made her feel like she was seeing something very few people ever saw.

It'd been months before she'd finally taken him. Long after he'd shaken his head in bemusement when she'd refused to take him to such a private place.

She'd told him she didn't think it was a smart idea to take a man she barely knew to an abandoned ridge thousands of feet over a cavern in the middle of the night.

But it hadn't stopped her from handing him a canvas wrapped in brown kraft paper weeks later. It'd been the picture that had hung over his desk until he'd returned to Vegas after Prague, and even though he'd taken it down, he hadn't found it in him to destroy it.

He would never tell her that he'd taken it to his apartment in Reno to hang it there so there was no way she could accidentally come across it.

At the ridge, Ethan leaned against the side of his car, his arms folded across his chest, watching as Genevieve knelt on the dusty ground with the black urn in front of her.

She was silent, though at times he saw her lips moving. Whatever she was saying, was for Vincent alone, but it had her brushing her hand across her face. Crying, he thought.

And then she was standing, holding the urn in one hand and the lid in the other. Slowly, she emptied the contents into the night and stood straight and tall, the outline of her slender form in her jeans and t-shirt making it look like she was a part of the night.

Captivated, Ethan stared. It was as if she'd become an extension of the mountain itself. He watched as a gentle breeze caught and sent the fine grains spinning up and around her before they disappeared completely.

Back in the car, she was silent, contemplative as she stared out of the window, her head resting against the glass.

"What is it?" he asked.

"I hate it here."

"What are you talking about?" he said dryly. "All vampires love Vegas."

"I don't see why. It's full of death, and blood, and pain. I don't see what there is to love about it."

The look he shot her was cynical. "And London didn't have any of those things?"

Her eyes were tired and her face worn when she turned her gaze from the window.

"It may have been," she said. "But at least I didn't have

to see it. I could live my quiet life and pretend it didn't exist."

Ethan tightened his grip on the steering wheel in response to her words. She'd never spoken like this before. Always, she'd been a glass-half-full rather than half-empty kind of person. Was grief driving these dark thoughts inside her? Or was it something else?

Up ahead, the lights changed. But instead of turning toward home as he intended, after a brief pause, he made a sharp turn and headed for the Night Mall.

This short detour wouldn't cost him anything.

"So, blissful ignorance is what you're longing for, then?"

She was silent for a beat.

"I miss normality, and painting, and parties that aren't filled with blood and sex. I miss Vince, miss my freedom, and not living in fear for my life. And Tess... I miss her too."

Pulling the car to a stop, he turned to face her. "So, are you coming in, or waiting here?"

He almost felt sorry for her at the confusion spreading across her face when she saw they were parked outside a coffee shop.

"What are we doing here?"

Pushing his car door open, he started to get out. "What does it look like? Come on, it's late and I have no desire to be locked in a coffee shop storage room all day while I wait for sunset."

"I'm coming." She scrambled to unbuckle her seatbelt. "I've never been here before. Is this the Night Mall?" she asked, eyeing the bright lights of the shop fronts as she climbed out of the car.

Outside, large balls of golden light linked together by sparkling ropes hung from streetlights, illuminating the dim streets. With it being so close to dawn, the streets and shops were mostly empty, but there were still a few vampire couples here and there, finishing up their shopping.

It was one of the biggest attractions in Vegas outside of the Strip. After all, where else could you do your shopping in designer shops owned, run, and frequented by vampires? There was nowhere else like it in the world.

"It is," he said, slamming his door shut and heading for the coffee shop entrance. He held the door open for her, and as she passed, he took the opportunity to brush a smear of red dirt off her cheek.

Startled steel-grey eyes met his, and he flipped his hand to show her the dirt he'd wiped off her face.

"Oh, thanks," she mumbled, absentmindedly rubbed her hand over her face as they headed for the counter.

"What do you want?" Ethan asked, scanning the menu.

"Uh, a cappuccino. With a caramel shot. And a cookie."

"A cookie?" he repeated, raising his eyebrow.

"Double chocolate chip cookie," she added. "And one for Rachel."

"It's her day off."

He could feel her surprise, but they waited until after he'd ordered and paid for their drinks and her sweet treat before resuming their conversation.

"She gets a day off?" she asked as they waited for the barista to make their drinks.

"Of course she gets a day off. What do you think I am?"

"Not all vampires give their VASS a day off. I mean, Vince and I did, but in London, it felt like we were more the exception than the rule," Genevieve said, watching the petite redhead behind the counter at the coffee machine.

"I know," Ethan said, finding it strange that he wasn't feeling enraged to hear Genevieve talking about her life with Vincent in London.

He couldn't say why, but all he was feeling was relaxed and calm as they watched the barista make their drinks.

Silence descended again, but it wasn't an awkward one.

"What is it?" he asked Genevieve, sensing she had a question.

After taking their prepared drinks from the barista, he held the door open for her as they left.

"Any word on Dante?"

"Dante doesn't want to be found," he said, opening his car door.

Inside, Genevieve took a sip of her coffee and sighed in pleasure.

"So why don't you use the Master-Childe bond?" she asked, snapping her seatbelt into place.

He handed her his coffee, black and unsweetened, as he started the car. "No."

"But he's your Master. There must be a way you can find him by—"

"He made me," Ethan said. "But he is not my Master. There is a difference."

Beside him Genevieve was silent, and he felt the tension rise in the car.

"Right. No bond. Got it," she said, turning to look out the window.

Ethan stared at her for a moment. For a second he debated saying something, but he wasn't sure what. In the end, he shook his head, started up the car, and pulled away from the coffee shop. He needed to get a handle on himself. One minute he was ready to kill Genevieve, and the next, being with her felt too much like the way they'd been before. Before Prague.

That way lay madness, and it was best he remembered why.

Ethan was back in his office, probably still trying to track down Dante, and she was unsuccessfully digging through the kitchen cabinets, still trying to work out what had happened between them early last morning.

He hadn't come to bed with her after their coffee, but he'd slept beside her. Again. The outline of his body was still there, but he'd been gone.

She couldn't get it out of her mind that it'd felt like a date, which wasn't what she'd been expecting. Not when she'd woken that night feeling a deep surge of sadness and wanting nothing more than to cry as she scattered Vince's ashes.

But Ethan hadn't left her, not even after. Instead, he'd taken her for coffee.

That was what people on dates did. They went for coffee and talked. And she and Ethan had done those things, right up until she'd mentioned the Master-Childe bond. Then he'd closed down, and whatever they'd had was suddenly over.

But before that. Before his closing down like that... it'd been nice. He'd been nice, and even though he'd warned her before that it was getting close to sunrise, he hadn't rushed her at the ridge. Instead, he'd given her the space and the time she'd needed to say a proper goodbye to Vince.

Did that mean he still cared about her? Loved her? She didn't know. But with Dante's presence still looming over them, not to mention that Ethan still wasn't talking to her about Prague, she knew they were still a long way away from reconciliation.

If that was even what she wanted.

"What are you doing?"

She grabbed at a cupboard door, just managed to stop herself from falling as she twisted around to face Ethan.

He leaned against the doorframe with his arms folded across his chest, and it was a battle she nearly lost keeping her eyes from dropping to the defined muscles of his arms and shoulders. Nothing good would come from noticing those, she thought, turning back around.

"Trying to find all the food you've hidden," she said, crawling along the kitchen counter to the next cupboard.

"I haven't hidden any food."

"Uh-huh," she muttered.

Empty. Urgh, every single cupboard was empty. But she wasn't ready to stop searching. Her gurgling stomach refused to let her.

She was a little taller than average, but all the cupboards in Ethan's kitchen were tall. Like, needing to climb on top of the counter to be able to see if there was anything on the highest shelves kind of tall.

"Why are you looking for food?" he asked, sounding like he'd come closer.

She moved to the next cupboard, found it empty, and kept on crawling. Still, she could feel his gaze on her back, sliding down to linger on her ass, and she forced herself to not turn around.

"I need sugar."

Ethan caught the back of her shirt and twisted her around, so she was sitting on the edge of the counter and he was standing in front of her with his legs wedged between hers. Then, leaning forward, he closed the open cupboard door beside her head.

All of which put them in the same position Selene and Max had been in when they'd been having sex on the bar at Eros. Carefully she tried not to think about it, or do anything that might clue Ethan in on where her mind had strayed. But going by the heat on her cheeks and his raised eyebrow as he stood with one hand curled around her hip, she doubted it'd worked.

Amusement lit his eyes. "You don't want sugar."

"I do."

After they'd gotten back from the coffee shop, she'd decided to save her cookie for later. It wasn't often she had a sugar craving, and it wasn't like she even needed to eat anymore. In fact, eating anything more than a few mouthfuls of food would only make her sick. Something she'd learned the hard way when Vince had taken her to Paris and she'd discovered macarons, despite Vince warning her not to eat the entire box in one sitting.

She'd spent the rest of the night hurling her guts up, and Vince had stayed with her, holding her hair from her face and passing her a glass of water to rinse her mouth out.

Vince had told her over time that the sugar cravings would disappear once her body got used to a different kind of nourishment, and sugar was one of the cravings that hung around the longest after being turned.

Even though it had been years since Paris, every now and again she still got a sudden urge for something sweet. As long as she made sure not to overindulge, she didn't pay the price for it.

This time her sweet craving hadn't been sated by her double chocolate chip cookie. If anything, the gurgling in her stomach and the painful emptiness she'd felt on waking had only gotten worse.

Eyes dipping to her mouth, Ethan brushed crumbs from her bottom lip. Feeling herself warm at the brush of his fingers on her mouth, she tried to lean away from his touch.

"You're hungry," Ethan said, his voice a low growl.

Though he couldn't have missed her trying to shift away, he left his hand on her face, his eyes still on her mouth. "But not for food."

She shook her head. She hadn't known why the cookie hadn't satisfied her, but she knew her body, and this felt like a sugar craving... if only a more intense version of it.

"I'm sure the cookie wasn't sweet enough, that's all."

Ethan finally moved his hand away, and when he raised his eyes to meet hers, they were dark and hooded. "You were never feeding enough before. Now your body is telling you what it needs and what it wants. And it's blood. My blood."

"I'm sure what it wants is another cookie."

Wrapping his hands around her waist, he lifted her down from the counter, the heat of his touch lingering for a moment before he released her to turn away. "It's time to feed. My office. Now."

Her heart stuttered at the huskiness of his order as she watched him walk away.

"Damn it," she swore under her breath. "Why couldn't it just be a cookie?"

It was only when she saw his shoulders shaking that she realized he'd heard her. Sighing, she followed.

CHAPTER TWENTY-TWO

*P*erched on the edge of his desk, Ethan watched with wry amusement as Genevieve stared at him with visible reluctance from his office doorway.

"Close the door behind you."

Although she looked as if she would've preferred to be on the other side of the door when she closed it, nevertheless she did it with a heavy sigh.

"Come here." His voice was low as he widened his stance, leaving just enough space between his legs for her to stand.

She didn't move.

"Genevieve." A hint of steel now.

"But I'm not hungry. I don't understand why—"

"I'm not going to repeat myself."

Sighing again, she drifted toward him. But when she stopped a few inches away, further away than he would've liked, he caught her by her upper arms and tugged her closer.

"I'm not going to..." He stopped when he realized what he'd about to say.

Her lips twitched. "Bite?"

Fighting the urge to smile, he shook his head. "You're here to feed, that's all," he said, as if they weren't both aware of how the last feeding had ended. As if he wasn't lying to himself about wanting more of the same.

Tension spread up her arms, and he stroked his hands down the length of them to ease her. Instead, his touch seemed to make her more tense. "What's wrong?"

Her words came out in a rush, even as her eyes focused on his throat. "Nothing."

"So feed," he said, tilting his head to one side. "Or should I sit down?"

She stared at him like he was crazy. "And have me sit in your lap?"

The image of her naked and straddling his lap as she drank from him had him swallowing hard as he waited with bated breath for her response.

"No. This is... this is fine," she said, drawing a deep breath into her lungs before releasing it, slow and controlled.

He watched her curiously as she repeated the action. "What are you doing?"

"Nothing."

"You look like you're psyching yourself up."

"And what's wrong with that?" she snapped, and then instantly looked contrite. "Sorry, I didn't mean to snap."

"Tell me what's wrong."

She fixed her gaze on his chest, one hand fiddling with

his buttons. "I don't want it turning into... you know, sex again."

He didn't respond. Just continued to study the top of her head as he absorbed her words. The sudden spike of disappointment surprised him, and he waited for the feeling to pass. He'd been too rough with her in the car. He'd known it at the time, and this just proved it.

But then she peeked up at him through her lashes.

"It's not because I don't want to," she said, lowering her head to his chest again. "I'm getting attached... to you. So, it's probably best we don't do that again. Since this claim is only temporary, right?"

"Yes," he lied. "It's only temporary."

She raised her head to meet his eyes. "That's good. So, I guess in the time we have left, we can concentrate on finding the killer, then?"

But his attention wasn't on her words. His eyes latched onto the soft curve of her lips, and the brush of her breasts against his chest. She was getting attached to him, and the thought of her craving him—craving this—made him draw her even closer.

He hadn't kissed her yet, and right now he knew he had to. He had to know how she tasted before he walked away from her, or he'd regret it.

"Ethan?" she murmured, her lips parting as she said his name.

He bent his lips toward her. "Shh."

She stood frozen in his arms. But the moment he brushed his lips across hers, it felt like every muscle in her body loosened, even as her eyes started to drift close. He felt her sigh against his mouth, a gentle breath as she exhaled. And then he was moving his lips against hers with more pressure, even as her hands slid down his chest and crept around his waist.

Closing his eyes, he wrapped his hands around her as he angled his head, and drew the tip of his tongue against the seam of her lips. When her mouth opened in a moan, he slid his tongue into her mouth and stroked his tongue against hers, groaning at the taste of her.

She tasted of spun sugar, chocolate cookie, and that indescribable taste that was only Genevieve. A taste that made his cock stir, at the same time making him want to wrap himself around her and never let go. He felt her trembling against him as he curved his hand around the nape of her neck and held her still against him.

Wanting more—needing more—he tugged her close enough so the softness of her belly was cradled against his hardness, wallowed in the sweetness of her mouth, of the gentle stroke of her tongue against his as their kiss deepened.

Groaning, he angled his head so he could explore every inch of her mouth. He craved more of her. His tongue probed hers, thrusting and then retreating in a pale echo of what his body wanted to do to hers.

The scent of her arousal tickled his nose, and for one brief moment he let himself thrust against the softness of her belly before he broke the kiss. When he opened his eyes and gazed down into eyes dark with hunger, and lips swollen from his kisses, he nearly gave in to temptation.

"You need to feed," he said, his voice low with need.

Her tongue darted out and licked her lower lip. He trembled as he fought the need to crush her against him.

But dropping his hands from her hips, he looked away from the mouth he was still greedy for. A mouth he hadn't had nearly enough of.

"I don't think that's a good idea." Her voice was breathless from their kisses as her eyes moved to his throat. But even as Ethan opened his mouth, an order on his lips, she was already nuzzling at his throat, her tongue lapping at his pulse.

His eyes slammed shut, and he shuddered at the feel of her hot, moist tongue on him. Body hardening at the graze of her teeth, he tensed in anticipation. He groaned loudly as she bit down, her mouth latching onto his skin, forming a tight seal. At the first pull of her mouth against him, he thrust hard against her. His fingers bit into the curves of her jean-clad bottom as he ground his cock against her, and her hands burrowed beneath his shirt to massage the muscles in his back.

It wasn't enough, not nearly enough. Stroking one hand up her back to tunnel into her hair, he cradled her head against him as she fed. His head tilted at a slight angle to give her room, and with the almost erotic feel of her silky hair brushing along the sensitive line of his throat, he gave himself up to the pleasure running through him.

He started figuring out where he would take her. Against the desk, or on the floor. Maybe he'd sit in his chair and drop her into his lap. He'd be able to taste her breasts that way.

Gritting his teeth, he fought the need to come. Fought the need to be inside the heated clasp of her sex. Because she was right. They couldn't keep doing this. She was too addictive, and as time went on, he was craving her more and more.

When she stopped drinking and sealed the bite with a stroke of her tongue, he was almost relieved when she rested her forehead against his chin.

His body was on fire, sweat dotted his forehead, and he suspected any movement Genevieve made would have him exploding right there. So, closing his eyes, hands curved possessively around her hips, he worked on easing himself down from the edge.

He didn't open his eyes when she lifted her head. Looking at her would be a mistake. Thinking she was backing away, he started to release her. But instead of retreating as he'd expected, she brushed her lips across his.

His heart stuttered. He went motionless. Opened his eyes to watch her.

She moved forward slowly, as if to give him a chance to move away, and he fixed his eyes on her lips—soft, warm and inviting. Her lips met his again, never taking her eyes from his.

But before she could dance away again, his arms clamped around her and he pulled her flush against him.

This time their kiss was desperate, a carnal possession that had him groaning into her mouth. Ethan never wanted it to end.

But when he tasted the metallic sharp bite of his blood, he stopped fighting his need. His hands tugged at the hem of her shirt, trying to find a way to the soft skin beneath.

She broke the kiss.

Panting, they stared at each other for a heartbeat.

"Take me to bed, Ethan. I want you. Now."

And then she was in his arms, his tongue plunging into her mouth as he moved with preternatural speed up the stairs.

Easing her down onto the bed, he pulled her shirt over her head before he followed her down, toeing off his shoes as he went. In between long, drugging kisses she tore the buttons off his shirt, pushing it off his shoulders as her hands stroked over his arms and back.

He kissed his way down her neck, stopping to nuzzle at her breasts. Smiling at the feel of her hands in his hair, holding her to him as he unclasped her bra and drew the beaded point of one breast, and then the other into his mouth. Her back arched, and the fingers in his hair were almost painful as she moaned beneath him. But he didn't stop there.

Her stomach tensed as he kissed a path over the softness of her belly, taking his time and making it clear which direction he was heading. He paused to unbutton her jeans and tugged, taking her panties with them as he slid them down her legs. And then he stopped.

He gazed down at her, stunned by the flushed curves of her body, the dark curls between her legs, and the knowledge that she was his. Unable to stop himself, he bent his head and inhaled the scent of her. His mouth watered.

He'd planned on taking his time, on feasting on the heat of her. But with his cock twitching in his pants, already beyond desperate to be inside her, he couldn't—didn't want to—wait. His mouth came down on her, his tongue lapping at her hungrily.

She came instantly, her scream piercing the silence of the room. The sweet taste of her flooded his mouth, and her hips jerked beneath him. But with his hands on her thighs, he easily held her down, giving her soft, hungry licks that made her shudder and her body undulate.

Soon her panting turned to soft murmurs of pleasure, and the hands in his hair started to loosen, her body sated now.

Finally, she stilled, and he rose above her, pausing to examine her flushed face. Her eyes were closed and a faint smile of contentment curved her lips. Unbuttoning his pants, hands shaking with need, he shoved them down his legs and eased himself between her parted legs, bracing himself on his hands above her head, his eyes never leaving her face.

Her eyes fluttered open and her sated, sleepy gaze watched him. Slowly, he sank into her wet heat. They both groaned. God, it was fucking indescribable being inside her. And for a long moment, he held himself still at the silky feel of her, giving her time for her body to adjust to his, muscles taut with strain as he forced himself to keep still. Then slowly, her eyes closed, and she wrapped her legs around his hips, her hands stroking up his back in a way that had him arching under her touch.

Desperate for the taste of her lips, he bent and took her mouth again. Slower this time, exploring every inch of her. When she started stirring restlessly against him, he let go of control, gripped her hips tightly, holding her where he wanted her, and he surged into her. A deep, powerful thrust that penetrated every inch of her.

Growling into her mouth, he drove into her with more

force. They quickly found a rhythm. He felt himself swell as she moaned and met each of his firm thrusts with her own. One of his hands drifted to her taut breasts, the perfect size to fit his hands, and plucked at the nipples. When the muscles of her sex clenched tightly around him, he turned to repeat the action with the other.

When she broke their kiss to toss her head, he didn't have to look into her face to know she was close. He could feel it in the clasp of her sex, could hear the soft sound she made as she struggled to catch her breath. And then her nails were cutting into his shoulders, her back arching, making him sink deeper inside her as she screamed out her release.

The grip of her muscles was like a vice, triggering his own release seconds later. Slamming his eyes shut, he gripped her hips tight, holding her still beneath him as he continued to thrust. Then he was growling as his cock jerked deep inside her, back bowing and body straining as if desperate to go deeper still. Lights exploded behind his eyes, and the sound of his racing heart was loud in his head.

Spent, he collapsed on top of her, careful not to crush her. He caught her jaw to give her a long, lingering kiss that seemed to go on forever. And then he stayed there, still deep inside her, her arms curled around him and their kisses languid until she relaxed against him, and drifted into a light sleep.

She lay on her front, the sheets he'd pulled over her stopping at her waist, and as he lay stretched out beside her, his fingers traced the smooth line of her back and down to the dip just above her ass.

By the time his fingers had trailed back up, her eyes were open and she was watching him with a smile of contentment on her face.

"That feels really good," she murmured, arching her back under his touch.

His voice was husky when he saw her eyes darken. "I'm guessing you'd like me to continue?"

"Mm," she said with half-closed eyes.

"And what will I get in return?"

Her eyes opened fully, and he felt the impact of her gaze as her eyes slid down his naked body laid stretched out on top of the sheets. They stopped at his semi-hard erection, and when she licked her lips, he hardened at the interest in her eyes. Smiling, she started toward him.

There was a knock at the door, and Genevieve froze.

"What is it, Rachel?" he shouted.

"You have a guest," Rachel said in her normal voice from the other side of the door.

She didn't shout. It wasn't like she needed to. Not when Ethan would've heard her if she'd whispered from the bottom of the stairs. He didn't know if she'd tried to call him from there already, but he'd been more than a little distracted at the time.

"Tell them to come back tomorrow," Ethan said, watching Genevieve with half-lidded eyes as she sat up and started crawling toward him. Tangling his hand in her hair, he started to pull her head down to kiss her.

"He told me to tell you he won't be in Vegas tomorrow," Rachel said.

It was his turn to freeze, and Genevieve glanced at him with a question in her eyes.

Sighing, he released her and got up. "I'll be right there."

Ethan heard Rachel walking back downstairs as he pulled his pants on and grabbed another shirt from his closet. Genevieve had managed to rip most of the buttons off his last one, just like the one before in the car, and he smiled at the thought.

"Who is it?" she asked, propping her pillows up behind her head and sitting back as she watched him dress. She seemed to be finding it a challenge to keep her gaze from drifting down to his bare chest. Not that he had a problem with having her eyes on him. She was lying naked in his bed, and he was finding it a struggle to keep his eyes to himself. He found he didn't mind it at all.

"Probably my attorney," Ethan lied.

He didn't have to try very hard to imagine what her reaction would be if he told her that Dante—the man who probably wanted her dead—was waiting for him in the room below them.

When Ethan bent to kiss her, she stopped him by digging the heel of her foot against his belly. "No kisses. Not when you're leaving me to go see your attorney," she said with mock outrage.

He caught her foot and pressed a kiss in the center before he gave it a quick massage, digging his fingers deep into her arches, watching with a smile on his lips as her breath caught and her head fell back against her pillows.

"Oh, my God. Don't stop," she moaned.

"I have to stop. But I'll be back. Wait right here. Just like this," he said, dropping her foot and backing toward the door.

Genevieve raised her eyebrow. "And if I get cold?"

"Only hungry vampires get cold, and you're positively glowing from your last feeding. I'll be right back. And I expect you to pick up where we left off," he warned her. "I won't be happy if I come back and find you sleeping."

She smiled brightly and flipped over. "You mean just like this?" At the sight of her ass and the barest hint of her sex, he stopped.

Her giggle was infectious and made the edges of his mouth kick up, but he forced himself to turn away from the temptation she offered. She was doing it on purpose, but he also knew if he didn't leave now, he never would.

Rachel was waiting for him at the bottom of the stairs. "He's in the lounge."

Nodding, he started there, only to pause when he saw the strange look on her face as she watched him. "What is it?"

She shook her head.

"Nothing," she said and headed for the front door. "I'll see you tomorrow."

"Tell me," he ordered.

Rachel stopped with her hand on the handle and a carefully blank expression on her face.

"I haven't seen you smile like that in a long time. I thought you'd forgotten how."

CHAPTER TWENTY-THREE

*H*ours later, Gen found Ethan in front of the sliding glass doors that led to the garden. Now wrapped in a sheet from their bed, she padded in and slipped her arms around his waist. He startled as if he hadn't heard her come in, and she smiled against his back.

"You didn't come back to bed," she murmured.

Ethan lifted one arm behind him and held her against him for a brief moment before he turned to face her. When she saw his face, she stopped smiling.

"What is it? Did something happen?"

"Nothing important. Just some unexpected news," Ethan said. Bending, he scooped her into his arms and started for the stairs.

"Come on, it's late."

Taking the stairs three at a time, he kicked the door closed behind him and deposited her on the bed.

"You can talk to me about it," she offered, watching as he shucked off his shirt and stepped out of his pants. For a second her eyes lingered on his hardness, semi-erect now but still impressive in girth, and her arousal stirred at how good it'd felt having him inside her. She didn't know what had happened to her, but all of a sudden, all she could think about was Ethan touching her, and her touching him.

"I could," Ethan said, closing the drapes and plunging the room into complete darkness. She waited for him to switch on the lamps beside the bed, but instead he left them off, climbed into bed, and nuzzled her throat.

"But I'd much rather kiss you instead. If you'll let me," he breathed against her neck.

"If I'll let you? You make it sound like I'm the one stopping you." She smiled as she wrapped an arm around his waist.

His mouth hovered tantalizingly close to hers as they lay side by side, their bodies close but not quite pressing against each other.

"Well," he murmured, his lips brushing against the corner of her mouth. "If you'd stop talking for a minute, then maybe..."

Gen kissed him. She could tell she'd caught him off guard, because he stilled for a second before his hands rose to frame her face, and then he was kissing her back. Her body softened, and all the while Ethan's drugging kisses were awakening a hunger in her for something more.

She wiggled closer and curled one leg around his waist. Ethan deepened the kiss, his tongue probing her mouth, and then he was slipping inside her. His hands moved from her face to grip her hips, tilting her at a slight angle that made every muscle tighten in response.

Gasping, she broke the kiss as she struggled to catch her breath. He gave her a second, and then his lips were back on hers, one hand on the back of her head as he continued to thrust inside her.

It was a slower loving, gentler than what had come before—and without quite knowing why, her eyes welled with tears and splashed onto her cheeks.

Ethan stilled. This time it was him breaking the kiss as he eased back, and though she had her eyes closed, she could still feel his eyes searching her face.

"Genevieve?" he whispered, his mouth feathering over the wetness on her face.

She shook her head and thrust against him, and though he caught her hips to try and still her, she felt the tremor in his hands, even as his cock swelled inside her.

"Don't stop," she begged. "Please, Ethan, don't..."

Finding his lips, and wrapping her arms tight around him, she rolled so he was braced over her, and he slipped further inside her.

He swore, and then he was thrusting again, his movements more insistent. They were close. Both of them on the edge. Ready to come apart. And then he tilted his hips, and his cock hit her at just the right angle.

Panting, she shifted restlessly beneath him. He hit that spot inside her again, and then she was shuddering, her muscles twitching with release even as he continued to thrust against her.

"I love you," she whispered into his mouth.

Above her, Ethan's body tensed. His hips pressed hers into the bed, and then she felt him coming. His body strained with the force of his release as he groaned and emptied himself into her, his arms braced above her head and her legs wound tight around his hips.

Maybe the darkness of the room made it easier for her to tell him. Maybe feeling Ethan wrapped around her so tightly, as if he was pressing every single inch of him against every inch of her, made her feel brave. She'd told him she loved him, and he was still beside her. He hadn't run away.

"Ethan?" Genevieve murmured against his shoulder.

"It's late. You need to rest," he said, sounding lazy and sated as he peppered soft kisses against her throat.

"I can't with you doing that," she admitted and felt his smile against her skin.

"I'll stop in a second," he said, his hands stroking over her curves. He was burrowed deep inside her, still hard, his body a comfortable weight as he pressed her into the softness of the bed. She never wanted to move, ever again.

"I never loved Vince, you know," she said.

Ethan's hands stilled.

"You never asked, and I know you heard what I said at his funeral."

He was silent, and she turned her face to his, though she didn't try to use her night-sight to see him in the dark. Somehow it felt less scary telling him when she couldn't see his expression, though she knew he could read hers.

"I always felt guilty about it. Because I knew how he felt about me, but I didn't... I couldn't be with anyone after you." Above her, she could feel his eyes still searching her face as she spoke.

Clearing her throat, she continued. "I knew he wanted more, but I told him I wasn't ready for him—for anyone, and I never knew why. Maybe a part of me knew you were alive, even if subconsciously I knew it couldn't be possible. It always felt like I was waiting for... something, you know. Only I didn't know what that something was. Now I know it was you. All this time, I was waiting for you."

Lying still below him, she waited for his response, waited to see what he would say, what he would do. She was tense, but she knew she'd regret it if she lost him again without telling him how she'd always felt about him.

He bent his head to her neck. Pressed a kiss against her throat and thrust his hips against hers. She moaned. Clutched at his back.

"I thought you said—" She stopped to moan when he thrust again. "That I should... rest?"

"Later," Ethan said, his voice husky. "But first..."

He sealed his lips against hers, and then there were no more words. Just his body moving against hers, and hers against his as the sun started its ascent across the sky.

The sun was still setting when he rose. Though the heavy drapes blocked out their harmful rays, and the ultra-blackout blinds prevented even a hint of light peeking through, he still felt the uncomfortable awareness that it wasn't yet time for him to rise. That he should still be sleeping.

Pausing, he studied Genevieve. To a human, she would appear as if she were dead with her lack of heartbeat. But with her radiant golden skin still flushed from her earlier feeding, to him she looked like a sleeping angel.

She'd told him she loved him for the first time, and though he hadn't repeated the words, he sensed that something had shifted deep inside him. The thought of letting her go, of imagining her in another man's bed, made him snarl, and he pressed a hard kiss to her dusky lips as if to reassure himself she was here, and she was his. He'd claimed her, and he intended to keep her.

Leaving Genevieve to sleep, he quickly showered, dressed, and made his way to his office. A spontaneous urge struck, a need to do something for her, and he knew exactly what it would be. It was a few minutes' work to organize his surprise for her, and then he turned his attention to Dante.

His arrival had been more than a little unexpected—but more than that, his words had disturbed him. So, leaning back in his chair, his thoughts drifted over the conversation they'd had.

"I see things are going well," Dante said in greeting as Ethan walked into the lounge. He was at the drinks tray, examining the bottles Ethan kept there.

"Where have you been?" Ethan said, closing the door behind him. The last thing he needed was for Genevieve to wander down and see the man he was convinced wanted her dead.

"Here and there. I thought I warned you to keep your distance from her."

"And I'm guessing that was the reason you sent the wolf? Well, she hasn't seen even one of your gifts, and she won't. I'll make sure of it." His voice was calm, unconcerned, like they

were discussing the weather instead of Dante's sick game designed to drive Genevieve away from him.

Dante glanced up at him. "What are you talking about? What wolf?"

"You know exactly what I'm talking about," Ethan said, looking Dante right in the eyes.

Dante didn't look away from the challenge. "No Ethan, I do not."

He sprawled on the couch, crossing one leg over the other. "The dead wolf you left on my doorstep? And before that, the rabbit. And before that, the dead mouse. Surely you must remember those gifts."

It was a deceptively casual pose. If he needed to move, he could be up and fighting in less than a quarter of a second.

Unfortunately for him, the vampire he was facing down was not only the one who'd made him, but also the one who'd taught him almost everything he knew. He would need the element of surprise to best his former Master. But he'd deal with that when the time came.

Although Dante must have seen the spark of violence in his eyes, he didn't react. Instead, he put down the bottle of aged whiskey he'd been examining and crossed the room to sit on the couch opposite him.

"Ethan. You know me well enough to know that's not my style. To play sick games like that is... something I neither have the time nor inclination for. It's the very reason I left all this behind me," *Dante said, waving his hand to indicate Vegas in general.*

"So, you're saying you're not trying to scare her away from me?" *Ethan asked, abandoning his casual recline to sit up.*

"If I wanted to scare Genevieve, I wouldn't need to send

dead animals to do it." Dante's voice was cold as he leaned toward him. *"And if I wanted her dead... well. I don't imagine there's anything you could do to stop me."*

Ethan felt the muscles in his face tense at the threat and the insult. The tension was like a living thing as it crackled in the air between them.

Then just like that, it dissipated at Dante's sigh. Sitting back in his seat, Dante ran a hand through his dark hair. "Look at me. Lashing out like a young wolf with no control."

He fixed his dark eyes on Ethan before he rose. "I have no wish to harm Genevieve. I came to warn you that I'm not the only one who's been hurt by something you've done, and there will be a reckoning."

Ethan watched him with a raised eyebrow. "A reckoning, you say?" he asked. "Are you sure it's not the Italian in you making you overly dramatic?"

Dante stared him down. "I come to warn you that yours and Genevieve's lives are being threatened, and this is how you respond?"

"Tell me, then," Ethan said, standing. "Just who this person is that wants to harm us."

"You know I do not involve myself in games between Masters and their Children."

"What Children are you talking about? You made me, and I made Genevieve. I have no other Childe to be concerned about. Unless you plan on visiting a little cemetery in Prague, that is?" Ethan quipped.

Dante stared at him with cold eyes.

Ethan's smile widened. "You don't find it funny? Surely you didn't come all the way from Italy to throw about vague warn-

ings and threats. Give me a name, if you're so sure about this threat."

"I can see that you do not believe me. I've said all I can."

"Enough with this dramatic bullshit, Dante. I didn't have any love for it before, and I certainly don't now. If you cannot stir yourself enough to give me some tangible evidence of what you're saying—something like a name—then get out. And this time, I'd appreciate it if you'd stay away. Italy can have you."

Dante nodded, his eyes sad. Sliding the glass door open, he paused with one foot outside. "I've always wished the best for you, Ethan. I just hope your arrogance and your pride don't result in the death of your Childe. She's a sweet girl," Dante said, his Italian accent thick with emotion.

Before Ethan could respond, Dante stepped out into the night.

He couldn't say how long he stood at the door after Dante had left, but then Genevieve was there, all warm and soft, and naked beneath the thin sheet she'd wrapped around herself. The last thing he'd wanted to do then was to dwell on the ramblings of a lonely old vampire.

But now, in the quiet of his office, once more Ethan's thoughts lingered over Dante's words. He'd spoken of games between Masters and their Children, and those words still haunted him. Both his first Childe and Vince were dead, so the only connection between Vince and Genevieve was Vince's Master.

If it wasn't Dante playing around with him, then it had to be Vince's Master who was responsible. After all, this was a Master who had publicly done nothing about the murder of his Childe, but perhaps secretly he blamed Genevieve...

No.

That didn't make sense. Not if Vince's Master had allowed her to assume responsibility for his funeral.

He shook his head. Dante was still playing games with him—it had to be him trying to turn his attention elsewhere. And Ethan had just let him walk away. So now Dante was free to continue with his games until either he grew bored with it, or more likely, Ethan stopped him.

At the knock on his door, he looked up. "Come in."

Rachel stepped in and closed the door behind her.

He raised his eyebrows. A closed door could only mean one thing. "You have something to say. Something you'd rather Genevieve didn't hear?"

She cleared her throat in what could only be nerves. "I do."

Ethan waited, intrigued.

"It's about something I saw."

"Fascinating. Go on."

"I didn't want to be the one to tell you, but if I don't, then no one else will. I don't want to see you hurt again."

"While I am intrigued," Ethan drawled, reminded of Genevieve and of her lying naked in his bed. Perhaps he might rejoin her, since Dante had slipped through his fingers. "I'm hoping you'll get to the point sooner rather than—"

"I caught her on the phone with Aidan."

He blinked in surprise. Well, that was... unexpected.

"I don't see how a phone call with Aidan is liable to hurt me," he said, his lips twisting in amusement as he rose from his desk.

Rachel's mouth tightened in a rare display of frustration. "She was acting suspicious as soon as she realized I was there, and she hung up so quickly, it was clear she didn't want me to hear what they were talking about."

Ethan sighed. While he knew how Rachel felt about him, he'd hoped to avoid confronting her with it, especially after he'd been so cruel to her about it once before.

"I know you have feelings for me," he said, noting her narrowed eyes. "But I thought you were above simple jealousy, Rachel."

"Fine," Rachel bit out. "Believe me. Don't believe me. I was only trying to look out for you. I won't bother in the future. Good night, Sire." Rachel turned, back stiff as a board, and walked out of his office, and then through the front door.

She hadn't sounded like she was lying, he thought as he watched her leave. He knew her well enough to be able to tell the difference between truth and lies. But she believed she was telling the truth, that much was certain.

Without pausing to think too much about what he was doing, he grabbed his phone and called Aidan's cell.

The phone rang and rang.

After leaving a message for Aidan to call him, he stood with the phone in his hand, feeling a growing sense of unease. He remembered Aidan telling him about his seeing someone. Who was this woman, and why had Aidan been so cagey about her?

CHAPTER TWENTY-FOUR

There was something wrong.

When Ethan touched her, it was only to nudge her away once she drank, and he made sure to keep a space between their bodies.

It'd been three nights since she'd told him she loved him, and now it was clear she'd made a big mistake. He hadn't been ready to hear it, and now he was pushing her away.

At first, she'd thought his distance was because of his meeting with his attorney. Maybe his investments weren't doing so well anymore. Maybe that was why he always had his phone when she saw him—when his office door wasn't closed, that is. But that seemed an excessive reason for his coldness toward her.

More than once she'd stood, poised to knock on his office door, and more than once she'd dropped her hand and walked away. But this couldn't go on forever. Soon the Council would accept that Ethan had taught her everything she needed to know, and then she'd be on her own trying to figure out who'd killed Vince and why.

Vince, who had taken a back seat to her and Ethan, she thought as guilt swept through her. She'd sworn to herself that she would keep him in the forefront of her thoughts, that he would be her focus. But instead, the moment Ethan started giving her a crumb of affection, she'd cast Vince aside as if he hadn't meant anything to her.

As if she'd forgotten about him. Some friend she was.

She hadn't heard from Aidan about Tess, and the only reason she hadn't called him was the fear that Rachel would catch her.

Rachel hadn't exactly been subtle with the way she stared at her when she was in the lounge, as if she expected to find her doing something she shouldn't have been.

But lying around trying to summon up the courage to ask Ethan what was wrong, and finding out what was going on with Dante, was wasting time she didn't have.

So, rising from the couch, she headed for his office, took a couple of deep breaths before she knocked, and pushed the door open.

"Can I come in?" she asked, poking her head around the door.

He looked up from his laptop and stared at her for a moment, his expression carefully blank. She wondered what he was thinking, what he didn't want her to read.

"What did you want?"

Taking that as a yes since he wasn't screaming at her to get out, she crossed his office and dropped into the chair opposite his before wrapping her arms around her legs as she gazed around the room.

While it hurt her to see that the picture of the sunrise he'd hung behind his desk was gone, it hurt a lot less to see he hadn't filled the space with something else. She couldn't help but wonder if he felt the same way about her. Gone from his life, but irreplaceable.

Why did she have to open her mouth? Why couldn't she have just enjoyed them being together in the moment, instead of ruining it?

"I wanted to see how you were. I miss you," she said softly.

A line formed between his eyebrows, but before he could speak, his cell phone started vibrating on his desk.

"Can this wait until later?" he asked, picking up his phone.

"Sorry, I didn't realize you were in the middle of something," she said, starting to stand.

He tapped out a quick text message and returned the phone to his desk.

"I was expecting a call. I'm trying to reach someone, but they're proving difficult to pin down," Ethan said, a strange note in his voice.

"Oh, I'm sorry. Is it about Dante? Or your attorney with more bad news?" she asked. Her heart was in her throat, hoping she'd been overacting and his change was something that had nothing to do with her.

"My attorney?" Ethan asked blankly. "What would—"

"From a few nights ago. You said you had some unexpected news."

His expression cleared. "Oh, it's nothing to do with that. Or Dante."

He studied her in silence, as if he were weighing up whether he would tell her something or not. Mouth dry and tension roiling through her, she clutched at the armrests of her chair and waited.

"It's Aidan." He was watching her with an odd look in his eyes. "I've been trying to reach him for days, but he's not answering any of my calls or returning my messages."

She blinked in surprise. That hadn't been what she'd been expecting. "And that's unusual for him?"

"Yes. For him to not get back to me like this is... out of character."

Genevieve tensed. First Tess, and now Aidan had dropped off the radar. What was going on?

Under the weight of Ethan's stare, she fixed a calm but curious expression on her face, trying to squash down the terror sparking to life inside her.

Everything in her was screaming at her that Aidan's disappearance had everything to do with her calling him, and with his offer to help her find Tess. Now, he'd stopped answering Ethan's calls. How could the two things not be related?

If something had happened to Aidan because of her... because she'd involved him, she'd never forgive herself. And neither would Ethan.

"Really?" She started to back out of his office, furiously running through her memory of the phone call. Had Aidan said he'd go looking for Tess, or had he only said he'd keep an eye out for her?

Ethan leaned back in his chair, his eyes lazily tracking

her retreat like a great hunting cat. "Really. You wouldn't happen to know—"

Jumping when his phone started ringing, she waited until he'd bent to answer it before beating a hasty retreat.

His eyes narrowed at her as she stepped out of the room. "Yes," he snapped into the phone.

Forcing a smile on her face, she pulled the door closed behind her and sagged in relief. She could hear him on the other side talking about high-risk investments, and in her mind, she doubted it would be a quick call.

Which was good. The longer he was on the phone, the more time she would have to figure out how she was going to tell him she was responsible for Aidan going missing.

Her nose itched, and she rubbed at it distractedly as she turned toward the source of the stench in the air. She knew it hadn't been there earlier. The intense rotten-apple odor was far too potent for that.

Leaning her head against the door, she tried to ignore the smell. She had to focus. What was she going to do about Aidan? She could try calling him, but if he wasn't answering the phone as Ethan said, there didn't seem to be much point. Going to the bar wouldn't work either, not when there was no way Ethan would miss her slipping out.

She'd promised obedience, and that wasn't being obedient. Not by a long shot. When he caught up to her, he'd be liable to kill her himself, if Dante didn't get to her first.

So, regardless of how reluctant she was to say something that would only add to her failings in his eyes, she was left with little choice but to tell him the truth and hope he didn't kill her.

But first, if only to distract herself from Ethan's looming explosion when he found out what she'd done, she decided to investigate the smell that was growing stronger the longer she lingered in the foyer. The closer she got, the fouler it became, until she was practically gagging at the ripeness. God, what was it?

When she swung open the front door and the putrid-sweet smell hit her full in the face, she clamped a hand over her mouth as her eyes watered.

Blinking back tears, she stared in surprise at the large silver-wrapped gift box with a shiny red bow that sat outside.

It was so beautifully decorated, she struggled to fathom how such a foul smell could come from something that pretty. But after glancing around the sloped driveway, she saw nothing else that could explain the source of the smell.

Eyeing a small silver envelope nestled in the bow, she started in surprise when she saw that it was addressed to her. Who would send her a gift? A gift that stank to high heaven, but a gift nonetheless.

With a hand still covering her nose and mouth, she lifted the lid.

"Genevieve!" Ethan's voice was a sharp order, coming at the same time she lifted the lid free. "Don't."

Turning, she saw him standing outside his office. His phone was in his hand, and a muffled voice from it told her he hadn't hung up yet. Then she saw Ethan's gaze was leveled not on her, but the box behind her.

But despite Ethan's warning, and some inner part of her trying to warn her that nothing good could ever come from a gift that smelled as bad as this—despite that, something compelled her to look.

Red. All she saw was red.

Fiery red strands of hair.

The distinctive cherry red hair she'd searched for and could never find in Hellfire.

She didn't know when she started screaming. Just that she suddenly was. The high-pitched sound was something she'd never heard herself make before.

And then Ethan had her in his arms, was pulling her in the house, slamming the door shut behind him as she fought him.

"Tess! No. I have to go to... let me go. I have to—"

"She's dead, Genevieve. She's dead."

He was forcing her away and up the staircase, holding her tight enough to leave bruises, but she didn't care. She fought with everything she had and more.

She had to get to Tess. Had to know it wasn't Tess out there, dead. Had to know she was wrong.

"How is she?" Rachel asked him.

"In shock," Ethan said, closing the bedroom door behind him. It'd been a battle to get her up the stairs and to lie down on the bed, and he sensed she still had fight left in her.

"Did you call the Council?" He didn't take his eyes

from the closed front door, to where the gift that'd likely traumatized Genevieve had been.

Luckily, Rachel had arrived while he was getting her up the stairs, so at least he'd known he could trust her to handle it.

"Yes. They came and took the..." Rachel paused, glanced at the bedroom door. "They came. It's... she's gone now," she murmured.

Ethan let out a heavy sigh. That was one less thing he had to worry about, at least. He didn't know exactly what Genevieve had seen but hoped he'd gotten to her before she'd seen too much. It'd taken him no more than a glance to know Tess had died in the same way all the other gifts had. A broken neck.

"Good," he breathed. "Good."

"Do you need me to do anything? I can—"

Genevieve pushed the bedroom door open and stepped out. Although Rachel watched her with pity in her eyes, she didn't seem to recognize that Rachel was even there.

Her red-rimmed eyes were fixed on him, and him alone.

"Genevieve, you need to rest," Ethan said softly, reached for her shoulder to guide her back inside. But she dodged his hand as she continued to stare at him.

"This is your fault," she said, voice husky with un-shed tears as she shoved at his chest. He didn't move.

"I tried to tell you something wasn't right. I tried to call her. I tried to... but you didn't care. You didn't even tell me she'd stopped working at the bar." She shoved at him again, with more force now, and he rocked back a little.

He caught at her arms. "Genevieve..."

"No," she snapped, yanking her arms free from his grip. "I had to find out from Aidan that she'd stopped going to work. Days ago. *Days!* She could've needed help. She could've needed *me,* and you didn't care enough to tell me. I told you something might be wrong."

"Aidan told you?"

"I called him on the off chance she'd be there—at Hellfire, and I'd missed her." Her laugh when it came was hard and brittle. "But you knew all along. He told me to ask you. You? You, who never want to tell me anything, unless it's to hurt me."

"That's why you called him," Ethan murmured.

He glanced at Rachel, and she flinched. She'd made a mistake about Genevieve, and he could see the moment of realization in her eyes, but it was too late to take it back.

Genevieve laughed louder.

He turned to her, and the look in her eyes chilled him. He'd never seen such a cold, flinty look on her before, and unease stirred at the sight of it

"And now it's happening to you."

"What's happening to me?"

"Aidan. He's behaving out of character, you said? Well, Tess would've answered her phone, even if it was to shout at me. And now we know why she wasn't answering, don't we?" She paused, her voice taunting. "What do you think is keeping Aidan from answering you?"

Ethan knew this wasn't Genevieve. This was the grief talking. She wasn't like this. She wasn't vindictive or cruel. But even knowing this, his anger—a volatile thing at the best of times—growled at him. Aidan was missing, could be dead already, and Genevieve was *taunting* him over it.

A smile, the mirror of her sharp-edged one, twisted his lips as he bent toward her. "We never would have turned her," he said, his voice hard. Cruel.

Genevieve blinked. Confusion swam in the depth of her eyes. "What?"

"Tess. You must have noticed all the bite marks. Did you think we would turn her when she served just fine as prey?"

Genevieve stared at him. She shook her head. No, it wasn't just her head shaking—it was her entire body that shook. Trembled. With anger or shock, he couldn't say.

"Surely you must've wondered why no vampire ever turned her? Other people were turned. *You* were turned. But not Tess. Never Tess. Didn't you ever wonder why?"

"I don't know why vampires do what they do," Genevieve said, her voice hard.

Ethan's smile was as hard as her voice. "What *we* do, Genevieve. Have you forgotten what you are? Why would we turn someone eager to be a perpetual source of food to us? Who would keep on coming back, again and again, happy to serve us regardless of how we treated them?"

"Stop it." Her voice was a whisper, a thread of sound.

Smiling, he continued. "Whether we made sure they felt pleasure or agonizing pain? Even if we fed so much, their roommate thought they'd die? Even then, they always came back for more."

"I said, stop it!" Her hand flew at his face, and he caught it easily. Gripping her wrist tightly, he met her gaze.

"Ethan, maybe..." Rachel's voice was hesitant.

"Do not interfere!" he snapped, keeping his eyes locked on Genevieve.

"I don't think—"

"That's right, Rachel. You don't think, do you?" He turned to face her now, still gripping Genevieve by her wrists as she struggled to pull free.

Rachel swallowed and glanced at Genevieve.

"Let me go," Genevieve whispered, her struggles slowing as if she realized there was little point in it. That he was too strong.

He never took his eyes from Rachel. Instead, he waited until she met his gaze.

"You can leave," he told her. It was nothing less than a cold dismissal.

"But I—"

"From what I remember," Ethan drawled, "you are my VASS. You have a signed contract with me. With VASS. And with the Council. Would you like me to inform them of your inability to follow the simplest of orders? Would you prefer I found someone more capable of serving me in the manner I wish?"

He watched as her resistance crumbled. She shook her head, swallowing hard. He knew Rachel, knew what buttons to press to bend her to his will. Being a VASS meant everything to her. She wouldn't give it up for anything.

"No, Sire," she said, falling back on stiff formality.

"Then leave. Now," Ethan said, impatient for her to be gone. Beyond furious at her turning him against Genevieve.

He didn't miss Rachel's long look at Genevieve, and Genevieve's complete disregard of it as she continued to watch him.

Rachel slipped past them and walked down the stairs without another word. Ethan waited until she'd stepped out of the front door and closed the door behind her, and then turned his attention to Genevieve.

"I want you to listen very carefully to me," Ethan said, his voice low.

Genevieve's expression was blank now. Shock was starting to set in again. He wasn't even sure she was listening to him. He shook her.

"Tess was happy at Hellfire. She was treated well there. She wouldn't have left for any other reason than a vampire convincing her they would turn her."

She blinked, confused. "But you said—"

"I was cruel. But my words were nothing less than the truth. We don't turn those who we regularly feed on. But some like to promise one thing and deliver another." He paused, waited until he could see she'd understood what he was hinting at.

"There are too many bites on her neck for them to only come from being fed on, and she had blood on her mouth. Someone was toying with her, letting her believe they'd turn her."

He could see the effect his words were having on her, but she needed to hear them. She deserved to know what had been done to Tess. It wasn't how he'd planned on telling her, but she needed to know.

A thought occurred to him, so suddenly he couldn't believe he hadn't seen it before.

"It couldn't have been Dante," he murmured. "Because he didn't even know Tess existed."

But Genevieve shook her head, and he knew then that he'd lost her. He doubted she'd even heard him.

All the fight seemed to have gone out of her, and as he led her into the bedroom, he could see in her eyes that there was little left in her but shock and grief.

He stripped her mechanically, not dwelling on her nakedness as he undressed her before slipping a t-shirt over her. All the while she stood unmoving, her gaze on the wall behind him, just as she'd been when he'd first brought her home.

Finally, picking her up, he deposited her in bed. She lay on her back, staring up at the ceiling with empty eyes.

He leaned over her. "It's time for you to rest."

A tear formed in her eyes, a pinkish-red drop that slid from the corners of her eye and down the sides of her face, disappearing into her dark hair.

He bent closer. "I said rest. Close your eyes. Now."

There was no give in him, no room for her to resist him. No acceptance for anything less than her complete and utter obedience. She could've fought him. But just like the time before, she gave herself over to the darkness without a fight. Closing her eyes, her heart stuttered, and then it stopped.

Kicking off his shoes, he sighed as he did what he should have done—what he'd been planning on doing before Rachel had interrupted, what Genevieve would never know he did. He lay down beside her, pulled her still body against his, and wrapped his arms around her, burrowing his face in her hair.

CHAPTER TWENTY-FIVE

*T*he memory of Tess's body, the smell, the things Ethan had said… all of it came flooding back the moment Gen opened her eyes.

He'd undressed her and put her to bed, and going by the indentations, he'd lain beside her. As if that would excuse any of his cruelty. But then she remembered what she'd said. How she'd laughed.

She couldn't believe that she'd tried to slap him. *Her.* The middle-school art teacher who didn't have an aggressive bone in her body had nearly lost her mind and tried to hit Ethan!

Was this her now? Was this the way she was going to be?

Squeezing her eyes shut, she concentrated on breathing deeply until the sick feeling, and the burning behind her eyes warning her she was about to cry, had passed.

When she felt she'd gotten herself under control, she opened her eyes and took in the clock on the bedside table. It told her it was nine at night, which was late for her to be rising when sunset was around five. But after everything she'd been through, it was a wonder she'd risen at all.

Since she was up, it was about time she showered and brushed her teeth. If nothing else, it might make her feel human... well, more alive, anyway.

She was coming out of the bathroom, a towel wrapped around her, when she found Rachel waiting beside the bed. A tall glass of blood sat on the bedside table, but she ignored both it and Rachel as she crossed over to the closet.

"I brought you something to drink."

"I can see that."

There was nothing she wanted to wear in the closet. Closing the door, she made her way over to the dresser instead. In the third drawer, she found where Ethan kept his sweats.

Dressing in his clothes didn't exactly appeal to her, but right now she craved comfort, and at least the clean sweat pants and T-shirt she pulled out were freshly laundered and didn't smell of him.

"He's gone to see if he can find Aidan," Rachel said.

Gen glanced at Rachel and found her eyeing the bruises on her wrist. "Did he ask you to tell me that?"

"Well, only if you asked."

"I didn't ask."

"I thought you might want to know where he is."

"And there you go," Gen said, pulling the sweatpants on under her towel. "Once again offering your opinion, whether or not it's needed or wanted."

Behind her, Rachel was quiet, but Gen could feel her gaze on her back as she dropped the towel and tugged the soft cotton t-shirt over her head.

Picking up her hairbrush from the dresser, she started brushing the tangles out of her hair. She hadn't bothered washing it. It'd been one more thing she didn't have the energy to deal with. Not tonight.

"I know you must think the worst of me."

Gen stopped brushing her hair and turned to face Rachel.

"You're wrong. I don't think the worst of you. I know you don't like me. I get that. You've made that perfectly clear, and right now, I don't particularly care why. But what I'd like to know is what you told Ethan."

She hadn't missed Ethan's words to Rachel, nor the look he'd given her, and it hadn't taken her long to figure out Ethan's change in mood had been the result of Rachel, instead of anything she'd done. When Rachel flushed with guilt, she realized her suspicions had been right.

"So, tell me. Did you tell him Aidan and I were doing the dirty behind his back?"

"I was trying to look out for him. I didn't mean—"

"You did mean. Instead of saying anything to me," Gen interrupted, "you ran straight to Ethan. You have no right to involve yourself, to insinuate yourself into his—or my —personal life like that."

Gen could read the hurt in her eyes, could see Rachel

was feeling guilty for the trouble she'd caused. But right now, she didn't care.

"I didn't want him to be hurt," Rachel said.

But Gen heard what else she wasn't saying. "By me again, like last time. Right? You seem so very interested in protecting Ethan from me. Why is that, Rachel?" she asked softly.

Rachel's silence was deafening, and Gen finally understood what Rachel would never admit out loud. She turned away and continued brushing her hair.

"You've done what you came here to do. So, you can go now."

She was being a bitch, and she knew it. But she wasn't feeling particularly sympathetic to anyone right now. Not when all she wanted was to be alone.

But Rachel didn't move. "Ethan said I should stay with you, in case you needed anything."

"The only thing I need is to be left alone. So please, leave."

Ethan had probably chewed her out over all the trouble she'd caused, but none of that had anything to do with her.

When the door clicked shut behind Rachel, she lowered her hairbrush and stood staring at the wall. Ethan was gone, but that didn't mean he wouldn't be back anytime soon.

Until then, Rachel would probably be hovering around her, but right now she needed room to breathe. And there was only one place in Vegas where she could do that.

Mind made up, she headed downstairs, past Rachel who hovered near the top of the stairs. Stepping into the lounge, she closed the door behind her, picked up the phone and called for a driver, then slipped out through the garden to the front of the house.

It was so peaceful on the ridge.

The only sound she heard was the air as it blew through the trees and the shrubs below her feet. Leaning back on her hands, with her legs dangling over the edge, she tilted her head back and closed her eyes.

Behind her, the driver waited quietly in his car parked a few feet away, and she appreciated how quiet he'd been, how patient. For over half an hour, she could just breathe and forget everything—Tess, Vince, Rachel, and Ethan. If she couldn't have her painting, then this was the next best thing, and it was a balm for her weary soul.

While Ethan wouldn't be happy with her for leaving the house, it wasn't like she'd walked out on her own. True, instead of telling Rachel where she was going, she'd slipped out the back door instead of the front. But it was only a matter of time before Rachel decided to check up on her in the lounge and found her gone.

Ethan would find her soon enough, and when he found her... he'd probably toss her over the edge of the ridge.

On the heels of her thought, she turned at the sound of a speeding car with a powerful engine tearing up the narrow, winding road to her ridge. She scrambled to her feet. It might be Ethan, and if it was, she'd rather be on her feet to face him down instead of sitting on the edge of what was essentially a cliff. And if it turned out not to be him—well, it didn't seem like the smartest thing in the world to be standing in the path of a speeding car.

As the car turned onto the ridge, she threw a hand over her eyes, for a second blinded by the bright headlights. By the time she could see again, the car had come to a stop and the driver was climbing out.

It was Ethan.

His face was a cold, expressionless mask, but she could guess what emotion he was keeping from her.

After Ethan's gaze took in her sweats, lingering on her bare feet, he turned away. He crossed over to her driver, who'd climbed out of his car and was on his way to meet him. Whatever words they exchanged were brief, before the driver was getting back into his car and driving away.

Then it was her and Ethan on a ridge high above Vegas, and she was standing at the edge of a thousand-foot drop. Vampire or not, she thought her chances of survival were slim to none if she fell, or was pushed.

Ethan's jaw was a hard line, and intense emotion radiated from him as he strode toward her, projecting cold determination.

"Ethan," she said, raising her hands. "I didn't come alone, so you really can't be too pissed at—"

She gasped as, retreating a step, her foot met thin air and she lost her balance. But Ethan was there, already catching her even before she was falling. One arm locked around her waist as tight as a vice, and he jerked her against him.

Raising her hands to his chest, she gasped as his other hand curved around the back of her head, his fingers tangling in her hair as his mouth slammed down on hers, his kiss a hot brand.

Surprise held her immobile, and Ethan took full advantage, his tongue invading her mouth.

Her eyes fluttered closed, and her hands drifted over his chest and slipped around his shoulders, moaning at the stroke of his tongue against hers.

She shouldn't be melting into his kiss like this. She should be shoving him away from her, or screaming into his face.

And she would... just not quite yet.

No one at Hellfire had been able to tell Ethan where Aidan was, only that he'd taken a few days off and the bar manager was in charge.

But finally, Ethan had tracked Aidan down at his home. If his friend's frequent glances at his front door hadn't given away what he'd been up to, then the musky scent of sex clinging to him would have.

"You haven't been returning my calls," he said.

"I might've been a little tied up," Aidan said, grinning as he flashed his wrists and the faint outline of handcuffs around them.

"It's been three days," he said dryly.

"And when was the last time I took a day off? Figured I'd reach out to you when I'm back at the bar tomorrow. What's going on? You never come out here."

It looked like his friend was actually taking a night away from his club, and he'd managed to find a bar manager he could actually trust to run the venue in his absence—something he'd struggled with since taking it on.

Aidan didn't live in any of the vampire enclaves overlooking the city. Instead, he'd chosen to make a home for himself near his downtown bar by taking a dilapidated old townhouse and turning it into a true home. It was surrounded, like the other homes alongside it, by towering cast iron black gates.

But since he'd moved out of his apartment near the Strip several years ago, he'd rarely spent any time at all here. So little, in fact, Ethan had almost forgotten he owned a home here—especially when he practically lived in the small apartment above his bar.

"Tess's dead," Ethan said bluntly as a couple of young women came to a sudden stop across from Aidan's home to stare at them. He doubted they'd leave anytime soon, given that he and Aidan sat on the top step leading up to his friend's townhouse, and Aidan was currently clad in nothing but a pair of black briefs.

"What? How?"

"Someone broke her neck and sent me her dead body, all packaged in a pretty box." Ethan narrowed his eyes in concentration at the two young women, watching as one tugged a cell phone from her pocket and aimed it at them.

He met her gaze for one brief second before turning his attention to her friend, and then, when both turned to walk back the way they'd come, he refocused his attention on Aidan.

"Genevieve got to the box before I could."

"Shit. That's... seriously messed up. And you still think Dante's responsible?"

Despite Aidan sounding relatively calm in spite of what Ethan had told him, Ethan made sure to observe his friend closely. Given Aidan's loss of control at the attack on his bar, it seemed like the smart thing to do.

"Not anymore, no. I'm starting to wonder if this is more to do with Genevieve, with someone wanting to hurt her, than it has to do with Vince."

"It does seem that way. Any ideas who?"

"Vince's Master, maybe, but that doesn't make sense either."

"Does she have any ideas?" *Aidan asked, scratching at his back. Ethan leaned back and whistled at the scratches that could only have come from a woman's nails running up and down his back.*

"Nope. And I don't plan on asking her."

"Why? You still think she fucked you over in Prague?"

Ethan was silent as he considered Aidan's question. Did he think she had him tortured and left to die?

He didn't know. He wanted to believe her, and she'd told him she loved him. Looking into her face, he couldn't see how she could be lying. But then again, what did someone like him know about love?

"I don't know," *he murmured.*

Aidan clapped him on the back so hard, Ethan nearly went flying off the top step. "Ah, you guys have turned the corner, I see?" *he said.*

He glared at Aidan. "Not quite."

"So there's even more domestic drama. What is it now?"

Ethan hadn't meant to bring it up, but Aidan had a way of getting him talking—except about one thing. His family. He never spoke about that with anyone.

"I believed Rachel when she told me she caught you and Genevieve on the phone."

A smile lit Aidan's eyes. "You believed Rachel... which

implies that she... you're not saying what I think you're saying, are you?"

"Shut up."

Aidan's lips twitched. "No, no. Please do go on. You were saying something about me and Gen having an illicit affair."

"Rachel was very convincing."

"I'm sure she was. You really must introduce me to the stern Rachel I hear so much about. I have to say, I'm intrigued."

"You're not allowed to be. She's a VASS, so hands off."

"Well, she's not my VASS, so I can do whatever I like."

"If you think you have a chance with Rachel, then—"

Ethan's phone vibrated in his pocket. Slipping it out, he glanced at the caller I.D.

"Ah, speaking of the lady," Aidan said teasingly, as he leaned over Ethan's shoulder to peer at the screen.

"Fuck off. Yes, Rachel, what is... wait, what? She's gone... why didn't you... Okay, I'm leaving now... No, stay there in case she comes back. And call me if she does."

Ethan was on his feet. Was already halfway down the front path with Aidan close beside him by the time he hung up.

"You need me to come with?" were the first words out of Aidan's mouth. "I can throw something on and be ready in a few seconds."

"No need. I think I know where she's gone."

"And if she's not there?"

Ethan ran a hand through his hair as he considered Aidan's question. He knew what Aidan was being careful not to say—what if whoever had been sending the deadly gifts had somehow managed to get their hands on Genevieve? What would they do to her? Could he expect a silver gift box with his name on it waiting outside his front door?

He shook his head to clear the disturbing image from his mind. No, that wouldn't happen. Not to Genevieve. He wouldn't let it.

Aidan clapped him again on his shoulder, only this time his hand squeezed it fondly. "She'll be there. And if she's not... we'll find her together, brother."

As soon as he spotted the car parked near the ridge, he knew he'd been right. Only then did he feel he could slacken the grip he had on the steering wheel, and only then did he feel like he could breathe.

She sat right at the edge of the ridge, leaning back, her long curls blowing about her face, her eyes closed and her expression tranquil.

A look of such quiet calmness on her face, it was only then he realized how long it'd been since he'd seen it.

And then he was making the final turn, and she was on her feet, her eyes turning wary. The familiar way she watched him now, as if he were a bomb primed to go off at any moment.

He got rid of the driver, and then he was there, catching her as she stepped back into nothing. She was alive, and she was safe in his arms as he kissed her, pouring out all of his fear and his anger... and everything else into that kiss.

In seconds she was softening against him, curling her arms around him as he lifted her off her feet and backing up, striding to his car.

The only thing he could think of was being inside her,

and he didn't hesitate for a moment before he yanked down her sweatpants, sat her on the hood of his car, and tore at the front of his pants.

Their teeth clashed. His hands widened her legs as he moved closer, and gripping her bare ass, he thrust into her. He groaned into her mouth as she, moaning, wrapped her legs around his waist and lay back on the car.

Beneath him, with her nails digging into his shoulders, she ground herself against him as again and again, he impaled himself on her.

Tearing his lips from hers, his mouth sought the sweat-dampened skin of her neck. He craved the taste of her in his mouth, was beyond desperate for the warm heat of her muscles clenching around him as he fed, his fangs bit into her soft throat.

"Ethan." A soft gasp. Almost begging, and then her back bowed. The muscles of her sex clamped so tight around him, all he could do was helplessly thrust inside her. His release followed close behind hers.

The force of her climax silenced her, and as he quietly fed, she lay still beneath him, her legs still wrapped around his hips and her fingers tunneling through his hair.

His tongue sealing the bite on her throat set her muscles rippling against his softening cock and drew a soft moan from her, but he was in no rush to pull out.

Not when being inside her felt like perfection. So, nuzzling his face between her breasts, they remained that way, still locked together in the still beauty of the night.

Then she started laughing. He felt the vibrations in her chest first, then the tremors in her arms, until her entire body was shaking from the strength of her soundless laughter.

Lifting his head, he observed her in silence.

"I thought you were going to throw me over the edge," she gasped.

He heard the tinge of something else lurking behind the laugh, something close to panic. But he didn't smile, just watched and waited for what he knew was coming.

When her breath caught, and she made a choked sound, he wasn't the least bit surprised. As she pressed her wet face against his throat, wailing over everything she'd lost, he said nothing as he held her.

He knew what she needed, and words weren't it.

CHAPTER TWENTY-SIX

At first, Gen thought he'd been avoiding her, assuming she'd found some new way to piss him off.

Since she'd been doing little else but cry in the nights since he'd found her on the ridge, she couldn't exactly blame him.

But when she'd gone to his office with her stomach gurgling to tell him she was hungry, she'd realized how wrong she'd been.

He'd been avoiding her—just not for the reason she thought.

Staring at her, his eyes had burned. Then he'd risen from his desk, and after asking her to wait, he'd come back with a glass of blood for her and an unmistakable bulge in his pants.

Then there was the pile of books and a brand-new laptop with Netflix set up, waiting for her in the lounge, and that was how she'd spent her nights. Cocooned in a blanket on the couch, either reading romance novels or binge-watching whatever she wanted on Netflix.

She'd started to ask Ethan about Tess, but he'd stopped her as soon as her eyes had filled with tears.

He'd told her he'd sent Tess's body back home, and that her parents would have more than enough money to give her whatever funeral they wanted.

Then the night before, he'd found her in the lounge, curled up on the couch with a book she'd been trying to read for several days but hadn't been able to finish.

"Come here," he'd told her, his expression giving nothing away. "I have something to show you."

Wary—because who wouldn't be, after her last surprise—she'd reluctantly put her hand in his and let him lead her to one of the downstairs reception rooms he never used.

Confused at his refusal to answer any of her questions, she'd finally pushed the door open and stepped inside, her mouth gaping open at what she found inside.

"I can't accept all this."

"Since none of it is returnable, I guess it's only going to end up in the trash if you don't find some use for it." His voice was indifferent as he leaned against the doorframe with his arms folded across his chest.

Although his face was blank, she knew he was laughing at her.

"You're joking," she said.

He shrugged.

She shook her head. "It's too much. Way, way too much. I'll never be able to use it all."

"So, don't use it all, then."

Turning her attention back to the room, she tried to absorb the sheer amount of... stuff, and found herself quickly becoming overwhelmed again.

Ethan had managed to empty an entire art supply store into the room, and the room wasn't exactly small to begin with. That was the only explanation for what she was seeing.

There were easels, paints, canvases propped against the wall, boxes of yet more supplies—and those were only the things in her line of sight.

Retrieving a drawing pencil from a pot sitting on one of the side tables, she brushed her thumb over the soft nib, and a spark of creativity flared inside her. She hadn't painted or drawn anything in months, but now she felt a burning desire to.

And it would help her heal in a way only her art could. She might even paint something Ethan would hang over his desk in his office. Something so beautiful, he'd never be able to get rid of it.

Examining her space with a more critical eye, she could see that she'd have to move a table bursting with supplies out of view. Maybe Ethan had a spare cupboard or closet she could use. Something unobtrusive.

She'd need to shift the easel near the sliding glass doors at the back of the room. That way, she could enjoy looking at the garden while she painted.

Then there was the glare of the overhead lights. She'd have to set up lamps with a softer light, so her work wasn't washed out by them.

"I'll leave you to it," Ethan said, breaking her out of her deep focus.

Blinking up at him, she realized she'd forgotten he was there.

"I'm sorry. I was being rude." Moving toward him, she stopped him with a hand on his arm. "I haven't even thanked you."

Hesitating for a brief second, she stretched up on her toes to brush her lips across his but pulled away before he could return the kiss.

The silence stretched between them as he gazed down at her, his eyes burning with some strong emotion. But then he shook his head and looked away.

"What are you going to paint first?"

"Well," she said, turning to remind herself of the gift Ethan had given her. "I was hoping I might paint you, actually."

He came to bed when she was already sleeping and was never there when she rose. But he always slept beside her.

Apart from that one night, what felt like a million years ago, when they'd nearly had sex and he'd left to sleep somewhere else, she always woke with the imprint of his body beside hers.

All except this rising.

This rising, she woke with the sight of Ethan's bare chest in front of her face.

With a room bursting full of art supplies, she'd decided to wake early so she could finish packing away the supplies in a cupboard Ethan had pulled from another room for her. That, and the true reason for her anticipation to rise—to start on her preliminary sketch of Ethan.

But at the sight of him sleeping beside her, her excitement about painting shifted into a different kind of excitement altogether.

Slowly, she pressed one finger on his chest, and when he didn't react, rested her palm flat against his heart, her eyes never moving from his face. His heart was silent as he slept.

Confident that she'd stop long before he discovered what she was doing, she lowered her gaze and smoothed her hand down the muscled plains of his pecs, and down to his six-pack abs.

Heart racing, she paused with a hand on his flat stomach, her eyes darting to his face to reassure herself that he still slept. Finding his eyes were still closed and no breath passed his lips, she slid her hand below the sheet.

Her hand continued its descent, and she realized she was holding her breath when she let it out in a heavy gasp when she saw, or rather felt, that he was naked beneath the sheet he'd draped over his hips.

Just as her fingers brushed against the barest tip of him, Ethan moved, and she found herself pinned below him, her hand caught between them. She raised her eyes from his chest and found him gazing down at her, a look of amusement on his face.

"And what," he murmured, his voice husky, "do you think you're doing?"

Swallowing, she fought the urge to look away as heat stole over her cheeks. "I'd tell you, but I think it's pretty obvious."

His eyes darkened, and something hard and hot stirred against her thigh.

"I would prefer for you to say it. Tell me. What do you want, Genevieve?" He shifted, and the hard press of him nudged her lower belly.

That was when it all started to make sense. He wanted her, which explained the way he'd been when she went to feed. Her drinking from him would lead to sex like it always had, so instead, he'd kept his distance from her.

He'd been waiting for her to tell him she wanted him.

He hadn't spoken about the end of... whatever it was that was happening between them. Not since her first night with him.

Neither had he said anything about her admitting that sex between them was making her more attached to him. Did that mean he was becoming attached to her, too? Did it mean he loved her?

She still grieved for Tess—was still grieving over the loss of her friend. She hadn't stopped thinking about why someone would want to kill Tess and Vince. But none of that meant she didn't want Ethan, that she didn't miss his touch. If anything, her need for him was more intense than ever.

Throughout her silent introspection, Ethan waited patiently for her to tell him what she wanted.

Finally, her mind made up, she took a deep breath and prepared herself to say something she'd never said before.

"I want you to make love to me. I want to... I want to make love to you."

"Because of the art supplies?" There was a hint of a smile on his lips.

She shook her head. "No. Not because of the art supplies. I always want to touch you." She felt her face flame, but she didn't stop. "But I want to kiss you too… everywhere."

Ethan's amusement faded and his face hardened.

Hurt by his reaction, at his unwillingness to hand over control in the bedroom for even a second, she started to move. "Never mind, it's not imp—"

His hand caught her wrist, halting her. "And where do you think you're going?"

She stared at his chest, still trying to get out of bed.

God, this is so humiliating.

"Uh, to have a shower, since you… well, since you don't want—"

His voice was a growl. "Will you stop struggling for a second? What makes you think I don't want this—that I don't want you?"

Still staring at the muscles of his chest she was desperate to touch and to kiss, she closed her eyes to temptation. "You looked angry. Like you didn't want—"

Again, he cut her off. This time it wasn't with anything he said.

Between one breath and the next, he'd tugged her hand caught between them and placed it on him. He was hard. Rock-hard. All but pulsing in her hand.

Her eyes shot up to his.

"Does that feel like someone who doesn't want you?"

Her mouth went dry at the heat in his eyes, and for a heart-stopping moment, they did nothing but stare at each other. Then her hand was closing around him, gently squeezing his rigid length.

He was so thick, she still couldn't believe he fit inside her—and the memory of how good it felt, how right it was, was enough to have a surge of wetness flooding her panties.

Growling low in his throat, he jerked her hand away from him and rolled over until he was lying on his back, his eyes closed as he breathed through his mouth.

"For the record, I think this is a terrible idea," he muttered.

Sitting up, Gen felt a smile twisting her lips as her gaze took in the tent his erection had made of the sheet. "So, you're saying yes?"

His eyes were slits as he shifted his gaze to her. "It's a yes," he grunted.

Grinning now, she walked on her knees toward him. "You're making it sound like I'm about to torture you."

"Before you start, how about you tell me where this is coming from?"

She placed a hand on his chest and slid her hand down to his stomach. Felt the muscles tense. "I know we don't dream, but I can't help but think I have been. Dreaming, that is. About what you taste like."

At her words, he closed his eyes and swallowed hard, his body shuddering. Then his eyes opened and she felt one of his hands stroke her back.

She shook her head. "No," she said, looking him in the eye. "I don't want you touching me. Not yet."

Without a word, he moved his hand away, and she turned her attention back to his chest. Bending over him with her hair brushing over his bare skin, she licked at his skin, flicking her tongue across his nipples. He sucked in a breath and groaned deep in his throat.

When he shifted restlessly beneath her, she paused to see what he would do. But he didn't touch her. Moving her head to his other pebbled nipple, she drew it into her mouth, sucking lightly at his skin, loving the taste of him.

Her fingers angled down, taking the sheet with it until he was stretched out beneath her, laid completely naked to her gaze.

The soft cotton of her T-shirt brushed against the beaded points of her breasts, making her catch her breath. All of a sudden, the material was uncomfortable, almost painful against her aching breasts.

So, easing back from Ethan, she caught the hem of her shirt and pulled it over her head, leaving her kneeling beside him in just her panties.

His eyes were a furnace as he stared at her breasts, his hands clenching the sheets as the veins in his arms stood out sharply, bearing testament to his effort to keep his hands to himself. But she thought that she could break his will. The idea that she could make him lose control made her feel powerful in a way she'd never felt before.

Bending over him, her fingers moved over his skin, her mouth following close behind, with the muscles in Ethan's stomach bunching as she crept closer to her true goal. Then, just before her fingers reached their destination, her mouth not far behind, she stopped.

Her eyes shot up to Ethan's face. His features were carved of granite, his eyes focused on her with a searing intensity as he stared down at her.

"Um," she started. "Despite what I said, I... I've never

done this before, so I'm not sure I know what to do. I mean, I get the mechanics, but—uh, I'm pretty sure I have no idea what I'm doing."

Despite the tension radiating from every line of his body, Ethan closed his eyes and shook with laughter. Without conscious thought, her lips curved into a smile as she stared down at him, stunned by the beauty of his smile.

She'd almost forgotten what he looked like when he laughed hard enough to reveal the dimple in his right cheek. He was like a dark angel.

"Genevieve…" Ethan said, once his laughter had died away. "I'm sure whatever you do, you'll do fine. Do what feels right. No pressure." He gazed up at her as if he was prepared to wait forever.

She turned her attention back to his erection. Taking him gently in one hand, she stroked him from root to tip in an easy glide. He hummed in pleasure beneath her, giving her the confidence to continue.

He'd always preferred to control the pace of their lovemaking. But being like this, touching him, using her hand to excite him… she liked the feeling of control it gave her.

"Harder," he growled.

It'd occurred to her that she might accidentally hurt him, but at his harsh command, she tightened her grip around him. He was velvet over steel in her hand, and the more she stroked him with increasing confidence, the hotter he became.

A bead of liquid formed at his tip as she watched, and bending, she took him into her mouth, hearing him swear as he thrust reflexively into her mouth.

Swirling her tongue around the droplets at the tip, she sucked and licked at the salty taste of him. He thrust again, his hips moving like he couldn't quite stop himself. The taste in her mouth was pure Ethan. Faintly salty, decadent, and with an earthy masculinity that made her hungry for more.

Closing her eyes, she tried to take as much of him as she could in her mouth, even knowing it was impossible. He was too long for her, too wide, but that didn't stop her from trying.

But she found by breathing only when she released him and holding her breath as she drew him deeper into her mouth, she could fit him deep enough for the tip of him to tickle against the back of her throat.

She lost track of time as she sucked and licked at him. But soon she became aware of the gentle tug of Ethan's hand in her hair, pulling her up, pushing her down as he thrust into her mouth.

"Genevieve," Ethan growled as she lapped at more of the salty taste of him spilling onto her tongue, a warning in his voice.

Raising her head, she found herself staring into eyes gone wild with need.

"You have to stop," he said. "You keep doing that, and touching yourself like that, neither of us are going to last much longer."

Confused, she glanced down. Found she'd slipped her hand into her panties and had been rubbing herself without even realizing it.

Pulling her hand free, she saw her fingers were moist and felt embarrassment stir. She felt the weight of Ethan's stare, and turning, found him staring at her hand like a starving man.

"Give me your hand."

Reluctantly she held out her hand. He took it, and with his gaze locked on hers, raised her hand to his mouth and sucked each digit, one at a time. Gen felt the pressure of each draw deep inside, felt a gush of liquid between her legs, and swallowed back a moan.

After he'd sucked each finger clean, Ethan rolled over, falling between her legs. His eyes never left hers as his hands tore her panties from her.

Grasping her tight around her waist, he thrust into her in one hard move that seated him deep enough for their hips to be pressed tightly against each other.

Her head fell back, eyes rolling to the back of her head as she moaned at the press of his hardness spearing into her, filling her completely.

For a second he didn't move, giving her a moment to adjust to his size. But when she opened her eyes, caught the side of his face, and brought him down for a kiss, he started moving.

Pressing her heels flat against the bed so she could meet the smooth glide of his powerful thrusts driving her into the bed, a heavy warmth started to settle between her legs.

His hands covered her breasts, stroking and tugging at her nipples, making her thrash at the strength in his fingers. She whimpered into his mouth, one of her feet coming up to dig into his ass, opening herself up more to him.

When she came, it was with a scream, every muscle in

her body seizing as she held herself against him while he found his own release, his body straining against hers.

But he didn't move, and after her heart had stopped pounding so loudly in her chest, she opened her eyes as Ethan settled more comfortably on top of her. His eyes were no less heated than before, and he was still hard inside her.

"I'll give you two minutes to catch your breath. And then we go again. I'm staying right here inside you, all night." His voice was full of dark promise.

She felt her muscles clench around him, and his wicked smile told her he'd felt it, and liked it. Less than a minute later, and he was moving again. Moaning, she lay her head back on the pillow and held on as he continued to surge inside her. She didn't have it in her to tell him it hadn't been even close to two minutes yet.

CHAPTER TWENTY-SEVEN

She was wearing the white lace dress Ethan had seen displayed in a Night Mall boutique window, on his way back from a meeting with his attorney.

Something about the demure knee-length dress, along with its revealing nature, had made him think of Genevieve. Perhaps it was the innocence of her sweet smile, and the dark sensuality emerging in her.

She didn't seem to be the slightest bit aware of the impact of her dress, and the tantalizing glimpses of golden skin it revealed. Her gaze, when it wasn't on the paintings lining the walls, was on him.

"You told me there was a Renoir here," she reminded him, her eyes on the grand staircase at the end of the hallway. "In one of the bedrooms."

"Ah, a bedroom. Of course, why didn't you say so before? What are we still doing here?" Ethan said.

"Not for that," Genevieve said, glancing around the

room as if making sure no one was listening. "I want to see the painting."

"A painting is now more important than bodily delights?" He glared down at her in mock outrage. "Are you sure you're a vampire? Maybe I made a mistake, and you're still—"

Genevieve rose onto her tiptoes and slipped her arms around his neck. Leaning close, she pressed her lips against his ear.

"If you show me this painting, I'll show you what I'm wearing under the very pretty but very revealing dress you bought me."

Her whisper was quiet, but not nearly quiet enough.

Curling an arm around her slender waist, he pressed a brief kiss against her neck, ignoring the glances suddenly turned toward them. "Good lord, woman. You must be trying to kill me."

Genevieve giggled. "What makes you think that?"

"Because I know exactly what you're wearing—or what you're *not* wearing, beneath that dress."

"Does that mean you don't want to see?" she asked, blinking up at him with perfect innocence.

"I guess we'd better go see this painting, then," Ethan sighed.

He guided her past the curious onlookers in the hallway and up the grand staircase of the private enclave party he'd brought her to.

With her attention focused on the promise of finally seeing the painting he'd told her about, it took her a lot longer than it should have to notice all the glances pointed her way. As it was, they were halfway up the staircase when she leaned into his chest.

"Why are people staring at us? And smiling like that? Is it the dress? Is it too much?" she murmured out of the side of her mouth as she smiled at a couple on their way down the stairs.

" They're just curious to know what it is you want to show me under that dress of yours. Though I'm sure a few of them may have already guessed," he said just as quietly.

Genevieve jerked to a sudden stop. Glancing down at her, his lips twitched when he saw the look on her face.

"Are you suggesting that they..." Her face flushed bright red.

"Heard? This is a room full of vampires, Genevieve. I doubt they'd miss even a whisper," he said, urging her up the stairs.

"But... but you said... stuff too. And you were whispering. Why would you whisper, if you knew they would hear you?" she asked, her face still aflame.

Ethan shrugged. "Because it's sex. There's nothing to be embarrassed about with sex."

"Well, I'd prefer everyone not knowing what we do in the bedroom. And if it's no big deal, why were they staring?"

Snagging her hand, he led her down a hallway and stopped at a set of double doors.

"Because you're beautiful, and people like to fantasize about having sex with beautiful people. I'm sure in a century, you won't even think about it either," he said, pushing the doors open and tugging her inside.

"And will we still be together in a century?" Genevieve asked, her voice very quiet.

He paused.

This wasn't the place to talk about their future. They could do that later, at home and in bed, with him wrapped around her naked body. Preferably with him inside her.

Shrugging, he continued into the room. "I don't see why not."

"I'm not spending a century in Vegas."

"So, we'll move somewhere else," he said, trying to hide his pleasure that she wasn't demanding a return to London. If anything, she was sounding as if their being together was set in stone, like it was a foregone conclusion.

"Just like that?"

"It's moving. People do it all the time, and vampires more than anyone. Who would want to spend hundreds of years living in one city, when you have the entire world to explore?"

Continuing to lead her through several adjoining bedrooms, he followed her through another door, turned, and locked the door behind them.

"Ethan, why are you locking the door?"

"So we're not disturbed while you're showing me the contents beneath your dress," Ethan said, tugging her closer to the huge monstrosity of a bed in the middle of the room.

"I didn't mean here. And even if I did, I doubt a locked door is going to keep a vampire out," she replied, trying to pull her hand from his.

"Probably not." He shrugged, tugging her more insistently toward the bed.

"I see how this is. You lied about the painting, didn't you? All so you could get me here in this room, where we could—"

Ethan mentally started counting down from five as he listened to her. He'd reached one when she turned to gesture at the enormous bed.

Her silence was sudden and almost deafening when she caught sight of the large, ornate frame above the bed. He knew then he'd lost her.

Sighing, he released her hand and watched as she drifted over to the painting with a dreamy look on her face, like she was sleepwalking. Coming to a stop in front of it, she stared up at the painting of a garden dotted with bright flowers, mesmerized.

Figuring he might as well make himself comfortable, since there was a bed right there, he climbed on and after closing his eyes, leaned his back against the headboard and let his mind wander as he waited for her to get her fill of the Renoir.

Genevieve could and would stay like that for hours if he let her. It wouldn't have been the first time he'd found her staring with a look of utter absorption at her canvas in her makeshift studio. She'd be standing with a paintbrush in hand, paint dripping on the sheet she'd placed at the foot of her canvas.

At first, he'd thought he could get away with slipping in, taking a quick peek at the painting she refused to let him see, and be gone again before she'd even noticed he was there. But the moment he took a step inside, she was alert again and shooing him out of the room, telling him it wasn't ready for him to see it yet.

"Okay, I'm ready to go home now," Genevieve said.

His eyes snapped open and he glanced down at his watch.

"It hasn't even been thirty minutes yet."

She raised her eyebrow in question.

"You can stare at a painting for two hours without moving and barely blinking. There're times I don't think you're even breathing," Ethan said, swinging his legs off the bed.

Although she glared at him, she couldn't quite manage to hide the humor he saw swimming in her eyes.

Taking advantage of her distraction to snatch her hand, he tugged her close enough so she was standing between his legs.

"I breathe. Jeez, you make me sound like I'm crazy or something."

"Or something," he agreed, urging her to wrap her arms around his neck.

"I'm not having sex with you here," she said, her voice firm.

He nodded and kissed her on the neck. At her soft sigh, he kissed her again, keeping it light. Doing nothing to give her even a hint of his intention.

"I'm being serious, Ethan. We're not having sex here."

"I'm never going back there ever again," she said, climbing out of the car and clutching her heels in one hand.

Her hair fell about her shoulders, a big difference from the artful updo she'd worn earlier. The plum lipstick she'd worn was mostly gone, and Ethan had a strong suspicion he was wearing more of it on his neck than she had on her lips.

"I doubt we were the only couple to go upstairs and do more than admire paintings."

"It was embarrassing walking down the stairs, knowing they all knew what we'd been doing. And did you have to pull all my pins out?" she asked, outpacing him as she stalked into the house.

Turning to shut the front door, he did his best to hide his grin. There was no point trying to deny he'd had the intention of doing a lot more than showing her the painting all along. She would know he was lying.

"I know you're smiling," she said, her tone severe. "So, you can quit trying to hide it."

He made sure to wipe all expression from his face before he turned to face her.

Narrowing her eyes at him in suspicion, she shook her head and started up the stairs. "I'm going to have a shower."

He started after her as the image of a naked and wet Genevieve invaded his mind. "Great idea, I'll join you."

"Ethan?" Rachel said, stepping out of his office.

"Yes?" He turned to face her, stopping Genevieve with a hand on her hip.

"You have some mail, and there are some contracts I need you to sign," Rachel said."

He'd felt the tension in Genevieve as soon as Rachel

appeared, and he wondered if it was time for him to cut Rachel loose.

It was getting harder and harder to ignore how much Rachel had hurt Genevieve—and him, with her suspicions about her and Aidan. The last thing he wanted was for her to be uncomfortable every time Rachel was around—which, as his VASS, would be every night but one. Sooner rather than later, he'd have to do something about that, no matter how much it would hurt Rachel to do it.

Then his brain caught up to what she'd said. "Mail?"

There'd been no more "gifts" since Tess's body, and Genevieve was finally starting to recover from it. The last thing he needed was for the gifts to start reappearing.

Soon, he knew, he'd have to try to figure out who was responsible. But the last few days of being with Genevieve, of them laughing and making love, had been so perfect, he hadn't wanted to leave her.

"Yes, from a law office on the Strip," Rachel said.

Ethan felt his tension ease. Turning, he continued up the stairs.

"I'll deal with it tomorrow. You can take the rest of the night off."

Ordinarily, Rachel would have pushed him. At any other time, she'd have insisted he sign the contracts so she could deal with them sooner rather than later. But perhaps sensing she was on shaky ground after the Aidan affair, she kept her silence.

"Yes, Sire," she said.

"Good night, Rachel," he said, his mind already on sharing a shower with Genevieve.

CHAPTER TWENTY-EIGHT

*G*en couldn't stifle her disappointment when she woke to find herself alone. But then she remembered the contracts Ethan had put off so he could spend the night with her. Stretching in bed, she smiled at the memory.

They'd spent over an hour soaking in the large spa bath and... well, doing other things as well. And after, it'd seemed like the most natural thing in the world to fall into bed together, even though they still had hours before dawn.

As she lay in bed, her thoughts turned to Tess and her funeral in their small Ohio town. If she'd still been human, she wouldn't have missed it for the world. But with the way Tess had died... most everyone in town would either say it was Tess's fault for seeking out vampires, or they'd blame her for not protecting her friend. They'd want nothing to do with her, or with Ethan's money.

But not Tess's parents. Long ago they'd accepted that

Tess's obsession with all things vampire would only lead to a violent end. She could see them now, planning a simple funeral with the money Ethan had sent, and then using the rest to move away from a town that would never let them forget the path their only daughter had taken.

Sighing, she rose. Thinking about Tess and her sad end would only depress her, and with the way things had been with Ethan, it was the last thing she wanted to be. That could come later, after the honeymoon period had ended. And Vince too. They still had to get to the bottom of who had killed him and why.

Heading for the bathroom, she showered and dressed in one of Ethan's white shirts and a pair of blue jeans. Then after running a brush through her wet hair, she left it down to dry and started downstairs. She'd been working on the painting of Ethan for days, and although she still had a lot left to do, if Ethan would stop distracting her by trying to sneak in and see it, she might have it finished in a couple of days.

"Ethan?"

There was no response, so she padded toward his office and stuck her head in—and was confused to find it empty, since he spent more of his time in there than anywhere else in the house. On his desk were his cell phone, a sheaf of papers she assumed were the contracts Rachel had been talking about, and a small stack of mail.

"Ethan?" she yelled, checking the lounge but finding it empty. "Where are you?"

He wasn't in the kitchen either—not that she'd expected him to be. She couldn't imagine he'd gone out, not with his cell phone on his desk. And if he had, he'd have left her a note, like the time he'd gone to meet with his attorney in the city.

Then a thought occurred to her.

She hadn't checked her makeshift studio yet, and she wouldn't put it past him to be in there. Her refusal to let him have even the tiniest peek until her painting was finished had only made his curiosity worse.

"You'd better not be in my studio," she shouted, really worried now that he'd see it when she wasn't there. She wanted to gauge his reaction when she showed it to him. Just in case he hated it. Even though she didn't. It was her best work, she thought, and she was proud of all the emotion she'd caught in his eyes. But she wanted to be with him when he saw it for the first time, so she could capture his first reaction.

"Why aren't you—"

Genevieve stopped outside her studio and raised her hand to her mouth in horror.

Her canvas had been so eviscerated, it was impossible to tell what the painting had been of. At seeing what had been done to it, she flinched as if she'd been struck. All her work, all of it gone—destroyed and lost forever, just like that.

But that wasn't all that was broken in her studio. It looked like a tornado had whirled through it.

The table she'd been using to hold her supplies had been tipped over, was cracked in half and spilling its smashed contents all over the wall and floor. Paint dripped from opened cans, and the blank canvasses she'd left propped against the wall, ready for her next projects, were like white confetti on the paint-splattered floor.

She was seeing, but not quite able to believe her eyes.

Ignoring the wet paint squelching between her toes, she stepped inside, aghast at all the damage. Everything, absolutely everything she could see had been rendered useless. Thousands of dollars' worth of art supplies gone, just like that. It was enough to bring tears to her eyes to see it.

What had happened? Had it been Dante, or whoever it was who'd killed Tess and Vince? How had they been able to cause so much damage without Ethan being aware of it? Gasping, panic surged through her.

Ethan.

He hadn't responded to any of her calls, and he had to have heard her. Had he been hurt? She swallowed, fresh tears filling her eyes—was he lying dead somewhere, like Vince and Tess, his body waiting for her to find?

At the sound of footsteps behind her, she spun around with her heart in her throat.

CHAPTER TWENTY-NINE

Genevieve visibly sagged in relief at the sight of Ethan in the doorway, lowering her hand from her mouth as she started toward him.

"Ethan, you scared me to death. What happened here? Did someone break in?" she asked, gazing anxiously up at him.

He didn't respond.

"What's wrong? I thought something had happened to you."

He tried to find the words to speak, but nothing—no words he could think of came close to adequately describing what he was feeling.

"Ethan?"

"It was me," he said, close to breaking point. "I did it."

"You? I don't... I don't get it, why would you...?" She looked so stunned, was so convincing in the role of victim she'd cast herself in that he turned and stalked away from her. He couldn't bear to even look at her.

"I need you to see something," he said.

"But the paint. I'm not going to leave paint all over the—"

"I don't give a fuck about the paint," he snarled.

Behind him, he felt her eyes on his back, and then he heard the sound of her wet feet on the marble floor.

They reached his office door at about the same time the front door opened and Rachel stepped in, closing the door behind her.

"Oh good, you're here," Rachel said, sparing Genevieve a brief nod of greeting before she turned to Ethan. "Did you sign those contracts?"

Ethan stopped outside his office. "I don't need you today, Rachel. You can go." He turned to Genevieve. "Inside," he told her.

"But today isn't my day off. And why is there paint all over the..." Confusion reigned as her eyes took in the paint Genevieve had tracked down the hallway, and then she caught sight of the destruction in the studio.

Her eyes widened, and she turned uneasily to face him. "Maybe I could stay and..."

"I told you you're not needed today. Go. Now."

Rachel's eyes returned to the studio, and she paused.

His patience starting to run out. He started to speak when Genevieve intervened.

"It's okay, Rachel," Genevieve said with a smile. "Ethan was going to show me something. I'm sure he'll get those contracts signed soon. Won't you, Ethan?"

Seeing that smile, remembering how many times she'd smiled at him just like that... he knew it now for what it was. A lie. Everything she'd said, telling him she loved him, what she'd said about Vince—all of it had been nothing more than lies.

His patience snapped. He'd warned Rachel about interfering, had warned her what would happen if she pushed him.

"Get out. You're fired."

"Wait. What?" At that moment her professionalism abandoned her and she gaped at him in shock, her eyes disbelieving. For the first time, Ethan had managed to blindside her. At any other time he'd be laughing, but not now. Not today.

Genevieve cleared her throat. "Uh, Ethan. Are you sure? That seems a bit harsh. I mean—"

He didn't take his eyes off Rachel. "As her contract holder, I can fire her any time I want, and I want. Get out."

Without a word Rachel turned to leave, her gaze lingering for a second on something in his office. Her expression turned thoughtful, and he could almost hear her thinking.

She was probably wondering if he'd signed the contracts, as if it even mattered anymore, he thought with a sneer.

But she didn't immediately leave. Instead, she spun to face Genevieve.

"Goodbye, Genevieve. I'm sorry again about... well, everything. Take care of yourself," she said, and without waiting for a response, she left.

When he heard Rachel start her car, he turned his attention back to Genevieve, who was gazing at him with her mouth still slack with disbelief. As if she hadn't believed he'd really meant to fire Rachel.

"Did Rachel do something wrong?"

He strode into his office. "I don't give a fuck about Rachel."

Crossing over to his desk, he snatched up the large brown envelope he'd opened earlier and thrust it at her.

"Take it," he snapped.

Eyeing him with growing unease, Genevieve followed him into his office and hesitantly took it from him, lowering her gaze as she emptied the contents into her hand.

"Where did you get this?" she asked, her voice unsteady.

He knew which photograph she gripped in her trembling hands.

After all, it hadn't been all that long ago since he'd held it in his own hands. It'd been burned into his mind's eye, the sight of Genevieve and Vincent's intimate embrace on a balcony, of his mouth pressed against her neck as he slid her bra down her arms, and of the line of blood on her neck that told him Vincent had been feeding on her.

It must have been that same night he'd nearly claimed her at Eros. The night she'd been wearing the peach gown, and Rachel's phone call had interrupted him. But he'd known what would happen between Vincent and Genevieve. Hadn't he seen all the signs Vincent would take her home and fuck her?

"You've barely even started," Ethan said, pacing around the office, struggling to get a handle on the rage bubbling up inside of him.

Genevieve glanced up at him, and he saw in her eyes the first traces of fear. Swallowing hard, she lowered her head and started flicking through the stack of photos in her hand.

Finally, she looked up at him, her eyes wide with shock.

"Where did you get these photos?" she asked, a tremor in her voice.

Smiling, he crossed over to his desk and sat in his chair. "I'm intrigued to know what you think of them, since you play such a prominent role in them."

"But they're not—"

"Genevieve, I've asked you to do something for me. Don't make me ask you again."

She shook her head, her voice coming out in a whisper. "She looks like me, but it's not—"

"Looks like you?" Ethan interrupted.

She nodded.

"So, the first photograph, the one of Vincent undressing you, you're telling me that isn't you?"

"Well, yes. That one is me, but it's not how it—"

"We'll get to that later. The other pictures, tell me about them."

"They look like they were taken in a club. I don't know which one."

"Go on."

"Vince and the woman in the picture are doing... things to each other in this club. And they're having sex. I don't know who she is, but I don't have—"

"You don't know who she is?" Ethan's voice was soft. "Even though she looks very much like you... I'd say the resemblance is uncanny, wouldn't you agree?"

Dropping the photographs on his desk as if she

couldn't bear to touch them for a second longer, she folded her arms across her chest.

"It's a dark club. From a distance, I guess she could be mistaken as being me. But she isn't—I don't go to clubs like that. I don't do things like that. Is this what all of this is about? Someone told you this was me?"

Instead of answering, Ethan rose to his feet without warning, smiling as she took a small step back from his desk—from him.

"I can tell you about this club, if you like, since you're so determined to play this game," he offered, folding his hands behind his back and starting to pace around the room.

"As you know, it's a London club. It moves around every couple of years, so it doesn't draw too much attention to what goes on inside." He never took his eyes from her as he circled the periphery of the room.

"It doesn't have a name. Just a symbol. A Greek letter only. But it's a notorious den of vice, as the British like to say. There are things that happen in there that you wouldn't find here in the States. For all the Brits' talk of us Americans being brash and uncivilized, you'd be surprised at what they're capable of. Well, maybe *you* wouldn't be surprised. How long did you and Vincent live in London, again? "

He could see she wanted to argue, but when he narrowed his eyes at her, she fell silent. "Answer the question."

"Nearly four years."

He nodded. "Four years. I guess you learned a lot about London over the years, and about what you liked. You never struck me as the type to like things like…" Trailing off, he nodded at the photographs on his desk.

"Tell me what you liked about London." His voice came out sharper than he'd expected.

"I liked the quiet, but you knew that. Ethan, please, stop this. Why are you—" She turned to watch him as he continued to pace a wide circle around the room, and around her.

His voice was gentle now, mild. "We're just talking, Genevieve. Aren't women always complaining that men don't want to talk? Well, you're finally getting what you want. Did you prefer London?"

"I liked the quiet parts. The parks… being in nature… my painting. I rarely went out. That was something Vince did. I wasn't interested in parties."

"Rarely? Hmm."

He nodded, impressed at her ability to pretend he'd gotten her all wrong. Evidently, he'd massively underestimated her ability to lie to his face. But if that was the way she wanted to play this game, he was happy to play it with her and see how far she wanted to take it.

Genevieve made no response.

Nodding as if she'd spoken, he continued his meandering pace.

"There is an old machine. Older than the club itself, I think. Rumored to have belonged to a legendary French lover—a connoisseur of pleasure who collected and even had a hand in creating machines like it. It has a series of levers and clamps, and ropes. and… well, the ability to deliver a great deal of pleasure, and pain if that's your sort of thing. Which, going by some of these pictures, it is."

He stopped his pacing in front of the desk, staring down at the photographs spread across the surface. Feeling Genevieve's eyes on his face as she stood in tense silence beside him.

In one of the photographs, Vince was tightening a scarf around a woman's neck—around Genevieve's neck, and her back was crisscrossed with raised red marks. Marks that could only have come from a whip. And the photographer had caught him mid-thrust as she lay face down on the surface, wrists tied, completely at Vincent's mercy.

He couldn't remember what his first response had been when he'd seen it. But now the only thing he felt was empty. That and disgust. At himself, and her. How had he been so wrong about her? How had he not seen what she was really like?

Wrapping his arm around her waist, he jerked her hard against him. She gasped.

"And you're sure you haven't ever experienced the wonders of this machine?"

She shook her head violently. "No. Ethan, please, I—"

"You know what? I think I really would prefer you to call me Master. I think I've been very lax in enforcing that. Don't you?"

He stepped closer, turning her in his arms so her back was to him, bent his face to her throat. "Maybe it's about time I finally clued you in on the reason I claimed you, hmm?"

"I don't understand. What are you talking about? You said the Council—"

"You think the Council gives a shit about you?" he snarled.

"I don't—"

"Maybe I wanted to give you a little taste of my pain. Of what it is to be tortured… to be toyed with, mmm?" He stroked up her body, cupped her breasts, teasing and rolling her nipples into hard points.

Her head fell back and she moaned, her hands coming up to cover his hands, even as she tried to step away.

At the sound of her breathy moan, his body hardened. Swearing, he gritted his teeth at the feel of her in his arms, of the press of her soft curves flush against him. He still wanted her, even after all her lies. Even after her betrayal.

"Please…" she whimpered.

Stepping forward, he bent her over his desk, grinding his cock against her. "Maybe it isn't the machine you're interested in. Maybe it's something else you want instead. From what I can see, you like nothing more than to be tied down with a cock in your ass."

Her voice was a whisper. "No."

"No?" His laugh was bitter in her ear. "I guess I'll just have to do my best to convince you then, won't I?"

His hands moved to his pants, and at the sound of his zipper, Genevieve started to struggle.

"Ethan, you have to stop this. It isn't me in those photos. I swear to you, I've never done that before—any of that. Not with anyone."

"Genevieve," he said, voice soft. "I've told you to call—"

She threw herself back without warning. Surprised, he stumbled back a step as the back of her head connected with his chin. Not that it did her much good—not when she seemed more stunned by it than he did.

Rage, pure hot rage, poured through him as he wrapped his arms tight around her.

"This isn't you," she stammered, trembling in his arms. "I don't know what's going on, but this isn't you. Please…"

The room was filled with the scent of her terror as she tried to tear herself from his grasp, and he choked on it. All he could smell was her fear, all he could hear was the pounding of her heart as she fought him.

His lip curling in self-disgust, he tore his hands away.

For a moment she was frozen, as if she couldn't quite believe he'd let her go. And then she was gone, the sound of her footsteps loud on the stairs, the crash of an upstairs door slamming shut.

Roaring, he spun around, grabbed the edge of his desk, and flung it away from him. The glass desk exploded, shards cutting into his face and neck, but he didn't feel a thing. All he could do was stand there panting, his eyes locked on the photographs of Genevieve and Vincent fucking spread out across his office floor.

CHAPTER THIRTY

As scalding hot water streamed over her, it failed to penetrate her numbness.

Ethan had lied to her about everything. He'd used Vince as a ploy to stop her from leaving. To torment her.

And she'd told him she'd loved him.

Was that a part of his game as well? To make her love him, and then throw her away?

Had he been the one to kill Vince?

Her legs gave out, and she found herself on the floor without warning. But she didn't get up. Wrapping her arms around herself, she stared at her knees, at the pink drops sliding down her legs.

She should have run straight out the front door, but instead she'd run up the stairs, and she didn't know why. Was it shock? Had she been so terrified he'd come after her that locking herself in a room had been the first thing she could think to do?

Probably.

By the time she'd realized her mistake, it'd been too late.

That was when she'd heard it.

The almighty smash in Ethan's office. It was his desk. The sound of glass exploding like that could only be his desk.

Leaving would mean passing his office. There'd be no way she could leave without him hearing her—seeing her.

Hurting her.

More pink drops landed on her raised knees and were washed away.

She had to stop crying.

She had to leave.

Fuck… fuck everything. She didn't care if someone wanted her dead. Or about being caught in the sun, or having nowhere to go, and not a cent to her name.

Somehow, she had to find a way to leave.

CHAPTER THIRTY-ONE

At the sound of a key in the front door, Ethan tensed but didn't turn around.

"What are you doing here?" Ethan said when Rachel stepped into his office.

Although she couldn't fail to notice his shattered glass desk, she chose not to comment on it. Other than picking up the photographs and stuffing them back in their envelope the night before, he hadn't done a thing about the mess.

All the rest of the night, and all through the day, he'd sat on the floor beside his office door, staring straight ahead. Then when the sun had set, he'd torn open the drapes covering the window and stared at the bright lights in the distance.

He'd expected her to try and run. But she hadn't.

For hours he'd heard the shower running. Long enough to know the hot water would have long since gone off. But hours had passed before it'd finally been turned off. And then there was nothing but silence upstairs.

"Where's Genevieve?" Rachel asked.

He ignored her question. "I asked you what you were doing here. I'm busy."

He heard the sound of jingling keys. "I came to return these."

"You could've had them couriered over," he said, still not turning to face her.

Behind him, he heard Rachel dropping into the chair that'd sat in front of his desk. When he'd had the desk there, that was.

Annoyed that she'd taken his words as a sign to make herself comfortable, he finally turned around.

She looked different in a pair of black jeans, a pale blue sweater, and leather ankle boots. He didn't think he'd ever seen her in anything other than office attire.

Rachel shrugged. "I could have. But with a killer running around, I didn't want anyone to get a hold of them—and anyway, couriers are expensive and I've lost my job."

Despite himself, curiosity stirred. "Killer? What are you talking about?"

She crossed her legs. "I'll get to that. But I also came because there was something I wanted to tell you. Something I thought it was important you knew."

"You do realize that I didn't invite you to sit down," he said.

She shrugged. "That envelope you were sent, the one with the Carter & Steed Law Office stamp?"

"What about it?"

"It didn't come from Carter & Steed at all."

He stared at her, waited for her to continue.

"But, since you're not looking to be in the most patient of moods, I'll get straight to the point, shall I?"

Glowering at her, he leaned against the window frame. He wasn't sure he liked this change in Rachel and the way she was speaking to him.

There was little of the VASS respect in her tone he was used to, and the warmth in her eyes when she looked at him had gone. Rachel had always had a soft spot for him, but looking into her eyes now, he knew she no longer did.

"I know the letter didn't come from there, because I went down there and spoke to them about it."

"You went down there...?"

"Yes. I went to their office on the Strip and spoke with the secretary there. I explained that my employer had received a letter, but it looked like it'd already been opened."

He opened his mouth to interrupt, but she raised her hand to stop him. Narrowing his eyes, he straightened. Was she... was his VASS shutting him up? Him?

"If you'll let me finish, I promise I won't take up much more of your time."

"As long as it doesn't take all night, as I said—"

"You're busy. As I was saying, I told her the letter looked like it'd already been opened, and my boss wasn't happy that someone had opened his private legal documents. And that I was there to find out which courier company they'd used so I could make a complaint. Imagine my surprise when the secretary checked their system and found that no one in the law offices had ever done business with you."

Ethan blinked at her. "The secretary must've been mistaken. I'm sure I've dealt with a law firm on the Strip before."

Rachel smiled and shook her head.

Ethan watched, and he waited. He knew what that small smile meant.

"She wasn't mistaken. Because although I don't open all your mail, I do pay attention to the mail you receive. When I left your mail on your desk, I noticed something about it that didn't click—not until I was on my way home after you'd fired me." Here, she paused.

"Are you going to tell me or not?" he snapped.

Her smile widened. "Of course I'm going to tell you. You see, that fancy stamp all the expensive attorneys on the Strip use on the corner of their letters was in the wrong corner."

Ethan stared at her. "Is that all you came here to tell me? That the letter couldn't possibly have come from Carter & Steed because some intern stamped the wrong corner, and a secretary told you I wasn't a client?"

Rachel's smile turned smug. "That, and the law firm's been closed this last week because the owners have taken all the partners on a work retreat. Since the only people at the office were a secretary and a skeleton staff, there was no reason for anyone to courier anything to someone who isn't even on their client list."

Rising, she dropped his keys on the chair and turned to leave.

"What the fuck did you say?"

Turning, he watched as her smile faded from her face. Pity shone in her eyes.

"I said that whoever sent you that letter, the letter that had you tearing Genevieve's studio apart like that... well, it wasn't anyone at the law firm."

He paced his office as Rachel flipped through the stack of photographs she'd asked to see. If it'd been anyone else, he would have killed them for asking. But Rachel was smart. She'd figured out something was wrong, and despite his firing her, had followed her intuition and found out what that something was.

Her shock had long since passed as she stared down at each photograph in turn. Her eyes were narrowed in concentration as she scanned each photograph for several seconds before shuffling it to the back and moving to the next. She was determined to take her time, and nothing he could say could get her to go any faster.

It'd been twenty long minutes since she'd started poring over the pictures, and he was running out of patience. He didn't know what she was looking for, and apparently neither did she.

"There's something here, Ethan, there has to be. When I see it, I'll know what it is."

As she started going through the stack for the second time, he was turning to make himself a drink when he she hummed beneath her breath.

"Mm, that's... not what I expected," she murmured.

He pierced her with a stare. "What? What is it?"

"Oh, it's nothing. Just... I'm sure it's nothing," she said.

"Tell me," he ordered.

Rachel looked up at him, a line between her eyes. "I never saw Genevieve as someone who'd ever get a tattoo."

"A tattoo?"

"Yeah. She was a middle-school teacher, right?"

When he nodded, she continued. "So, I imagine they had rules about tattoos. But I don't remember seeing her with one before. I mean, I guess since it's only small, maybe it's okay if it's tiny and not anywhere super visible. But still..."

Sighing, she bent her gaze back to the photographs in her hand again, as if to remind herself of their contents. "I just don't see Genevieve ever getting one. This is all so wrong. Like, I know I don't know her all that well, but still... these photographs, the things here are just... wrong. None of it seems like anything she'd ever do. Are you sure it's her?"

Ethan folded his arms across his chest and leaned back against the wall. That'd been the first thought that crossed his mind when he'd opened the envelope. But by the third and fourth picture, doubt had started to set in. By the last photograph, all doubt had been eradicated.

He was feeling a pounding pressure in his head. "What does this tattoo look like?" he murmured.

Rachel's eyes turned wary at the softness of his voice. That was the thing about Rachel. She knew him, knew his moods almost as well as he knew hers.

"Rachel!" he snapped.

She jumped. "Okay, okay. It's small. It's on her inner wrist. Looks like a circle with something going through it... a line, maybe? I'm not sure." She squinted down at it, leaning so close that her nose nearly touched it.

"It could be Latin or Greek? God knows you vampires do love your Latin," she muttered under her breath.

Then apparently realizing he would have heard her despite her low voice, her eyes shot up to his, and she flushed. "Uh, sorry. No offense meant."

But he was too distracted to pull her up on it. Crossing over to her, he held his hand out until she placed the picture in his hand.

He saw the tattoo right away. In fact, he couldn't believe he'd missed it. How had Rachel seen what he had not? Him, with his hundreds of years of life? With his enhanced sight, and smell, and speed?

Returning the picture to her without a word, he made his way to the side table where he kept a decanter of whiskey and a couple of glasses. After pouring himself a large drink, he leaned against the wall, crossing one ankle over the other as he took a long draw.

Through it all he felt Rachel's eyes on him, waiting for him to speak.

"It's Phi, a Greek symbol for the number twenty-one. It's also the name, or rather the symbol, of this club that represents the twenty-one rooms of pleasure available, each with its own distinctive flavor. Each of the workers has this tattoo as a way for guests to identify them as staff."

His gaze was fixed on the wall opposite him as he spoke. Blinking, he remembered what Rachel had said when she'd first arrived.

"You said something about a killer earlier. What were

you talking about?" he asked, concentrating on his breathing.

He couldn't let himself think about anything else. Not about the photographs, or Genevieve, and especially not on what he'd nearly done. On what he *had* done to her. All because he hadn't taken the time to look at the photographs, or to believe she'd been telling the truth.

"Yes. Paul's body was found."

"Paul?"

What would he say to Genevieve? How could he make it right? Was it even possible?

"Genevieve and Vince's VASS. He came to Vince's funeral," Rachel said. "I wasn't the most welcoming to him, if I'm completely honest, and…"

But he was barely listening to Rachel now. He needed to figure out what he was going to say to Genevieve. Would he let her go now? Could he? What could he do or say to make her forgive him?

"I mean, he had to have been mistaken, right? The account holder had to be Vince or Genevieve," Rachel was saying.

"What did you say?"

"The VASS account for Vince and Genevieve. Paul was trying to tell her it wasn't Vince, and she was convinced it had to be. If it wasn't them, then who could it have been?" Rachel repeated.

"Are you telling me that it was neither of them?"

"Yes. Which is weird. Because apparently Paul spoke with the account owner and was going to meet with them about another contract extension. It's all rumors at this point, though, but it looks like if he did, then whoever held the contract was the last person to see him alive—and possibly the one to kill him."

"Yeah," Ethan said. "It looks like it does."

"And not only that," Rachel said, her expression neutral. "But I think I stopped him from revealing to Genevieve that the account holder was a woman."

He stared at her.

That had been what she'd been trying to tell him. And more than once. She'd tried to tell him it was a woman, since there was no male vampire who'd have any reason to do any of this. But he hadn't listened to her. Just as he hadn't listened to Genevieve.

But the *who* still eluded him.

Who was this person—this woman who wanted to hurt Genevieve, and was determined to make him think the worst of her?

CHAPTER THIRTY-TWO

"Genevieve?"

She ignored Ethan. Instead, she kept her eyes on her feet as she made her way down the stairs.

All she could think about, all she could focus on, was taking one step at a time.

"Genevieve."

Reaching the bottom of the staircase, she kept going. The front door couldn't be more than a handful of steps away. But to get there, she'd have to walk past Ethan.

It'd taken hours before she could stop crying, and she had no intention of starting again. Not ever. Especially not in front of Ethan.

"Genevieve. Can we talk?"

She stopped. Clenching her hands into tight fists, she looked up for the first time. Struggled to choke back the fury at Ethan's words, at seeing him.

He leaned against the wall with his arms folded across his chest. His eyes moved over her, eyelids flickering when he saw she was wearing the cream angora sweater and jeans she'd been wearing when he'd first brought her here.

Rachel must have had it dry cleaned at some point, but here and there were still splashes of pink. Tears. She'd been crying after she'd found Vince's body and it seemed it'd been impossible to remove the stains from the sweater.

She hadn't been able to find her shoes in the closet, and despite wanting nothing Ethan had bought her, she'd been forced to settle on a pair of four-inch-high heeled ankle boots.

It was either that or go barefoot and have to deal with the attention it brought her. More attention than she was prepared to handle in her present state of mind.

"No," she said, no give in her voice.

Turning to the front door, she kept walking.

Out of the corner of her eye, she caught his hand stretching toward her and shrank away from him. "Don't touch me."

Her voice was shrill, and he froze.

"I won't hurt you." His voice was low, anguished as he re-folded his arms.

She swung to face him, laughing. "Why? Because you've already done what you brought me here to do?"

He flinched, his mouth flattening at her words. Then he sighed.

"I'm sorry I didn't believe you. Rachel was here, she figured out—"

Her words were as harsh and bitter as her laugh had been. "Oh, so you needed physical evidence to believe something you should've known already?"

"I know I should have. I know—"

"That first photograph," she interrupted. "That was Vince groping me on the balcony. About a second after someone took that picture, I was fighting him off. I figured he was drunk, or whatever. It doesn't matter anymore, since someone killed him, and it's not worth my energy to be angry at someone who was never anything but kind to me before. But at least he had an excuse. You... you have none."

Ethan's eyes darkened. "He did what?"

She laughed. "As if you care. Not when what you did was a million times worse."

She took another step toward the front door, stopping when he stepped in front of her and blocked her path.

"Get out of my way, Ethan."

"You don't have anywhere to go."

She glared up at him. "I don't care."

His eyes flashed with something that resembled panic. "But don't you want to get to the bottom of this? Of who was doing this, and who sent the photographs? About Vince and—"

"Oh, so you're happy to use Vince to get me to do what you want again?" she sneered and kept walking, moved to step around him. "Vince wouldn't want me to stay in this toxic, fucked-up situation for a second longer."

She'd surprised him, swearing like that. She could see it in his face.

It wasn't like her to swear, but if there was a time to start dropping the f-bomb, she figured now was it.

"Gen, please, let me—"

She turned to him with a snarl. "Don't you *dare* call me

Gen. My friends call me Gen. People I love, and whom I love, call me Gen. You are *none* of those things."

He was backing up now as she stalked toward the front door. The hint of panic she'd seen in his eyes had now morphed into full-blown desperation.

"If you just—"

His phone started ringing, and he swore. Yanking it out of his back pocket, he answered it without looking.

"What!" he snapped.

She stared at him in disbelief.

Was he seriously answering his phone in the middle of this? Did he really think a phone call was more important than her?

She started for the lounge. If he wouldn't move out of her way, she'd leave through the garden.

"Aidan, now isn't the—Genevieve, where are you going?"

He was following her, but she didn't turn around. But he must have put two and two together pretty quickly when she stepped into the lounge and heading for the sliding glass doors.

"Are you sure? What—" Then Ethan was there, blocking her from leaving.

She looked up into his face. "You need to get out of my way. You can't—"

And then his face changed, and she stopped and shut up.

She just stared into his face as he continued to listen with his eyes narrowed in concentration to whatever Aidan was saying. His eyes remained locked on her face, and she saw the lines there.

He hadn't slept, she thought. He'd probably stayed awake all this time to make sure she didn't leave. Not that it would matter in the end. He couldn't force her to stay, and she made sure he saw the truth of it in her eyes.

He'd lost her.

He hung up the phone without another word and tucked it in his back pocket, his eyes never leaving hers as he ran a hand through his hair.

At any other time, she'd want to straighten it, to smooth down the ends, if just for the chance to bury her fingers in the softness of his hair. But now all she could think about was getting as far away from him as possible.

Forever.

"That was Aidan. He said he's found something out. About who's doing this."

She opened her mouth to tell him she didn't care anymore, but he must have known what she'd been about to say, because he spoke quickly before she could.

"About who killed Vince and Tess."

She stared at him. "You're lying. You're just trying to trick me into staying. Again."

He flinched. Briefly closed his eyes. "No. No, I'm not. I wouldn't… I wouldn't lie about this. If you believe nothing else, you have to believe that."

Folding her arms across her chest in a pose that mirrored his, she edged back a step so they weren't standing so close together. "And if I do choose to believe you, then what? You expect me to wait here while you go meet Aidan?"

But he was already shaking his head. "No. Aidan wants

to meet with both of us. On the Strip. He says it's important that we meet with him now."

She hesitated. This was what she wanted. Ethan knew—he must have known there was only one thing that would make her hesitate, and this was it. Seeing her indecision, some of the tension left his shoulders as relief flashed across his face.

He thought he'd won. That she'd stay because this was what she'd always wanted. To find out who'd killed Vince, and now Tess as well.

Spinning around, she strode back the front door. "Fine. We'll go meet Aidan. After that, we can all go our separate ways."

For a second it was as if she'd stepped out of her own body, as if she were watching herself, hearing it all from high above. It was like she was observing a stranger, wondering who this person fueled by nothing but rage and pain was.

Her hand grabbed the door handle and twisted. But from out of nowhere, Ethan's hand flashed out and landed on the edge of the door, above her head and to her right, holding the door closed.

When he spoke, she felt his breath stirring at the hair on the back of her head, making her shiver.

"It's not safe for you to go off alone. To be alone," he said.

Her hand tightened around the door handle. "It's not safe for me to be with you either, is it?" she asked and yanked the door open.

His hand fell away and she stepped outside, feeling him follow close behind.

Ethan pulled up outside a restaurant on the Strip, and Gen was relieved that at least he hadn't tried to talk to her on the drive. He'd left her to stare in silence out of her window as she counted down the minutes until they reached their destination.

After unsnapping her seatbelt, she shoved her car door open and started for the restaurant, not bothering to wait for Ethan.

On her way to the entrance, she heard Ethan bark out a few words to someone, probably to the valet in the lime green vest and white shirt who'd rushed past her.

But somehow, by the time she was stepping into the entryway, Ethan had not only caught up to her but made it look like they'd walked up to and into the restaurant together.

Guiding her inside the busy restaurant with his hand on the crook of her elbow, she did her best to ignore his firm grip.

It was tight enough for her not to even bother struggling. They were in public, and trying to break free of his hold would only cause a scene.

Instead, she tried to distract herself from Ethan pacing beside her by looking around, struggling to understand why Aidan would want to meet them in a busy restaurant full of human tourists. Why hadn't he asked them to meet him at Hellfire, or even come to Ethan's house?

Their arrival hadn't gone unnoticed, and as they followed one of the waiters who'd taken one look at them and told them their party was expecting them, she tried to ignore the stares and whispers around them.

"This way, please." Their server led them through the main dining floor, up to a mezzanine level where the cut of the dining guests' clothes was of a higher quality.

"Your table," the server said with a flourish.

Gen winced and twisted to glare at Ethan when his hand tightened painfully around her arm. But he wasn't looking at her. He wasn't paying her the slightest bit of attention.

Instead, his gaze was fixed on the table that the waiter had indicated, and the look on his face was one she'd never seen before.

Before she could ask Ethan what was wrong, or tell him to take his hand off her, a woman spoke. "Hello."

Turning, she found herself staring at a striking woman with long jet-black hair falling like a dark river over her shoulders, her eyes a glittering sapphire. A woman who looked strangely familiar, only she couldn't place where she'd seen her before.

"Ethan. Genevieve. Please sit. Unfortunately, Aidan won't be joining us. He's in a bit of a bind." A trace of amusement tinged her cut-glass British accent, and Gen found herself unnerved by her without quite knowing why.

Glancing at Ethan, she could see he'd yet to recover from whatever it was about the woman that held him immobile. But as she watched, slowly the mask of utter disbelief was replaced by dawning awareness.

"Lily, you're alive," he murmured.

The name had Gen widening her eyes. It wasn't the

first time she'd heard it. Vince had mentioned a woman called Lily, a woman she'd believed was his first love. Was this the woman he meant? And just who had she been to him, and to Ethan?

"Don't mind Ethan. He's had a bit of a shock to the system. I'm sure in a moment or two, he'll be right as rain," the woman said with a smile, indicating the empty seat opposite from her.

Sparing Ethan one more look, Gen tugged her arm free from Ethan's grip to sit, and examined the woman curiously.

"I'm sorry, I didn't even introduce myself. I'm—"

"You're supposed to be dead, Lily. What are you doing here?"

Ethan made no attempt to speak quietly, and Gen both saw and felt the couple from the neighboring table direct their attention to them.

"Not quite so loudly. You're causing a scene, ruining these delightful couples' romantic meal," Lily admonished with a hint of a smile on her lips.

"Sit down, please. I'd much prefer it if you would sit beside me," Lily said when Ethan moved to sit beside Gen.

Gen glanced in surprise at the steel in Lily's voice, and then she looked to Ethan to see what he would do. He stared down at Lily, and then without breaking eye contact, he pulled the chair out from under the table and sat down beside her.

Although Lily's lips flattened briefly, she didn't respond.

"You're British," Gen said after a lengthy silence. And then she remembered where she'd seen her before. "You were in the boutique when Vince and I were shopping. That's where I saw you."

"I am British, and yes, I was doing a little bit of shopping. Go on," Lily urged, "I can see there's something else you want to say."

"Yes," Gen said, the pieces slotting together. "You're Vince's Master."

Lily giggled, a happy girlish trill, seeming not to notice the way Ethan watched her warily, as if she were a bomb about to go off.

"I was expecting a man," Gen said.

"And what makes you think—oh, I see. I'm assuming Ethan might've had something to do with this belief of yours?" Lily asked, leaning her elbows on the table and turning her smile between Ethan and Gen.

"What are you doing here, Lily?" Ethan asked.

Sighing, Lily fanned her face. "That sexy voice. Oh, how I've missed that husky, sexy voice."

"Stop fucking around and tell me what the hell you want," Ethan snarled.

But Lily just laughed again, looking happy and relaxed, as if she didn't have a care in the world.

Tossing her hair back over her shoulder, she turned those cold blue eyes on Gen. "Has he told you about why he hates to be alone yet? What about how close he was to that big family of his—and those delightful brothers and sisters, how devastated he was when they—"

"Lily!" Ethan's voice was low with warning.

Between Ethan's growls and Lily's loud giggles, they were fast becoming the central focus of the diners around them, and Gen could feel the sharpness of their attention as they trained their sights on their table. Then there was the energy she was feeling, a rising tension that was increasing the longer she and Ethan stayed.

"I ask Genevieve this because it's a rather important piece of information she needs, in order to understand exactly why I'm here. You see, Genevieve, Ethan has this rather..." Lily frowned, waved her hand around as if looking for the right word "... long-sighted, if not unusual, way of dealing with his loneliness. He finds a girl that he thinks he likes—"

"Lily!" Ethan growled.

Gen took in the predatory gleam in Lily's eyes and knew she wasn't going to like what she was about to hear.

"It could almost be a fairy tale, if the ending was a little happier. You see, a long time ago, Ethan met and fell in love with a girl—well, at least he thought it was love. Turns out he was wrong. Anyway, he met and fell and love, but that wasn't enough for him. You see he had to make the girl fall in love with him so deeply, she was prepared to give up everything for him. She gave up her family, her friends, her job, even her humanity to be with him. But then he realized it wasn't love he felt after all. So, he threw her away and moved on to the next girl. A rather pretty American girl. Does this sound at all familiar to you, Genevieve? Or did I miss the mark?" Lily smiled.

Gen felt her lips curving into a smile despite the sharp agony of something twisting in her heart. "No, Lily. You hit the mark exactly. Thank you," she said.

And then she stood.

Ethan reached his hand out to stop her. "Genevieve…"

But she was moving before she'd even realized. At that

moment she knew, was certain, that the last thing she wanted was for Ethan to ever touch her again.

She dodged his hand with little effort. Ignoring a sharply indrawn breath from the table beside her, she took a step back.

All of this—the pain, the death, all of it—had nothing to do with her. She could see now that it had only ever been about Ethan and Lily.

"You know what? I'm done. Whatever this is…" She waved an arm around. "Clearly has nothing to do with me. I'll leave you to it."

She walked away and heard Ethan push his chair back.

"Gen—" Ethan said.

Lily's voice was sharp. "I wouldn't get up if I were you, Ethan. You're going to want to hear what I have to say."

CHAPTER THIRTY-THREE

*E*than stared across the table at Lily, conscious that Genevieve had walked away…was still walking away. But since it was her and not Aidan sitting opposite him, he needed to know why. He had to know why she was back from the dead, and what game she was playing. Because with Lily, there was always a game.

Now that he wasn't threatening to leave, Lily's smile turned coy. "How did you like the photographs?"

Ethan stared at her in silence.

She sighed. "Oh, come on, Ethan, don't be such a spoilsport. Tell me, did I manage to fool you?"

He continued to say nothing.

He couldn't afford to lose it in front of a restaurant full of tourists, and Lily knew it. While the Council would, and often did turn a blind eye to a few bodies in the alley, it was another thing entirely to expect them to deal with the bloody fallout of a vampire brawl in a packed restaurant.

"How long before you realized it wasn't Genevieve?"

Lily said with that sweet, sunny smile that revealed nothing of who she was, and what she was capable of.

"Was it before or after you lashed out at her?"

He clenched his jaw so tight, it was almost painful.

But Lily had known him a long time. Perhaps longer than anyone, so much so that he hadn't needed to respond. She read enough from his expression to guess what his reaction to the photographs had been.

"So after, then? Poor Genevieve. Poor, sweet Genny. Is that why she was so eager to leave?"

"What goes on between me and Genevieve has nothing to do with you. Why did you kill your Childe?"

If she'd been the one to send him the photographs, she must have been the one to send all the other 'gifts' as well. No wonder she'd worked so hard at masking her identity. He hadn't had any idea she was alive—because if he did, she'd have been the first person he'd have suspected.

Lily shrugged. "He'd served his purpose."

"Purpose?"

Ethan knew even before Lily answered what she would say, and he could guess why Vincent had been behaving so out of character on the balcony. Lily would have been there to enthrall Vince, ready to take a photograph that would reveal the very opposite of what was actually happening.

Not all vampires could be enthralled, but some could, and Masters often could and did have the ability to enthrall their Childe. A thing he had never, and would never have done to Genevieve, or even to Lily.

There were some lines he would not cross. But Lily... Lily had never cared about anything except her own pleasure, and her own happiness. It was a pity he had failed to see it until it was too late.

"To be Genevieve's knight in shining armor, of course. But falling in love? That was not part of the plan. And then trying to run away with Genevieve when everything was finally coming together..." Lily wagged her finger back and forth.

Ah. So, she had been the cloak-covered guest, then. That had been the reason there had been something familiar about her stride.

"No, I couldn't have him starting to grow a backbone. Not when I was already so busy with all the other cogs and wheels."

"Aidan," Ethan murmured.

Aidan had started seeing a woman from his past, a woman who'd wanted to remain hidden. A woman whose idea it'd been to send him the email with pictures from his New Year's Eve party. Pictures that had included Vincent and Genevieve, which had been the reason he'd returned to Vegas in the first place.

He knew now why Aidan hadn't sounded like himself on the phone. Lily must have forced him in some way to call him and arrange the meeting in the restaurant. But he'd been so distracted trying to stop Genevieve from leaving, he hadn't thought too much about it. Now, unease spread through him.

"And who did you tell him you were, exactly?"

"Just an old friend. It helped that you didn't tell him as much about me as I thought you would. Why is that, when we spent so many happy years together?"

"Pretending you didn't exist was always my preferred

way of dealing with you. What have you done with Aidan?"

A brief flash of irritation sparked in her eyes. "You're ruining all my fun, Ethan. Don't you want to hear about how I was keeping Aidan's bed warm while you were pouring your heart out to him?"

He realized something he should've picked up on long before now. Lily had always worn rose-scented perfume, with Chanel being her favorite—subtle but unmistakably her. But this close to her, all he could smell was the clean scent of someone freshly showered.

"You stopped wearing your perfume?"

She grinned. "Of course I did. I couldn't have you smelling me on Aidan, or before you could reach my table. Do you miss it?"

"Tell me about Tess. I'm assuming you promised to turn her, then."

Lily shrugged as if Tess didn't matter. And to her, she wouldn't. Not when Lily hadn't even reached her twentieth year of being turned before she was looking down at anyone and anything not vampire.

When he'd labeled humans as prey, he'd wanted to make Genevieve uncomfortable—though he'd never thought of them that way, not really. But he knew Lily did.

"I saw them together at a playground, and she was so desperate to be turned... well, it was something to help pass the time."

"And Aidan? What have you done with Aidan?" His voice was expressionless, revealing nothing of what was simmering beneath the surface.

If she'd killed Aidan... he wouldn't care if the entire world were watching while he cut her head off.

She sighed. "Ethan, you're not being any fun at all."

"Tell me," he bit out. "Now."

"He's fine."

He stared at her.

"Maybe he's a little bruised and battered around the edges. But he was still breathing when I left him in his bed."

Ethan pulled his cell phone out to call Rachel. She answered after the first ring. "Head over to Aidan's house, now. Something's happened to him."

Lily sighed. "It was only a bit of harmless fun."

"Don't forget I know you, Lily. You don't know the meaning of harmless, and your idea of fun leaves something to be desired. Now, why are you here? How are you even still alive?"

Staring down at the table, she started to trace a finger around her knife and fork. "I'd quite forgotten how demanding you can be. So many questions, so much judgment. Maybe I'm just here to have a little fun."

"Lily," he grated warningly.

"Oh, come on, you have to admit it was all so very brilliant of me. You had no idea I was even alive, and it was such fun making sure Vince kept your sweet Genevieve sheltered, rather like a pet. Knowing nothing, keeping her innocent and ignorant—and dare I say it, stupid—all so I could serve her up to you. Tell me, how did I do?"

Ethan's jaw locked.

He'd been the stupid one. The signs had been there all along for him to see. He'd wondered how Genevieve could know so little despite being a vampire for so long. And he'd been happy to take advantage of her ignorance so he could hurt her, but one thing he hadn't done was put two and two together.

"Did you enjoy tormenting her? I'm sure you must have, taking out all your years of frustrations, putting your plans of revenge in motion against poor, clueless Genny."

"Why, Lily?" he bit out. "Why did you do this?"

"Because you're mine. Or rather, you were mine first."

As he continued to observe Lily, he started to consider her end goal. Lily had always liked games. The higher the stakes, the more likely it was to cause someone—anyone—pain, the more it seemed to excite her. He didn't know how she'd managed to hide her true nature from him for so long, but somehow, she had.

"What else are you up to, Lily? What do you really want?"

"Maybe I'm here to solve a problem for you. It seems pretty clear to me that you and Genevieve aren't exactly friends right now." She peered up at him innocently before dropping her gaze back to the table as she continued to trace the outline of her spoon. "I thought I might be able to help you with that."

"Help me with what?"

"Are you sure we can't talk about how much fun we used to have in—"

"Lily, get to the point."

"Genevieve doesn't like Vegas very much. I heard her say it herself, when she was shopping with Vincent."

He kept his expression carefully blank. "You were following her."

"I was multi-tasking, but I have to say I agree with her. London is so much better," she said, peeking up at him again through her lashes as if to gauge his reaction.

"Go on," he said, wondering where she was going with all this.

"Well, I know what you're like, Ethan. Below that sexy alpha male exterior beats the heart of a gentleman. Don't deny it. I know it's there. So, I understood your predicament at once. The moment you claimed Genevieve, I knew you'd hold yourself to it. So now you have a Childe who wants nothing to do with you, and one you're not about to leave to die on the streets of Vegas."

Lily paused to give him a look laced with pity. "Especially with how you've treated her."

It all became clear to him at that moment. How Lily had been manipulating him all this time, how she'd made Genevieve a betrayer in his eyes.

Had Genevieve been paying the price for his inability to see what was right in front of him all along? For god's sake, Dante had warned him, had all but told him the person responsible was his Childe.

"But I've always been more than generous, wouldn't you agree? Since we both know Genevieve wouldn't last a night on her own—friendless, homeless, and all but penniless, not to mention being a little too trusting—I wouldn't like to see anything bad happen to her."

Ethan stiffened at Lily's implied threat. "I'm assuming you're going to want something in return."

Beaming at him as if he'd said what she'd been waiting

for him to say all along, she leaned across the table. "Come back to London with me."

"I'm afraid I can't do that"

Sighing with evident disappointment, she lowered her gaze back to the table. "That's a shame. Poor, sweet Genevieve."

"What did you say?"

Raising her head, her gaze settled on something over his shoulder. "I said, poor, sweet Genevieve. Despite how you treated her, and I'm sure you weren't exactly kind, you never have been to those who betray you, I can't help but think she looks a little torn."

Ethan spun around and saw, to his surprise, Genevieve in the restaurant entryway, bent over the contents of a thick white envelope.

"What's going on? Where did she get that envelope?"

"Just a little something from me to her," Lily said happily.

"And that means what exactly?"

"A new start. Details of an account with more than enough money for her to start again, directions to a driver waiting outside who will take her to the private airfield, and who will fly her anywhere she wants to go. And the most important thing—a new passport for the start of her new life. I think I'm being very generous, don't you?"

Ethan stood.

The people sitting nearby seemed to sense something was about to happen, because they stopped talking and turned to him.

Around him, other conversations died until there was nothing but silence. Silence and stares.

"You've gone too far," he said. He knew Lily. If she'd gone to this much trouble, she must be serious about getting him back. Which meant there was no way she would just let Genevieve go.

Somewhere down the line, there'd be some game involving Genevieve—some game that would end in her death.

"I won't let you hurt her," he said, facing Lily head-on.

"I have no intention of hurting Genevieve. I just want what we had before, for you to come with me. As painful as it is for me to admit, it never was the same without you. Come with me, and Genevieve can live whatever life she wants to live, wherever she wants to live it. You heard her… she doesn't want you, anyway."

"The only place I'm going is after Genevieve. But not before I make sure you can never hurt her."

"Fine, then. Go ahead and kill me, since you're so set on it."

"But?"

"What do you mean, but?" Lily asked, the hint of a smile on her lips.

He narrowed his eyes. "There's always a 'but' with you."

"Is there? Well, since I never could hide anything from you…"

"Except you faking your death?" Ethan drawled.

Lily rose from her chair, graceful, unconcerned about the threat he posed. "Except that. Look, the way I see it, you have two choices here."

Pushing his chair back, he rounded the table. "And what are my choices?"

"If you don't want to come with me, your choice is

this, Ethan: Stay to kill me and lose Genevieve forever." She circled the table in the other direction, glancing behind him as she did. "Or you can try and catch Genevieve now, only so you can lose her later."

Ethan spun around. The entryway was empty.

Genevieve was gone.

"Tick-tock, Ethan. You have time to do one, but you're almost out of time for the other. What will it be, Ethan? What will you choose?"

To continue Ethan and Gen's story
Pre-order DEEPEST PAIN here.

EXCERPT OF DEACON: THE BLADED
(SPIN-OFF SERIES)

The humans who served as Bladed were good for one thing and one thing only: guarding the feeding rooms from nosey human tourists who viewed rules as nothing more than suggestions.

At least, that was what the vampires had always told Deacon Chase.

But they expected him to play personal guard to a stuck-up vampire princess from the highest enclave above the city? A position which came with a bonus on completion big enough to have him eyeing the supervisor of Bladed recruits, his boss and sometimes friend with suspicion as he waited for the other shoe to drop.

But it was tempting. The bonus. And the challenge too; he couldn't say he wasn't tempted by it. And it would be a change from the tourists sticking cameras in his face or sidling up to him to sneakily take selfies as if he were one of those British guards who for some absurd reason couldn't move.

This wasn't England. It wasn't even America anymore.

Not since the vamps had taken over ownership. Vegas was in the hands of the vamps now, and over the years, people had learned vampires had no hesitation about using force whether or not it was called for.

It'd been one of the first things he'd learned after he'd signed up. That, and the Bladed issued wakizashi short sword could cut through just about anything. Intrigued, he'd stayed—and been the only human in a group of twenty who had.

Deacon was under no illusions about the job. Even if he took it, things wouldn't change for him. Soon, he'd find himself right back where he started. Stuck in the same tiny apartment he'd been in since he'd moved in five years ago. Still earning less. Much less than his vampire counterparts, with no promotion or even the hint of one on the horizon.

But his boss had singled him out for the assignment.

Maybe he'd seen the writing on the wall that he wanted out, and was ready for this year to be his last as a Bladed, since nothing had gone the way he thought it would when he'd come to Vegas in search of a fresh start after the Marines.

At least, outside of Vegas he could work his way up to something better. Here you were nothing unless you had money or you knew someone who did. Being a vampire didn't hurt either.

Pierce was holding something back. Something his boss hadn't wanted to talk about at Bladed headquarters. Narrowing his eyes, Deacon leaned toward him.

"Who's the girl, Pierce? And why does she need a guard, especially up there?"

"Big wedding, haven't you heard? A uniting of dynasties." Pierce slid a black folder across the table, but Deacon ignored it.

"You're fucking shitting me! They realize it's the twenty-first century, right?"

"Keep your voice down." Despite the sternness of his voice, the brief flash of amusement in Pierce's cool gray eyes reassured Deacon that Pierce's supervisory role training up recruits hadn't fully deprived him of his sense of humor. Not yet, at least.

Picking up his beer, Deacon leaned back in the cracked leather booth of the downtown British-style pub that the human contingent of the Bladed liked to spend their downtime in. What little they had of it, that is.

As he took a healthy swig of his lager, his eyes roamed over the pub. Other than an old man nursing a pint of Guinness who looked about to tip off his barstool at the counter, and the bartender who rested his head on a bent elbow and looked close to drifting off, he and Pierce were alone.

The tourists wanted nothing to do with such a worn-down pub where vampires had no interest in visiting. They came to Vegas for the vampires, the gambling, and the clubs—excitement, in short. When the tourists wandered into The Rising Sun Pub, it was to use the bathroom or ask for directions. Not in search of a good time.

"Why me?" he asked, returning his gaze to his boss.

"You've made an impression on the right people. Or wrong." He shrugged. "Who knows, you might like it better than the door work. So, you gonna take a look?"

Pushing his bottle aside, Deacon flipped open the file.

He had no recollection of picking up the photograph in it, but suddenly it was in his hand. His eyes locked on the beautiful—no, the word didn't do her justice—redhead who looked to be in her early twenties, all long flowing hair and sensuous curves standing front and center. Fierce arousal spiked as blood went straight to his cock, and in no time whatsoever he was primed and ready to go.

Between the long waves of her red-gold hair, and the expanse of creamy peaches-and-cream skin on show in a pale green slip dress, he wasn't sure where to look first. And that was before he even caught sight of the size of the sparkling diamond on her left hand.

The photographer had caught her leaving a bar, mid-laugh, with her head half-turned to a pale dark-haired woman beside her in a leather dress.

But her eyes…

As his gaze fixed on the green-hazel of her eyes, fringed by long, dark lashes, he saw in them something that had him frowning. Triggered a deeper need than simple lust. A need—his need to protect.

"Who is she?" he murmured, distracted.

"Ophelia Mortlake."

His head snapped up to meet his boss's eyes as he lowered the picture but didn't release his grip on it. So that was the catch then. The reason for the big bonus. He'd be playing personal guard to August Mortlake's daughter, the sole vampire Councilor who'd chosen to make his identity publicly known. "Mortlake, huh?"

"Yep."

"Why me?" Despite himself, Deacon found his eyes

drawn back to the photograph in his hand. Why couldn't he stop looking at her? "I'm human. I'd have thought he'd want only the best for his little girl."

"You're handy with a sword."

"But I'm human," Deacon repeated, louder this time. In case his boss had missed it.

Pierce's snort had Deacon raising his head. "Quit fishing for compliments, Chase. If August Mortlake wants you guarding his daughter, that's what he gets."

"And I don't get a say in this?"

A smile twisted the corner of Pierce's lips. "With a bonus this big and the hungry way you're eyeing the photo, you don't look like a man about to say no. Or am I wrong?"

EXCERPT OF COLD-BLOODED ALPHA

My bare knees sink into soil still damp from last night's rain, and the touch of the moon on my back is like a soft kiss. Cool, but welcome. And even though my wolf is strangely silent, I know the moon soothes her as it always has me.

Opening my eyes, I stare down at the space between my hands, my shoulder-length hair forming a shield between me and the sharp gazes that surround me—surround us. My new mate, Dayne and I.

It's over now. Done. Yet I don't move, and neither does he. Instead, he curves the long line of his body over mine, and a hot muscled arm settles between my bare breasts as he buries his face in the joint of my neck and shoulders. His hot breath has tension coiling, anticipation thrumming through me.

But he doesn't do what I'm expecting. He doesn't bite me. Just holds me, as he works to steady his harsh breaths in the aftermath of our joining.

He's not alone in fighting for breath in this midnight

darkness, as smoky-white tendrils of airy lighted breath stir around us like spirits.

I can't quite believe this is real. Any of it.

My first time, with anyone, and it's at my moon-blessing ceremony in front of my pack, and with a virtual stranger.

If uncle had been kind, he'd have let Dayne and I meet before the ceremony so we could get to know each other a little beforehand. Then, I could've told him I'd only ever played with the boys in my pack. I'd certainly never gone any further than that.

But no one could ever accuse Uncle Glynn of being kind, least of all to me.

I shift restlessly, unable to silence the rising tension Dayne has awakened, a fierce need I'm desperate for him to satisfy. Only I can't speak, or rather I don't dare to.

Making demands of anyone has only gotten me a slap, or worse. Usually worse.

So, while Dayne found his release, I don't dare to ask for more.

I have a mate now. That should be enough, and I can finally leave. Wanting more is just being greedy.

When the pack throws their head back in a howl to mark the joining of a newly mated pair, startled, I jerk my head up. For the first time my face is no longer obscured by layers of dark-brown hair.

Dayne takes it as a sign the ceremony is over and jerks to his feet so fast I'm not expecting it, nor am I prepared for his sudden absence. Which is when I realize he was the only thing keeping me upright. Without the strength of his arms around me, the muscles in my arms give out and I slump to the ground, at the last possible second stopping myself from face planting.

Great Talis. In front of the pack. In front of Dayne. Just fucking great.

But Dayne isn't paying the least bit of attention to me or to my watching pack. No. Out of the corner of my eye I observe him stalking away, toward the heavily wooded forests, and the pack's house a couple of minutes walk away. Head proudly tossed back, completely uncaring of his nudity.

"Say your goodbyes. We leave tonight," Dayne announces in his low rumbling voice, just shy of a growl, before the thick forests swallow up his tall muscled figure and he disappears from view.

Struggling to my feet on shaking knees, all I'm conscious of is that I'm naked while all around me my pack have the benefit of their wolf shape to preserve their modesty. With not even a second going by before the hot flush of embarrassment is staining my cheeks.

We shifters aren't usually so embarrassed by sex or nakedness since it's part of who we are. Changing shape means there will always be a time before we shift, and just after when others will see our naked form. Except me. I don't change shape anymore. It's not safe. For anyone, least of all for me.

It takes everything I have to not rush over and snatch up my white silk robe from the ground. Instead, I force myself to appear nonchalant as I casually stride over to the material lying neglected between me and the wolves who stare with eyes that glitter silver in the night.

Former pack, I correct myself. After tonight they will be my pack no longer.

Bending down to retrieve it, a bare foot beats my fingers by a hairbreadth. Disbelieving I stare at it. I would recognize that foot anywhere.

Lifting my head, I meet my uncle's eyes. They glitter with malice.

So, nothing new there then.

"You'll have to do better than that," he smirks, "If you want to keep a hold of your new mate."

I flinch at the stinging lash of my uncle's words, since I can hardly ignore the fact that seconds after our mating ceremony, my new mate is stalking away from me without a single backward glance.

The barbs that hurt the most, the ones I can never shake free are always the ones mired with truth.

"Yes, Uncle," I murmur.

"Alpha!" he snaps, inching forward.

Crossing my arms over my chest, I ease back a step, forcing my eyes from his and to the ground.

The rest of the pack are watching me. They've mostly all changed back to human now. All except the submissives and those lower down in the pack hierarchy since it takes them much longer than the mere seconds it takes my uncle—and Alpha to shift.

Predatory anticipation fills the air as they wait to see what my uncle will do to me this time. How will he punish me for whatever preconceived wrong or slight I've done?

DEEPEST RAGE

With Dayne's declaration we're leaving tonight—now, he's snatched any opportunity for my uncle to strike out at me one last time. If he wants to do anything to me, it has to be now.

"Yes, Alpha," I tell the foot he still has on my robe.

His hand comes from nowhere, and suddenly I'm choking, my fingers scrabbling at his tight grip around my neck.

I go from standing to balancing on the very tip of my toes in a heartbeat as he forces my heels from the ground. "Is that mockery I hear?"

Since I'm struggling to breathe, there's no way I can answer him. All I can do is hope he either drops me soon, or my new mate comes back. But what he'll do, I don't know. The idea of Dayne Blackshaw saving anyone least of all me is ludicrous.

"Answer me!" Uncle snaps as if I'm able to speak a single word at all.

Desperately, I shake my head no.

The sound that emerges from my throat is barely a gasp, and the edge of my vision is darkening as I sink into unconsciousness. Since this isn't the first time for it to happen, I can read the signs before anyone.

"Is there a problem?"

ALSO BY EVE BALE

Voracious Vampires of Las Vegas
The Lottery
Hellfire
Deepest Rage
Deepest Pain (July 2021)
Deepest Love (August 2021)

The Bladed
Deacon
Julian (August 2021)
Hunter (October 2021)

Cold-Blooded Alpha
Cold-Blooded Alpha (June 2021)
Hot-Blooded Alpha (July 2021)

THANK YOU

Thank you so much for you picking up Deepest Rage.

If you'd like to never miss a new release, and pick up your subscriber exclusive story The Lottery set in the Voracious Vampire World, you can keep updated by joining my mailing list here: www.evebale.com/newsletter

You can also "like" my Facebook page at: www.facebook.com/AuthorEveBale

As a new indie author, reviews mean a lot. So, if you enjoyed Deepest Rage and would like to share that with other readers, it would mean the world to me if you'd leave a review.

XOXO

Printed in Great Britain
by Amazon